The Round House

ALSO BY LOUISE ERDRICH

NOVELS

Love Medicine
The Beet Queen
Tracks
The Crown of Columbus (with Michael Dorris)
The Bingo Palace
Tales of Burning Love
The Antelope Wife (1997; revised edition, 2012)
The Last Report on the Miracles at Little No Horse
The Master Butchers Singing Club
Four Souls
The Painted Drum
The Plague of Doves
Shadow Tag

STORIES

The Red Convertible: New and Selected Stories, 1978–2008

POETRY

Jacklight
Baptism of Desire
Original Fire

FOR CHILDREN

Grandmother's Pigeon
The Birchbark House
The Range Eternal
The Game of Silence
The Porcupine Year
Chickadee

NON-FICTION

The Blue Jay's Dance
Books and Islands in Ojibwe Country

Constable & Robinson Ltd
55–56 Russell Square
London WC1B 4HP
www.constablerobinson.com

The Round House

LOUISE ERDRICH

First published in the US by HarperCollins, 2012

First published in the UK by Corsair,
an imprint of Constable & Robinson Ltd, 2013

Grateful acknowledgement is made to the editors of *The New Yorker*, where the section 'Linda's Story' was published in slightly different form as 'The Years of My Birth'.

A copy of the British Library Cataloguing in Publication data is available from the British Library

ISBN: 978-1-47210-816-6 (hardback)
ISBN: 978-1-47210-815-9 (trade paperback)

Printed and bound by CPI Group (UK) Ltd, Coydon, CR0 4YY

1 3 5 7 9 10 8 6 4 2

To Pallas

The Round House

CHAPTER ONE

1988

Small trees had attacked my parents' house at the foundation. They were just seedlings with one or two rigid, healthy leaves. Nevertheless, the stalky shoots had managed to squeeze through knife cracks in the decorative brown shingles covering the cement blocks. They had grown into the unseen wall and it was difficult to pry them loose. My father wiped his palm across his forehead and damned their toughness. I was using a rusted old dandelion fork with a splintered handle; he wielded a long, slim iron fireplace poker that was probably doing more harm than good. As my father prodded away blindly at the places where he sensed roots might have penetrated, he was surely making convenient holes in the mortar for next year's seedlings.

Whenever I succeeded in working loose a tiny tree, I placed it like a trophy beside me on the narrow sidewalk that surrounded the house. There were ash shoots, elm, maple, box elder, even a good-sized catalpa, which my father placed in an ice cream bucket and watered, thinking that he might find a place to replant it. I thought it was a wonder the treelets had persisted through a North Dakota winter. They'd had water perhaps, but only feeble light and a few crumbs of earth. Yet each seed had managed to sink the hasp of a root deep and a probing tendril outward.

My father stood, stretching his sore back. That's enough, he said, though he was usually a perfectionist.

I was unwilling to stop, however, and after he went into the house to phone my mother, who had gone to her office to pick up a file, I continued to pry at the hidden rootlings. He did not come back out and I thought he must have lain down for a nap, as he did now sometimes. You would think then that I would have stopped, a thirteen-year-old boy with better things to do, but on the contrary. As the afternoon passed and everything on the reservation grew quiet and hushed, it seemed increasingly important to me that each one of these invaders be removed down to the very tip of the root, where all the vital growth was concentrated. And it seemed important as well that I do a meticulous job, as opposed to so many of my shoddily completed chores. Even now, I wonder at the steepness of my focus. I wedged my iron fork close as I could along the length of the twiglike sprout. Each little tree required its own singular strategy. It was almost impossible not to break off the plant before its roots could be drawn intact from their stubborn hiding place.

I quit at last, sneaked inside, and slipped into my father's study. I took out the law book my father called The Bible. Felix S. Cohen's *Handbook of Federal Indian Law.* It had been given to my father by his father; the rust-red binding was scraped, the long spine cracked, and every page bore handwritten comments. I was trying to get used to the old-fashioned language and constant footnotes. Either my father or my grandfather had placed an exclamation point on page 38, beside the italicized case, which had naturally interested me also: *United States v. Forty-three Gallons of Whiskey.* I suppose one of them had thought that title was ridiculous, as I did. Nevertheless, I was parsing out the idea, established in other cases and reinforced in this one, that our treaties with the government were like treaties with foreign nations. That the grandeur and power my Mooshum talked about wasn't entirely lost, as it was, at least to some degree I meant to know, still protected by the law.

I was reading and drinking a glass of cool water in the kitchen when my father came out of his nap and entered, disoriented and yawning. For all its importance Cohen's *Handbook* was not a heavy book and when he appeared I drew it quickly onto my lap, under the table. My father licked his dry lips and cast about, searching for the smell of food perhaps, the sound of pots or the clinking of glasses, or footsteps. What he said then surprised me, although on the face of it his words seem slight.

Where is your mother?

His voice was hoarse and dry. I slid the book on to another chair, rose, and handed him my glass of water. He gulped it down. He didn't say those words again, but the two of us stared at each other in a way that struck me somehow as adult, as though he knew that by reading his law book I had inserted myself into his world. His look persisted until I dropped my eyes. I had actually just turned thirteen. Two weeks ago, I'd been twelve.

At work? I said, to break his gaze. I had assumed that he knew where she was, that he'd got the information when he phoned. I knew she was not really at work. She had answered a telephone call and then told me that she was going in to her office to pick up a folder or two. A tribal enrollment specialist, she was probably mulling over some petition she'd been handed. She was the head of a department of one. It was a Sunday—thus the hush. The Sunday afternoon suspension. Even if she'd gone to her sister Clemence's house to visit afterward, Mom would have returned by now to start dinner. We both knew that. Women don't realize how much store men set on the regularity of their habits. We absorb their comings and goings into our bodies, their rhythms into our bones. Our pulse is set to theirs, and as always on a weekend afternoon we were waiting for my mother to start us ticking away on the evening.

And so, you see, her absence stopped time.

What should we do, we both said at once, which was again upsetting. But at least my father, seeing me unnerved, took charge.

Let's go find her, he said. And even then as I threw on my jacket, I was glad that he was so definite—find her, not just look for her, not search. We would go out and find her.

The car's had a flat, he declared. She probably drove someone home and the car's had a flat. These damn roads. We'll walk down and borrow your uncle's car and go find her.

Find her, again. I strode along beside him. He was quick and still powerful once he got going.

He had become a lawyer, then a judge, and also married late in life. I was a surprise to my mother, too. My old Mooshum called me Oops; that was his nickname for me, and unfortunately others in the family found it funny. So I am sometimes called Oops to this very day. We went down the hill to my aunt and uncle's house—a pale green HUD house sheltered by cottonwood and gentrified by three small blue spruce trees. Mooshum lived there too, in a timeless fog. We were all proud of his superlongevity. He was ancient, but still active in the upkeep of the yard. Each day, after his exertions outside, he lay by the window on a cot to rest, a pile of sticks, lightly dozing, sometimes emitting a dry, sputtering sound that was probably laughter.

When my father told Clemence and Edward that my mother had had a flat and we needed their car, as if he actually had knowledge of this mythical flat tire, I almost laughed. He seemed to have convinced himself of the truth of his speculation.

We backed down the gravel drive in my uncle's Chevrolet and drove to the tribal offices. Circled the parking lot. Empty.

Windows dark. As we came back out the entrance, we turned right.

She went to Hoopdance, I'll bet, said my father. Needed something for dinner. Maybe she was going to surprise us, Joe.

I am the second Antone Bazil Coutts, but I'd fight anyone who put a junior in back of my name. Or a number. Or called me Bazil. I'd decided I was Joe when I was six. When I was eight, I realized that I'd chosen the name of my great-grandfather, Joseph. I knew him mainly as the author of inscriptions in books with amber pages and dry leather bindings. He'd passed down several shelves of these antiquities. I resented the fact that I didn't have a brand-new name to distinguish me from the tedious Coutts line—responsible, upright, even offhandedly heroic men who drank quietly, smoked an occasional cigar, drove a sensible car, and only showed their mettle by marrying smarter women. I saw myself as different, though I didn't know how yet. Even then, tamping down my anxiety as we went looking for my mother, who had gone to the grocery store—just that, surely, a little errand—I was aware that what was happening was in the nature of something unusual. A missing mother. A thing that didn't happen to the son of a judge, even one who lived on a reservation. In a vague way, I hoped *something* was going to happen.

I was the sort of kid who spent a Sunday afternoon prying little trees out of the foundation of his parents' house. I should have given in to the inevitable truth that this was the sort of person I would become, in the end, but I kept fighting it. Yet when I say that I wanted there to be *something*, I mean nothing bad, but something. A rare occurrence. A sighting. A bingo win, though Sunday was not a bingo day and it would have been completely out of character for my mother to play. That's what I wanted, though, something out of the ordinary. Only that.

Halfway to Hoopdance, it occurred to me that the grocery store was closed on Sunday.

Of course it is! My father's chin jutted, his hands tightened on the wheel. He had a profile that would look Indian on a movie poster, Roman on a coin. There was a classic stoicism in his heavy beak and jaw. He kept driving because, he said, she might have forgotten it was Sunday, too. Which was when we passed her. There! She whizzed by us in the other lane, riveted, driving over the speed limit, anxious to get back home to us. But here we were! We laughed at her set face as we did a U-turn there on the highway and followed her, eating her dust.

She's mad, my father laughed, so relieved. See, I told you. She forgot. Went to the grocery and forgot it was closed. Mad now she wasted gas. Oh, Geraldine!

There was amusement, adoration, amazement in his voice when he said those words. Oh, Geraldine! Just from those two words, it was clear that he was and had always been in love with my mother. He had never stopped being grateful that she had married him and right afterward given him a son, when he'd come to believe he was the end of the line.

Oh, Geraldine.

He shook his head, smiling as we drove along, and everything was all right, more than all right. We could now admit we had been worried by my mother's uncharacteristic absence. We could be jolted into a fresh awareness of how we valued the sanctity of small routine. Wild though I saw myself in the mirror, in my thoughts, I valued such ordinary pleasures.

So it was our turn, then, to worry her. Just a little, said my father, just to let her in for a taste of her own medicine. We took our time bringing the car back to Clemence's house and walked up the hill, anticipating my mother's indignant question, Where were you? I could just see her hands knuckled on her hips. Her smile twitching to jump from behind her frown. She'd laugh when she heard the story.

We walked up the dirt driveway. Alongside it in a strict

row, Mom had planted the pansy seedlings she'd grown in paper milk cartons. She'd put them out early. The only flower that could stand a frost. As we came up the drive we saw that she was still in the car. Sitting in the driver's seat before the blank wall of the garage door. My father started running. I could see it too in the set of her body—something fixed, rigid, wrong. When he got to the car, he opened the driver's side door. Her hands were clenched on the wheel and she was staring blindly ahead, as she had been when we passed her going the opposite way on the road to Hoopdance. We'd seen her intent stare and we'd laughed then. She's mad at the wasted gas!

I was just behind my father. Careful even then to step over the scalloped pansy leaves and buds. He put his hands on hers and carefully pried her fingers off the steering wheel. Cradling her elbows, he lifted her from the car and supported her as she shifted toward him, still bent in the shape of the car seat. She slumped against him, stared past me. There was vomit down the front of her dress and, soaking her skirt and soaking the gray cloth of the car seat, her dark blood.

Go down to Clemence, said my father. Go down there and say I am taking your mother straight to the Hoopdance Emergency. Tell them to follow.

With one hand, he opened the door to the backseat and then, as though they were dancing in some awful way, he maneuvered Mom to the edge of the seat and very slowly laid her back. Helped her turn over on her side. She was silent, though now she moistened her cracked, bleeding lips with the tip of her tongue. I saw her blink, a little frown. Her face was beginning to swell. I went around to the other side and got in with her. I lifted her head and slid my leg underneath. I sat with her, holding my arm over her shoulder. She vibrated with a steady shudder, like a switch had been flipped inside. A strong smell rose from her, the vomit and something else, like gas or kerosene.

I'll drop you off down there, my father said, backing out, the car tires screeching.

No, I'm coming too. I've got to hold on to her. We'll call from the hospital.

I had almost never challenged my father in word or deed. But it didn't even register between us. There had already been that look, odd, as if between two grown men, and I had not been ready. Which didn't matter. I was holding my mother tightly now in the backseat of the car. Her blood was on me. I reached onto the back window ledge and pulled down the old plaid quilt we kept there. She was shaking so bad I was scared she would fly apart.

Hurry, Dad.

All right, he said.

And then we flew there. He had the car up past ninety. We just flew.

My father had a voice that could thunder out; it was said he had developed this. It was not a thing he'd had in his youth, but he'd had to use it in the courtroom. His voice did thunder out and fill the Emergency entrance. Once the attendants had my mother on a gurney, my father told me to call Clemence. Then wait. Now that his anger was the thing filling the air, crackling clean, I was better. Whatever had happened would be fixed. Because of his fury. Which was a rare thing and got results. He held my mother's hand as they wheeled her into the emergency ward. The doors closed behind them.

I sat down in a chair of orange molded plastic. A skinny pregnant woman had walked past the open car door, eyeing my mother, taking it all in before she registered herself. She slumped down next to a quiet old woman, across from me, and picked up an old *People* magazine.

Don't you Indians have your own hospital over there? Aren't you building a new one?

The emergency room's under construction, I told her.

Still, she said.

Still what? I made my voice grating and sarcastic. I was never like so many Indian boys, who'd look down quiet in their anger and say nothing. My mother had taught me different.

The pregnant woman pursed her lips and looked back at her magazine. The old woman was knitting the thumb of a mitten. I went over to the pay phone, but I didn't have any money. I went to the nurse's window, asked to use the phone. We were close enough for the call to be local, so the nurse let me use it. But there was no answer. So I knew my aunt had taken Edward up to adore the sacrament, which got them out of the house on Sunday nights. He said that while Clemence adored the sacrament, he meditated on how it could be possible that humans had evolved out of apes only to sit gaping at a round white cracker. Uncle Edward was a science teacher.

I sat back down in the waiting room, as far from the pregnant lady as I could get, but the room was very small, so that wasn't far enough. She was thumbing through that magazine. Cher was on the cover. I could read the words beside Cher's jaw: *She's made* Moonstruck *a megahit, her lover is 23 and she's tough enough to say "mess with me and I'll kill you."* But Cher did not look tough. She looked like a surprised plastic doll. The bony, bulgey woman peeked around Cher and spoke to the knitting lady.

Looked like that poor woman had a miscarriage or maybe—her voice went sly—a rape.

The woman's lip lifted up off her rabbit teeth as she looked at me. Her ratty yellow hair quivered. I looked right back, into her lashless hazel eyes. Then I did something odd by instinct. I went over and took the magazine out of her hands. Still staring at her, I tore off the cover and dropped the rest of the magazine. I ripped again. Cher's identical eyebrows parted. The lady who was knitting pursed her lips, counting stitches. I gave the cover back and the woman accepted the pieces. Then suddenly I felt bad about Cher. What had she done to me? I got up and walked out the door.

I stood outside. I could hear the woman's voice, raised, triumphant, complaining to the nurse. The sun was almost down. The air had gone cold, and with the darkness a stealthy chill entered me. I hopped up and down and swung my arms. I didn't care what. I was not going back in until that woman was gone, or until my father came out and told me that my mother was all right. I could not stop thinking about what that woman had said. Those two words stabbed my thoughts, as she had meant them to do. Miscarriage. A word I didn't altogether understand but knew had to do with babies. Which I knew were impossible. My mother had told me, six years before, when I'd pestered her for a brother, that the doctor had made sure that after me she could not get pregnant. It just could not happen. So that left the other word.

After a while, I saw a nurse take the pregnant lady back in through the emergency doors. I hoped they would not put her anywhere near my mother. I went in and again called my aunt, who said that she'd leave Edward to watch Mooshum and drive right over. She also asked me what had happened, what was wrong.

Mom's bleeding, I said. My throat shut and I couldn't say more.

She's hurt? Was there an accident?

I got it out that I didn't know and Clemence hung up. A poker-faced nurse came out and told me to go back to my mother. The nurse disapproved that my mother had asked for me. Insisted, she said. I wanted to run ahead, but I followed the nurse down a bright-lit hall, into a windowless room lined with green glass-fronted metal cabinets. The room had been dimmed and my mother was wearing a flimsy hospital gown. A sheet was tucked around her legs. There was no blood, anywhere. My father was standing at the head of her bed, his hand on the metal rail of the headboard. At first I didn't look at him, just at her. My mother was a beautiful woman—that's something I always knew. A given among family, among strangers. She and Clemence had coffee-cream skin and hot black glossy curls. Slim even after their children. Calm and direct, with take-charge eyes and movie-star lips. When overcome with laughter, they lost all dignity, however, and choked, snorted, burped, wheezed, even farted, which made them ever more hysterical. They usually sent each other into fits, but sometimes my father, too, could make them lose control. Even then, they were beautiful.

Now I saw my mother's face puffed with welts and distorted to an ugly shape. She peered through slits in the swollen flesh of her lids.

What happened? I asked stupidly.

She didn't answer. Tears leaked from the corners of her eyes. She blotted them away with a gauze-wrapped fist. I'm all right, Joe. Look at me. See?

And I looked at her. But she was not all right. There were scrapes of blows and the awful lopsidedness. Her skin had lost its normal warm color. It was gray as ash. Her lips were seamed with dried blood. The nurse came in, raised the end of the bed with a crank. Laid another blanket over her. I hung my head and leaned toward her. I tried to stroke her wrapped wrist and cold, dry fingertips. With a cry, she snatched her hand away as though I'd hurt her. She went rigid and closed her eyes. This action devastated me. I looked up at my father and he gestured for me to come to him. He put his arm around me, walked me out of the room.

She's not all right, I said.

He looked down at his watch and then back at me. His face registered the humming rage of a man who couldn't think fast enough.

She's not all right. I spoke as if to tell him an urgent truth. And for a moment I thought he'd break. I could see something rising in him, but he conquered it, breathed out, and gathered himself.

Joe. He was looking strangely at his watch again. Joe, he said. Your mother was attacked.

We stood in the hallway together under patchy, buzzing, fluorescent lights. I said the first thing I thought of.

By who? Attacked by who?

Absurdly, we both realized that my father's usual response would have been to correct my grammar. We looked at each other and he said nothing.

My father has the head, neck, and shoulders of a tall and powerful man, but the rest of him is perfectly average. Even a little clumsy and soft. If you think about it, this is a good physique to have as a judge. He looms imposingly seated at the bench, but when conferring in his chambers (a glorified broom closet) he is nonthreatening and people trust him. As well as thunderous, his voice is capable of every nuance, and sometimes very gentle. It was the gentleness in his voice now that scared me, and the softness. Almost a whisper.

She doesn't know who the man was, Joe.

But will we find him? I asked in that same hushed voice.

We will find him, my father said.

And then what?

My father never shaved on Sundays, and a few tiny stubbles of gray beard showed. That thing in him was gathering again, ready to burst out. But instead he put his hands on my shoulders and spoke with that reedy softness that spooked me.

I can't think that far ahead right now.

I put my hands on his hands and looked into his eyes. His leveling brown eyes. I wanted to know that whoever had attacked my mother would be found, punished, and killed. My father saw this. His fingers bit into my shoulders.

We'll get him, I said quickly. I was fearful as I said this, dizzy.

Yes.

He took his hands away. Yes, he said again. He tapped his watch, bit down on his lip. Now if the police would come. They need to get a statement. They should have been here.

We turned to go back to the room.

Which police? I asked.

Exactly, he said.

The nurse didn't want us back in the room yet, and as we stood waiting the police arrived. Three men came through the emergency ward doors and stood quietly in the hall. There was a state trooper, an officer local to the town of Hoopdance, and Vince Madwesin, from the tribal police. My father had insisted that they each take a statement from my mother because it wasn't clear where the crime had been committed—on state or tribal land—or who had committed it—an Indian or a non-Indian. I already knew, in a rudimentary way, that these questions would swirl around the facts. I already knew, too, that these questions would not change the facts. But they would inevitably change the way we sought justice. My father touched my shoulder before he left me and approached them. I stood against the wall. They were all slightly taller than my father, but they knew him and leaned down close to hear his words. They listened to him intently, their eyes not leaving his face. As he spoke, he looked down at the floor occasionally and folded his hands behind his back. He looked at each of them in turn from under his brows, then cast his eyes down at the floor again.

Each police officer went into the room with a notebook and a pen, and came out again in about fifteen minutes, expressionless. Each shook my father's hand and swiftly exited.

A young doctor named Egge was on duty that day. He was the one who had examined my mother. As my father and

I were going back to Mom's room, we saw that Dr. Egge had returned.

I don't suggest that the boy . . . , he began.

I thought it was funny that his domed, balding, shiny head was eggish, like his name. His oval face with the little round black eyeglasses looked familiar, and I realized it was the sort of face my mother used to draw on boiled eggs so that I would eat them.

My wife insisted on seeing Joe again, my father told Dr. Egge. She needs him to see that she is all right.

Dr. Egge was silent. He gave my father a prim little piercing look. My father stepped back from Egge and asked me to go out into the waiting room to see if Clemence had arrived yet.

I'd like to see Mom again.

I'll come get you, said my father urgently. Go.

Dr. Egge was staring even harder at my father. I turned away from them with sick reluctance. As my father and Dr. Egge walked away from me, they spoke in low voices. I didn't want to leave, so I turned and watched them before I went out into the waiting room. They stopped outside my mother's room. Dr. Egge finished speaking and jabbed his eyeglasses up his nose with one finger. My father walked to the wall as if he were going through it. He pressed his forehead and hands against the wall and stood there with his eyes shut.

Dr. Egge turned and saw me frozen at the doors. He pointed toward the waiting room. My father's emotion was something, his gesture implied, that I was too young to witness. But during the last few hours I had become increasingly resistant to authority. Instead of politely vanishing, I ran to my father, flailing Dr. Egge aside. I threw my arms around my father's soft torso, held him under his jacket, and I fiercely clung to him, saying nothing, only breathing with him, taking great deep sobs of air.

*

Much later, after I had gone into law and gone back and examined every document I could find, every statement, relived every moment of that day and the days that followed, I understood that this was when my father had learned from Dr. Egge the details and extent of my mother's injuries. But that day, all I knew, after Clemence separated me from my father and led me away, was that the hallway was a steep incline. I went back through the doors and let Clemence talk to my father. After I'd sat for about half an hour in the waiting room, Clemence came in and told me that my mother was going into surgery. She held my hand. We sat together staring at a picture of a pioneer woman sitting on a hot hillside with her baby lying next to her, shaded beneath a black umbrella. We agreed that we had never really cared for the picture and now we were going to actively hate it, though this was not the picture's fault.

I should take you home, let you sleep in Joseph's room, said Clemence. You can go to school tomorrow from our house. I'll come back here and wait.

I was tired, my brain hurt, but I looked at her like she was crazy. Because she was crazy to think that I would go to school. Nothing would go on as normal. That steeply inclined hallway led to this place—the waiting room—where I would wait.

You could at least sleep, said Aunt Clemence. It wouldn't hurt to sleep. The time would pass and you wouldn't have to stare at that damn picture.

Was it rape? I asked her.

Yes, she said.

There was something else, I said.

My family doesn't hedge about things. Though Catholic, my aunt was not one to let butter melt in her mouth. When she spoke, answering me, her voice was quick and cool.

Rape is forced sex. A man can force a woman to have sex. That's what happened.

I nodded. But I wanted to know something else.

Will she die from it?

No, said Clemence immediately. She won't die. But sometimes—

She bit down on her lips from the inside so they made a frowning line and she squinted at the picture.

—it's more complicated, she said finally. You saw that she was hurt, real bad? Clemence touched her own cheek, sweetly rouged and powdered from going to church.

Yes, I saw.

Our eyes filled with tears and we looked away from each other, down at Clemence's purse as she dug in it for Kleenex. We both let ourselves cry a bit as she got the Kleenex. It was a relief. Then we put the tissues to our faces and Clemence went on.

It can be more violent than other times.

Violently raped, I thought.

I knew those words fit together. Probably from some court case I'd read in my father's books or from a newspaper article or the cherished paperback thrillers my uncle, Whitey, kept on his handmade bookshelf.

Gasoline, I said. I smelled it. Why did she smell like gas? Did she go to Whitey's?

Clemence stared at me, the Kleenex frozen beside her nose, and her skin went the color of old snow. She bent over suddenly and put her head down on her knees.

I'm okay, she said through the Kleenex. Her voice sounded normal, even detached. Don't worry, Joe. I thought I was going to faint, but I'm not.

Gathering herself, she sat up. She patted my hand. I didn't ask her about the gasoline again.

I fell asleep on a plastic couch and someone put a hospital blanket over me. I sweated in my sleep and when I woke, my cheek and arm were stuck to the plastic. I peeled myself unpleasantly up on one elbow.

Dr. Egge was across the room talking to Clemence. I could tell right away that things were better, that my mother was better, that whatever had happened with the surgery was better, and in spite of how bad things were, at least for now the picture wasn't getting any worse. So I put my face down on the sticky green plastic, which now felt good, and I fell back asleep.

CHAPTER TWO

Lonely Among Us

I had three friends. I still keep up with two of them. The other is a white cross on the Montana Hi-Line. His physical departure is marked there, I mean. As for his spirit, I carry that around with me in the form of a round black stone. He gave it to me when he found out what had happened to my mother. Virgil Lafournais was his name, or Cappy. He told me that the stone was one of those found at the base of a lightning-struck tree, that it was sacred. A thunderbird egg, he called it. He gave it to me the day I went back to school. Every time I got a pitying or curious look from another kid or a teacher that day, I touched the stone Cappy gave me.

It was five days since we had found my mother sitting in the driveway. I'd refused to go to school before she came back from the hospital. She was anxious to get out, relieved to be home. She said good-bye to me that morning from my parents' bed in their upstairs bedroom.

Cappy and your other friends will miss you, she said.

I should go back to school, even though there were just over two weeks left until summer. When she was better, she would make us a cake, she said, and sloppy joes. She had always liked to feed us.

My other two friends were Zack Peace and Angus Kashpaw. Back in those days, the four of us were more or less together whenever it was possible, though it was understood that Cappy and I were closest. Cappy's mother had died when he was young, leaving Cappy and his older brother, Randall, and his father, Doe Lafournais, to a life that had worn itself into bachelor grooves and a house of womanless chaos. For although Doe became involved with women from time to time, he never did remarry. He was both a janitor of the tribal offices and, on and off, the chairman of the tribe. When he was first elected in the 1960s, he was paid just enough money to take his janitor job down to half-time. When too exhausted to run for a term, he picked up extra hours as the night watchman. It wasn't until the seventies that the feds put money into tribal government, and we started figuring out how to run things. Doe was still chairman, on again, off again. The way it worked was, people voted Doe into office whenever they got mad at the current chairman. But as soon as Doe was in, the buzz began, the complaints, the gossip machine, the inexorable teardown that is part of reservation politics and the lot of anyone who rises too far into any spotlight. When it got bad enough, Doe would decline to run. He'd pack up his office, including the tribal chairman stationery that he always had printed on his own dime: *Doe Lafournais, Tribal Chairman*. For a few years, we'd have lots of drawing paper at Cappy's house. Inevitably, his successor went through the same treatment. Eventually Doe's contrite and pleading constituents would work on him until he threw his hat back in the ring. 1988 was an out-of-office year for Doe, which meant he did a lot of fishing with us. We'd spent half the winter in Doe's icehouse, pulling in northerns and sneaking beers.

Zack Peace's family was split up now for the second

time. His father, Corwin Peace, was a musician on perpetual tour. His mother, Carleen Thunder, ran the tribal newspaper. His stepdad, Vince Madwesin, was the tribal police officer who had interviewed my mother. Zack was almost a decade older than his baby brother and sister, because his parents had married young, divorced, then given it a second try and found out they were right the first time they divorced. Zack was musical, like his father, and always brought his guitar to the icehouse. He said he knew one thousand songs.

As for Angus, he was from a part of the reservation that was hard-core poor. The tribe had acquired the money to put in subsidized project housing—large, tan city-style apartment buildings just outside of town. They were surrounded by hummocks of weedy earth, no trees or bushes. The money had run out before steps were built, so people used ramps of plywood or just hoisted themselves in and jumped out of their houses. His aunt Star had moved Angus, his two brothers, her boyfriend's two children, and a changing array of pregnant sisters and bingeing or detoxing cousins into a three-bedroom unit. Aunt Star managed an epic amount of craziness. It didn't help that besides no steps the building itself was a low-bid nightmare. The contractor had skimped on insulation, so in winter Star had to keep the oven on all night with the door open and the water in the kitchen trickling, or the pipes would freeze. There were rags stuffed between the walls and windows, because the Sheetrock had shrunk away from the cheap-john aluminum combination storm frames. The windows soon fell apart, lost their screens. Nothing worked. The plumbing kept backing up. I even became an expert in sealing the toilet with wax and duct tape. Star was always bribing us with frybread to do house repairs or rig up satellite reception off a dented hubcap or some such thing.

Actually, once she had taken up with her big love, Elwin, we did manage the satellite. Star had a fancy television bought with the one lavish bingo win she'd managed in her lifetime. Together with Elwin we MacGyvered some old equipment together and got signals from Fargo, Minneapolis, even Chicago or Denver. The satellite was hooked up in September of 1987, just in time for the season premieres of all the network shows. We improved reception to the point where we sometimes even got the shows syndicated out of certain cities, ever-changing according to the weather and the magnetism of the planets. We had to hunt them down, but I don't think we ever missed one episode of *Star Trek*. Not the old one, but *The Next Generation*. We loved *Star Wars*, had our favorite quotes, but we lived in *TNG*.

Naturally, we all wanted to be Worf. We all wanted to be Klingons. Worf's solution to any problem was to attack. In the episode Justice we found out Worf didn't enjoy sex with human females because they were too fragile and he had to show restraint. Our big joke around pretty girls was *Hey, show some restraint*. In Hide and Q the ideal Klingon girl jumped Worf and she was grotesquely hot. Worf was combustible, noble, and handsome even with a turtle shell on his forehead. Next to Worf, we liked Data because he mocked white people by being curious about stupid things that the crew would do or say, and because when gorgeous Yar got drunk he declared himself fully functional and had sex with her. Wesley, the one you'd think we'd identify with, our age and a genius, and with a careless mom who let him get into trouble, did not interest us because he was a bumbling white town-baby and wore ludicrous sweaters. We were in love of course with the empathic half-Betazoid Deanna Troy, especially when the show let her hair go long and curly. Her jumpsuits were low-cut, her red V belt pointed you-know-where, and her big head and short curvy body drove us wild. Commander Riker was supposedly hot for her, but he was wooden, implausible. Better once a beard hid his baby cheeks, but we still wanted to be Worf. As for Captain Picard, he was an old man, though a French old man, so we liked him. We also liked Geordi because it turned out he was always in pain because he wore the eye visor, and that made him noble too.

The reason I go into this is that because of this show we set ourselves apart. We made drawings, cartoons, and even tried to write an episode. We pretended we had special knowledge. We were starting to get our growth and were anxious how we'd turn out. In *TNG* we weren't skinny, picked on, poor, motherless, or scared. We were cool because no one else knew what we were talking about.

The first day I went back to school, Cappy walked me home. It is unusual to see people walking places on the reservation now, except on the special walking paths created to promote fitness. But in the late eighties young people still walked places, and as both Cappy and I lived less than a mile from school, we often flipped a coin to see whose house we'd go to. His was livelier, as Randall always had his friends around, but mine had a television and box so that we could play Bionic Commando, a game we were fanatical about.

Cappy had given me the thunderbird egg in the school hallway, and he told me about it on the way back to the house. He said that when he had found it the tree was still smoking. I pretended I believed him. Without saying anything, it was clear that Cappy was just walking me home and would not go inside. I would not have let him anyway. My mother didn't want anyone to see her. Although my father was about to take a leave of absence and had called in another judge from retirement, he was still finishing up some paperwork at his office. He had already told me that he'd keep checking in all that day, but that my mother would be glad when I got home.

As we walked up the drive, Clemence came out the front door and said she'd got a call from a neighbor that Mooshum was out in the yard. I assumed from her rush that he'd left his pants in the house. She got in her car and swerved away. Cappy turned around for his own house once we'd reached mine, and I walked to the back door. As I rounded the corner, I saw the twiggy treelets with their shriveled leaves, still laid out in a row on the concrete to die. I put down my books and gathered them up, one by one, and stashed them at the edge of the yard. It was in me at that moment to feel sorry for the little trees and to be aware also that I dreaded going into my house. I had never felt that before. Then I tried to open the door and found it was locked.

I was so surprised at first that I kicked at the door, thinking it was stuck. But the back door was really locked. And the front door locked automatically—Clemence had probably forgotten that. I got the key from its hiding place and went in slowly, quiet, not banging the door and slamming my books on the table as I ordinarily would have. On any other day, my mother wouldn't have been home yet and I would have felt the sort of elation that a boy feels when he steps into his house knowing that for two hours it is all his. That he can make his own sandwich. That if there is TV reception, there might be afterschool reruns for him to watch. That there might be cookies or some other sweet around, hidden by his mother, but not hidden too well. That he can rifle through the books on his father and mother's bedroom bookshelves for a book like *Hawaii*, by James Michener, where he might learn interesting but ultimately useless tips on Polynesian foreplay—but there, I have to stop. The back door had been locked for the first time I ever recall, and I'd had to fish the key from underneath the back steps where it had always hung on a nail, used only when the three of us returned from long trips.

Which was the sense I had now: that just going to school had been a long trip—and now I had returned.

The air seemed hollow in the house, stale, strangely flat. I realized that this was because in the days since we'd found my mother sitting in the driveway, nobody had baked, fried, cooked, or in any way prepared food. My father only made coffee, which he drank day and night. Clemence had brought us casseroles that were still sitting, half eaten, in the refrigerator. I called for my mother softly, and walked halfway up the stairs until I could see that the door to my parents' bedroom was shut. I eased back down the stairs into the kitchen. I opened the refrigerator, poured myself a glass of cold milk, and took a big swallow. It was grossly sour. I dumped the milk, rinsed the glass, filled it, and gulped down the iron water of our reservation until the sour taste was gone. Then I stood there with the empty glass in my hands.

Part of the dining room set was visible through the open door, a roan maple table with six chairs around it. The living room was divided off by low shelves. The couch sat just outside a small room lined with books—my father's den, or study. Holding the glass, I felt the tremendous hush in our little house as something that follows in the wake of a huge explosion. Everything had stopped. Even the clock's ticking. My father had unplugged it when we came home from the hospital the second night. I want a new clock, he'd said. I stood there looking at the old clock, whose hands were meaninglessly stopped at 11:22. The sun fell onto the kitchen floor in golden pools, but it was an ominous radiance, like the piercing light behind a western cloud. A trance of dread came over me, a taste of death like sour milk. I set the glass on the table and bolted up the stairs. Burst into my parents' bedroom. My mother was sunk in such heavy sleep that when I tried to throw myself down next to her, she struck me in the face. It was a forearm back blow and caught my jaw, stunning me.

Joe, she said, trembling. Joe.

I was determined not to let her know she'd hurt me.

Mom . . . the milk was sour.

She lowered her arm and sat up.

Sour?

She had never let the milk go sour in the refrigerator before. She had grown up without refrigeration and was proud of how clean she kept her treasured icebox. She took the freshness of its contents seriously. She'd bought Tupperware even, at a party. The milk was sour?

Yes, I said. It was.

We have to go to the grocery!

Her serene reserve was gone—a nervous horror welled across her face. The bruises had come out and her eyes were darkly rimmed like a raccoon's. A sick green pulsed around her temples. Her jaw was indigo. Her eyebrows had always been so expressive of irony and love, but now were held tight by anguish. Two vertical lines, black as if drawn by a marker, creased her forehead. Her fingers plucked at the quilt's edge. Sour!

They have milk now at Whitey's gas station. I can bike down there, Mom.

They do? She looked at me as though I'd saved her, like a hero.

I brought her purse. She gave me a five-dollar bill.

Get other things, she said. Food you like. Treats. She stumbled over the words and I realized that she'd probably been given some sort of drug to help her sleep.

Our house was built in the 1940s, a sturdy bungalow-style. The BIA superintendent, a pompous, natty, abnormally short bureaucrat who was profoundly hated, had once lived in it. The house had been sold to the tribe in 1969 and used as office space until it was scheduled to be torn down and replaced by actual offices. My father had bought it and moved it onto the little plot of land near town that had belonged to Geraldine's late uncle, Shamengwa, a handsome man in an old-fashioned framed picture. My mother missed his music, but his violin was buried with him. Whitey had used the rest of the land that Shamengwa had owned to put up his gas station on the other side of town. Mooshum owned the old allotment about four miles away, where Uncle Whitey lived. Whitey had married a younger woman—a tall, blonde, weather-beaten ex-stripper—who now worked the gas station cash register. Whitey pumped the gas, changed oil, inflated tires, did unreliable repair work. His wife did the books, restocked the shelves of the little store with nuts and chips, and told people why they could or could not charge gas. She had recently bought a large dairy cooler. She kept a smaller cooler filled with bottles of orange and grape Crush. Sonja was her name, and I liked her the way a boy likes his aunt, but I felt differently about her breasts—on them I had a hopeless crush.

I took my bicycle and a backpack. I had a battered black five-speed with trail-bike tires, a water-bottle clip, and a silver scrawl on the crossbar, Storm Ryder. I took the cracked side road, crossed the main highway, circled Whitey's once, and slid sideways to a halt, hoping that Sonja had her eye on me. But no, she was inside counting Slim Jims. She had a great big flashy radiant white smile. She looked up and turned it on me when I walked in. It was like a sunlamp. Her cotton-candy hair was fluffed up in a swirly yellow crown and a glossy two-foot ponytail hung out of it, down her back. As always, she was dramatically outfitted—today a baby blue running suit with sequin piping, the top three-quarters unzipped. I caught my breath at the sight of her T-shirt, a paler fairy-wing-transparent tissue. She wore white unmarred spongy track shoes and crystals in her ears big as thumbtacks. When she wore blue, as she did quite often, her blue eyes zapped with startling electricity.

Honey, she said, putting down the Slim Jims and taking me in her arms. There was nobody at the pump or in the store at that moment. She smelled of Marlboros, Aviance Night Musk, and her first drink of the late afternoon.

I was lucky: I was a boy doted on by women. This was not my doing, and in fact it worried my father. He made valiant attempts to counteract feminine coddling by doing manly things with me—we played catch, threw a football, camped out, fished. Fished often. He taught me to drive the car when I was eight. He was afraid all the doting I experienced might soften me, though he'd been doted on himself, I could see that, and my grandma doted plenty on him (and me) in those years before she died. Still, I'd hit a lull in our family's reproductive history. My cousins Joseph and Evelina were in college when I was born. Whitey's sons from his first marriage were grown, and Sonja's relationship with her daughter, London, was so stormy she said she'd never want another. There were no grandchildren in the family (yet, thank god, said Sonja). As I said, I was born late, into the aging tier of the family, and to parents who would often be mistaken for my grandparents. There was that added weight of being a surprise to my mother and father, and the surging hopes that implied. It was all on me—the bad and the good. But one of the chief goods, one I cherished, was the proximity I was allowed to Sonja's breasts.

I could press against her breasts for as long as she hugged me. I was careful never to push my luck, though my hands itched. Full, delicate, resolute, and round, Sonja's were breasts to break your heart over. She carried them high in her pastel scoop-neck T-shirts. Her waist was still trim and her hips flared softly in tight stonewashed jeans. Sonja massaged her skin with baby oil, but all her life she had harshly tanned and her cute Swedish nose was scarred by sunburn. She was a horse lover and she and Whitey kept a mean old paint, a fancy quarter horse/Arabian mix, a roan Appaloosa with one ghost eye named Spook, and a pony. So along with the whiskey and perfume and smoke, she often exuded faint undertones of hay, dust, and the fragrance of horse, which once you smell it you always miss it. Humans were meant to live with the horse. She and Whitey also had three dogs, all female, ferocious, and named in some way after Janis Joplin.

Our dog had died two months ago and we hadn't got a new one yet. I opened my backpack and Sonja put in the milk and other things I'd picked out. She pushed back my five dollars and gazed at me from under her delicate, pale-brown, plucked eyebrows. Tears flooded her eyes. Shit, she said. Let me at the guy. I'll waste him.

I did not know what to say. Sonja's breasts made most thoughts leave my head.

How's your mom doing? she said, shaking her head, swiping at her cheeks.

I tried to focus now; my mother was not fine so I could not answer *fine*. Nor could I tell Sonja that half an hour ago I'd feared my mother was dead and I had rushed upon her and got hit by her for the first time in my life. Sonja lit a cigarette, offered me a piece of Black Jack gum.

Not good, I said. Jumpy.

Sonja nodded. We'll bring Pearl.

Pearl was a rangy long-legged mutt with a bull terrier's broad head and viselike jaws. She had Doberman markings, a shepherd's heavy coat, and some wolf in her. Pearl didn't bark much but when she did she became very worked up. She paced and snapped the air whenever someone violated her invisible territorial boundaries. Pearl was not a companion dog and I wasn't sure I wanted her, but my father did.

She's too old to teach to fetch and stuff, I complained to him when he got home that night.

We were sitting downstairs, eating heated-up casserole brought once again by Clemence. My father had made his usual pot of weak coffee and he was drinking it like water. My mother was in the bedroom, not hungry. My father put down his fork. From the way he did it (he was a man who liked his food and to stop eating was usually a relinquishment, though these days he wasn't eating much), I thought he was angry. But although his gestures of recent were abrupt and he often clenched his fists, he did not raise his voice. He spoke very quietly, reasonably, telling me why we needed Pearl.

Joe, we need a protection dog. There is a man we suspect. But he has cleared out. Which means he could be anywhere. Or, he might not have done it but the real attacker could still be in the area.

I asked what I thought was a police TV question.

What evidence do you have that this one guy did it?

My father considered not answering, I could tell. But he finally did. He had trouble saying some of the words.

The perpetrator or the suspect . . . the attacker . . . dropped a book of matches. The matches were from the golf course. They give them out at the desk.

So they're starting with the golfers, I said. This meant the attacker could be Indian or white. That golf course fascinated everyone—it was a kind of fad. Golf was for rich people, supposedly, but here we had a course of scraggly grass and natural water pits. With a special introductory rate. People passed their clubs around and everybody seemed to have tried it—except my dad.

Yes, the golf course.

Why'd he drop the matches?

My father rubbed a hand across his eyes and again had trouble speaking.

He wanted to, tried to, he was having trouble lighting a match.

A book match?

Yes.

Oh. Did he get it lit?

No . . . the match was wet.

So then what happened?

Suddenly my eyes began to water and I bent over my plate.

My father picked his fork back up. He quickly shoveled Clemence's well-known macaroni and tomato sauce/hamburger concoction into his mouth. He saw that I had stopped eating and was waiting, and he sat back. He drained another cup of coffee from his favorite heavy white china diner mug. He put a napkin to his lips, shut his eyes, opened them, and looked at me directly.

All right, Joe, you're asking a lot of questions. You are developing an order to things in your mind. You're thinking this out. So am I. Joe, the perpetrator couldn't light the match. He went to look for another book of matches. Some way of lighting a fire. While he was gone, your mother managed to escape.

How?

For the first time since we'd pulled out those trees the Sunday before, my father smiled, or it was some version of a smile, I should say. There was no amusement in it. Later on, if I had to classify that smile, I would say it was a smile like Mooshum's. A smile of remembrance of lost times.

Joe, do you remember how I used to get so exasperated when your mother locked herself out of her car? She had—still has—a habit of leaving the car keys on the dashboard. After she parks, she always gathers her papers or groceries off the passenger seat, then she puts her keys on the dash, gets out, and locks the car. She forgets that she left her keys in the car until she needs to go home. Then she rummages through her purse and can't find her keys. Oh no, she says, not again! She goes out, sees her car keys are on the dashboard, locked inside, and then calls me. Remember?

Yeah. I almost smiled too as he described what had been

her habit, the whole rigmarole we went through. Yeah, Dad, she calls you. You use a mild swear word, then you get the extra set of keys and take a long walk over to the tribal offices.

Mild swear word. Where'd you get that?

Damn, I don't know.

He smiled again, put his hand out and nicked at my cheek with his knuckle.

I never really minded, he said. But one day it occurred to me that your mom would be really stuck if I wasn't home. We don't go many places. Our schedule is pretty boring. But if I wasn't home, or you weren't, to bike her keys over.

That's never happened.

But see, you might have been outside. Not heard the telephone. I thought, What if she really gets stuck somewhere? And thinking this, about two months ago I glued a magnet onto the back of one of those little metal boxes Whitey sells mints in. I saw someone else had a key holder like it. I put a car key in the box and stuck it inside the car's frame just over the left rear tire. That's how she escaped.

What? I said. How?

She managed to reach under the car; she got the car key. He came at her. She locked herself in the car, then she started the car and drove away.

I took a deep breath. I couldn't help a sense of her fear from slashing through me and it made me weak.

My father started eating again, and this time he was clearly going to finish his meal. The subject of what had happened to my mother was closed. I went back to the dog.

Pearl bites, I said.

Good, said my father.

He's still after her then.

We don't know, said my father. Anybody could have picked up those matches. Indian. White. Anybody could have dropped them. But probably it was someone from around here.

*

You can't tell if a person is an Indian from a set of fingerprints. You can't tell from a name. You can't even tell from a local police report. You can't tell from a picture. From a mug shot. From a phone number. From the government's point of view, the only way you can tell an Indian is an Indian is to look at that person's history. There must be ancestors from way back who signed some document or were recorded as Indians by the U.S. government, someone identified as a member of a tribe. And then after that you have to look at that person's blood quantum, how much Indian blood they've got that belongs to one tribe. In most cases, the government will call the person an Indian if their blood is one quarter—it usually has to be from one tribe. But that tribe has also got to be federally recognized. In other words, being an Indian is in some ways a tangle of red tape.

On the other hand, Indians know other Indians without the need for a federal pedigree, and this knowledge—like love, sex, or having or not having a baby—has nothing to do with government.

It took me another day to find out that it was already going around that there were suspects—basically anyone who acted strange or had not been seen or had been seen walking out of his back door with loaded black garbage bags.

I found out by going over to my aunt and uncle's house to pick up a pie on Saturday afternoon. My mother had told my father that she thought she had better get up, bathe, get dressed. She was still on pain pills, but Dr. Egge had told her that bed rest wouldn't help. She needed mild activity. Dad had announced that he was cooking dinner from a recipe. But he could not manage dessert. Thus, the pie. Uncle Whitey was sitting at the table with a glass of iced tea. Mooshum sat across from him, hunched and frail, wearing ivory-colored long underwear, and a plaid robe over the long johns. He refused to dress in street clothes on Saturday because he needed a day of comfort, he claimed, to get ready for Sunday, when Clemence made him wear suit pants, a pressed white shirt, and sometimes a tie. He too had a glass of iced tea, but he was glaring at it.

Bunny piss, he griped.

That's right, Daddy, said Clemence. It's an old man's drink. It's good for you.

Ah, swamp tea, said Uncle Whitey, swirling the glass appreciatively. Good for everything that ails you, Daddy.

Cures old age? said Mooshum. Takes the years off?

All but, said Whitey, who knew he could have a beer as soon as he got home and quit pretend-drinking with Mooshum, who was lonely for the old days when Clemence poured smooth whiskey. She'd become convinced that it was harming him and was always trying to cut him off.

This goes down hard, my daughter, he said to Clemence.

Cleans out your liver good, though, said Whitey.

Here, Clemence, pour a little swamp tea for Joe.

Clemence poured me a glass of iced tea and went to answer the phone. People were calling her constantly for news, gossip really, about her sister.

Maybe the pervert really is an Indian, said Uncle Whitey. He was carrying an Indian suitcase.

What Indian suitcase? I said.

The plastic garbage bags.

I leaned forward. So he left? But from where? Who is he? What's his name?

Clemence came back in and flared her eyes at him.

Awee, said Uncle Whitey. Guess I'm not supposed to talk.

Or have even a little glass of whiskey. Or piss in the sink, as I will do until she no longer pours swamp tea. A man's kidneys overflow, said Mooshum.

You piss in the sink? I asked.

When given tea, always.

Clemence went into the kitchen, came out with a bottle of whiskey and three stacked shot glasses. She arranged them on the table and poured two a quarter full. She poured the third half full and tossed it back. I was astounded. I'd never seen my aunt toss back a whiskey like a man. She held her drained glass delicately for a moment, regarding us, then put the glass down with a short smack and walked outside.

What was that? Uncle Whitey asked.

That was my daughter pushed too far, said Mooshum. I pity Edward when he returns. The whiskey will have set by then.

Sometimes whiskey sets Sonja too, Uncle Whitey said, but I have tricks.

What kind of tricks, said Mooshum.

Old Indian tricks.

Teach them to Edward, eh? He is losing ground.

The pie began to scent the air with a sweet amber fragrance. I hoped my aunt hadn't got so angry she'd forget the pie.

The golf course. Is that where it happened? I looked straight at Whitey, but he dropped his eyes and drank.

No, it didn't happen there.

Where did it?

Whitey raised his sad and permanently bloodshot eyes. He wasn't going to tell me. I couldn't hold his gaze.

Mooshum's grip, so unsteady on the tea glass that he'd slopped it on the table, tightened now. He lifted the shot and took a neat sip. His eyes shone. He had not taken in our exchange. His brain was still fixed on women.

Ah, my son, tell Oops and me of your beautiful wife. Red Sonja. Paint the picture. What does she do at present?

Whitey shifted his eyes off me. When he grinned, the devil's gap between his front teeth showed. Red Sonja was my aunt's exotic dance persona not so long ago. She'd worn revealing barbarian armor, which was bits of studded plastic. Tattered scarves flowed from her hips. The transparent material looked to have been chewed and clawed by desperate men or pet wolves. Zack had found the picture in a Minneapolis publication and made me a gift of it. I kept it deep in my closet, in a special folder I had made that said HOMEWORK.

These days Sonja works behind the cash register, my uncle said now, the whiskey adding its soft glow. She is always adding numbers. Today she is figuring out exactly what we must reorder for the next week.

Mooshum closed his eyes, held the whiskey at the back of his tongue, and nodded, conjuring her up, bent over the accounts. I could see her suddenly, too, breasts riding like clouds over the long columns of neat little figures.

And what will she do, asked Mooshum dreamily, when she has the sums and figures for the day, when she is finished?

She will leave the desk and go outside with a bucket of water and the long-handled squeegee. She cleans the glass every week.

Mooshum wasn't wearing his flashy dentures and his collapsed smile spread. I closed my eyes and saw the pink sponge side of the squeegee drip its window-solution suds down the plate glass. Sonja stretched up on her tiptoes. Cappy's big brother, Randall, said girls looked so good stretching up on their tiptoes that he liked to sit watching down the rows in the school library. Randall used to put all the good books on the top shelves. Mooshum sighed. I saw Sonja pressing the rubber blade hard against the glass, drawing the dust and the smudges down with the liquid and leaving a sparkling clarity.

Clemence came back in, breaking my thoughts, and I heard the creak of the oven door. Then the slide of the rack as she removed two pies from the oven. I heard her set the pies out to cool. The oven door clanged and the screen door whined open and clapped shut. In a moment, the faint crispness of a burning cigarette wafted through the screen. I'd never known my aunt to smoke before, but she had started since the hospital.

The scent of Clemence's newly taken up smoking sobered both of the men.

They turned to me and Uncle Whitey's face was grave as he asked how my mother was.

She's coming out of her room tonight, I told Whitey. I'm supposed to take a pie home. My dad is cooking.

Mooshum stared at me, an edge of harsh brilliance in his gaze, and I knew he had been told something, at least, of what had occurred.

That's good, he said. Hear me now, Oops. She gotta come out. Don't leave her to sit. Don't let her alone too much.

Clear spring shadows spread like water across the road. Down past the quiet slough, engines rumbled up to and away from the liquor store's drive-up window. From yards invisible behind stands of willow and chokecherry, the short, vibrant cries of women rang, calling their children home. A car slowed next to me and Doe Lafournais nodded at the empty passenger seat. Doe had a quiet face, a crooked nose, kind eyes. He had powerful arms and stayed strong through constant hard labor—besides being the chairman and janitoring, he had built their house from scratch. He and his sons had messed it up from scratch, too. The place was layers of junk on interesting junk now. He drove on when I shook my head and called out that I'd see him later—I was helping out that evening at Randall's sweat lodge. Clemence had put the pie in the bottom of a shallow cardboard box. The steam from the warm apples threaded from the slit crust. The evening wasn't cooling off, but I didn't care. I'd sweat to eat that pie. I turned down the driveway and Pearl popped out of the lilacs. She gave one deep-chested bark of recognition and, after sniffing the air about me, she accompanied me, at a space of about three feet, up to the back door of the house. There she left me and went back to lie underneath her bush.

My father let me in. The hot kitchen smelled of some violent experiment.

Perfect timing, he said, and put the pie on the counter. Let's keep this as a surprise. The pièce de résistance. She'll be down in a minute, Joe. Wash up.

While I was in the little toilet off the study, I heard the stairs creak. I stayed in there, washing and drying my hands slowly. I didn't really want to see my mother. It was terrible, but it was true. Even though I understood perfectly why she had struck me, I resented that I had to pretend it hadn't happened or didn't matter. The blow had not left a visible bruise and my cheekbone was only slightly tender, but I kept touching the place and reviving my sense of injury. When I finished washing, I refolded the towel for perhaps the first time in my life and hung it carefully upon its rail.

In our dining cove, my mother was standing behind her chair with her hands nervous on the wooden back. The fan was on, stirring her dress. She was admiring the meal laid out on the plain green cloth. I looked at her and was immediately ashamed of my resentment—her face was still garishly marked. I busied myself. My father had made a stew. The collision of smells that hit me when I'd entered the kitchen were the ingredients—sour turnips and canned tomatoes, beets and corn, scorched garlic, unknown meat, and an onion gone bad. The concoction gave off a penetrating reek.

My father beckoned the two of us to sit down. There were potatoes, nearly cooled, way overcooked, disintegrating in an undrained pot. He ceremoniously heaped our shallow bowls. Then we sat looking at the food. We didn't pray. For the first time, I felt the lack of some ritual. I couldn't just start eating. My father sensed this and spoke with great emotion, looking at us both.

Very little is needed to make a happy life, he said.

My mother took a sharp breath, and frowned. She shrugged

away what he'd said, as if it irritated her. I guessed she'd heard his Marcus Aurelius quote before, but looking back on it, I also know she was trying to build up her shield. To not feel things. Not refer to what had happened. His emotion grabbed at her.

With no ceremony, she picked up her spoon and plunged it into the stew. She choked her first gulp down. I sat poised. We both looked at my father.

I added caraway seeds, he said gently. What do you think?

My mother took a paper napkin from the pile my father had laid in the middle of the table, and she held it to her lips. Deep violet streaks and the yellow of healing contusions still marred her face. The white of her left eye was scarlet and her eyelid drooped slightly, as it would from then on, for the nerve had been tampered with and the damage was irreversible.

What do you think? my father asked once more.

My mother and I were silent, staring in shock at what we had tasted.

I think, she said at last, that I should start cooking again.

My father cast his eyes down, put out his hands, the picture of a man who had tried his best. He pouted a little and dug into his bowl, with a pretend heartiness that grew labored. He swallowed once, twice. I was aghast at his strength of mind. I filled up on bread. His spoon slowed. My mother and I probably realized at the same time that my father, who had taken care of my grandmother for many years and certainly knew how to cook, had faked his ineptitude. But the stew with its gagging undertone of rotted onion was so successfully infernal that it cheered us up, as my mother's decision to cook had done. When I cleared away the awful dinner and the pie was produced, my mother smiled slightly, just an upward movement of her lips. My father divided the pie into three equal pieces and laid a slab of Blue Bunny vanilla on top of each piece. I got to finish my mother's. She started teasing my father about the stew.

Exactly how old were those turnips?

Older than Joe.
And where did you get that onion?
That's my little secret.
And the meat, roadkill?
Oh god, no. It died in the backyard.

I wasn't particularly worried about missing dinner that night because I knew after Randall's sweat lodge that Cappy and his sidekick, me, would eat top-shelf. We were the fire keepers. Cappy's aunts, Suzette and Josey, who had made Doe's boys their pets, always fixed the food. On ceremony nights they'd leave a feast put up neatly in two big plastic coolers alongside the garage. Farther back, nearly in the woods, the sweat-lodge dome of bent and lashed-together saplings, covered by army-surplus tarps, humidly waited, gathering mosquitoes. Cappy had already made the fire. The rocks, the grandfathers, were superheating in the middle. Our job was to keep that fire going, hand in the sacred pipes and the medicines, bring the rocks to the door on long-handled shovels, close and open the flaps. We'd also throw tobacco into our fire when someone in the lodge yelled for it, to mark some special prayer or request. On crisp nights it was a good job—we'd sit talking around that fire, staying warm. Sometimes we'd secretly roast a hot dog or marshmallow on a stick even though the fire was sacred and one time Randall had caught us. He'd claimed we'd taken the sacredness out of the fire with our hot dogs.

Cappy looked at him and said, How sacred can your fire be if we sucked out its holiness with just our puny wieners? I couldn't stop laughing. Randall threw up his hands and walked off. It was too hot to roast anything now, besides we knew we'd eat hugely at the end. Food was our pay, besides sometimes driving Randall's beat-up Olds. It was usually a pleasant enough job. That night, however, instead of cooling off, it grew muggy. There was no breeze. Even before sunset, whining clouds of mosquitoes swarmed us. Their attacks made us sit closer to the fire, in order to take advantage of the smoke, which only made us sweat enticingly. They just kept sucking on us through the salty, smoky layers of Off.

Randall's friends, who all belonged to a powwow drum or danced like Randall, showed up laughing. Two of them were baked, but Randall didn't notice. He was obsessive about setting everything up perfectly—the rack for the pipes, the star quilt blanket smoothed out beside the entrance, the abalone shell for burning sage, the glass jars of powdered medicine, the bucket and dipper. He seemed to have a little measuring stick in his head for lining up these sacred items. It drove Cappy nuts. But other people liked Randall's style and he had friends from all over Indian Country—just that day he'd opened a package from a Pueblo friend which contained a jar of medicine that was now sitting with the others. He was humming a pipe-loading song and putting his pipe together, concentrating so hard he didn't notice that the back of his neck was covered with gorging mosquitoes. I swiped them off.

Thanks, he said distractedly. I'm gonna pray for your family.

That's cool, I said, though it made me uncomfortable. I didn't like being prayed for. As I turned away I felt the prayers creeping up my spine. But that was Randall, too, always ready to make you feel a little uncomfortable with the earnest superiority of all that he was learning from the elders, even your own elders, for your benefit. Mooshum had instructed Doe on how to set up this lodge and Doe had passed it down to Randall. Cappy saw my look.

Don't worry about it, Joe. He prays for me too. And he gets a lot of girls with his medicine. So he's gotta keep in practice.

Randall had a stony profile, smooth skin, and a long braided ponytail. Girls, especially white ones, were fascinated with him. A German girl had camped in their yard for a whole month one summer. She was pretty, and wore the first earth sandals ever seen on our reservation, so Randall got teased about them. Somebody got a good look at the label and it was Birkenstock, which became Randall's nickname.

The heat grew worse and we guzzled dippers of the sacred sweat-lodge water. I envied the guys going into the lodge because they would get so hot that this outside heat would seem like a cool breeze when they came out. Plus the fiercer heat from those grandfathers would wilt the mosquitoes. They all went in. Cappy and I brought the rocks to the door with the long-handled shovels. Randall took them off the shovels with a pair of deer antlers and placed them in the center pit. We handed in all of their stuff and closed the flap. They started singing and we sprayed ourselves again with Off.

We had finished three rounds and passed in the last of the grandfathers. We'd gone up to the house to refill the water cooler and were coming out, standing on the back deck, when there was an explosion. We didn't even hear anyone yell, *Door*, signaling us to open it. The top of the sweat lodge just billowed up and heaved with guys fighting to get out. They raged and flailed in the tarps. There was muffled howling. Then they popped out any way they could—gasping, yelling, and rolling naked in the grass. The mosquitoes dive-bombed. We ran down with the water cooler. Randall and his buddies made gestures at their squeezed-up faces and we doused their heads. As soon as they could jump up, each one of them staggered or ran toward the house. Cappy's aunts were driving up just then with extra frybread for the feast, so they saw eight naked Indians trying to grope their way across the yard. Suzette and Josey just stayed in the car.

It took a long while, everyone sitting in the house amid the piles of bachelor junk, for the men to emerge from shock and figure out what happened.

I think it was, said Skippy at last, that Pueblo medicine. Remember just before you threw a big handful on the rocks you thanked your buddy down there, then you said a longish prayer?

A long, long prayer, Birkenstock. Then you ladled on that water . . .

Oooh, said Randall. My friend said it was Pueblo medicine. I was praying for his situation with a Navajo woman. Cappy, go and get that jar.

Don't order me.

Okay, please, younger brother, seeing as we're all butt naked and traumatized, would you go out and get that jar?

Cappy went out. He came back. There was a label on the jar.

Randall, said Cappy, the word medicine has quote marks around it.

The jar was filled with a brownish powder that didn't smell very strong to us—not like bear root or wiikenh or kinnikinnick. Randall held the jar and frowned. He sniffed it like a fancy wine taster. At last, he licked his finger, stuck it in the jar, and put his finger in his mouth. Tears spurted instantly.

Aah! Aah! He stuck his tongue out.

Hot pepper, said the others. Special Pueblo hot pepper. They watched Randall dance around the room.

Man, look at his feet fly.

We should give him Pueblo medicine next powwow.

For sure, man. They took long drinks of water. Randall was at the sink with his tongue sticking out under the water tap.

Randall placed that medicine down on the rocks, said Skippy, but when he threw down four big ladles of water, then, man, it vaporized into our eyes and we were breathing that shit in! It burnt like hell. How could Randall have done that to us, man?

They all looked at Randall with his tongue under the faucet.

I hope he puts more clothes on finally, said Chiboy Snow.

We remembered the aunts when we heard them pull out of

the driveway. We looked out. They'd left behind two bags of fresh frybread. The grease was darkening the paper sacks in delicate patches.

If you bring our clothes in, Skippy said to us, and hand in that feast, I'd pay youse.

How much? said Cappy.

Two each.

Cappy looked at me. I shrugged.

We hauled their stuff in and as we were all eating Randall came and sat next to me. His face was rugged and raw like all the other guys. His eyes were swollen red. Randall had most of his college education, and sometimes he talked like he was addressing me as a social service case, and other times he treated me like his little brother. This was one of those close familial Randall times. His friends were already laughing and eating. They'd forgotten to be mad at Randall now and everything was funny.

Joe, he said, I saw something in there.

I filled my mouth with taco meat.

I saw something, he went on, and he sounded genuinely troubled. It was before the hot pepper blew things up that I saw it. I was praying for your family and my family and all of a sudden, I saw a man bending over you, like a police maybe, looking down at you, and his face was white and his eyes deep down in his face. He was surrounded by a silver glow. His lips moved and he was talking, but I could not hear what he said.

We sat there quietly. I stopped eating.

What should I do about it, Randall? I asked in a low voice.

We'll both put down tobacco, he said. And maybe you should talk to Mooshum. It had a bad feeling, Joe.

My mother cooked all the next week, and even made it outside, where she sat on a frayed lawn chair scratching Pearl's neck, staring into the chokecherry bushes that marked the boundaries of the backyard. My father spent as much time home as possible, but he was still called to finish out some of his responsibilities. He was also meeting daily with the tribal police, and talking to the federal agent who was assigned to the case. One day he traveled to Bismarck and back to talk with the U.S. attorney, Gabir Olson, an old friend. The problem with most Indian rape cases was that even after there was an indictment the U.S. attorney often declined to take the case to trial for one reason or another. Usually a raft of bigger cases. My father wanted to make sure that didn't happen.

So the days went by in that false interlude. On Friday morning, my father reminded me that he would need my help. I often earned a few dollars by biking to my father's office after school and "putting the court to bed for the weekend." I swept out his small office, spray-wiped the glass top of his wooden desk. I straightened and dusted the diplomas on his wall—University of North Dakota, University of Minnesota Law School—and the plaques recognizing his service in law organizations. He had a list of places he was admitted to practice that went all the way up to the U.S. Supreme Court. I was proud of that. Next door, in his closet-turned-chambers, I did a sweep-out. President Reagan, ruddy cheeks and muddled eyes, B-movie teeth, grinned off the wall in his government-issue portrait. Reagan was so dense about Indians he though we lived on "preserves." There was a print of our tribal seal and one of the great seal of North Dakota. My father had framed an antiquified copy of the Preamble to the U.S. Constitution, plus the Bill of Rights.

Back in his office, I shook out his brown wool rug. I put away and straightened up his books, which included all the later editions of the old Cohen *Handbook* at home. There was the 1958 edition, issued during the era when Congress was intent on terminating Indian tribes—it was always left on the shelf, its disuse a mute rebuke to the editors. There were the

1971 facsimile edition and the 1982 edition—big, heavy, well worn. Next to those books there was a compact copy of our own Tribal Code. I also helped my father file whatever his secretary, Opichi Wold, hadn't put away. Opichi, whose name meant Robin, was a dour little skinny woman with pin-sharp eyes. She functioned as my father's set of reservation eyes and ears. Every judge needs a scout out there. Opichi gathered tidbits, call it gossip, but what she knew often informed my father's decisions. She knew who could be released on recognizance, who'd run. She knew who was dealing, who was only using, who was driving without a license, who was abusive, reformed, drinking, dangerous, or safe with their own children. She was invaluable, though her filing system was opaque.

We kept all papers next door in a larger room walled with tan metal filing cabinets. A few files were always left on top of the cabinets because my father had expressed an interest in reading them over, or was adding notes. That day I noticed large stacks were left out—chestnut brown cardboard files with the labels neatly typed and fixed on by Opichi. Most were notes on cases, summaries and thoughts, drafts that preceded a final published judgment. I asked if we were going to file them, thinking there were too many to finish before suppertime.

We're taking them home, said my father.

This was a thing he did not do. His study at home was his retreat from all that went on in tribal court. He was proud of leaving the week's turmoil where it belonged. But today, we loaded the files into the backseat. We put my bike in the trunk and drove home.

I'll take those files in myself after dinner, he said on the way. So I knew he did not want my mother to see him bring those files into the house. After the car was parked we took my bike out and I wheeled it around back. My father entered before me. Walking through the kitchen door, I heard a splintering crash. And then a keen, low, anguished cry. My mother was backed up to the sink, trembling, breathing heavily. My father was standing a few feet before her with his hands out, vainly groping in air the shape of her, as if to hold her without holding her. Between them on the floor lay a smashed and oozing casserole.

I looked at my parents and understood exactly what had happened. My father had come in—surely Mom had heard the car, and hadn't Pearl barked? His footsteps, too, were heavy. He always made noise and was as I have mentioned a somewhat clumsy man. I'd noticed that in the last week he'd also shouted something silly when returning, like, I'm home! But maybe he'd forgotten. Maybe he'd been too quiet this time. Maybe he'd gone into the kitchen, just as he always used to, and then he'd put his arms around my mother as she stood with her back turned. In our old life, she would have kept working at the stove or sink while he peered over her shoulder and talked to her. They'd stand there together in a little tableau of homecoming. Eventually, he'd call me in to help him set the table. He'd change his clothes quickly while she and I put the finishing touches on the meal, and then we would sit down together. We were not churchgoers. This was our ritual. Our breaking bread, our communion. And it all began with that trusting moment where my father walked up behind my mother and she smiled at his approach without turning. But now they stood staring at each other helplessly over the broken dish.

It was the kind of moment, I see now, that could have gone several ways. She could have laughed, she could have cried, she could have reached for him. Or he could have got down on his knees and pretended to have the heart attack that later killed him. She would have been jolted from her shock. Helped him. We would have cleared up the mess, made sandwiches for ourselves, and things would have gone on. If we'd sat down together that night, I do believe things would have gone on. But now my mother flushed darkly and an almost imperceptible shudder coursed over her. She took a gasping breath, and put her hand to her wounded face. Then she stepped over the mess on the floor and walked carefully away. I wanted her to shout, cry out, throw something. Anything would have been better than the frozen suspension of feeling in which she mounted the stairs. She was wearing a plain blue dress that night. No stockings. A pair of black Minnetonka moccasins. As she walked up each riser she looked straight ahead and her hand was firm on the banister. Her steps were soundless. She seemed to float. My father and I had followed her to the doorway, and I think as we watched her we both had the sense that she was ascending to a place of utter loneliness from which she might never be retrieved.

We stood together even after the bedroom door clicked shut. At last we turned and without a word we went back into the kitchen and scraped up the casserole and broken dish. Together we brought the mess outside to the garbage. My father paused after he closed the bin. He bowed his head and at that moment I was first aware that he exuded a desolation that would grip him with increasing force. When he remained there motionless, I truly became frightened. I put my hand urgently on his arm. I couldn't say what I was feeling, but that time, at least, my father looked up.

Help me get those files in. His voice was hard and urgent. We'll start tonight.

And so I did. We unloaded the car. Then we slapped together a few rough sandwiches. (He prepared one of the sandwiches with more care and put it on a plate. I cut up an apple, arranged the slices around the bread, meat, and lettuce. When my mother didn't answer my tap on the bedroom door, I left it just outside.) Holding our food in our hands, we went into my father's study and crammed our mouths as we frowned at the files. We brushed our crumbs to the floor. My father turned on the lamps. He settled himself at his desk and then nodded at me to do the same in the reading chair.

He's there, he said, nodding at the heavy stacks.

I understood that I was going to help. My father was treating me as his assistant. He knew, of course, about my surreptitious reading. I glanced instinctively at the Cohen shelf. He nodded again, raised his eyebrows a fraction, and lip-pointed at the stack near my elbow. We began to read. And it was then that I began to understand who my father was, what he did every day, and what had been his life.

Over the course of the next week, we culled several cases from the corpus of his work. During this time, which was the last week of school, my mother was unable to leave her room. My father brought her food. I sat with her in the evenings and read to her from *The Family Album of Favorite Poems* until she slept. It was an old maroon book with a ripped cover picturing happy white people reading poems in church, to their children at bedtime, whispering into a sweetheart's ear. She would not let me read anything inspirational. I had to read the endless story poems with their ornate words and clunking rhythms. "Ben Bolt," "The Highwayman," "The Leak in the Dike," and so on. As soon as her breathing evened out, I slunk away, relieved. She slept and slept, like she was sleeping for a sleeping marathon. She ate little. Wept often, a grinding and monotonous weeping that she tried to muffle with pillows but which vibrated through the bedroom door. I'd go downstairs, into the study, with my father, and continue reading through the files.

We read with a concentrated intensity. My father had become convinced that somewhere within his bench briefs, memos, summaries, and decisions lay the identity of the man whose act had nearly severed my mother's spirit from her body.

CHAPTER THREE

Justice

August 16, 1987
Durlin Peace, Plaintiff
v.
The Bingo Palace, Lyman Lamartine, Defendants

Durlin Peace is a janitor at the Bingo Palace and Casino, and reports directly to Lyman Lamartine. He was fired on July 5, 1987, two days after an argument with his boss. A witness testified that the argument was overheard by several other employees and involved a woman dated by both men.

On July 4, the employee cookout was held in the back courtyard patio of the Bingo Palace. During this cookout, Durlin Peace, who had been repairing some equipment earlier that day, walked off the premises. He was stopped by Lyman Lamartine and asked to empty his pockets. In one pocket, six washers were found, worth about 15 cents apiece. Lyman Lamartine then accused Durlin Peace of attempting to steal company property, and fired him.

Durlin Peace said that the washers belonged to him. As there were no distinguishing marks on the washers, which were examined by Judge Coutts, there was no proof that the washers belonged to the Bingo Palace. As there was no valid basis upon which Durlin Peace could be fired, it was ordered that he be reinstated at the Bingo Palace.

Washers? I said.

What about them? said my father.

I looked back down at the file.

Although this was not one of the cases we marked out as important, I remember it well. Here it was. The weighty matters on which my father spent his time and his life. I had, of course, been in court when he handled these sorts of cases. But I'd thought I was being excluded from weightier matters, upsetting or violent or too complex, because of my age. I had imagined that my father decided great questions of the law, that he worked on treaty rights, land restoration, that he looked murderers in the eye, that he frowned while witnesses stuttered and silenced clever lawyers with a slice of irony. I said nothing, but as I read on I was flooded by a slow leak of dismay. For what had Felix S. Cohen written his *Handbook*? Where was the greatness? the drama? the respect? All of the cases that my father judged were nearly as small, as ridiculous, as petty. Though a few were heartbreaking, or a combination of sad and idiotic, like that of Marilyn Shigaag, who stole five gas station hot dogs and ate them all in the gas station bathroom, none rose to the grandeur I had pictured. My father was punishing hot dog thieves and examining washers—not even washing machines—just washers worth 15 cents apiece.

December 8, 1976
Before Chief Judge Antone Coutts, also Justice Rose Chenois and Associate Justice Mervin "Tubby" Ma'ingan.
Tommy Thomas et al., Plaintiffs
v.
Vinland Super Mart et al., Defendants

Tommy Thomas and the other plaintiffs in this case were Chippewa tribal members, and Vinland was and is a non-Indian-owned gas and grocery business, which, though located primarily on fee (former purchased allotment) land, is surrounded by tribal trust land. The plaintiffs alleged that during commercial transactions occurring at Vinland Super Mart a 20% surcharge was added to transactions involving tribal members showing signs of age-related dementia, innocence of extreme youth, mental preoccupation, inebriation, or general confusion.

The owners, George and Grace Lark, did not deny that on some occasions a 20% surcharge had been added to cash register receipts. They defended their action by insisting it was a way to recoup losses from shoplifting. The defendants claimed that the Tribal Court did not have personal jurisdiction over them or subject matter jurisdiction over the transactions, which were the basis for the plaintiffs' complaint.

The Court found that although the gas station building itself was located on allotment #122093, the parking lot, garbage Dumpster, sidewalk, pumps, fire hydrants, sewage system, leach field, concrete parking barriers, outside picnic tables, and decorative flower planters were all located on tribal trust land, and that in order to enter the Vinland Super Mart, customers, 86% of whom were tribal members, had to drive and then to walk across tribal trust land.

This court claimed jurisdiction over the case and as there was no evidence presented to deny the surcharge had taken place found in favor of the plaintiffs.

My father had kept this one aside.

It seems like an ordinary enough case, I said. I tried to keep the disappointment out of my voice.

I was able in that case to claim limited jurisdiction over a non-Indian-owned business, said my father. The case held up on appeal. There was some pride in his voice.

That was satisfying, he went on, but that is not the reason I've pulled the case. I've marked it out to examine it further because of the people involved.

I looked back at the file.

Tommy Thomas et al. or the Larks?

The Larks, though Grace and George are dead. Linda survives. And their son, Linden, who is not mentioned or involved here, but who figures in another action, one more emotionally complicated. The Larks are the sort of people who trot out their relationships with "good Indians," whom they secretly despise and openly patronize, in order to prove their general love for Indians, whom they are engaged in cheating. The Larks were bumbling entrepreneurs and petty thieves, but they were also self-deceived. While their moral standards for the rest of the world were rigid, they were always able to find excuses for their own shortcomings. It is these people really, said my father, small-time hypocrites, who may in special cases be capable of monstrous acts if given the chance. The Larks, in fact, were shrill opponents of abortion. Yet at the birth of their twins, they had been willing to put to death the weaker and (as they thought at the time) deformed member, a baby girl. The whole reservation knew about it because one of the nurses at the hospital removed the damaged twin. A tribal member, Betty Wishkob, who was a night janitor, succeeded in adopting the infant. Which brings us to the other case.

In the Matter of the Estate of Albert and Betty Wishkob

Albert and Betty Wishkob, both enrolled members of the Chippewa Tribe and residents on the reservation, died intestate and with four children, Sheryl Wishkob Martin, Cedric Wishkob, Albert Wishkob Jr., and Linda Wishkob, who was born Linda Lark. Linda was informally adopted by the Wishkobs and raised among their family as an Indian. At the death of her adoptive parents, the other children, who had moved off reservation, agreed to let Linda continue living as she had in the home of Albert and Betty, which is situated on allotment #1002874, consists of 160 acres, and was returned to Tribal Trust after the Indian Reorganization Act of 1934. On January 19, 1986, the biological mother of Linda Lark Wishkob, Grace Lark, appealed to this court to allow her to assume guardianship of her now middle-aged daughter, Linda, in order to manage her affairs.

Grace Lark claimed that an illness contracted after Linda underwent a difficult medical procedure left Linda severely depressed and mentally confused. Grace Lark openly stated that she was interested in developing the 160 acres that she claimed had been left to Linda after her adoptive parents' death.

The last paragraph was handwritten, an aside for my father's eyes only.

As Linda is non-Indian by blood, as there is no legal evidence that the Wishkobs formally adopted Linda, as Grace Lark made no attempt to contact the other three inheriting children involved, and as, moreover, Linda Lark Wishkob, in the opinion of the court, was not only mentally competent but more sane than many who have come before this court, including her biological mother, this case was dismissed with prejudice.

Strange, I said.

It gets stranger, said my father.

How can it?

What you see is only the tip of a psychodrama that for some years consumed both the Larks, who gave their child up, and the Wishkobs, who in their kindness rescued and raised Linda. When the Wishkob children caught wind of the action, a clumsy, greedy, mean-minded attempt to raid and profit from an inheritance that never was, and land that never could be passed out of tribal ownership, they were furious. Linda's older sister by adoption, Sheryl, took direct action and organized a boycott of Lark's gas station. Not only that, she helped Whitey apply for a business grant. Everybody goes to Whitey's now. Whitey and Sonja have put the Larks out of business. During this time, Mrs. Lark's son, Linden, lost his job in South Dakota and returned to help his mother run the failing enterprise. She died of a sudden aneurysm. He blames the Wishkobs, his sister, Linda, Whitey and Sonja, and the judge in this case, me, for her death and his near bankruptcy, which seems now inevitable.

My father frowned at the files, passed his hand over his face.

I saw him in the courtroom. People say he's quite a talker, a real charmer. But he didn't say a word during the trial.

Could he be the . . . ? I asked.

Attacker, I don't know. He's troubling for sure. After his

mother died, he got into politics for a while. During the trial, he probably became unpleasantly aware of the jurisdiction issues on and surrounding the reservation. He wrote a crank letter to the *Fargo Forum*. Opichi clipped it. I remember it was full of the usual—let's dissolve reservations; he used that old redneck line, "We beat them fair and square." They never get that reservations exist because our ancestors signed legal transactions. But something must have sunk in because, next I heard, Linden was raising money for Curtis Yeltow, who was running for governor of South Dakota and shared his views. I've also heard—through Opichi, of course—that Linden is involved in a local chapter of Posse Comitatus. That group believes the powers of the highest elected official of government should reside with the local sheriff. Lark lives in his mother's house, last I heard. He lives very quietly and goes away a lot. Down to South Dakota, it's supposed. He's become secretive. Opichi says a woman is involved, but she's only been seen a few times. He comes and goes at odd hours, but so far, no sign he's dealing drugs or in any way breaking the law. I do know that the mother had a way of inciting emotional violence. Other people absorbed her anger. She was a frail-looking little old white lady. But her sense of entitlement was compelling. She was venomous. Maybe Lark moved on, or maybe he absorbed her poison.

My father went out to the kitchen to fill his mug. I stared at the files. Perhaps it was then that I noticed that every one of my father's actual published opinions was signed with a fountain pen, the ink a lyric shade of indigo. His handwriting was meticulous, almost Victorian, that spidery style of another age. I've learned since that there are two things about judges. They all have dogs, and they all have some special quirk to make them memorable. Thus, I think, the fountain pen, even though at home my father used a ballpoint. I opened the last file on the desk and began reading it.

September 1, 1974
Francis Whiteboy, Plaintiff
v.
Asiginak, Tribal Police, and Vince Madwesin,
Defendants

William Sterne, Attorney for the appellant, and
Johanna Coeur de Bois, Attorney for the respondents.

On August 13, 1973, a Shaking Tent ceremony was conducted at the old round house just north of Reservation Lake. The Shaking Tent is one of the most sacred of Ojibwe ceremonies, and will not be described here except to say that the ceremony served to heal petitioners and to answer spiritual questions.

That night there were over a hundred people in attendance, several of whom, at the edge of the crowd, were drinking. One of those who were drinking was Horace Whiteboy, brother of Francis, the appellant in this case. The leader of the ceremony, Asiginak, had asked Vince Madwesin of the local tribal police to act as security for the ceremony. Vince Madwesin asked Horace Whiteboy and the others who were drinking to leave the premises.

It is culturally unacceptable, even offensive, to drink at a Shaking Tent ceremony, and Madwesin behaved appropriately in asking the drinkers to leave. Several of the drinkers, realizing they were in gross breach of sacred etiquette, did leave the grounds. Horace Whiteboy was seen to stumble away from the ceremony with those drinkers, down the road. However, as affirmed by several witnesses, the spirit in the tent inhabited by Asiginak warned those listening that Horace Whiteboy was in danger.

Horace Whiteboy was found dead on the afternoon following the ceremony. Having apparently left the group of drinkers on the road, he had turned around and attempted to return to the round house. At the bottom of the hill, he apparently decided to lie down. He was found beneath some low bushes, lying on his back, and had choked to death on his own vomit.

Francis Whiteboy, brother of Horace, charges negligence in the actions of Asiginak (who was in the tent and had knowledge from the spirits that his brother was in trouble) and Vince Madwesin (who was off-duty in his capacity as security and not paid).

The court found that Asiginak's only responsibility was to allow the spirits to voice, through his presence, what they knew. This responsibility was carried out.

Vince Madwesin's actions to guarantee the security of the Shaking Tent ceremony were appropriate and as he was off-duty and unpaid this case cannot be brought against the tribal police. Madwesin's responsibility was to make certain that inebriates were warned away. He was not responsible for the actions of the drinkers.

An individual who drinks himself into a state of stuporous sickness runs the risk of succumbing to accidental death. The death Horace Whiteboy suffered, though tragic, was the outcome of his own actions. While compassion for alcoholics should be the rule, caring for them as one must care for children is not the law. Horace Whiteboy's behavior resulted in his death and his own decisions guided his fate.

The court ruled in favor of the defendants.

Why this one? I asked, when my father returned.

It was late. My father sat down, took a sip of coffee,

removed his reading glasses. He rubbed his eyes, and perhaps in his exhaustion spoke without thinking.

Because of the round house, he said.

The old round house? Did it happen there?

He did not answer.

What happened to Mom, did it happen there?

Again, no answer.

He shuffled away the papers, stood up. The light caught the lines in his face and they deepened to cracks. He looked a thousand years old.

CHAPTER FOUR

Loud as a Whisper

Cappy was a skinny guy with big hands and scarred-up, knobby feet, but he had bold cheekbones, a straight nose, big white teeth, and lank, shiny hair hanging down over one brown eye. Melting brown eye. The girls loved Cappy, even though his cheeks and chin were always scraped and he had a gap in one eyebrow where his forehead had been opened by a rock. His bike was a rusted blue ten-speed Doe had picked up at the mission. Because their house rattled with tools on every surface, Cappy kept it halfway fixed. Still, only first gear worked. And the hand brakes gave out unexpectedly. So when Cappy rode you'd see a spidery kid pedaling so fast his legs blurred and from time to time dragging his feet to stop or, if that didn't work, throwing himself suicidally over the crossbar. Angus had a beat-up pink BMX that he meant to paint before he realized the color kept it from getting stolen. Zack's bike was new, and a cool black, because his dad brought it after he had not shown up for two years. Since we couldn't drive legally (although of course we drove whenever we could), the bikes gave us freedom. We didn't have to rely on Elwin or on Whitey's horses, though we did ride the horses, too, when we could. We didn't have to ask Doe or Zack's mom for a ride, which was good on the morning after school let out because they wouldn't have taken us where we wanted to go.

Zack had confirmed, from listening in on his stepfather's burping police radio (he did this constantly), where the crime against my mother had taken place. It was the round house. A two-track bush road led to the old log round house on the far side of Reservation Lake. Early that morning, I got up and stepped quietly into my clothes. I slipped downstairs and let Pearl out. Together, we peed outside, in the back bushes. I didn't want to flush the noisy inside toilet. I sneaked back in, barely opening the screen door so it wouldn't whine, easing it slow so it wouldn't whap shut. Pearl entered with me and watched silently as I filled a bag with peanut butter sandwiches. I put them in my pack together with a jar of my mother's canned dill pickles and a water jug. I had agreed to write a note to tell my dad where I was—all summer, he made me swear. I wrote the word LAKE on the legal pad he'd left for me on the counter. I tore off half a sheet and wrote another note that I stuck in my pocket. I put my hand on Pearl's head and looked into her pale eyes.

Guard Mom, I said.

Cappy, Zack, and Angus were supposed to meet me in a couple of hours at a stump we used—just off the highway, across the ditch. There, I left the other note, telling them I'd gone ahead. I had planned this because I wanted to be alone at the round house when I first got there.

It was a lofty June morning. The dew was still cold on the wild rose and sage in last fall's mowed stubble, but I could tell that by afternoon it would be hot. Hot and clear. There would be ticks. Hardly anyone was out this early. Only two cars passed me on the highway. I turned off onto Mashkeeg Road, which was gravel, enclosed by trees, running partway around the lake. There were houses by the lake, screened by bush. An occasional dog popped up but I was pedaling fast and I came and went so quickly through their territories that few barked and none followed me. Even a tick, spinning through the air off a tree, hit my arm and could barely cling. I flicked him off and pedaled even faster until I reached the narrow road that led to the round house. It was still blocked by construction cones and painted oil drums. I guessed that was the work of the police. I walked my bike, looking carefully at the ground and beneath the leaves of the bushes along the way. The area had leafed in thickly during the past weeks. I was looking for anything that other eyes might have missed, as in one of Whitey's crime novels. I didn't see a thing out of place, though, or rather, since it was the woods and everything was out of place and wild, I didn't see a thing in place. A neatened area. Something that did not look or feel right. An empty jar, a bottle cap, a blackened match. This place had been minutely combed clean of what didn't belong already and I reached the clearing where the round house was set without finding anything of interest or use.

The grass had not been mowed yet, but the area where cars parked was covered with scrubby little plants. Horses had pulled all the good plants up by the roots and now tense little weeds rasped beneath the tires of my bike. The log hexagon was set up on top of a slight rise, and surrounded by rich grass, vivid green, long and thick. I dropped my bike. There was a moment of intense quiet. Then a low moan of air passed through the cracks in the silvery logs of the round house. I started with emotion. The grieving cry seemed emitted by the structure itself. The sound filled me and flooded me. Finally, it ceased. I decided to go forward. As I climbed the hill, a breeze raised hairs on the back of my neck. But when I reached the round house, the sun fell like a warm hand on my shoulders. The place seemed peaceful. There was no door. There had been one, but the big plank rectangle was now wrenched off and thrown to the side. The grass was already growing through the cracks between the boards. I stood in the doorway. Inside, it was dim although four small busted-out windows opened in each direction. The floor was tidy—no empties or papers or blankets. All had been picked up by the police. I caught the faint odor of gasoline.

During the old days when Indians could not practice their religion—well, actually not such old days: pre-1978—the round house had been used for ceremonies. People pretended it was a social dance hall or brought their Bibles for gatherings. In those days the headlights of the priest's car coming down the long road glared in the southern window. By the time the priest or the BIA superintendent arrived, the water drums and eagle feathers and the medicine bags and birchbark scrolls and sacred pipes were in a couple of motorboats halfway across the lake. The Bible was out and people were reading aloud from Ecclesiastes. Why that part of the Bible? I'd once asked Mooshum. Chapter 1, verse 4, he said. *One generation passeth away, and another generation cometh, but the earth abideth forever.* We think that way too. Sometimes we square-danced, said Mooshum, our highest Mide' priest was a damn fine caller.

There was one old Catholic priest who used to sit down with the medicine people. Father Damien had sent home the superintendent. Then the water drums and feathers and pipes had returned. The old priest had learned the songs. No priest knew those songs now.

From Zack's report of his stepdad's radio conversation, and my father's silence after he mentioned the round house, I knew the general location of the crime. But I didn't know the exact whereness of it. At that moment, a certainty entered. I knew. He had attacked her here. The old ceremonial place had told me—cried out to me in my mother's anguished voice, I now thought, and tears started into my eyes. I let them flood down my cheeks. Nobody was there to see me so I did not even wipe them away. I stood there in the shadowed doorway thinking with my tears. Yes, tears can be thoughts, why not?

I concentrated on the escape itself, just as my father had described. Our car was parked at the base of the rise, just past a scraggle of bushes. Nobody would come up the road that way, anyway. There was a beach farther down that you could get to easier by a road along the lakeshore, around the other side. Of course the rapist—except I didn't use that word: I used attacker—the attacker had bet on this lonely place remaining deserted. Which meant he had to have known something about the reservation, and meant more planning. People drank down on that beach at night, but to get there from the round house you had to cross a barbed-wire fence and then bushwhack. The attack had happened approximately where I was standing. He'd left her here, to get a new book of matches. I blocked out the thought of my mother's terror and her scramble for the car. I imagined how far away the attacker had to have gone to fetch the matches, in order not to run back in time to catch her.

My mother had gotten up and bolted through the doorway, down the hill to her car. Her attacker would have walked down the opposite side of the hill, to the north, not to have seen her. I walked the way he must have gone, through the grass to that barbed-wire fence. I lifted the top line and side-legged through. Another fence line led down through the heavy tangle of birch and popple to the lake. I followed that fence all the way down to the edge of the lake and then kept walking to the water.

He must have had a stash somewhere or maybe another car—one parked near the beach. He'd gone back for more matches when his got wet. Probably, he was a smoker. He'd left behind extra matches or a lighter. He followed that fence down to the lake. He'd reached his stash. Heard the car door slam. Ran back up to the round house and after my mother. But too late. She'd managed to start the engine, stomp on the accelerator. She was gone.

I continued walking, across the narrow sand beach, into the lake. My heart was beating so hard as I followed the action in my understanding that I did not feel the water. I felt his overpowering frustration as he watched the car disappear. I saw him pick up the gas can and nearly throw it after the vanishing taillights. He ran forward, then back. Suddenly, he stopped, remembering his stuff, the car, whatever he did have, his smokes. And the can. He could not be caught with the can. However cold it was that May, the ice out but the water still freezing, he'd have to wade partway in and let water fill the can. And after that, as far out as possible, he had surely slung the water-filled tin and now, if I dived down and passed my hands along the muddy, weedy, silty, snail-rich bottom of the lake, there it would be.

My friends found me sitting outside the door of the round house in full sun, still drying off, the gas can placed in the grass before me. I was glad when they came. I had now come to the understanding that my mother's attacker had also tried to set her on fire. Although this fact had been made plain, or was at least implicit in Clemence's reaction at the hospital and my father's account of my mother's escape, my understanding had resisted. With the gas can there before me, I began shaking so hard my teeth clacked. When I got upset like that, sometimes I puked. This hadn't happened in the car, in the hospital, even reading to my mother. Maybe I was numbed. Now I felt what had happened to her in my gut. I dug a hole for the mess and covered it with a heap of dirt. I sat there, weak. When I heard the voices and bikes, the drag of Cappy's braking feet, the shouts, I jumped up and started slapping at my arms. I couldn't let them see me shaking like a girl. When they got to me I pretended it was the cold water. Angus said my lips were blue and offered me an unfiltered Camel.

They were the best cigarettes you could steal. Star's man usually smoked generics, but he must have come into some cash. Angus slipped them from Elwin's pack, one at a time, so he would not get suspicious. For this occasion, he'd taken two. I broke my cigarette carefully in half and shared with Cappy. Zack and Angus shared the other. I dragged on the end until it scorched my fingers. We didn't speak while we were smoking and when we were done we flicked the shreds of tobacco off our tongues, the way Elwin did. The gas can was a battered dull red with a gold band around the top and the bottom. There was a long, crooked spout. Written in thick black script across a flame shape, bright yellow with a blue center and a white dot in the center of the blue, there was a scratched logo: CAUTION.

I wanna get him, I said to my friends. Watch him burn. They were also staring at the can. They knew what it was about.

Cappy picked a splinter off the broken door and stabbed the ground with it. Zack chewed a piece of grass. I looked at Angus. He was always hungry. I told him I'd brought sandwiches and fished the bag out of my pack to divide them up.

First, we unstuck the bread slices carefully from the peanut butter. Next we tucked in my mother's famous little crunchy pickles. Last, we closed the sandwiches back up. The pickle juice salted the peanut butter, cut the stickiness so you could swallow each bite, and added just the right hot, sour bite to the nuts. After the sandwiches were gone, Angus drank most of the pickle brine and put the hot red pepper in his mouth. Cappy took the dill and chewed the end of the stalk. Zack looked away—sometimes he was fastidious, and then he would surprise you.

We passed around the water jar and then I told them I had thought of how the attack had happened. Here's how it went, I said without blinking. He did it here. I tipped my head back to the round house. He did it, then he wanted to burn her inside the place. But his matches got wet. He went over the hill and down toward the lake for dry matches. I told them exactly how my mother had escaped. I said I'd thought that the attacker must have kept some of his stuff in the woods, and that I'd followed the fence posts to the lake and then out into the lake to where he'd sunk the can. I said that he was probably a smoker because he'd gone after the extra matches, or maybe he'd had a lighter. He had to have left something in the woods. If he'd left a pack of stuff out there, he'd maybe even slept out there. He could have smoked, dropped a butt. Or field-stripped the cigarette the way Whitey did, rolling away the threads of the filter, forming the end of the paper into a tiny ball. What we'd look for would be threads, tracks, any foreign material, anything at all.

We all nodded. Looked at the ground. Cappy raised his head, stared at me evenly.

Make it so, he said. Starboy?

Okay, said Angus, whose nickname that was, let's see what we get.

What we got was wood ticks. Our reservation is notorious for them. We made a grid of the woods, crisscrossed the area from the fence going south along the lake about thirty feet. In the spring, when you hit a tick hole, which is where a huge bunch have hatched, they swarm you. But they swarm slow. You can shake some off but you can't really crawl them off. We were crawling through tick hole after tick hole.

Zack yelled once, panic in his voice. He jumped up and I could see a few flung off him onto Angus and into Cappy's shiny hair.

Shut up, you baby! said Angus. Fleas are a hell of a lot worse.

Yeah, fleas, said Zack. Remember when your mom flea-bombed your place and forgot you were inside?

Oh man, they shut the whole place up and flea-bombed the hell out of it, said Angus, squinting at what looked like a bit of plastic wrap, then tossing it. Forgot I was asleep in the corner and left me there overnight. All the fleas jumped onto me for safety and I was only four. They had one last drink of blood and died in my clothes. It was lucky they didn't suck me dry.

They sucked your brain dry, said Zack. Look what you threw at me. He pinched a matted condom by the edge and swung it back and forth. It had obviously been there through the winter. Older kids made fires on the beach.

I held out the bread bag and Zack dropped in the petrified condom. And then we found dozens more and so many beer cans that Angus brought them to a rock and started crushing them to take back and redeem. What looked from a distance like leafy new undergrowth actually hid a dump. There were countless cigarette butts. The bread bag quickly filled with condoms and butts. There were also candy wrappers and old balls of toilet paper. Either the police did not consider this area relevant, or they had just given up.

People are disgusting, said Zack. This is way too much evidence.

I knelt on the ground with the bread bag. Ticks were crawling all over me. I said we should quit and drown the ticks in the lake. So we left the woods and stripped down on the beach. The ticks were mainly still in our clothes and not many were attached yet, except that Angus had one stuck on his balls.

Hey, Zack, I need some help!

Oh, fuck you, said Zack.

Cappy laughed. Why don't you let him stay on till he gets really big? They'll call you Three Balls.

Like Old Man Niswi, I said.

He really had three. It's true. My grandma knows, said Zack.

Shut up, said Cappy. I can't take hearing about your grandma doing it with a three-balled man.

We were in the water now, splashing around, diving and mock-fighting. We'd been so hot and sweaty and itchy it felt wonderful. I reached down to make sure no tick had gotten me where that one had got Angus. I went underwater and stayed as long as I could. When I came up, Zack was talking.

She said they tapped against her ass like three big ripe plums.

Your grandma says all kinds of things, said Cappy.

She told me all about it, Zack said.

There are Indian grandmas who get too much church and Indian grandmas where the church doesn't take, and who are let loose in their old age to shock the young. Zack had one of those last sort. Grandma Ignatia Thunder. She had been to Catholic boarding school but it just hardened her, she said, the way it hardened the priests. She spoke Indian and talked about men's secrets. When she and Mooshum got together to reminisce about the old days, my father said they talked so dirty the air around them turned blue.

When the water numbed us, we got out and made fun of one another's shriveled dicks.

Zack laughed at me, Aren't you a little short for a Storm Trooper?

Size matters not. Judge me by my size, do you?

Zack had a Darth Vader, circumcised, and I did too. Cappy's and Angus's still had their hoods, so they were Emperors. We argued over whether it was better to be an Emperor or a Darth Vader—which one girls liked better. We made a fire. We sat around it, naked, on logs already carved with the names of other boys, picking ticks off our clothing and flicking them into the fire.

Worf's an Emperor, said Angus.

For sure, said Cappy.

Nah, I said. Anyhow, the important one would be Data's, because they'd give an android the kind girls like best, right? And he would definitely be a Darth Vader. I don't see him as anything but a Darth.

I think everyone on that ship's a Darth, said Cappy, except for Worf.

But hey, said Zack, a Klingon? You'd think hung, man, but there's no bump in his uniform.

Do you question Klingon power? said Cappy, standing up. He looked down. Rise, my friend.

No response. We started laughing at him. Cappy laughed too. After a while, we wished we had another cigarette and we were hungry again. Angus went off to take a piss. He walked into the lake and went around the fence, into the woods.

Holeee, he yelled.

Then he marched out of the woods with two full six-packs of Hamm's beer. One in each hand. Cappy and Zack whooped with joy. I ran toward him. Every other can we'd crushed or bottle we'd found had been Old Mill or Blatz, the reservation beer of the time. In spite of the dancing, drumming, feather-wearing Indian bear in the Hamm's commercial, we were a Blatz people.

Drop that, I yelled. Angus froze. He laid the six-packs carefully on the ground.

I think he left those, I said. I think it's evidence. There will be fingerprints.

Uh . . . I could see that Angus was thinking as fast as he could. He talked fast, too. Does water erase fingerprints? I found these in an open cooler. The beer was covered with water.

You found his stash, I said.

Can I pick up the beer? asked Angus.

I guess, I said.

Can I crack one open?

I looked at my friends. Yeah, I said.

Their hands shot out and pulled cans from the plastic ring.

If there's no fingerprints then the main evidence is that he is a Hamm's drinker, I said. Make of that what you will. I took a beer. The can was wet and icy. I held it as I followed Angus back to where he'd found the stash. I said we shouldn't get too close yet and destroy the evidence, that we should probably crawl up to this thing and collect what we could find all around it.

Crawl? Again? said Angus.

The cooler, cheap Styrofoam, sat against a tree. There was a heap of clothes to one side.

Cappy said that he'd prefer to drink the beer first and get a buzz, then crawl over to gather evidence before he jumped back in the lake and drowned his ticks off again. We drank our beers.

Went down good, said Angus. He attempted to crush his can against his thigh. Ow, he said.

We fanned out and crawled in a circle, closing in on the cooler. It was on the edge of that cow pasture and there were dried cow pies here and there. We'd drunk the beers fast, to get buzzed, knowing that we each had two more waiting, cold, and we'd drink our next beers slower by the fire. The crawling around was definitely easier on us this time, though Angus lifted his leg and flared a boogid at me.

No boogid wars, said Zack.

Aw, said Angus, cracking another fart.

All of a sudden, Cappy tossed a cow pie into the open pasture like a Frisbee and started laughing.

Why did the Indian ignore the cow pie?

Nobody said anything.

He didn't know shit!

Ha-ha, said Zack. You're gonna turn into a powwow MC like your dad.

How much is four bucks and four bucks?

An Indian bar fight, groan, said Angus. He lifted his leg but he had no gas left.

It was true that at home Doe, Randall, and Cappy sometimes just sat around inventing bad Indian jokes.

As we crawled along, I noticed us. My skin was very light brown. Cappy's was more brown. Zack's a deeper brown. Angus's was white but already tanned. Cappy was getting his growth, I was next, Zack and Angus were both shorter than me.

Between us, we had so many scars that it was hard to count.

How come the four naked Indians in the woods were laughing, said Cappy.

Don't encourage him, I said.

They got tick-led.

Sore. I laughed. For a handsome guy that girls loved, Cappy was not cool.

Angus was crawling away from me. I kept my distance. His butt was packed with purple marks where his brother had shot him with a BB gun. We were bumbling around at random now, not following any grid. There was hardly any trash on this side of the fence. I'd guessed that the attacker had gone in the lake, too, around the end of the fence, and put his stash away from the beach area. We got close to the cooler and I used a stick to prod at the pile of blankets and clothes.

The blankets were made of crummy polyester. There was a rotted-looking shirt, a pair of jeans. It all stank like behind the Dead Custer Bar.

Maybe we should leave this to the police, I said.

If we tell them, then we have to say we were here, said Zack. They will figure out that I listen to Vince's radio and phone calls. I'll be in deep shit.

Also, said Angus, there's the beer.

Drinking half the evidence doesn't look good, said Cappy.

Let's get rid of it all, said Zack.

Okay, I said.

We went back, around the fence, and built up the fire. Then we ran down to the lake and jumped back in and got rid of the new ticks. Zack showed the place where he'd got speared in the armpit. He could have died, they said. The stitches had healed like a tiny white railroad track running mysteriously up his rib, under and along his arm. We put our clothes on and felt normal again. We sat by the fire and popped open the rest of the evidence.

Was his third ball the same size as the other two? Angus asked Zack.

Don't start that again, said Cappy.

I wonder, I said, if we should even talk to the cops. I mean, they missed the gas can. They missed the cooler. They missed the pile of clothes.

That pile stinks. It smells like piss.

He pissed himself, said Angus.

We should torch that stuff, I said.

My throat burned and I was invaded by a stab of feeling so acute that I wanted to cry—again. Suddenly, we froze. We heard what sounded like a high-pitched eagle-bone whistle up the hill through the riffle of woods. The wind had changed direction, and a series of notes sounded as the air poured through the gaps in the mud chinking of the round house.

Cappy stood up and stared at the round house.

Angus made the sign of the cross.

Let's bug out, said Zack.

We crushed the Hamm's cans along with the others, piled them in a piece of plastic, and tied them together to bring back for Angus to sell. Then we put the fire out and buried the rest of the trash. I tied the gas can to my bike with a shoestring and we took off. The shadows were long, the air was cooling off, and we were hungry the way boys get hungry. Irrationally hungry so that everything we saw looked tasty and all we could talk of on the way home was food. Where we could get food, and eat food, a lot of food, and quick. That was our concern. Zack's mom would be at bingo. Aunt Star was either flush or broke, never in between, and it was a Saturday. By now, she'd have spent what she had and probably not on food. Things were lean that week at Cappy's house, though his dad possibly had stew. Doe's bachelor stews were a crapshoot, though. Once he added commodity prunes to his chili. Another time he left some bread dough overnight and a mouse burrowed into it. Randall got a slice with the head and Cappy got the tail. Nobody could find the middle. My friends didn't mention my house, though before what happened we would definitely have showed up there on a raid mission. Whitey and Sonja's place was on the way, but I hated it when my friends talked about her. Sonja was mine. So I said they would be working at the gas station. Our other prospect was Grandma Thunder. She lived at the retirement home in a one-bedroom apartment with a full kitchen. She liked to cook for us; her closet was bursting with commodities that others traded to her.

She'll make frybread and meat, said Zack.

She always has canned peaches, said Angus. His voice was reverent.

She has her price, said Cappy.

Just don't anybody bring up balls or say the word twat.

Who would say that word around their grandma?

It could come out by mistake.

Come? Don't say come.

Don't even mention cats. She'll say pussy.

Okay, I said. The list of topics not to mention while we stuff ourselves at Grandma's is balls, cats, pussies, dicks.

Don't say head, ever.

Don't say wiinag, don't say anything that rhymes with the f-word or the word cock.

Don't say crotch, prick, snatch, you know, like snatch at something. She will take it wrong, believe me.

Don't say horny, don't say hard.

Don't say hot or tit or virgin.

I have to get off my bike, said Angus.

We all did. We put our bikes down. Avoiding one another's eyes, we mumbled something about going off to take a piss and each went off alone and in three minutes relieved ourselves of all those words and then came back and got on our bikes and continued riding onward, taking the back road past the mission. When we got into town we rode over to the retirement home. I was feeling guilty about having written just LAKE to my dad, so I called home from the lobby. Dad answered on the first ring, but when I told him that I was at Grandma Thunder's, he sounded glad and told me that Uncle Edward was showing him my cousin Joseph's latest science article and they were eating some leftovers. I asked, even though I knew, where Mom was.

Upstairs.

She's asleep?

Yes.

I love you, Dad.

But he had hung up. The words *I love you* echoed. Why had I said those words and why into the phone just as I knew he was replacing it on the cradle? That I had said those words now made me furious and that my father had not responded singed my soul. A red cloud of anger floated up over my eyes. My head was light with hunger, too.

Come on, said Cappy, coming up behind me, startling me so my eyes filled yet again that day, which was too much.

Shut the fuck up, I said.

He put his hands up and walked away. I followed him down the hall. Just before we got to Grandma's apartment I spoke to his back, Cappy, I'm . . .

He turned around. I put my hands in my pockets and scuffed my shoes on the floor. My dad had refused on principle to buy me the type of basketball shoes I had wanted in Fargo. He said I didn't need new shoes, which was true. Cappy had the shoes I wanted. He had his hands in his pockets too, and he was looking at the floor, ducking his head back and forth. Strangely, he said what I had been thinking, though he lied.

You got the shoes I wanted.

No, I said, you got the shoes I wanted.

Okay, he said, let's trade.

We traded shoes. As soon as I put his on, I realized that his feet were a size bigger. He walked away from me on pinched feet. He had heard what I'd said on the phone.

We went into Grandma's and sure enough the meat was already frying, and with an onion. The smell had a wonderful power and my stomach jumped. I wanted to grab anything that I could put in my mouth. There was a stack of jam sandwiches on the table, to tide us over. I ate one. Her back was to the stove and on her table there was a bowl of sweet little dried apples. There was an apple tree behind the senior citizens and Grandma always harvested the apples. She picked every apple out of the tree and she pared the apples into thin slices and dried them out in her oven and sprinkled them with sugar and cinnamon. I ate another jam and white bread sandwich. She had set plates on the table and more paper towels on the plates to soak up the frybread grease.

Wiisinig, she said, without turning around.

I took some apple slices and put them on my tongue. I looked at Cappy. We ate another jam sandwich each and just stood there watching in mesmerized hunger until she started lifting out the frybreads. Then we each took a plate and stood beside her. She took the hot frybreads out of the bubbling lard with tongs and put the lumpy golden rounds on our plates. We said thank you. She salted and peppered the meat. She dumped in a can of tomatoes, a can of beans. We kept standing there, our plates out. She heaped spoons of the crumbled meat mix on top of the frybreads. On the table, there was a block of commodity cheese. The cheese was frozen so it was easy to grate on top of the meat. We were so hungry we sat down right at the table. Zack and Angus were outside, through her sliding doors, in the courtyard. She made their Indian tacos now like ours, called them in, and they sat on the couch and ate.

For a long time, nobody said anything. We just ate and ate. Grandma hummed as she cooked at the stove. She was short and skinny and she always wore a flowery pastel dress, flesh-colored stockings rolled down as if it were a fashion accent to do that, and moccasins that she made herself out of deerhide. Cappy's two aunts tanned hides in their backyards. Their backyards stank, but the hides came out perfectly. Every summer they gave a soft buckskin to Grandma. Her moccasins were beaded with small pink flowers. She clipped her long, thin, white hair up in a barrette, and wore white shell earrings. Her face was gnarled and sly and her eyes were sharp little shining black marbles. Her eyes were never soft or affectionate, but always alert and cold. This seemed odd for someone who cooked for boys. But then, she had survived many deaths and other losses and had no sentiment left. As we filled up, we ate more slowly. We all wanted to finish at exactly the same time, to eat and run. But Grandma Thunder made us seconds, and we started all over again, eating even more slowly now, still not talking. When I finished, I thanked her and brought my plate to the sink. I was just about to tell her that I had to get home when Mrs. Bijiu came in without knocking. The worst of them all! A hefty, jiggling, loud woman, she took my chair at the table immediately and said, Oooohph!

Eyah, they ate good, said Grandma Thunder.

Top shelf, said Angus.

We must go now, Kookum, said Zack.

Apijigo miigwech, said Cappy. Minopogoziwag ingiw zaasakok waanag. He knew that to really make the old ladies happy, he should talk Indian, even if he wasn't sure the words were right.

Just listen to that Anishinaabe! They were indeed pleased with him.

Just go . . . Grandma waved her hand toward the door, satisfied that we had come to her.

This one, this one here, said Mrs. Bijiu, lip pointing at me suddenly, fiercely. He is bony!

Our hearts sank at the word.

Bony! Grandma Thunder's voice cracked. She reared up in her chair. I'll tell you who's got a bone in his pants these days!

Holy Jesus! said Mrs. Bijiu. I know who you're talking about. Napoleon. That akiwenzii goes scratching around at night and it's not me who lets the old man in. He's in good shape, though, never drank. Worked hard all his life. Now gets himself laid by a different woman every night!

You boys listen up, said Grandma Ignatia. You want to learn something? Want to learn how to keep your little peckers hard all your life? Go and go? Live clean like old Napoleon. Liquor makes you quicker and that's no good. Bread and lard keep you hard! He is eighty-seven and he not only gets it up easy, he can go five hours at a stretch.

We wanted to sneak away but were pulled back by that last piece of information. Maybe we were each thinking of our three minutes in the woods.

Five hours? said Angus.

For he never tomcatted around and wasted his juice, cried Mrs. Bijiu. He was faithful to his wife!

That's what she thought, said Grandma Ignatia, taking a hankie from her sleeve.

The two started laughing so hard they almost choked and we nearly made it out the door.

In addition, he swears by his secret formula.

Our heads turned back.

Look at them swivel necks, the two old ladies laughed. Should we give them Napoleon's secret formula?

If the bread and lard don't work, he takes red-hot pepper, rubs it on his . . . down there. Mrs. Bijiu made a certain hand motion over her lap, so vigorous it made us leap right out the door. The two old women's cackling excitement followed us down the hall. I thought of what the red pepper had done to Randall and his buddies. No sign whatsoever of Napoleon's formula at work as they bolted buck-naked across the quack grass.

I think I'd like a medical opinion before I tried the pepper, I said to myself. But Angus heard it. *A medical opinion* became one of those ridiculous fake-smart lines I got teased for. Joe needs a medical opinion. Joe, have you asked your doctor if you should do that? I knew as we walked down the hallway I'd never hear the end of it, like Oops. Just before we went out the retirement home doors, I said to wait. I took off Cappy's shoes.

Thanks, I said.

We switched back. But I still believe that if it would have helped me, Cappy would have kept on walking in my tight old shoes.

Endless June summer light and silence in the dirt yards—everyone fallen back into their beds or kitchens as I wandered my bike up the road. Pearl met me as I came around the corner of the house. She stood alert, gazing at me, and never barked. You knew it was me, I said. You did good. She came up to me and wagged her tail just four times. She had a beautiful creamy plume of a tail that didn't go with the short-haired middle of her—even though it matched her long, furry, wolfish ears. She sniffed at my hand. I scratched her ears until she shook my hand away. She was hungry. I'd taken one of Grandma's jam sandwiches as I left and now I gave it to Pearl. Inside, I heard voices. I put away my bike and slipped inside. Uncle Edward was still there, in the study with my father. The kitchen was a shambles, so they'd probably fixed themselves a snack. I sneaked in and stopped outside the study. They were talking just loud enough for me to hear them from the couch. I could listen in, then pretend to be asleep if they came out. I could tell right away from the clink of ice, the glasses, that they were drinking together. It would be the Seagrams V.O. from the bottle behind the dishes on the highest shelf. I craned to hear what they would say.

In all the years we've been married we have never once slept apart until now, said my father.

This of course both repelled and fascinated me. I held my breath.

She is isolating herself even from Joe. Doesn't talk to anyone from work, of course. Won't see visitors, even her old friend from boarding-school days, LaRose.

Clemence says she is cutting her off, too.

Geraldine. Oh, Geraldine! She dropped a casserole, then this. Well, I know that wasn't it. I frightened her, triggered her terror of the event.

The event. Bazil.

I know. But I cannot refer to it.

There was silence. At last my father said, the attack. The rape. I must be going crazy, too, Edward. I keep losing track of Joe.

He'll be all right. She'll come out of it, said Edward.

I don't know. She's drifting out of grasp.

What about church? said Edward. Would it help if Clemence took her to church? You know what I think about it, of course, but there's a new priest she seems to like.

I don't think Geraldine would find comfort there, after all these years.

We all knew that my mother had stopped going to church after she returned from boarding school. She never said why. Clemence never tried to get her to go, either, that I knew of.

What about this new priest, though, my father asked.

Interesting. Good-looking, I suppose. If you like the type. Central casting.

For what?

War movie. B western. Man on a doomed mission. Of all things, he's an ex-Marine.

Oh god, a trained killer turned Catholic.

A dead silence opened between the two men and went on for so long it suddenly seemed loud.

My father rose. I heard him shuffle about. I heard the silken pour of liquor.

Edward, what do we know of this priest?

Not much.

Think.

Pour me another. He's from Texas. Dallas. The Catholic martyr on our kitchen wall. Dallas. That's where this priest is from.

I don't know Dallas.

More correctly, he's from a little dried-up town outside of Dallas. He's got a gun and I saw him out popping prairie dogs.

What? That's odd for a Benedictine. They strike me as a more genteel and thoughtful bunch.

True, generally, but he's new, recently ordained. He's different from—but oh, who remembers Father Damien? And, ah, he's searching. He gives very questioning sermons, Bazil. Sometimes I wonder if he's entirely stable, or then again, if he might be simply . . . intelligent.

I hope he's not like the one before him who wrote that scorching letter to the paper about the deadly charms of Metis women. Remember how we laughed about it? God!

If only it were about God. Sometimes when I'm at the Adoration with Clemence, I see double, just like now.

What do you see then?

I see two priests, one dispensing holy water from a silver aspergillum, the other with a rifle.

Just an air rifle, surely.

Just an air rifle, yes. But he was fast with it, deadly, and accurate.

Gopher count?

Dozen or so. All laid out on the playground.

The men paused, thinking, then Edward continued, Still, that does not make him . . .

I know. But the round house. Symbol of the old pagan ways. The Metis women. Setting it all on fire together—the temptation and the crime all burned up as in a fire offering . . . oh god.

My father's voice caught.

Now Bazil, now Bazil, said Edward. This is just talk.

But I thought the priest's guilt sounded plausible. That night, from the couch, where I listened and they never knew, I thought I had perhaps heard the truth. All we needed was proof.

I must have fallen asleep for a good hour. Uncle Edward and my father woke me as they passed into the kitchen, rattling their glasses and flipping on and off the lights. I heard my father open the door and say good-bye to Uncle Edward, and I heard Pearl come in. He spoke to her in a calming way. He didn't sound drunk at all. I heard him pour food into Pearl's dish. Then her businesslike crunching and gnashing. It sounded like Dad put a dish or two in the sink, but then quit cleaning. He turned off the light. I squeezed back into the couch pillows as he passed, but he wouldn't have noticed me anyway.

My father was looking so intently at the head of the stairs as he climbed, step by deliberate step, that I crept around the couch to see what he was peering at—a light beneath the bedroom door, perhaps. From the foot of the stairs, I watched him shuffle to the bedroom door, which was outlined in black. He paused there, and then went past. To the bathroom, I expected. But no. He opened the door to the cold little room my mother used for sewing. There was a narrow daybed in that room, but it was only for guests. None of us had ever slept in it. Even when one of my parents had the flu or a cold, they slept in the same bed. They never sought protection from each other's illnesses.

The sewing-room door shut. I heard my father rustling about in there and hoped that he'd emerge again. Hoped he had been looking for something. But then the bed creaked. There was silence. He was lying in there with the sewing machine and the cardboard boxes of neatly folded fabric, with the Peg-Boards he'd screwed to the wall that held a hundred colors of silken thread, with the scissors in graduated sizes, with the neatly coiled tape measure and the heart-shaped pincushion.

I went upstairs and undressed sleepily, but once my head hit the pillow I realized my father hadn't even made sure I was home. He'd forgotten all about me. I lay in my bed, sleepless, outraged. Over and over, I replayed the day's events. The day had been packed with treacherous findings and information. I went through it all over again. Then I went farther back, to the night of the dropped casserole. To the mournful tension of repressed feeling as my mother had floated up the stairs, to my father's hushed anxiety as we read together in the lamplight. With all my being, I wanted to go back to before all this had happened. I wanted to enter our good-smelling kitchen again, sit down at my mother's table before she'd struck me and before my father had forgotten my existence. I wanted to hear my mother laugh until she snorted. I wanted to move back through time and stop her from returning to her office that Sunday for those files. I kept thinking how easily I could have gotten in the car with her that afternoon. How I could have offered to do that errand. I had entered that furrow of remorse—planted with the seeds of resentment—peculiar to young men.

When I got to the resentment, I resented everything I could think of, including that file my mother had returned for. That file. Something nagged at me. The file itself. No one had mentioned it. Why had she gone back for a file? What was in it? I was back to weak regret. But I would ask her. I would find out more about what had drawn her back on a Sunday. There was, now I remembered it, a phone call. There'd been a call and the sound of her voice answering the call. And then she'd walked around, cleaning things, clattering dishes, agitated, though I hadn't connected it with the call until now.

Then she'd left, mentioning the file.

Eventually my brain slowed, sifting thoughts into images. I was half asleep when I heard Pearl walk to my bedroom window. Her claws clicked on the bare wooden floor. I turned toward the window and opened my eyes. Pearl was standing fixed, ears pointing forward, her senses focused on something outside. I pictured a raccoon or a skunk. But the patient recognition with which she watched, not barking, wakened me entirely. I crept out of bed to that tall window, the sill just a foot or so from the floor. The moonlight illuminated the edges of things, made suggestions out of shadows. Kneeling next to Pearl, I could make out the figure.

It was standing at the edge of the yard, in the tangle of branches. As we watched, its hands parted the branches, and it looked up at my bedroom window. I could make out its features clearly—the lined, somewhat sour countenance, the deep-set eyes under a flat brow, some dense silver hair—but I could not tell whether this being was male or female, or for that matter, whether it was alive or dead or somewhere in between. Although I was not exactly alarmed, I had the clear notion that what I was seeing was unreal. Yet it was neither human nor entirely inhuman. The being saw me and my heart jumped. I could see that face close up. There was a glow behind its head. The lips moved but I couldn't make out words except it seemed to be repeating the same words. The hands drew back and the branches closed over it. The thing was gone. Pearl turned in a circle three times and settled herself on the rug again. I fell asleep as soon as I lay my head on the pillow, perhaps exhausted by the mental exertion required to admit that visitor into my consciousness.

*

My father had bought an ugly new clock, and it was ticking again in the quiet kitchen. I was up before him. I made myself two pieces of toast and ate them standing, then made two more and put them on a plate. I hadn't progressed yet to eggs, nor had I learned to mix pancakes. That would come later, after I became accustomed to the fact that I had begun to lead a life apart from my parents. After I began to work at the gas station. My father came in while I was sitting with my toast. He mumbled, and didn't notice that I gave him no answer. He hadn't started on his coffee yet. Soon he would be brought to life. He made his brew the old way, measuring the ground coffee into a speckled black enamel camp pot and throwing in an egg to set the grounds. He laid a hand briefly on my shoulder. I shrugged it off. He was wearing his old blue wool robe with the funny gilded crest. He sat down to wait for his coffee and asked if I'd slept well.

Where? I said. Where do you think I slept last night?

On the couch, he said, surprised. You were snoring your fool head off. I covered you up with a blanket.

Oh, I said.

The coffeepot hissed and he got up, turned down the burner, and poured himself a cup.

I think I saw a ghost last night, I told my father.

He sat down again across from me and I looked into his eyes. I was sure he would explain the incident and tell me just how and why I'd been mistaken. I was sure he'd say, as grown-ups were supposed to, that ghosts did not exist. But he only looked at me, the circles under his eyes swollen, the dark creases becoming permanent. I realized that he had not slept well, or at all.

The ghost was standing at the edge of the yard, I said. It looked almost like a real person.

Yes, they're out there, my father answered.

He rose and poured another cup of coffee to take up to my mother. As he left the room, I experienced an alarm that quickly turned to fury. I glared at his back. Either he had purposely not cared to quiet my fear by challenging me, or he had not listened to me at all. And had he really covered me with a blanket? I had not noticed the blanket. When he came back into the room, I spoke belligerently.

Ghost. I said ghost. What do you mean they're out there?

He poured more coffee. Sat down across from me. As usual, he refused to be perturbed by my anger.

Joe, he said. I worked in a graveyard.

So what?

There was an occasional ghost, that's what. Ghosts were there. Sometimes they walked in, looking just like people. I could recognize one occasionally as a person I had buried, but on the whole they didn't much resemble their old selves. My old boss taught me how to pick them out. They would look more faded out than living people, and listless, too, yet irritable. They'd walk around, nodding at the graves, staring at trees and stones until they found their own grave. Then they'd stand there, confused maybe. I never approached them.

But how did you *know* they were ghosts?

Oh, you just know. Couldn't you tell the thing you saw was a ghost?

I said yes. I was still mad. That's just great, I said. Now we have ghosts.

My father, so strictly rational that he'd first refused the sacrament and then refused to attend Holy Mass at all, believed in ghosts. In fact he had information of ghosts, things he'd never told me. If Uncle Whitey had said these things about ghosts walking around looking like real people, I'd have known he was pulling my leg. But my father had very different ways of teasing and I knew in this case he wasn't teasing. Because he took my ghost seriously, I asked him what I really wanted to know.

Okay. So why was it there?

My father hesitated.

Because of your mother, possibly. They are attracted to disturbances of all kinds. Then again, sometimes a ghost is a person out of your future. A person dropping back through time, I guess, by mistake. I've heard that from my own mother.

His mother, my grandmother, was from a medicine family. She'd said a lot of things that would seem strange at first but come true later in life.

She would have said to watch for that ghost. It could be trying to tell you something.

He put down his cup of coffee and now I remembered that last night he'd slept next to the sewing machine instead of my mother, and that he and Uncle Edward had figured out the priest was a suspect, and that they'd probably figured out even more than I realized because I'd fallen asleep. The priest and the gas can and the pile of stinking clothes and the court cases all collected in a tangled skein. My throat went dry and I couldn't swallow. I sat there. He sat there. The ghost had come for my mother, or to tell me something.

The last thing I want to know is something that a ghost wants to tell me, I said.

At that moment it struck me that Randall also had seen something similiar, which relieved me. If this ghost, or whatever, was looking for Randall, he could fix it with his medicine. He'd put out tobacco. I would put out tobacco. The ghost would leave, or it might even help my mother. Who knew? She was upstairs with the coffee on her side table, cooling off. I knew she wouldn't touch the cup and it would be there later on. An oily sheen would have formed on the cold, repugnant stuff. It would leave a black ring in the cup. Everything we gave her came back and left a ring or a crust or went cold or congealed or went hard. I was sick of bringing down her wasted food.

My father bent his head down and rested his forehead on

his fist. He closed his eyes. There was the ticking of the clock in that sunny kitchen. Around the face of the clock there was a kind of sunburst. But the rays were plastic squiggles and the thing looked more like a gilded octopus. Still, I kept looking at the clock because if I looked down I would have to see the top of my father's head. To see the egg-brown scalp and thin patch of gray hairs would put me over the edge. I'd snap, I thought, if I looked down.

So I said, Hey, Dad, it's just a ghost. We can get rid of it.

My dad reared up and wiped his face with both hands. I know, he said. It has no damn message and it hasn't really come for her. She's going to get better, to get over this. She'll start working again next week. She said something about it. And she's reading books, I mean she's reading a magazine anyway. Clemence brought some light reading into the house. *Reader's Digests*. But that's good, isn't it? The ghost. How do you mean we'll get rid of it?

Father Travis, I said. He can bless the yard or something.

My father took a sip of coffee and his eyes gauged me over the rim of the cup. I could see an energy fill him now. He was something like his old self. He knew when he was hearing bullshit.

So you were awake, he said. You heard us.

Yes, and I know more, I said. I went to the round house.

CHAPTER FIVE

The Naked Now

When the warm rain falls in June, said my father, and the lilacs burst open. Then she will come downstairs. She loves the scent of the lilacs. An old stand of bushes planted by the reservation farm agent bloomed against the south end of the yard. My mother missed its glory. The flimsy faces of her pansies blazed and then the wild prairie roses in the ditches bloomed an innocent pink. She missed those too. Mom had grown her bedding plants from seeds every year I could remember. She'd had her paper milk carton planters arranged on the kitchen counter and on the sills of all south-facing windows in April—but the pansy seedlings were the only ones that lived to get planted outside. After that week, we'd forgotten to take care of all the others. We found the spindly stalks dried to crisps. Dad had dumped the seedlings and dirt in the back and burned the bottoms of the milk cartons with the trash, destroying signs of our neglect. Not that she noticed.

The morning I told my father about the round house, he pushed his chair back, stood, and turned from me. When he turned around, his face was calm and he told me that we'd talk later. We were going to put in my mother's garden. Now. He'd bought expensive bedding plants from a tumbledown hothouse twenty miles off the reservation. Cardboard flats and plastic trays were set out in the shade. There were red, purple, pink, and striped petunias. Yellow and orange marigolds. There were blue forget-me-nots, Shasta daisies, lavender calendula, and red-hot poker flowers. Dad gave me directions. I set the plants one by one into the flower beds. She had a tractor tire painted white and filled with dirt, and matching rectangles of dirt beside the front steps. I added lobelia and candytuft to the pansies in the narrow beds that lined the driveway. I kept all of the flimsy plastic plant markers for her to see. From time to time, as I worked, I thought of the files. The ghost. The bits and pieces of confusion. The round house. I was beginning to dread the talk with my father. The files again. And the nagging thought of the priest, then the Larks, then the priest again. Behind the house her vegetable garden lay—still heaped with straw. After I'd planted the flowers, I went around back of the house to stack the plastic pots and put away the tools.

Keep those out. We're going to turn over the dirt in your mother's vegetable garden, said my dad.

For what?

He just gave me back the shovel I had dropped, and pointed to the edge of the yard, where onion sets and tomato sprouts and packets of bush bean and morning glory seeds waited. We worked together for another hour. When we'd finished with half the soil, it was time for lunch. He left to buy the rest of the plants. I went inside. I was supposed to watch over my mother. I looked around the kitchen. There was a tin of minced ham on the counter, a key fixed to the top to roll the cover back. I made myself a sandwich, ate it, and drank two glasses of water. There was a package of cookies with red jam in the center. I ate a handful. Then I made another sandwich and put it on a plate with two cookies to decorate it. I walked upstairs with the plate of food and a glass of water. Pearl had learned to watch for and wolf down food left outside the bedroom door, so we always brought it into the room now. I balanced the plate on top of the glass of water, and knocked. There was no answer. I knocked harder.

Come in, said my mother. I went in. It had now been over a week since she had walked up those stairs, and the bedroom had taken on a fusty odor. The air was heavy with her breath, as if she'd sucked out the oxygen. She kept the shades pulled. I wanted to set the sandwich down and run. But she asked me to sit.

I put the sandwich and water on the square bedside table from which I had removed so many stale sandwiches and half-drained glasses and bowls of cold soup. If she'd eaten anything I'd not seen it. I dragged a light chair with a cushioned seat close to the bed. I assumed that she wanted me to read to her. Clemence or my father chose the books—nothing sad or upsetting. Which meant the books were either boring romances (Harlequin) or old *Reader's Digest Condensed Books* (better). Or those *Favorite Poems*. Dad had checked "Invictus," and "High Flight," which I'd read. They made my mother emit a dry laugh.

Now I reached forward to switch on her bedside lamp—she wouldn't want the shade drawn up, light to pour through the window. Before I could touch the switch, she gripped my arm. Her face was a pale smudge in the dim air, and her features were smeared with weariness. She'd become weightless, all jutting bones. Her fingers bit hard into my arms. Her voice was fuzzy, as if she'd just woken.

I heard you two. What were you doing out there?

Digging.

Digging what, a grave? Your father used to dig graves.

I shook her arm off and drew back from her. The spidery look of her was repellent, and her words so strange. I sat down in the chair.

No, Mom, not graves. I spoke carefully. We were digging up the dirt in your vegetable garden. Before that, I was planting flowers. Flowers for you to look at, Mom.

Look at? Look at?

She turned over, away from me. Her hair on the pillow was greasy strings, still black, just a few streaks of gray. I could see her spine clearly through the thin gown, each vertebra jutted, and her shoulders were knobs. Her arms had wasted to sticks.

I made you a sandwich, I said.

Thank you, dear, she whispered.

Do you want me to read to you?

No, that's all right.

Mom, I need to talk to you.

Nothing.

I need to talk to you, I said again.

I'm tired.

You're always tired, but you sleep all the time.

She didn't answer.

It was just a comment, I said.

Her silence got to me.

Can't you eat? You'd feel better. Can't you get up? Can't you . . . come back to life?

No, she said immediately, as if she'd thought about this too. I can't do it. I don't know why. I just cannot do it.

Her back was still turned and a slight tremor began in her shoulders.

Are you cold? I stood and drew the blanket up over her shoulders. Then I sat back down in the chair.

I planted those stripey petunias you like. Here! I emptied my pockets of the little plastic identifying sticks, scattered them on the bed. Mom, I planted all different kinds of flowers. I planted sweet peas.

Sweet peas?

I hadn't really planted sweet peas. I don't know why I

said it. Sweet peas, I said again. Sunflowers! I hadn't planted sunflowers either.

Sunflowers will get huge!

She turned over in bed and stared at me. Her eyes were sunk in gray circles of skin.

Mom, I've got to talk to you.

About the sunflowers? Joe, they'll shade out the other flowers.

Maybe I should plant them in another place, I said. I've got to talk to you.

Her face dulled. I'm tired.

Mom, did they ask you about that file?

What?

She stared at me in sudden dread, her eyes riveted to my face.

There was no file, Joe.

Yes, there was. The file you went to get on the day you were attacked. You told me you went to get a file. Where is it?

The dread in her face became an active fear.

I didn't tell you. You imagined that, Joe.

Her lips trembled. She coiled in a ball, put her shrunken fists to her mouth, and squeezed her eyes shut.

Mom, listen. Don't you want us to catch him?

She opened her eyes. Her eyes were black pits. She did not answer.

Mom, listen. I'm going to find him and I'm going to burn him. I'm going to kill him for you.

She sat up suddenly, activated, like rising from the dead. No! Not you. Don't you. Listen, Joe, you've got to promise me. Don't go after him. Don't do anything.

Yes, I'm going to, Mom.

This jolt of strong reaction from her triggered something in me. I kept goading her.

I'll do it. There is nothing to stop me. I know who he is and

I'm going after him. You can't stop me because you're here in bed. You can't get out. You're trapped in here. And it stinks. Do you know it stinks in here?

I went over to the window and was about to pull the shade up when my mother spoke to me. What I mean is, my before-mother, the one who could tell me what to do, she spoke to me.

Stop that, Joe.

I turned away from the window. She was sitting up. There was no blood in her face at all. Her skin had a pasty, sunless quality. But she stared at me and spoke in an even and commanding tone.

Now you listen to me, Joe. You will not badger me or harass me. You will leave me to think the way I want to think, here. I have to heal any way I can. You will stop asking questions and you will not give me any worry. You will not go after him. You will not terrify me, Joe. I've had enough fear for my whole life. You will not add to my fear. You will not add to my sorrows. You will not be part of this.

I stood before her, small again.

This what?

All of this. She swept her arm toward the door. It is all a violation. Find him, don't find him. Who is he? You have no idea. None. You don't know. And you never will. Just let me sleep.

All right, I said, and left the room.

As I descended the stairs my heart grew cold. I had a sense that she knew who had done the thing. For sure, she was hiding something. That she knew who did it was a kick in the stomach. My ribs hurt. I couldn't get my breath. I kept walking straight into the kitchen and then out the back door, into the sunshine. I took great gulps of sunshine. It was as though I had been locked up with a raging corpse. I thought of ripping out every single flower I had planted and of stomping those blossoms into the earth. But Pearl came up to me. I felt my anger blazing out.

I'm going to teach you to play fetch, I said.

I went over to the edge of the yard to pick up a stick. Pearl trotted across the yard with me. I reached down and got the stick and straightened up to throw it, but a blur swept by and the stick was wrenched violently out of my hand. I whirled around. Pearl was standing a few paces away with the stick in her mouth.

Drop it, I said. Her wolf ears went back. I was mad. I walked over and grabbed the stick to take it from her mouth but she gave a meaningful growl and I let go.

All right, I said. So that's your game.

I walked a few feet away and picked up another stick. Brandished it to throw. Pearl dropped her stick and streaked toward me with the clear intention of tearing off my arm. I dropped the stick. Once the stick was on the ground, she sniffed at it, satisfied. I tried once more. I bent down to pick the stick back up and just as I closed my fingers on it Pearl stepped up to me and caught my wrist in her teeth. I slowly released the stick. Her jaws were so powerful she could have snapped the bone. I stood warily, my hand empty, and she released my arm. There were pressure marks, but not a tooth had broken flesh or scratched me.

So you don't play fetch, I see that now, I said.

My father pulled up then and took another cardboard flat of expensive nursery plants out of the car's trunk. We took them out back and set them alongside the vegetable garden plot. For the rest of the afternoon, we took off the old straw, then spaded and raked black earth. We sifted out the old roots and dead stalks and broke up the clods so the earth was fluffy and fine. The dirt was moist deep down below the surface. Rich. I began to like what I was doing. The ground drained my rage. We lifted out the pot-bound plants and gently loosened the roots before we set them in holes and packed the dirt around their stems. Afterward, we hauled buckets and watered the seedlings and then we stood there.

My father took a cigar from his front pocket, then looked at me and replaced it.

The gesture made me mad all over again.

You can smoke that if you want to, I said. I'm not gonna start. I'm not gonna be like you.

I waited for his anger to snuff mine out but was disappointed.

I'll wait until later, he said. We have not finished talking, have we?

No.

Let's put the lawn chairs out.

I set up two lawn chairs where we could overlook our work. While he was gone, I got the empty gas can out from under the steps and I put it underneath my chair. Dad brought out a carton of lemonade and two glasses. I knew from the length of time it took that he'd taken a glass upstairs, too. We sat down with our lemonade.

You don't miss a damn thing, Joe, he said after a time. The round house.

I took the gas can from under my chair, and set it between us on the ground.

My father stared down at it.

Where . . . ? he said.

This was straight down through the woods from the round house. About fifteen feet out, in the lake.

In the lake . . .

He'd sunk it in the lake.

Almighty God.

He reached down to touch the can, but drew his hand back. He put his hand on his chair's aluminum armrest. He squinted out at the neatly planted little seedlings in the garden, then slowly, very slowly, he turned and stared at me with the unblinking all-seeing gaze I used to think he turned on murderers before I found out he only dealt with hot dog thieves.

If I could just tan your hide, he said, I would do that. But it just . . . I could never do you harm. Also, I am pretty certain that if I did tan your hide the hiding wouldn't work. In fact, it might set your mind against me. It might cause you to do things secretly. So I am going to have to appeal to you, Joe. I am going to have to ask you to stop. No more hunting down the attacker. No more clue gathering. I realize it is my fault because I sat you down to read through the cases I pulled. But I was wrong to draw you in. You're too damn inquisitive, Joe. You've surprised the hell out of me. I'm afraid. You could get yourself . . . if anything happened to you . . .

Nothing's going to happen to me!

I had expected my father to be proud. To give me one of his low whistles of surprise. I'd expected that he would help me plan what to do next. How to set the trap. How to catch the priest. Instead, I was getting a lecture. I sat back in my chair and kicked at the gas can.

Heart to heart, Joe. Listen, this is a sadist. Beyond the limits, someone who has no . . . way beyond . . .

Way beyond *your jurisdiction*, I said. There was an edge of juvenile sarcasm in my voice.

Well, you understand a bit about jurisdiction issues, he said, catching my scorn, then ignoring it. Joe, please. I am asking you now as your father to quit. It is a police matter, do you understand?

Who? Tribal? Smokies? FBI? What do they care?

Look, Joe, you know Soren Bjerke.

Yes, I said. I remember what you said once about FBI agents who draw Indian Country.

What did I say? he asked warily.

You said if they're assigned to Indian Country they are either rookies or have trouble with authority.

Did I really? said my father. He nodded, almost smiled.

Soren is not a rookie, he said.

All right, Dad. So why didn't he find the gas can?

I don't know, said my father.

I know. Because he doesn't care about her. Not really. Not like we do.

I had worked myself into a fury now, or planted myself into one with every puny hothouse plant that would not succeed in gaining my mother's attention. It seemed that anything my father did, or said, was calculated to drive me crazy. I was strangling there alone with my father in the quiet late afternoon. A rough cloud had boiled over me—I wanted all of a sudden nothing else but to escape from my father, and my mother too, rip away their web of guilt and protection and nameless sickening emotions.

I gotta go.

A tick started crawling up my leg. I pulled up the cuff of my trousers, caught it, and ripped it savagely apart with my nails.

All right, my father said quietly. Where do you want to go?

Anywhere.

Joe, he said carefully. I should have told you I am proud of you. I am proud of how you love your mother. Proud of how you figured this out. But do you understand that if something should happen to you, Joe, that your mother and I would . . . we couldn't bear it. You give us life . . .

I jumped up. Yellow spots pulsed before my eyes.

You gave *me* life, I said. That's how it's supposed to work. So let me do what I want with it!

I ran for my bike, jumped on it, and pedaled right around him. He tried to catch at me with his arms but I swerved at the last moment and put on a burst of speed that put me out of his reach.

I knew my father would call Clemence and Edward's. The gas station was out for the same reason. Cappy's and Zack's parents both had telephones. That left Angus. I pedaled straight over to find him outside, crushing last night's haul of beer cans. None of the cans were Hamm's. Angus had a scraped cheek and a fat lip. The fact is, sometimes Star would belt him. And when drunk, Elwin had a sly way of trapping Angus and slapping him up—it just about killed Elwin laughing. We wished it would. Besides that, there was a bunch of other guys who didn't like Angus's hair, or something, anything. Angus was glad to see me.

Those assholes again?

Nah, he said. So I knew his aunt or Elwin had done it.

As I helped Angus stomp the cans flat in the rock-hard dirt behind the building, I told him all that I'd overheard my father and Edward say about the priest the night before.

If we could find out that the priest drank Hamm's, I said. Do priests even drink?

Do they drink? said Angus. Hell, yes. They start with wine at mass. After that, I think they get shitfaced every night.

Every time Angus stamped down a can, his hair flew up in a brown mat. Angus had a round face and innocent long eyelashes. He had a crazy disarray of big, gleaming, dangerous-looking teeth. His fat bottom lip bared them in a helpless snarl.

I want to go to mass, I said.

Angus stopped with his foot in midair. What? You wanna go to mass? What for?

Is there a mass?

Sure, there's a five o'clock. We could just make it.

Angus's aunt was as pious as Clemence, though I doubted she'd confessed to slugging Angus.

We could check that priest out, I said.

Father Travis.

Right.

Okay, man.

Angus went up to his aunt's apartment and brought down the bike seat for his pink BMX. He attached it to the hollow rod with a bolt. He put the wrench in his pocket. Whitey had suggested this tactic and given him the wrench when his second mission bike was stolen. Next time someone steals your bike he'll get his ass reamed anyway, said Whitey. We took off and pedaled the long way to stay out of sight of the gas station, and we made it to the doors of Sacred Heart just before mass started. I followed Angus's lead, genuflected, and sat down. We took front-row seats. I had meant to observe the priest with a cool and objective calm—the same way, say, Captain Picard viewed the murderous Ligonian who had abducted Chief Security Officer Yar. I summoned to my face Picard's motionless yet searching gaze as the bell rang to draw the worshippers to their feet. I thought I had prepared myself. But when Father Travis swept in wearing a green robe that looked like a rough blanket, my head seemed to balloon out and fill with bees.

Hey, Starboy, my head is buzzing like a fucking hive, I whispered to Angus.

Shut up, he said.

The little group of twenty or so people began to murmur and Angus thrust a folded paper into my hands. It bore a typed set of responses and the words to hymns. My eyes stuck to Father Travis. I'd seen him before, of course, but I had never really looked at him closely. Boys called Father Travis Pan Face for his expressionless features. Girls called him Father What-a-Waste because his pale eyes glowed over romance-novel cheekbones. His skin was markless and had that redhead's milky pallor except for the snake of livid scar tissue that traveled up his neck. He had close-set little ears, a grave slash of a mouth, and a buzz-cut cap of fox-colored hair that receded back from his temples but came to a slashing point in the center. His teeth did not show when he talked and his boxy chin remained motionless so that the lips alone moved in his still face and the words seemed to wiggle out. Now, the mechanical regularity of his features in which the ever-moving slot of a mouth worked made me dizzy enough to sit down. I had the presence of mind to drop the paper so that I could pretend to search for it between my knees. Angus kicked me.

I'll puke if you do that again, I hissed. As soon as we could, pretending to find the end of the line for Holy Communion, we slipped out of the church and went down to the playground. Angus had a cigarette. We painstakingly halved it and I smoked my piece even though it brought back the whirling sense of misery. I must have looked as bad as I felt.

I'm gonna go find Cappy.

Yeah, I said. Why don't you. Tell him I ran away from my dad and to bring some food.

You ran away? Angus frowned. I'd always had the perfect family—loving, rich by reservation standards, stable—the family you would never run away from. No more. His eyes went sharp with pity and he rode off. I wheeled my bicycle into a ruffle of brush and spindly trees, mowed underneath, that marked the edge of the church's land. I leaned my bike against the tree and lay down in spite of the ticks. I shut my eyes. As I lay there I felt the earth pulling at my body. It seemed I could actually feel the gravity, which I pictured somehow as a huge molten magnet sitting at the center of the earth. I could feel it drawing on me and draining me of strength. I was going past limits, boundaries, to where nothing made sense and Q was high judge in red velvet robes. I fell into a drowse sudden as a fainting spell. Then woke to the vibrations of a quick-moving set of footsteps. I opened my eyes and stared straight up the flowing lines of black cloth to the wooden cross and Father Travis's rope belt. Above his rigid torso, broad chest, and undercliff of chin, his colorless eyes shone on me under the flat lids.

There's no smoking on the playground, he said. One of the nuns saw you.

I opened my lips and a hoarse little sound emerged. Father Travis continued.

But you are welcome at Holy Mass. And if catechism interests you, I teach Saturdays at ten a.m.

He waited.

Again, I made some sound.

You're Clemence Milk's nephew . . .

The drawing flow of gravity suddenly reversed and I sat straight up, filled with an electric energy of purpose.

Yes, I said. Clemence Milk is my auntie.

Now, remarkably, I found my legs under me. I stood. I actually stepped toward the priest, a small step, but toward him. My father's phrasing left my mouth.

May I ask you a question?

Shoot.

Where were you, I asked, between three and six o'clock on the afternoon of May fifteenth?

What day was that?

The grave mouth tucked at the corners.

It was a Sunday.

I suppose I was officiating. I don't really remember. And then after mass there was the Adoration. Why?

Just asking. No reason.

There is always a reason, said Father Travis.

Can I ask you another question?

No, said the priest. One question per day. His scar jumped to life on the side of his throat. It glowed red. You're a good kid, I hear from your aunt, get good grades. You don't give your parents trouble. We would love to have you in our youth group. He smiled. I saw his teeth for the first time. They were too white and even to be real. Young as he was, but with false teeth! And that scar like a thick rope of paint up his neck. He put his hand out. The callow artist's rendering of features resolved. Too handsome to be handsome, Clemence had said. We stood there. The sheen off his cassock reflecting up into his eyes spooked me. He held his hand out steady. I tried to hold back but my hand reached out of its own accord. His palm was cool. The callus smooth and tough, like Cappy's dad.

So we'll see you then. He turned away. Then looked back with the hint of a grin.

Cigarettes will kill you.

I stood rooted until he'd entered the church basement door far up the hill. I put my back against a tree and leaned there—not slumping. I was filled with that odd energy. I was allowing the tree to help me think. I decided first of all not to hate myself for what had just passed between the priest and me, that moment. I could hardly have refused. To refuse to shake a person's hand on the reservation was like wishing them dead. Although I did wish Father Travis Wozniak dead and wanted to burn him alive, even, my wish was contingent on secure proof that he was my mother's attacker. Guilty. My father would not have condoned a conclusion bereft of factual support. I scratched my back with the ridged tree bark and stared at the place where the priest had disappeared. The door to the church basement. I intended to get those facts, and when my friends came, I would have help.

Cappy appeared with Angus. He had a bread bag half full of potato salad and a plastic spoon. I made a bowl out of the bag by folding down the top, then I ate the salad. It was the kind with mustard in the mayonnaise and pickles and eggs. Cappy's aunts must have made the salad. My mother made it that way. I scraped my spoon against the inside of the bag. Then I told Cappy and Angus about the conversation I had overheard and how my father's suspicion had landed on the priest.

My dad said he was in Lebanon.

Whatever, said Cappy.

He was a Marine.

So was my dad, said Cappy.

I'm thinking we should find out if he drinks Hamm's beer, I

said. I was going to ask him but figured I'd give away the game. I did get his alibi. I have to check it.

Angus said, His what?

His excuse. He says he officiated at mass that Sunday afternoon. All I have to do is ask Clemence.

Should we set some Hamm's on his doorstep and see if he drinks it? said Angus.

Anybody would drink free beer, especially you, Starboy, said Cappy. We got to catch him drinking Hamm's in private. Spy on him.

Look in a priest's window?

Yes, said Cappy. We'll bike around back of the church and convent up to the old cemetery. Then we can slip around through the fence, take our bikes down through the graves. The back of the priest's house faces the cemetery, and the fence is padlocked, but you can slip through. When it's dark, we'll sneak up to the house.

Do the priests have a dog? I asked.

No dog, said Angus.

Good, I said. But at the moment I wasn't actually afraid of getting caught by the priest. It was the cemetery that unnerved me. I had recently seen a ghost. One was enough, and my father had told me how they visited the cemetery when he worked. This cemetery was the place where Mooshum's father, who had fought at Batoche with Louis Riel, was buried after he was killed years later racing a fast horse. It was where Mooshum's brother Severine, who had briefly served at the church as a priest, was buried in a plot specially marked off by white-painted brick. One of the three who were lynched by a mob in Hoopdance were also buried there—they'd taken the boy's body there because he was only thirteen. My age. And hanged. Mooshum remembered it. Mooshum's brother Shamengwa, whose name meant the Monarch Butterfly, was buried there. Mooshum's first wife, alongside whom he would be buried, was marked by a gravestone covered with fine gray lichen. His mother was buried in that place, the one who'd stopped talking entirely for ten years after Mooshum's baby brother died. And there was my father's family too, my grandmother's family and her mother's family, some of whom had converted. The men were buried to the west with the traditionals. They vanished into the earth. Small houses had been built over them to house and feed their spirits, but those had collapsed in advance of everything else, into nothingness. I knew the names of our ancestors from Mooshum and from my mother and father.

Shawanobinesiik, Elizabeth, Southern Thunderbird. Adik, Michael, Caribou. Kwiingwa'aage, Joseph, Wolverine. Mashkiki, Mary, The Medicine. Ombaashi, Albert, Lifted By Wind. Makoons, The Bearling, and Bird Shaking Ice Off Its Wings. They lived and died too quickly in those years that surrounded the making of the reservation, died before they could be recorded and in such painful numbers that it was hard to remember them all without uttering, as my father did sometimes as he read local history, *and the white man appeared and drove them down into the earth*, which sounded like an Old Testament prophecy but was just an observation of the truth. And so to be afraid of entering the cemetery by night was to fear not the loving ancestors who lay buried, but the gut kick of our history, which I was bracing to absorb. The old cemetery was filled with its complications.

To approach the cemetery from the back we had to go past an old lady who had dogs. You never knew how many dogs or what kind of dogs. She fed the rez dogs. Therefore her house was unpredictable and we always made a detour around it. As we got near, we prepared. Cappy had his pepper can. I grabbed up a heavy stick, thinking of how Pearl hated it, and why. Angus stripped some willow wands for a whip. We got our battle plan together and decided that I would go first with the stick and

Cappy would bring up the rear with the pepper. The woman's name was Bineshi and she was tiny and hunched as was her rickety little frame house. There were two wrecked cars in the yard where the dogs lounged. We thought we might make it if we had enough speed and zoomed past. But as soon as we turned onto the dirt road that ran along the edge of her yard, the dogs came bounding out of the wrecked cars. Two were gray with short legs, three were big, one was huge. They flashed up to us, barking with a vicious intensity. A small gray dog darted in and seized Angus by the pants cuff. Angus expertly kicked it, lashed its face with his whip, and kept riding.

They sense fear, yelled Cappy. We laughed.

The dogs were growing bolder now, as often happened if one made a move. Angus gave a hideous yell. A filthy whitish dog went for his arm and Angus dropped his whips and punched it square in the snout. The dog did not whimper and slink off, but sprang again. Once more Angus connected his blow, but as the dog twisted away, its head came down on Angus's leg and it tore his pants.

Get him off me!

Cappy turned. Dust flew. He scraped his feet in the dirt and pulled up beside Angus with the open pepper can, took a handful and flung it in the dog's face. It yipped and disappeared. But the others now surrounded us, clamoring for blood, their ears laid back. They snapped and gnashed like land sharks. We couldn't drop our bikes and run since we'd just have to retrieve the bicycles later. Anyway the dogs were quicker and would catch us before we could build up speed. Awkwardly, sticking close together, we climbed off and walked our bikes. Cappy peppered another dog. I clobbered two. The peppered dogs recovered and jumped back, drooling for revenge. They formed a circle and advanced, stiff-legged. Cappy dropped the can of pepper on the road and it spilled.

Ah shit, he said. We're gonna die.

We need fire, cried Angus. I clubbed a dog. It popped up. All of a sudden the dogs' heads turned. Their ears perked. As one pack they loped off. We heard the door of the little house slam.

She must be feeding them, said Cappy.

Maaj! cried Angus. We jumped back on our bikes and flew up the rest of the road, hardly noticing the rise. Then we ran our bikes down through the woods and hoisted them over the chain-link fence. We were safe in the graveyard. It was nearly dusk. Through the thick pines below we could make out a fractured glow from the windows of the priest's house. We wheeled our bikes down toward it. The fear I'd had of passing through the graveyard was eclipsed by relief. The dogless dead felt safe. We lingered on our stroll until it was almost dark, pointing out landmark gravestones. We each had ancestors in common, dotted here and there. The air was beginning to stir and a rainbird called over and over in the blue woods.

It's time, said Cappy when we reached the bottom.

The gate was loosely held together by the padlocked chain. We pulled it wide and eased our bikes through. With trepid stealth we rolled them to the far edge of the churchyard. The grass was clipped short, the stubble cool with evening dew. We slipped up beside the small cottage, just a one-story modernized cabin. Father Travis lived there by himself. We crouched into a scraggly bush. The low mutter of a television came from inside the house. We crawled around the far side to the window where the sound was loudest.

I wanna look in, whispered Angus.

He'll see you, I said.

There's blinds. Angus raised his head.

He came down quick.

He's sitting there watching!

Did he see you?

I dunno.

We went back around to the most hidden side of the house. There were footsteps inside and a sudden spill of light out the window just above our heads. There was a pause. The priest's silhouette loomed behind the curtain. We pressed ourselves to the clapboard. Just behind our heads a gentle splattering started.

Cappy mouthed the question Taking a piss? I shrugged because it sounded more like someone had taken the cap off a bottle and was gently shaking a delicate stream of water into the toilet. It took a long time and there were pauses. Then the toilet flushed, the faucet went on and off, the light went out, a door shut.

He's a low-key pisser, said Cappy.

Well, he is a priest, said Angus.

Do they piss funny?

They don't have sex, said Angus. With no regular use, maybe the plumbing could get rusty.

Like you know, said Cappy.

You guys stay here.

I crawled around the side of the house to the bluish TV glow. Anyone who came into the yard or passed beneath the black pines would have seen me. I stood and leaned slowly to the edge of the window. It was open, to catch the June breeze. I could see the back of Father Travis's head. He was sitting before the television in an easy chair and at his elbow there was a city beer, a Michelob. I couldn't tell what he was watching at first, and then I realized it was a movie. Not a television movie.

I sank down and crept back.

He's got a VHS player!

What's he watching?

This time Cappy went to look and after a little while he came back and said it was *Alien*, which had played two hours south of our reservation and which we'd only heard brain-bending stories of because we had no way down there and besides were too young to get in. There were no rental places on the reservation yet.

He must own it, I said, forgetting the open window.

He owns a copy? Owns it?

Shut up, you guys, whispered Cappy. He's got his screens in.

Angus leaned back against the foundation of the building and drew his legs up to his chest. We put our heads together and spoke low.

Could you see it very good?

I could see it fine. He's got a thirty-inch.

So that's how we finally saw *Alien*—standing at the window behind the young priest we suspected of an unspeakable crime. Father Travis even turned the sound up so we could hear the whole movie. When the credits started to roll, he switched it off and we ducked down and crawled around to where the bedroom had to be. We were still in delicious shock. Angus lay down and poked his fist up from his stomach and jerked his legs. The light went on in the bathroom again and there was the trickling noise. Then toothbrushing and gargling noises. Then the light went on in the bedroom. We edged along the foundation. Slowly rose. There were curtains and rolled-down shades, but there was a gap where the shade met the window. The curtains were transparent panels. We could see just fine. We watched Father Travis take off his wizardly cassock and hang it up. He had big hard muscled shoulders and rocklike pecs. Crazed scars looped down the divided slabs of his stomach. He shed his boxers and stood butt-naked, then turned around. His scars all connected in a powerful tangle around his penis and balls. His equipment was there, but obviously *sewn back on*, said Angus later, awed, telling Zack. Everything down there was scar tissue—ridged, slick, gray, purple.

We panicked, scrambled away. The lights went out. We darted toward our bikes but Father Travis was unbelievably swift out the door and with a sure bound he seized Angus. Cappy and I kept running.

Come back here, you two, said Father Travis in an even voice that carried perfectly. Or I'll rip off his head.

Angus yelped. We slowed and looked back. He had Angus by the throat.

He means it!

Say your Hail Marys, said the priest.

Hail Mary, Angus choked.

Silently, said Father Travis.

Angus's mouth began to move. Cappy and I turned and walked back. The night wind came in and the pines sighed around us. The flickering yard lamps that lighted the church parking lot didn't reach beneath the black trees. Father Travis walked Angus before him, to the house. Behind us. He ordered Cappy to open the door and once we were in he threw a dead bolt and kicked a chair up to the door.

As you know, there's no back way out, he said. So you might as well make yourselves comfortable.

He flung Angus at the couch and we jumped forward and sat down on either side of Angus, hands folded in our laps. Father Travis pulled a plaid shirt on and grabbed his easy chair. He turned it to face us. Then he sat down. He was wearing the boxers and the plaid shirt hung open. His chest was massive. I noticed a set of free weights on the floor and barbells in the corner.

Long time no see, he said to me and Angus.

We were petrified.

Got an eyeful, huh? You dumb monkeys. Whaddya think?

He kicked me in the shin, and although he was barefoot my leg went numb and I rocked backwards.

Say something.

But we couldn't.

Okay, dogface, he said to Cappy. You tell me why you were

spying on me. I know these two, but I don't know you. What's your name?

John Pulls Leg.

A jolt of admiration shot straight through me. That Cappy could give a fake name at this moment.

Pulls Leg. What kind of frickin' name is that?

It's an old traditional name, Sir!

Sir? Where'd you get that Sir!

My father was a Marine, Sir!

Then you've disgraced him, you puling ass-wipe shit. Son of a Marine spying on a priest. What's your dad's name?

Same name, Sir!

So you're Pulls Leg Junior?

Yes, Sir!

Well, Pulls Leg Junior, how's this?

Father Travis reached out and yanked Cappy off the couch with one streaming jerk of his leg. Cappy hit the floor hard but didn't cry out.

Pulls Leg, huh? Is that how you got your dumb-shit name?

He loomed down and Cappy put his dukes up but the priest just reached down and threw Cappy back on the couch.

All right, Pulls Leg Junior, what's your real traditional old-time name?

Cappy Lafournais.

Doe's your father?

Yeah.

Good man. He pointed a thick finger at Angus. And I know who your aunt is.

He stuck his finger in my face next. I couldn't breathe.

I know your dad, and I think I know why you pathetic scum-butts are here, spying on me. You. I started thinking about your question earlier this evening. Why you would ask me what I was doing on Sunday, May fifteenth, at such and such a time. Like you were asking for my alibi. I thought it was funny. Then

I remembered what happened to your mom. And bingo.

Our knees, our feet, our shoes, had taken on a profound significance. We were studying them closely. We could feel his hammered silver eyes on us.

So you think I hurt your ma, he said softly. Well? Answer.

He kicked me again. The numbness turned to pain.

Yeah. No. I thought maybe.

Maybe. Then the answer came in a flash, so to speak, huh? Im-poss-ee-bley. So you know. And just for your information, you little rat-pukes, you cat farts, you jerk-off freaks, I wouldn't use my dick that way even if I still could. You yellow-shit horndogs, I have a mother and I have a sister. I also had a girlfriend.

Father Travis leaned back. I glanced up at him. He was watching us from under his brow, his hands folded in his lap. His eyes had taken on that cyborg gleam. His cheekbones looked like they were going to break right through his skin. Not only did he own a copy of *Alien*, not only did he have an amazing and terrible wound, but he had called us humiliating names without actually resorting to the usual swear words. Besides that there was the deft speed with which he'd caught Angus, the free weights beside the television, the fancy Michelob. It was almost enough to make a boy want to be a Catholic.

You had a girlfriend?

Father Travis's face tightened to bone-white. I could not believe Cappy's nerve. For a moment I thought he was dead. But Cappy hadn't asked it in a taunting or sarcastic way at all. That was the thing about Cappy. He really wanted to know. He'd asked the question the way I know now a good lawyer might interview a potential witness. To find out about the other person. To hear his story.

Father Travis didn't speak for a time, but Cappy maintained a silent willingness to listen.

Yes, said Father Travis, at last. His voice was thicker now, and low. You skinny creamers don't know about women yet. You may think you do, but you don't. I was engaged to a real one. Extremely beautiful. Faithful. Never faltered. Not even when I got hit. She would have stayed. I was the one who . . . Do you boys like girls?

I do, said Cappy, the only one who dared answer.

Don't waste your time on sluts, said Father Travis. You in high school?

Going into high school, Cappy said.

All the better. There's a beautiful girl nobody else has noticed. You be the one to notice her.

All right, said Cappy.

So, said Father Travis. So.

He spread his hands over the arms of the chair. He watched us in silence until finally we raised our eyes to meet his lock-in stare.

You want to know how it happened. You want to know how I deal with it. You want to know things that you have no right to know. But you're not bad boys. I can see that now. You wanted to find out who hurt your mother, his mother. He stared at me.

I was at the U.S. Embassy in '83 and got lucky. I'm here, right? The spigot works. I have to take extremely good care of it. Otherwise, infections. Some sex drive. All sublimated. I was in seminary school before becoming a Marine. Had a spell of anger. Came home like this, a sign. Finished up. Ordained. Shipped here. Any questions?

I told him no priest here had ever shot the gophers.

Sisters gas 'em. You like to be gassed in a tunnel? Better thing to die clean, outside. They die like that. He snapped his fingers. Turn over and look at the sky, huh? The clouds.

He wasn't looking at us. He wasn't looking at anything now. He waved his hand, dismissing us. We half rose. He was far away. He steepled his hands together and lowered his forehead to rest against his fingers. We edged past him to the door, quietly moved the chair, and undid the dead bolt. We shut the door carefully and then we walked over to our bikes. The wind was blowing harder now. Beating the hood of the yard light so it flickered. The pines groaned. But the air was warm. A south wind, brought by Shawanobinesi, the Southern Thunderbird. A rain-bearing wind.

CHAPTER SIX

Datalore

The wind passed over us in a rolling mass of clouds that just kept moving until the sky went clear. Just like that, as if nothing had happened between us, my father and I began to talk. He told me he'd had an interesting conversation with Father Travis, and I froze up. But it was all about Texas and the military; Father Travis hadn't ratted on us. Whatever suspicions my father had expressed that night to Edward were gone, or submerged. I asked my father if he'd talked to Soren Bjerke.

The gas can? I asked.

Pertinent.

Now that Father Travis was off the list, I'd been thinking about the cases and bench notes my father and I had pulled. I asked my father if Bjerke had questioned the Larks, brother and sister.

He's talked to Linda.

My father tensely frowned. He had promised himself not to involve me, or confide in me, or collaborate with me. He knew where it went, what I might get into, but he didn't know the half of it. And here was the thing I didn't understand then but do now—the loneliness. I was right, in that there was just the three of us. Or the two of us. Nobody else, not Clemence, not even my mother herself, cared as much as we did about my mother. Nobody else thought night and day of her. Nobody else knew what was happening to her. Nobody else was as desperate as the two of us, my father and I, to get our life back. To return to the Before. So he had no choice, not really. Eventually, he had to talk to me.

I should visit Linda Wishkob, he said. She stonewalled Bjerke. But maybe . . . you want to come?

Linda Wishkob was magnetically ugly. Her pasty wedge of a face just cleared the post office counter. She regarded us with mooncalf, bulging eyes; her wet red lips were curls of flesh. Her hair, a cap of straight brown floss, quivered as she pulled out commemoratives. She displayed them for my father. She reminded me of a pop-eyed porcupine, even down to her fat little long-nailed paws. My father chose a set of fifty states of the union and asked if he could buy her a cup of coffee.

There's coffee in back here, said Linda. I can drink it free. She regarded my father warily, although she knew my mother. Everyone knew what had happened but nobody knew what to say or what not to say.

Never mind about the coffee, said my father. I'd like to have a word with you. Why don't you get someone to cover for you? You aren't busy.

Linda opened her wet lips to protest but could not think of a good excuse. In a few moments she had cleared things with her supervisor and came from around the counter. We walked out of the post office and across the street to Mighty Al's, which was a little soup can of a place. I couldn't believe my father was going to question someone in the close quarters of Mighty's, which had six scrounged tables crammed together. And I was right. My father asked no questions of

Linda but proceeded to have a useless conversation about the weather.

My father could out-weather anybody. Like people anywhere, there were times when it was the only topic where people here felt comfortably expressive, and my father could go on earnestly, seemingly forever. When the current weather was exhausted, there was all the weather that had occurred in recorded history, weather lived through or witnessed by a relative, or even heard about on the news. Catastrophic weather of all types. And when that was done with, there was all the weather that might possibly occur in the future. I'd even heard him speculate about weather in the afterlife. Dad and Linda Wishkob talked about the weather for quite a while and then she got up and left.

You really put her through the wringer, Dad.

The blackboard menu today advertised Hamburger Soup, all U could eat. We started on our second bowls of steaming hot soup: ground meat, commodity macaroni, canned tomatoes, celery, onion, salt, and pepper. It was especially good that day. Dad had also ordered Mighty's coffee, which he called the stoic's choice. It was always burnt. He kept drinking it expressionlessly after we'd finished the soup.

I wanted to get a feel for how she was doing, said my father. She's been through the wringer enough, for real.

I wasn't sure what coming down to talk with Linda Wishkob was about, but apparently some exchange I didn't understand took place.

Dad had finally allowed Cappy to come over that day. It was a grueling hot afternoon so we were inside playing Bionic Commando, quietly as we could, with the fan on. As always, my mother was sleeping. There was a soft tap. I answered the door, and there was Linda Wishkob, her bulging eyes, her tight blue uniform, her sweaty, dull, makeup-less face. Those long fingernails on the stubby fingers suddenly struck me as sinister, though they were painted an innocent pink.

I'll just wait for her to wake up, said Linda.

She surprised me by stepping past me into the living room. She nodded at Cappy and sat down behind us. Cappy shrugged, and as we hadn't played our game for a while and were not going to quit for any small reason, we continued: For years our people have struggled to resist an unstoppable array of greedy and unstable beings. Our army has been reduced to a few desperate warriors and we are all but weaponless and starving. We taste the nearness of defeat. But deep in the bowels of our community our scientists have perfected an unprecedented fighting weapon. Our bionic arm reaches, crushes, flexes, feints, folds. It pierces armor and its heat-seeking sensors can detect the most well-defended foe. The bionic arm combines the power of an entire army in itself and must be operated by one and only one soldier who can meet the test. I am that soldier. Or Cappy is that soldier. The Bionic Commando. Our mission takes us through the land of a thousand eyes, where death awaits us around every corner and through every window. Our destination: enemy headquarters. The heart of our hated foe's impregnable fortress. The challenge: impossible. Our resolve: unflagging. Our courage: quitless. Our audience: Linda Wishkob.

She watched us in such utter silence that we forgot about her. She hardly breathed or moved a muscle. When my mother left her room and went to the upstairs bathroom I didn't hear that either, but Linda did. She padded to the foot of the stairs and before I could say or do anything, she called my mother's name. Then she started walking up the stairs. I quit playing and jumped up, but already Linda's soft round body was at the top of the stairs and she was greeting my mother as if my mother weren't skinnily tottering away from her, disoriented, discovered, and invaded. Linda Wishkob did not seem to notice my mother's agitation. With a kind of oblivious simplicity she just followed her into her room. The door remained open. I heard the bed creak. The scrape of Linda's chair. And then their voices, as they started to talk.

A few days later there was finally a steady downpour of rain and I stayed inside for the second time that summer, playing my games, drawing cartoons. Angus had been working on his second portrait of Worf, but Star had called up and told him to borrow a plumber's snake from Cappy's place. They were over at Angus's now, probably, drinking Elwin's Blatz and pulling goop out of a stinking drain. My pictures bored me. I thought of sneaking the *Cohen* handbook, but reading my father's cases and notes had set up a despair in me. On a day like this I might have gone upstairs, locked myself in my room, and paged through my hidden HOMEWORK folder. My mother's presence upstairs had killed that habit off. I was thinking of slogging over to Angus's or even of taking out the third and fourth Tolkien books my father had got me for Christmas, but I wasn't sure I was desperate enough to do either thing. The rain was that endless, gray, pounding kind of rain that makes your house feel cold and sad even if your mother's spirit isn't dying right upstairs. I thought it might wash all of the plants out of the garden, but of course that wouldn't worry my mother. I took her a sandwich, but she was asleep. I took out the Tolkien set. I had just started reading as the rain came down and down, when out of the drumming pour, like a drenched hobbit, Linda Wishkob arrived again to visit.

Upstairs she went, with hardly a look at me. She had a little package in her hands, probably some of her banana bread—she bought black bananas and was known for her bread. A whole lot of murmuring went on upstairs—so mysterious to me. Why my mother chose to speak to Linda Wishkob might have bothered me or set me on alert or at least made me wonder. I didn't. But my father did. When he came home and learned that Linda was upstairs, he said to me in a soft voice, Let's trap her.

What?

You be the bait.

Oh, thanks.

She'll talk to you, Joe. She likes you. She likes your mother. Me, she's wary of. Listen to them upstairs.

Why do you want her to talk?

We need every piece of information—we need to know what she can tell us about the Larks.

But she's a Wishkob.

Adopted, remember. Remember the case, Joe, the case we pulled.

I don't think it's relevant.

Nice word.

But finally, I agreed to do it and Dad had fortunately bought some ice cream. It was Linda's favorite food.

Even on a rainy day?

He smiled. She's cold-blooded.

So when Linda came down the stairs I asked if she wanted a bowl of ice cream. She asked what flavor. I told her we had the striped stuff. Neapolitan, she said, and accepted a bowl. We sat down in the kitchen and Dad casually closed the door, saying that Mom needed her rest and how good it was of Linda to visit and how much everyone had enjoyed her banana bread.

The spice is excellent, I said.

I only use cinnamon, said Linda, and her pop eyes swelled with pleasure. Real cinnamon I buy in jars, not cans. From a foreign food section down in Hornbacher's, Fargo. Not the stuff you get here. Sometimes I use a little lemon zest or orange peel.

She was so happy we liked the banana bread that I thought maybe Dad wouldn't need me to get her to talk, but he said, Wasn't it good, Joe? And then I said how I'd eaten it for breakfast and how I'd even stolen a piece because Mom and Dad were hogging it all.

I'll bring two loaves next time, Linda said lovingly.

I spooned ice cream into my mouth and tried to let my father draw her out, but he raised his eyebrows at me.

Linda, I said, I heard. You know I wonder. I guess I'm asking a personal question.

Go right ahead, she said, and her pale features went rosy. Maybe nobody asked her personal questions. I thought quickly and let my tongue fly.

I have friends, you know, whose parents or cousins were adopted out. Adopted out of the tribe, and that is hard, well I've heard that. But I guess nobody ever talks about getting . . .

Adopted in?

Linda showed her little rat teeth in such a simple, encouraging smile that I was reassured now, and suddenly found I really wanted to know. I wanted to know her story. I ate more ice cream. I said I really did like the banana bread, and that I was surprised I had, because the truth was usually I hated banana bread. What I mean is suddenly I forgot my father and really started talking to Linda. I went past pop eyes and sinister porcupine hands and wispy hair and just saw Linda, and wanted to know about her, which is probably why she told me.

Linda's Story

I was born in the winter, she started, but then stopped to finish her ice cream. Once she'd pushed away the bowl, she started for real. My brother was born two minutes before me. The nurse had just wrapped him in a blue flannel warming blanket when the mother said, *Oh god, there's another one*, and out I slid, half dead. I then proceeded to die in earnest. I went from slightly pink to dull gray-blue, at which point the nurse tried to scoop me into a bed warmed by lights. The nurse was stopped by the doctor, who pointed out my crumpled head, arm, and leg. Stepping in front of the nurse and me, the doctor addressed the mother, telling her that the second baby had a congenital deformity, and asking if he should use extraordinary means to salvage it.

The answer was no.

No, let it die. But while the doctor's back was turned, the nurse cleared my mouth with her finger, shook me upside down, and swaddled me tight in another blanket, pink. I took a blazing breath.

Nurse, said the doctor.

Too late, she answered.

I was left in the nursery with a bottle strapped onto my face while the county decided how I would be transported to some sort of transitional situation. I was still too young to be admitted to any state-run institution, and Mr. and Mrs. George Lark refused to have me in their house. The night janitor at the hospital, a reservation woman named Betty Wishkob, asked for permission to hold me on her break. While cradling me, with her back turned to the observation window, Betty—Mom—nursed me. As she fed me, Mom molded and rounded my head in her powerful hand. Nobody in the hospital knew that she was nursing me at night, or that she was doctoring me and had decided to keep me.

This was five decades ago. I'm fifty now. When Mom asked if she could take me home, there was relief and not a lot of paperwork involved, at least in the beginning. So I was saved and grew up with the Wishkobs. I lived on the reservation and went to school as an Indian person would—first at the mission and later at the government school. But before then, around the age of three, I was taken away for the first time. I still remember the smell of disinfectant, and what I call *white despair*, into which there came a presence, someone or something who grieved with me and held my hand. That presence stayed with me. The next time a welfare officer decided to find a more suitable home for me, I was four. I stood beside Mom holding her skirt—green cotton. I hid my face in the scent of heated cloth. Then I was in the backseat of a car that sped soundlessly in some infinite direction. I woke alone in another white room. My bed was narrow and the sheets were tucked tightly down, so I had to struggle to get out. I sat on the edge of the bed for what seemed like a long time, waiting.

When you are little, you do not know that you are screaming or crying—your feelings and the sound that comes out of you is all one thing. I remember that I opened my mouth, that is all, and that I did not shut it until I was back with Mom.

Every morning, until I was about eleven years old, Mom and my dad, Albert, tried to round my head and work my arms and legs. They made me lift a little bag filled with sand that Mom sewed into a weight. They woke me first and brought me into the kitchen. The woodstove was going and I drank a glass of thin, blue milk. Then Mom sat in one kitchen chair and put me in her lap. She rubbed my head, then cupped her powerful fingers and pulled my skull into shape.

You're gonna see things sometimes, Mom told me once. Your soft spot stayed open longer than most babies. That's how spirits get in.

Dad sat across from us in another chair, ready to stretch me from head to toe.

Put your feet out, Tuffy, he said. That was my nickname. I put my feet in Dad's hands and he pulled me one way while Mom held tight around my ears and pulled the other.

My brother Cedric had given me the name Tuffy because he knew once I went to school I would get a nickname anyway.

He didn't want it to refer to my arm or head. But my head—so misshapen when I was born that the doctor had diagnosed me for an idiot—was changed by Mom's squeezing and kneading. By the time I was old enough to look in a mirror, I thought I looked beautiful.

Neither Mom nor Dad ever told me I was wrong. It was Sheryl who gave me the news, saying, *You are so ugly you're cute.*

I looked in the mirror the next chance I got and noticed that Sheryl was telling the truth.

The house we lived in still has a faint smell of rotted wood, onions, fried coot, the salty smell of unwashed children. Mom was always trying to keep us clean, and Dad was getting us dirty. He took us into the woods and showed us how to spot a rabbit run and set a snare. We yanked gophers from their holes with loops of string and picked pail after pail of berries. We rode a mean little bucking pony, fished perch from a nearby lake, dug potatoes every year for school money. Mom's job had not lasted. Dad sold firewood, corn, squash. But we never went hungry, and there was affection in our house. I knew I was loved because it was complicated for Mom and Dad to get me from the welfare system, though I'd helped out their efforts with my endless scream. All of which is not to say they were perfect. Dad drank from time to time and passed out on the floor. Mom's temper was explosive. She never hit, but she yelled and raved. Worse, she could say awful things. Once, Sheryl was twirling around in the house. There was a shelf set snugly in the corner. It held a cut-glass vase that was very precious to Mom. When we brought her wildflower bouquets, she would put them in that vase. I had seen her washing the vase with soap and polishing it with an old pillowcase. Then Sheryl's arm knocked the vase off the shelf and it struck the floor with a bright sound and shattered into splinters.

Mom had been working at the stove. She whirled around, threw her hands out.

Damn you, Sheryl, she said. That was the only beautiful thing I ever had.

Tuffy broke it! said Sheryl, bolting out the door.

Mom began to cry, harshly, and put her forearm to her face and cheek. I moved to sweep up the pieces for her, but she said to leave them, in such a heartsick voice that I went to find Sheryl, who was hiding in her usual place on the far side of the henhouse. When I asked why she'd blamed me, Sheryl gave a hateful look, and said, Because you're white. I didn't hold anything Sheryl did then against her, and we became close later on. I was very glad for that, as I have never married, and needed to confide in someone when, five years ago, I was contacted by my birth mother.

I lived in an addition tacked on to the tiny house until my parents died. They went one right after the other, as the long married sometimes do. It happened in a few months. By then, my brothers and sister had either moved off reservation or built new houses closer to town. I stayed on, in the quiet. One difference was I let the dog, a descendant of one that growled at the welfare lady, live inside with me. Mom and Dad had stationed the television in the kitchen. They had watched it after dinner, bolt upright on their kitchen chairs, hands folded on the table's surface. But I prefer my couch. I've had a fireplace installed with a glass front and fans that throw the heat off into a cozy circle, and there I sit every winter night, with the dog at my feet, reading or crocheting while I listen to the TV muttering for company.

One night the telephone rang.

I answered it with a simple hello. There was a pause. A woman asked if this was Linda Wishkob speaking.

It is, I said. I experienced a strange skip of apprehension. I knew that something was about to happen.

This is your mother, Grace Lark. The voice was tight and nervous.

I set the phone back down in the cradle. Later, that moment struck me as very funny. I had instinctively rejected my mother, left her in the cradle the way she'd left me in mine.

As you know, I am a government employee. At any time, I could have found out the address of my birth parents. I could have called them up, or hey, I could have gotten drunk and stood in their yard raving! But I didn't want to know anything about them. Why would I? Everything I did know hurt and I have always avoided pain—which is maybe why I've never married or had children. I don't mind being alone, except for, well . . . That night, after I'd hung up the phone, I made a cup of tea and busied myself with solving word puzzles. One stumped me. The clue was double-goer, twelve spaces, and it took me the longest time and a dictionary to come up with the word doppelganger.

I had always identified the visitations of my presence as one of those spirits Betty's doctoring let into my head. It first came when I was taken from Betty for that brief time, and put into the white room. At other times, I had the sensation that there was someone walking beside me, or sitting behind me, always just beyond the periphery of my vision. One of the reasons I let the dog live inside was that it kept away this presence, which over the years had grown to seem anxious, needy, helpless in some way I could not define. I had never before thought of the presence in relation to my twin, who'd grown up not an hour's drive away, but that night the combination of the call out of the blue and the twelve-letter word in my puzzle set my thoughts flowing.

Betty told me she had no idea what the Larks had named the baby boy, though she probably knew. Of course, as we were different genders, we were fraternal twins and supposedly no more alike than any brother and sister. The night my birth mother called, I decided to hate and resent my twin. I'd heard her voice for the first time, shaky on the phone. He'd heard it all of his life.

I had always thought I hated my birth mother, too. But the woman had called herself, simply, mother. My brain had perfectly taped the words she said. All that night and the next morning, too, they played on a loop. By the end of the second day, however, the intonation grew fainter. I was relieved that on the third day they stopped. Then, on the fourth day, the woman called again.

She began by apologizing.

I am sorry to bother you! She went on to say that she had always wanted to meet me and been afraid to find out where I was. She said that George, my father, was dead and she lived alone and that my twin brother was a former postal worker who had moved down to Pierre, South Dakota. I asked his name.

Linden. It was an old family name.

Was mine an old family name as well? I asked.

No, said Grace Lark, it just matched your brother's name.

She told me that George had quickly written my name down on the birth certificate and that they had never seen me. She went on talking about how George had died of a heart attack and she had nearly moved down to Pierre to be near Linden but she couldn't sell her home. She told me she hadn't known that I lived so close or she would have called me long before.

The light, conversational chatter must have caused a dream-like amnesia to come over my mind, because when Grace Lark asked if we could meet, if she could take me out to dinner at Vert's Supper Club, I said yes and agreed on a day.

When I finally hung up the telephone, I stared for a long time at the little log fire set going in the fireplace. Before the call, I'd laid the fire and looked forward to popping some corn. I would throw kernels high in the air and the dog would catch them. Perhaps I'd sit in the kitchen and watch a movie at the table. Or maybe I'd stay by the fire and read my novel from the library. The dog would snore and twitch in his dreams. Those had been my choices. Now I was gripped by something else—a dreadful array of feelings yawned. Which should I elect to overcome me first? I could not decide. The dog came and put his head in my lap and we sat there until I realized that one of the reactions I could have was numbness. Relieved, feeling nothing, I put the dog out, let him in, and went to bed.

So we met. She was so ordinary. I was sure that I had seen her in the street, or at the grocery, or the bank perhaps. It would have been hard to have missed seeing anyone, sometime, in a person's life around here. But she would not have registered as my mother because I could detect nothing familiar, or like myself, about her.

We did not touch hands or certainly hug. We sat down across from each other in a leatherette booth.

My birth mother stared at me. You aren't . . . her voice fell off.

Retarded?

She composed herself. You got your coloring from your father, she said. George had dark hair.

Grace Lark had red-rimmed blue eyes behind pale eyeglasses, a sharp nose, a tiny, lipless bow of a mouth. Her hair was typical for a woman of seventy-seven—tightly permed, gray-white. She wore stained dentures, big earrings made of cultured pearls, a pale blue pants suit, and square-toed lace-up therapy shoes.

There wasn't anything about her that called to me. She was just any other little old lady you wouldn't want to approach. I've noticed people on the reservation don't go toward women of her sort—I can't say why. A mutual instinct for avoidance, I guess.

Would you like to order? Grace Lark asked, touching the menu. Have anything you like, it's all on me.

No, thank you, we will split the check, I answered.

I had thought about this in advance and concluded that if my birth mother wanted to assuage her guilt in some way, taking me out to dinner was far too cheap. So we ordered, and drank our glasses of sour white wine.

We got through the dinner of walleye and pilaf. Tears came into Grace Lark's eyes over a bowl of maple ice cream.

I wish I'd known you were going to be so normal. I wish I hadn't ever given you up, she wept.

I was alarmed at the effect that these words had on her, and quickly asked, How's Linden?

Her tears dried up.

He's very sick, she said. Her face became sharp and direct. He's got kidney failure and is on dialysis. He's waiting for a kidney. I'd give him one of mine but I'm a bad match and my kidney is old. George is dead. You are your brother's only hope.

I put my napkin to my lips and felt myself floating up, off the chair, almost into space. Someone floated with me, just barely perceptible, and I could feel its anxious breathing.

Now is the time to call Sheryl, I thought. I should have called her before. I had a twenty-dollar bill with me and when I landed I put that money on the table and walked out the door. I got to my car but before I could get in, I had to run to the scarp of grass and weed that surrounded the parking lot. I was throwing up, heaving and crying, when I felt Grace Lark's hand stroking my back.

It was the first time my birth mother had ever touched me, and although I quieted beneath her hand, I could detect a stupid triumph in her murmuring voice. She'd known where I lived all along, of course. I pushed her away, repelled with hate like an animal sprung from a trap.

Sheryl was all business.

I'm calling Cedric down in South Dakota. Listen here,

Tuffy. I'll get Cedric to pull the plug on this Linden and you can forget this crap.

That's Sheryl. Who else could make me laugh under the circumstances? I was still in bed the next morning. I'd called in sick for the first time in two years.

You're not seriously even considering it, Sheryl said. Then, after I didn't answer, Are you?

I don't know.

Then I really am calling Cedric up. Those people ditched you, they turned their backs on you, they would have left you in the street to die. You're my sister. I don't want you to share your kidneys. Hey, what if I need one of your kidneys some day? Did you ever think of that? Save your damn kidney for me!

I love you, Sheryl said, and I said it back.

Tuffy, don't you do it, Sheryl warned, but her voice was worried.

After we hung up, I called the numbers on the card Grace Lark had put in my pocket, and made hospital appointments for all the tests.

While down in South Dakota, I stayed with Cedric, who was a veteran, and his wife, whose name is Cheryl with a *C*. She put out little towels for me that she had appliquéd with the figures of cute animals. And tiny motel soaps she'd swiped. She made my bed. She tried to show me that she approved of what I was doing, although the others in the family did not. Cheryl was very Christian, so it made sense.

But this was not a do-unto-others sort of thing with me. I already said that I do not seek pain and I would not have contemplated going through with it unless I couldn't bear the alternative.

All my life, knowing without knowing, I had waited for this thing to happen. My twin was the one just out of sight, right beside me. He did not know he had been there, I was sure. When the welfare stole me from Betty and I was alone in the whiteness, he held my hand, sat with me, and grieved. And now that I'd met his mother, I understood something more. In a small town people knew, after all, what she had done in abandoning me. She would have to have turned her fury at herself, her shame, on someone else—the child she'd chosen. She'd have blamed Linden, transferred her warped hatreds to him. I had felt the contempt and triumph in her touch. I was thankful for the way things had turned out. Before we were born, my twin had the compassion to crush against me, to perfect me by deforming me, so that I would be the one who was spared.

I'll tell you what, said the doctor, an Iranian woman, who gave me the results of the tests and conducted the interview, you are a match, but I know your story. And so I think it only fair that you know Linden Lark's kidney failure is his own fault. He's had not one but two restraining orders taken out against him. He also tried to suicide with a massive dose of acetaminophen, aspirin, and alcohol. That's why he is on dialysis. I think you should take that into account when making your decision.

Later that day, I sat with my twin brother, who said, You don't have to do this. You don't have to be a Jesus.

I know what you did, I told him. I'm not religious.

Interesting, said Linden. He stared at me and said, We sure don't look alike.

I understood this was not a compliment, because he was nice-looking. I thought he'd got the best of his mother's features, but the deceitful eyes and sharky mouth, too. His eyes shifted around the room. He kept biting his lip, whistling, rolling his blanket between his fingers.

Are you a mail carrier? he asked.

I work behind the counter, mostly.

I had a good route, he said, yawning, a regular route. I could do it in my sleep. Every Christmas my people left me cards, money, cookies, that sort of thing. I knew their lives so well. Their habits. Every detail. I could have committed the perfect murder, you know?

That took me aback. I did not answer.

Lark pursed his lips and looked down.

Are you married? I asked.

Nooooh . . . but maybe a girlfriend.

He said this like, poor me, self-pity. He said, My girlfriend's been avoiding me lately, because a certain highly placed government official has started paying her to be with him. Offering compensation for her favors. You get my drift?

I went speechless again. Linden told me that the girl he liked was young, working with the governor, that she got good grades and stood out, a model high-school sweetheart picked to intern. An Indian intern making the administration look good, he said, and I even helped her get the job. She's really too young for me. I was waiting for her to grow up. But this highly placed official grew her up while I was stuck in the hospital. He's been growing her up ever since.

I was uncomfortable and blurted out something to change the subject.

Did you ever think, I said, there was someone walking your route just beside you or just behind you? Someone there when you closed your eyes, gone when you opened them?

No, he said. Are you crazy?

That was me.

I picked up his hand and he let it go limp. We sat there together, silent. After a while, he pulled his hand out of mine and massaged it as though my grip had hurt him.

Nothing against you, he said. This was my mother's idea.

I don't want your kidney. I have an aversion to ugly people. I don't want a piece of you inside me. I'd rather get on a list. Frankly, you're kind of a disgusting woman. I mean, I'm sorry, but you've probably heard this before.

I might not be a raving beauty queen, I said. But nobody's ever told me I'm disgusting.

You probably have a cat, he said. Cats pretend to love whoever feeds them. I doubt you could get a husband, or whatever, unless you put a bag on your head. And even then it would have to come off at night. Oh dear, I'm sorry.

He put his fingers on his mouth and looked slyly guilty. He gave his face a mock slap. Why do I say these things? Did I hurt your feelings?

Did you say those things to drive me away? I asked. I had begun to float around again, the way I had in the restaurant. Maybe you want to die. You don't want to be saved, right? I'm not saving you for any reason. You won't owe me anything.

Owe you?

He seemed genuinely surprised. His teeth were so straight that I was sure he'd had orthodontic work done when he was young. He started laughing, showing all of those beautiful teeth. He shook his head, wagged his finger at me, laughing so hard he seemed overcome. When I bent down awkwardly to pick up my purse, he laughed so hard he nearly choked. I tried to get away from him, to get to the door, but instead I backed up against the wall and was stuck there in that white, white room.

My father sat silently at the table, hands folded and head lowered. I couldn't think of what to say at first, but then the silence went on so long I said the first thing that came into my head.

Lots of pretty women own cats. Sonja? I mean, the cats live

out in the barn, but she feeds them. You don't even have a cat. You have a dog. They are picky. Look at Pearl.

Linda beamed at my father and said that he had raised a gentleman. He thanked her and then said he had a question for her.

Why did you do it? he asked.

She wanted it, said Linda. Mrs. Lark. The mother. By the time the whole procedure was settled, I abhorred Linden—that's the word. Abhorred! But he cozied up to me. Plus, it was ridiculous because now *I* felt guilty about hating him. I mean, on the surface he was not all bad. He gave to charity cases, and sometimes he decided on a whim, I guess, that I needed his charity. Then he gave me presents, flowers, fancy scarves, soaps, sentimental cards. He told me how sorry he was when he was mean, temporarily charmed me, made me laugh. Also, I can't explain the hold that Mrs. Lark could exert. Linden was sullen to her and insulting behind her back. Yet he'd do anything she said. He consented because she forced him. And after that, as you know, I became very ill.

Yes, said my father, I remember. You contracted a bacterial infection from the hospital and were sent to Fargo.

I contracted an infection of the spirit, said Linda precisely, in a correcting tone. I realized that I had made a terrible mistake. My real family came to my rescue, got me on my feet again, she went on. And Geraldine too, of course. Also, Doe Lafournais put me through their sweat lodge. That ceremony was so powerful. Her voice was wistful. And so hot! Randall gave me a feast. His aunts dressed me in a new ribbon dress they made. I started healing and felt even better when Mrs. Lark died. I suppose I shouldn't say that but it's the truth. After his mother was gone, Linden moved back to South Dakota and soon he cracked again, or so I heard.

Cracked? I asked. What do you mean by that?

He did things, said Linda.

What things? I asked.

Behind me, I could feel the force of my father's attention.

Things he should have got caught for, she whispered, and closed her eyes.

CHAPTER SEVEN

Angel One

Although he was often to be found at the corner of the house sitting on a chipped yellow kitchen chair, watching the road, this was not how Mooshum spent his day but merely a pause to rest his stringy old arms and legs. Mooshum eagerly wearied himself with an endless round of habitual activities that changed with the seasons. In autumn, of course, there were leaves to rake. They came from everywhere to settle on Mooshum's patch of scrawny grass. He sometimes even plucked them off with his fingers and threw them in a barrel. It delighted him to burn them up. There was a short hiatus after the leaves and before the snow fell. During that time, Mooshum ate like a bear. His belly rounded and his cheeks puffed out. He was preparing for the great snows. He owned two shovels. A broad blue plastic rectangle that he used for the fluffy snow and a silver scoop with a sharp edge for snow that had packed or drifted. He also had an ice chipper, a hoelike instrument with a blade that ran straight down instead of curving over. He sharpened this one with a file until it was so keen it could easily slice off a toe.

Mooshum's battle array stood ready in the back entry through October. When the first snow fell, he put on his galoshes. Clemence had glued sandpaper of the roughest grade to the bottoms. Every other night or so she changed the paper and let the boots dry on the radiator. Mooshum's galoshes fit over his rabbit-fur-trimmed moccasins and insulated socks. He wore work pants lined with red flannel and a puffy, fluorescent orange parka that Clemence had given him so that he could be found if he got lost in the snow. Moosehide mitts lined with rabbit fur and a brilliant blue stocking cap with a wild pink pompom concluded this outfit. He went out every single day in his flamboyant gear and labored with incremental ferocity. He was antlike, he hardly seemed to be moving. Yet he shoveled trails to the garbage cans, cleared the snow not only from the walking paths around the house but completely off the driveway and away from the sides of the steps. He kept the snow scraped down to the ground and the concrete and never allowed it to accumulate. When there was no new snow and only the glare of ice, he hacked away with the lethal ice chipper. During the time when everything melted but the ground could not yet be prepared for the garden, he again ate constantly, putting back the flesh he'd lost to his winter war.

Spring and summer involved weeds that grew with vicious alacrity, pilfering animals, bugs, vicissitudes of weather. He used the push mower the way most his age would use a walker, but incidentally clipping the yard down to the nub. He tended a large vegetable garden with invisible zeal, rooting out quack grass, pigweed, and hauling bucket loads of water for the squash hills, again without ever seeming to move. He didn't care much for the flower garden, but Clemence had a raspberry patch gone wild that mingled with a stand of Juneberry bushes. When the berries began to ripen, Mooshum rose at dawn to defend them. A living scarecrow, he sat in his yellow chair sipping his morning tea. To frighten off the birds, he'd also rigged up a clothesline of tin-can lids. He'd pierced the can tops with a hammer and nail and knotted them close enough to clatter in a breeze. He secured these jangling lines all about the garden, and I was always very careful to note where he hung them as the edges of the cans were sharp and a boy who bicycled through the yard too carelessly might have his throat cut.

By means of this ceaseless and seemingly quixotic activity, Mooshum stayed alive. When he was past the age of ninety years, cataracts were removed from his eyes and false teeth refitted to his shriveled gums. His ears were still keen. He heard so well that he was bothered by the periodic judder of Clemence's sewing machine down the hall and by my uncle Edward's habit of humming dirges while he corrected school papers. One morning in the June heat I rode to their house. He heard my bicycle while I was still on the main road, but then I'd clothespinned a playing card to a spoke. I liked the cheerful clatter and also the ace of diamonds was good luck. Anybody might have heard me, but no one would have been so happy at that moment to see me as Mooshum. For he had tangled himself in a large piece of bird netting that he had been attempting to throw over the highbush pembina berries, even though they were nowhere near ripe.

I leaned my bike against the house and untangled him. Then I folded the net back up. I asked him where my auntie was and why he'd been left alone, but he hushed me and said she was inside the house.

She don't like me to use the net. The birds get tangled up and die in it, or lose their feet.

Indeed, from the folds of the net, at that moment, I picked out a tiny bird's leg, its minute claw still clenched around a strand of plastic webbing. I undid it carefully and showed it to Mooshum, who peered at it and worked his mouth back and forth.

Let me hide that, he said.

I'm keeping it.

I put the claw in my pocket. I won't tell Clemence. Maybe it's got luck in it.

You need some luck?

We put the net away in the garage and walked to the back door. The day was heating up and it was almost time for Mooshum to take his morning nap.

Yes, I need luck, I said to Mooshum. You know how things are. My father had grounded me for three days after I biked off without leaving a note. I'd been at home with my mother all that time. And there was still that ghost I'd never had a chance to figure out. I wanted to ask Mooshum what it meant.

Mooshum's eyes watered but not from pity. The sun was beginning to glare. He needed the Ray-Ban sunglasses that Uncle Whitey had given him for his last birthday. He took out a balled-up and faded bandanna and touched the rag to his cheekbones. Strings of hair hung around his face.

There's better ways of getting luck than from a bird's leg, he said.

We went inside. My aunt, who was dressed to go out and clean the church, in a set of high heels, a ruffled white shirt, and tight, streaky jeans, immediately put a pitcher of iced tea and two glasses on the table.

I wanted to laugh and ask how she was going to clean church in heels, but she saw me looking at them and said, I take them off, wrap my feet in rags, and polish the floor.

What's this? Mooshum pursed his mouth in displeasure.

The same medicine tea you drink every single day, Daddy.

Everyone around Mooshum was taking credit for his longevity, and the fact that he still had his wits about him. Or what passed for wits, Clemence said when he angered her. His next birthday was coming up and Mooshum claimed he would be 112. Clemence was focused especially hard on keeping him alive so that he could enjoy his party. She was making big preparations.

Pour me summa that cold slough water, Mooshum said to me as we sat.

Daddy! This peps you up.

I don't need no more pep. I need a place to put my pep.

How about Grandma Ignatia? I wanted to get him going.

She's all dried out.

She's younger than you, said Clemence in a frosty voice. You old buggers think you're made for young women. That's what's wrong with you.

That's what's keeping me alive! That and my hair.

Mooshum touched the long, slick, scrawny white mane he'd been growing for years. Clemence kept trying to braid or tie Mooshum's hair back, but he preferred to let it course in matted strings down the sides of his face.

Oh yai. He took a big gulp of tea. If Louis Riel had let Dumont ambush the militia back then, I'd be a retired prime minister. Clemence here might be governing our Indian nation instead of wiping the priest's floor. She'd have no time to make me drink these endless buckets of twig juice. The stuff runs right through me, my boy. Oops! Ha-ha. That's what I'll say when I shit my pants. Oops!

Don't you dare, said Clemence. Stay with him till I get back and make sure he gets to the toilet, him. She said she'd be back by noon or one.

I nodded and drank the tea. It had the sharp taste of bark. With Clemence gone, we could get down to business. I needed to find out about the ghost, first of all. Then I needed luck. I asked Mooshum about the ghost and described it. I told him that the same ghost had come to Randall.

It's not a ghost, then, Mooshum said.

What is it, then?

Someone's throwing their spirit at you. Somebody that you'll see.

Could it be the man?

What man?

I took a breath. Who hurt my mother.

Mooshum nodded and sat motionless, frowning.

No, probably not, he said at last. When somebody throws their spirit at you they don't even know it, but they mean to help. For weeks *mon père* dreamed that horse trampled him. Twice, I saw the angel that came to take my Junesse. Be careful.

Then help me get my luck, I said. How should I start?

You go to your doodem first, Mooshum answered. Find the ajijaak.

My father and his father were ceremonially taken into the crane clan, or Ajijaak. They were supposed to be leaders and have good voices, but beyond that I'd been given no special knowledge. I told this to Mooshum.

That's okay. You just go straight to your doodem and watch. It will show you the luck, Joe.

He drank the tea, made a face. Then his head tipped down on his chest and he fell into the instant sleep of the ancient and the very young. I helped him stand up and with his eyes shut he was willing to be led to the cot in the living room where he dozed in the daytime, right beside the picture window. It was placed so that when he woke up he could gaze at the hot eternal sky.

When Clemence came back, I left the house and biked to a slough outside of town. It was shallow all along the edges, and I'd seen a heron there last time I went. All the herons and cranes and other shorebirds were my doodemag, my luck. There was a dock of gray boards, some missing. I lay down on the warm wood and the sun went right into my bones. I saw no herons at first. Then I realized the piece of reedy shore I was staring at had a heron hidden in its pattern. I watched that bird stand. Motionless. Then, quick as genius, it had a small fish, which it carefully snapped down its gullet. The heron went back to standing still, this time on one leg. I was getting impatient for the luck to show itself.

Okay, I said, where's the luck?

With a flare of long, pointed wings, it vaulted into the air and flapped to the other side of the lake, where the round house was, as well as the cliff and drop-off, a place we liked to swim. The prevailing winds drove waves, junk, and scudding foam to this side of the lake. I turned around, disappointed, edged up over one of the missing boards, and looked down into the shadow of the dock through the clear water of the lake. There were usually baby perch, water skimmers, tadpoles, and maybe even a turtle to watch. This time a child's face stared up at me. Startling, but I knew it was a doll right off, a plastic doll sunk wide-eyed into the lake. Smirking like it had a secret, blue eyes with bits of sparkle in the iris catching points of sun. I jumped up, wheeled around, then kneeled back down for a better look. It occurred to me that if there was a toy there might be a real child attached to it, and that child might be wedged underneath the dock. A cloud passed over the sun. I thought of going after Cappy, but finally I got too curious and looked down again, peering through gaps between the boards. There was just the doll. A girl baby doll floating calmly along the lake bottom wearing a blue checked dress, puffy panties, and that naughty smile. As soon as I'd truly made sure there was no real child to go with it, I fished out the doll and shook it so the water trickled out the seam where the head met the molded plastic body. I wrenched the head off the doll to dump out the rest of the water, and there was my luck. Right there. The doll was packed with money.

I pushed the head back on the doll. I looked around. All was quiet. Nobody in sight. I took off the head and examined it more closely. The doll's head was stuffed with neatly rolled-up bills. I was thinking one-dollar bills. A hundred, maybe two. My pack was hanging behind my bike seat. I threw the doll in and pedaled toward the gas station. As I rode along I thought about my luck—there was a feeling of guilt attached. I assumed that the person who'd hidden the money in the doll was a girl, maybe even somebody that I knew. She had saved up her whole life, bills scavenged here and there, little job money, birthday money, dollars from drunk uncles. Everything she had was in that doll and she had lost it. I thought that my luck was probably temporary. There would be a pitiful ad tacked up somewhere or even in the newspaper, a hopeless message describing this doll and asking to have it back.

When I got to the gas station, I propped my bike up by the door and put the doll underneath my shirt. Sonja was taking care of a customer. I looked at the bulletin board. There were ads for bull semen and wolf puppies, offers to sell blown-out stereo equipment, hopeful snapshots and descriptions of quarter horses, pintos, and used cars. No doll. The customer finally left. I was still cradling the doll underneath my shirt.

What'cha got there? Sonja asked.

Something I have to show you in private.

I've heard that one before.

Sonja laughed and I went red.

C'mon, in here.

We went behind the counter to the tiny closet she called her office. There was a small metal desk, chair, cot, and lamp squeezed in. I took the doll from beneath my shirt.

Weird, said Sonja.

I took the head off.

Holy fuck.

Sonja shut the closet door. She used her long pink nails to tug the roll of bills from the neck. Then she uncurled a couple. They were hundred-dollar bills. Sonja rolled the bills back up, tightly, jammed them into the doll, and put the head back on. She went out, shutting the door behind her, and got three plastic bags. Then she came back in and rolled the doll into one of the bags and wrapped another bag around that one, then used the third bag as the carrier. She was looking down at me in the dim office. Her eyes were round and their blue was dark as rain.

Those bills are wet.

The doll was in the lake.

Anybody see you fish it out? Anybody see you with the doll?

No.

Sonja took the canvas deposit pouch out of a drawer. I knew about the pouch because she took the money to the bank twice a day. A sign at the register said, “No Money on the Premises!” Another next to it read, “Smile, You’re on Candid Camera.” That the camera was fake was a big secret. Sonja got out the tan aluminum cash box that locked with a little key. She thought a moment, then she took a stack of white business envelopes out of a drawer and put them in the tin box.

Where’s your dad?

Home.

Sonja dialed the home number and said, Mind if I take Joe with me doing errands? We’ll be back late afternoon.

Where are we going? I asked.

To my house, first.

We took the doll in the plastic bag, the deposit pouch, and the tan box to the car. Sonja kissed Whitey as we passed and told him that she was making the deposit and was going to buy me some clothes and stuff. The implication was that she was doing for me the things that my mother would have done if she was able to get up and out.

Sure, said Whitey, waving us off.

Sonja always made certain that I buckled myself in and rode safe. She had an old Buick sedan that Whitey kept running, and she was a careful driver, though she smoked, flicking the ashes into a messy little pull-out ashtray. The rest of the car was vacuumed spotless. We rode out of town and turned down the road to the old place, past the horses in the pasture, who looked up at us and started forward. They must have known the sound of the car. The dogs were standing at the house, waiting. They were Pearl's sisters—Ball and Chain. Both were black with burning yellow eyes and patches of cottontail brown here and there in their ruffs and tails. The male dog, Big Brother, had run off about a month before.

Whitey had put a stairway and deck on the front of the house. It was made of treated lumber that hadn't lost its sick green color yet. The house was a floaty blue. Sonja said she'd painted it that blue because of the name of the color: Lost in Space. The trim was spanking white but the aluminum storm door and solid-core interior door were old and battered. Inside, the house was cool and dim. It smelled of Pine-Sol and lemon polish, cigarettes and stale fried fish. There were four small rooms. The bedroom had a saggy double bed topped with a flowered comforter, and the window looked out on the sloping pasture and the horses. The pinto and the Appaloosa had come close to the wire at the edge of the yard. Spook whinnied, a love sound. I followed Sonja into the bedroom, where she opened her closet. Perfume wafted out. She turned around with a clothes iron in her hand and plugged it into the wall beside the ironing board. The board was set right before the window, where she could watch the horses.

I sat down on the edge of the bed, took the doll's head off, and gave Sonja bill after bill. She carefully ironed each one flat and dry, testing the bottom of the iron often with her finger. They were all hundreds. At first we put five bills carefully in each envelope, and folded down the flap but didn't seal it, and put the envelope on the bed. Then we got low on envelopes and put ten bills in each one. Then twenty. Sonja gave me a tweezers and I fished the last bills out of the wrists and ankles of the doll. Sonja used a flashlight to peer down the doll's neck. At last, I put the head back on.

Put it back in the bag, said Sonja.

She wiped her wrist across her forehead and upper lip. Her face was covered with beads of sweat although the heat hadn't reached inside the house yet.

She flapped her arms up and down, patted her armpits.

Phew. Go out in the kitchen and get me some water. I gotta change my shirt.

I went out to the kitchen and opened the refrigerator. The well on the place sucked up sweet water. Sonja always kept a jug of it cold. I poured water into a Pabst Blue Ribbon glass—they collected beer glasses—and drank it down. Then I filled it back up for Sonja. I guess I wanted her to drink out of the same glass as me, though I really wasn't thinking about that. I was thinking about how much money might be in the envelopes. I went back in and Sonja had a fresh shirt on—pink and gray stripes that pulled wide across her chest. The shirt had a stiff white collar and a buttoned tab. She drank the water.

Whew, she said.

We put the envelopes into the cash bag and put the bag in the aluminum box. Sonja went to the bathroom and brushed her hair and so on. She didn't entirely shut the door and I sat there in the kitchen looking at the bathroom wall. When she came out she had on fresh lipstick, a pink that exactly matched her fingernails and the stripes on her shirt. We went out to the car. Sonja took the doll with her in the plastic bag. She locked it in the trunk.

We're going to open a bunch of college savings accounts for you, said Sonja.

First we drove to Hoopdance and were ushered past the teller to talk with a bank manager in back. Sonja said that she was opening an account for me, a savings account, and we both signed printed cards while the woman typed out the passbook in my name with Sonja as a co-signer. Sonja handed over three of the envelopes, and the woman opening the account gave her a sharp look.

They sold his land, Sonja shrugged.

The woman counted out the money and typed it into the passbook. She put the passbook into a little plastic envelope and gave it pointedly to me.

I walked out with the passbook, and we drove to the other bank in Hoopdance, where we did the same thing. Only this time Sonja mentioned a big bingo win.

I'll say, said the bank manager.

We kept going, drove to Argus. At one bank she said I had inherited money from my senile uncle. At another she mentioned a racehorse. Then she went back to the bingo win. It took all afternoon, us driving through the new grass pastures and crops just beginning to show. At a roadside rest stop, Sonja stopped and opened the trunk. She took out the doll in its plastic bags and dropped it in a trash can. After that, we stopped in the next town and got take-out hamburgers and french fries. Sonja wouldn't let me drink a Coke but had some idea that orange soda was better for me. I didn't care. I was so happy to be in a car where Sonja had to watch the road and I could glance at her breasts straining at those stripes before I looked up at her face. Every time I talked to her, I looked at her breasts. I kept the cash box on my lap and stopped thinking about the money, actually, as money. But at last when we had deposited it all and were driving toward home I went through each of the passbooks and added the numbers up in my head. I told Sonja there was over forty thousand dollars.

It was a full-size baby doll, she said.

How come we couldn't keep out at least one bill? I asked. Once I thought about it, I was disappointed.

Okay, said Sonja. Here's the thing. Wherever that money

came from? They are gonna want it back. They will kill to get it back, you know what I'm saying?

I shouldn't tell anybody. Duh.

But can you do that? I've never known a guy who could keep a secret.

I can.

Even from your dad?

Sure.

Even from Cappy?

She heard me hesitate before I answered.

They'd whale on him too, she said. Maybe kill him. So you zip it and keep it zipped. On your mother's life.

She knew what she was saying. She knew without looking that tears started in my eyes. I blinked.

Okay, I swear.

We have to bury the passbooks.

We turned down a dirt road and drove until we came to the tree that people call the hanging tree, a huge oak. The sun was in its branches. There were prayer flags, strips of cloth. Red, blue, green, white, the old-time Anishinaabe colors of the directions, according to Randall. Some cloths were faded, some new. This was the tree where those ancestors were hanged. None of the killers ever went on trial. I could see the land of their descendants, already full of row crops. Sonja took the ice scraper out of her glove compartment and we put the passbooks in the cash box. She pushed the key into her front jeans pocket.

Remember the day.

It was June 17.

We traced down the sun to a point on the horizon and then walked in a straight line from where the sun would set, fifty paces back into the woods. It took us what seemed like forever to scrape out a deep hole for the box, using just that ice scraper. But we got the box in and covered it up and fit the divots back on top and scattered them with leaves.

Invisible, I said.

We need to wash our hands, said Sonja.

There was some water in the ditch. We used that.

I get it about not telling anybody, I said as we drove home. But I want shoes like Cappy's.

Sonja glanced over at me and almost caught me looking at the side of her breast.

Yeah, she said. And how would you explain where you'd got the money to buy them?

I'd say I had a job at the gas station.

She grinned. You want one?

Pleasure flooded into me so that I couldn't speak. I hadn't realized until then how much I wanted out of my house and how much I wanted to be working somewhere I could see and talk to other people, just random people coming through, people who weren't dying right before your eyes. It frightened me to suddenly think that way.

Hell, yes! I said.

You don't swear on the job, said Sonja. You're representing something.

Okay. We drove for a few miles. I asked what I was representing.

Reservation-based free market enterprise. People are watching us.

Who's watching us?

White people. I mean, resentful ones. You know? Like those Larks who owned Vinland. He's been here, but he's nice to me. Like, he's not so bad.

Linden?

Yeah, that one.

You should watch out for him, I said.

She laughed. Whitey hates his guts. When I'm nice to him, he gets so jealous.

How come you wanna make Whitey jealous?

All of a sudden, I was jealous too. She laughed again and said that Whitey needed to get put in his place.

He thinks he owns me.

Oh.

I was awkward, but she suddenly glanced at me, sharp, with a naughty smirk like the one on that doll's face. Then she looked away, still smiling with manic glee.

Yeah. Thinks he owns me. But he'll find out he don't, huh? Am I right?

Soren Bjerke, special agent for the FBI, was an impassive lanky Swede with wheat-colored skin and hair, a raw skinny nose, and big ears. You couldn't really see his eyes behind his glasses—they were always smudged, I think on purpose. He had a droopy houndlike face and a modest little smile. He made few movements. There was a way he had of keeping perfectly still and watchful that reminded me of the ajijaak. His knobby hands were quiet on the kitchen table when I walked in. I stood in the doorway. My father was carrying two mugs of coffee to the table. I could tell I'd interrupted some cloud of concentration between them. My legs went weak with relief because I understood Bjerke's visit was not about me.

That Bjerke was here anyway went back to Ex Parte Crow Dog and then the Major Crimes Act of 1885. That was when the federal government first intervened in the decisions Indians made among themselves regarding restitution and punishment. The reasons for Bjerke's presence continued on through that rotten year for Indians, 1953, when Congress not only decided to try Termination out on us but passed Public Law 280, which gave certain states criminal and civil jurisdiction over Indian lands within their borders. If there was one law that could be repealed or amended for Indians to this day, that would be Public Law 280. But on our particular reservation Bjerke's presence was a statement of our toothless sovereignty. You have read this far and you know that I'm writing this story at a removal of time, from that summer in 1988, when my mother refused to come down the stairs and refused to talk to Soren Bjerke. She had lashed out at me and terrified my father. She had floated off, so that we didn't know how to retrieve her. I've read that certain memories put down in agitation at a vulnerable age do not extinguish with time, but engrave ever deeper as they return and return. And yet, quite honestly, at that moment in 1988, as I looked at my father and Bjerke at our kitchen table, my brain was still stuffed with money like the head of that trashed doll with manufactured mischief in her eyes.

I walked past Bjerke into the living room but then I didn't want to walk upstairs. I didn't want to walk past my mother's shut door. I didn't want to know that she was lying in there, breathing in there, and with her constant suffering sucking all the juice out of the excitement of the money. But because I did not want to walk past my mother's door, I turned and went back to the kitchen. I was hungry. I stood in the doorway fidgeting until the men again stopped talking.

Maybe you want a glass of milk, said my father. Get yourself a glass of milk and sit down. Your aunt made a cake for us. A small round chocolate cake, neatly iced, was set on the counter. My father waved me to it. I carefully cut four pieces and put them on saucers with a fork beside. I brought three of the pieces to the table. I poured myself a glass of milk.

I'll take that up to your mother later on, said my father, nodding at the last piece of cake.

So I sat down with the men. And I realized I had made a mistake. Now that I was sitting in their proximity, the truth would pull at me. Not the gas can truth. But when they seemed to wait for me to speak, I threw that out, nervously, asking if it could be evidence.

Yes, said Bjerke. His no-flinch gaze pierced the scum on his eyeglasses. We'll do an affidavit. All in time. If we have a case.

Yes, sir. Well, I gathered my courage, maybe we should do it now. Before I forget.

Is he the forgetful type? asked Bjerke.

No, said my father.

Still, I ended up talking into a little tape recorder and signing a paper. After that, there were some politely well-meant questions about what I was up to that summer and how tall I was growing and which sports I'd go out for in junior high school. Wrestling, I said. They struggled to not look skeptical. Or maybe cross-country? That seemed more believable. I could tell that both men were glad to have me there but also fending off some large morose silence of confusion between them that probably stemmed, now that I think back to that day and that hour, to their impasse. They were out of ideas and had no suspects and no sure leads and no help at all from my mother, who now insisted that the event itself had passed from her mind. The money was still pushing at me to talk, to reveal.

There's something, I said.

I put down my fork and looked at my empty plate. I wanted another piece, this time with ice cream. At the same time, I had a sick sense of what I was about to do and thought that I might never eat again.

Something? said my father. Bjerke wiped his lips.

There was a file, I said.

Bjerke put down his napkin. My father peered at me over the rims of his eyeglasses.

Joe and I went through the files, he said to Bjerke, by way of explaining my unexpected remark. We pulled the possible court cases where someone might have—

Not that kind of file, I said.

The two of them nodded at me patiently. Then I saw my

father realize there was something he did not know in what I was about to say. He lowered his head and stared at me. That gilded octopus ticked on the wall. I took a deep breath, and when I spoke I whispered in a childish way that I immediately found shameful but which riveted them.

Please don't tell Mom I said this. Please?

Joe, said my father. He took off his glasses and set them on the table.

Please?

Joe.

All right. That afternoon when Mom went to the office there was a phone call. When she put the phone down, I could tell she was upset. Then about an hour afterward she said she was going after a file. A week ago, I remembered about the file. So I asked her if they found the file. She said there was no file. She said that I should never mention a file. But there was a file. She went after it. That file is why this happened.

I stopped talking and my mouth hung open. We stared at one another like three dummies with crumbs on our chins.

That is not all, said my father suddenly. That is not all you know.

He leaned over the table in that way he had. He loomed, he seemed to grow. I thought about the money first, of course, but I was not about to give that up and anyway to speak about it now would also implicate Sonja, and I would never betray her. I tried to shrug it off.

That's it, I said. Nothing else. But he just loomed. So I gave up a lesser secret, which is often the way we satisfy someone who knows, and knows that he knows, as my father did then.

All right.

Bjerke leaned forward too. I pushed my chair back, a little wildly.

Take it easy, said my dad. Just tell what you know.

That day we went out to the round house and found the gas

can, well, we found something else there too. Across the fence line, down by the lakeshore. There was a cooler and a pile of clothes. We didn't touch the clothes.

What about the cooler? asked Bjerke.

Well, I believe we opened that.

What was in it? asked my father.

Beer cans.

I was about to say they were empty and then I looked at my father and knew that a denial was beneath me and a lie would embarrass both of us in front of Bjerke.

Two six-packs, I said.

Bjerke and my father looked at each other, nodded, and sat back in their chairs.

Just like that I ratted out my friends in order to hide the fact of the money. I sat stunned at how quickly it had happened. I was also shocked at how perfectly my admission covered up the forty thousand dollars I had just secured that very day with Sonja's help. Or under Sonja's direction. It was me helping Sonja, after all. She was the one who'd had the idea. She was the one who hadn't gone to my father or to the police. She was an adult and so theoretically she was responsible for what had happened that day. I could always take refuge in that, I thought, and that I had this idea surprised and then humiliated me so that, sitting there before my father and Bjerke, I began to sweat and I felt my heart quicken and my throat seize tight.

I jumped up.

I gotta go!

Did he smell like beer? I heard my father ask.

No, said Bjerke.

I locked myself in the bathroom and could hear them talking out there. If there'd been a window easy to open I might have jumped out and run. I put my hands under the water and muttered words and very deliberately did not look into the mirror.

When I came back out and slunk to the table, I saw a slip of paper next to my empty cake plate and milk glass.

Read it, said my father.

I sat down. It was a citation, though just on scrap paper. Underage drinking. It mentioned juvenile detention.

Should I cite your friends too?

I drank both six-packs. I paused. Over time.

Where would we find the cans? asked Bjerke.

They're gone. Crushed up. Thrown out. They were Hamm's.

Bjerke didn't seem to think the brand was remarkable. He didn't even jot this down.

That area was under surveillance, he said. We knew about the cooler and the clothes, but they don't belong to the attacker. Bugger Pourier came home from Minneapolis to see his dying mother. She kicked him out, as usual, and he moved in down there. We were hoping he'd come get his beer. But I guess you drank it first.

He said this in a remote but somehow sympathetic tone and I felt my head begin to swim with the sudden drain of adrenaline. I stood up again and backed away with the paper warning in my hands.

I'm sorry, sir. They were Hamm's. We thought . . .

I kept backing up until I reached the doorway and then I turned around. Leaden, I climbed the stairs. I went past my mother's door without looking in on her. I went into my own room and shut the door. My parents' bedroom took up the front of the upstairs and had three windows that normally let in the first sunlight of morning. The bathroom and sewing room took up small spaces on either side of the stairway. My room at the back of the house caught the long gold of sunset and in summer especially it was comforting to lie in my bed and watch the radiant shadows climb the walls. My walls were painted a soft yellow. My mother had painted the walls while she was pregnant and always said she'd chosen the color because it would be right for either a girl or boy, but that halfway through the painting she knew I was a boy. She knew because each time she worked in the room a crane flew by the window, my father's doodem, as I have said. Her own clan was the turtle. My father insisted that she had arranged for the snapping turtles she'd hooked on their first date to scare him into asking her to marry him without delay. I only learned later that they'd caught the very snapper whose shell my mother's first boyfriend had carved with their initials. That boy had perished, Clemence had told me. The turtle's message had been about mortality. How my father should act with swiftness in the face of death. As the light crept down the sides of the walls, turning the yellow paint to a deeper bronze, I thought about the awful doll and the money. I thought about Sonja's left breast and right breast, which after continual surreptitious observation I had concluded were slightly different, and I wondered if I'd ever know exactly how. I thought about my father sitting in the welling gloom downstairs, and my mother in the black bedroom with the shades drawn against tomorrow's sunrise. There was that hush on the reservation that falls between the summer dusk and dark, before the pickup trucks drag between the bars, the dance hall, and the drive-up liquor window. Sounds were muted—a horse neighed over the trees. There was a short, angry bawl way off as a child was dragged in from outdoors. There was the drone of a faraway motor chugging down from the church on the hill. My mother hadn't ever realized that cranes are very predictable and cease their hunting at a certain hour and return to their roosts. Now the crane my mother used to watch, or its offspring, flapped slowly past my window. That evening it cast the image not of itself but of an angel on my wall. I watched this shadow. Through some refraction of brilliance the wings arched up from the slender body. Then the feathers took fire so the creature was consumed by light.

CHAPTER EIGHT

Hide and Q

My mother's job was to know everybody's secrets. The original census rolls taken in the area that became our reservation go back past 1879 and include a description of each family by tribe, often by clan, by occupation, by relationship, age, and original name in our language. Many people had adopted French or English names by that time, too, or had been baptized and received thereby the name of a Catholic saint. It was my mother's task to parse the ever more complicated branching and interbranching tangle of each bloodline. Through the generations, we have become an impenetrable undergrowth of names and liaisons. At the tip of each branch of course the children are found, those newly enrolled by their parents, or often a single mother or father, with a named parent on the blank whose identity if known might shake the branches of the other trees. Children of incest, molestation, rape, adultery, fornication beyond reservation boundaries or within, children of white farmers, bankers, nuns, BIA superintendents, police, and priests. My mother kept her files locked in a safe. No one else knew the combination of the safe and there was now a backlog of tribal enrollment applications piled up at her office.

*

Special Agent Bjerke was in our kitchen the next morning to approach the problem of questioning my mother about the particular file.

Would it help if we had a woman? To talk? We can get a female agent to drive over from our Minneapolis office.

I don't think so.

My father fiddled with the tray he'd fixed for my mother's breakfast. There was an egg fried the way she'd liked, toast buttered just so, a dab of Clemence's raspberry jam. He had already brought her coffee with cream and was encouraged that she'd sat up for him and had a sip.

I went upstairs with the tray and set it down on one of the chairs next to the bed. She had put down the coffee and was pretending to sleep—I could tell by the infinitesimal tension in her body and her fake deep breaths. Perhaps she knew that Soren Bjerke had returned, or perhaps my father had said something about the file already. She would feel betrayed by me. I didn't know if she would ever forgive me, and I left her room wishing that I could go straight to Sonja and Whitey's and pump gas in the hot sun or wash windshields or clean the scummy restroom. Anything but go back upstairs, into the bedroom. My father said it was important I be there so that she couldn't deny it.

We'll have to break through her denial, is how he put it, and I felt a miserable dread.

The three of us went upstairs. My father first, then Bjerke, me last. My father knocked before entering her room, and Bjerke, looking at his feet, waited outside with me. My father said something.

No!

She cried out and there was the crash of what I knew was the breakfast tray, a clatter of silverware skidding across the floor. My father opened the door. His face was glossy with sweat.

We'd best get this over with.

And so we entered and sat down in two folding chairs he'd pulled up next to her bed. He lowered himself, like a dog that knows it isn't welcome, onto the end of the bed. My mother moved to the far edge of the mattress and lay hunched, her back to us, the pillow childishly held over her ears.

Geraldine, said my father in a low voice, Joe's here with Bjerke. Please. Don't let him see you this way.

What way? Her voice was a crow's jeer. Crazy? He can take it. He's seen it. But he'd rather be with his friends. Let him go, Bazil. Then I'll talk to you.

Geraldine, he knows something. He's told us something.

My mother crunched herself into a smaller ball.

Mrs. Coutts, said Bjerke, I apologize for bothering you again. I'd much rather solve this and let you alone, leave you in peace. But the fact is I need some additional information from you. Last night we learned from Joe that on the day you were attacked you received a telephone call. Joe thinks he remembers that this telephone call was upsetting to you. He says that after a short time you told him that you were going after a file and then you drove to your office. Is this true?

There was no movement or sound from my mother. Bjerke tried again. But she waited us out. She didn't turn to us. She didn't move. It seemed an hour that we sat in a suspense that quickly turned to disappointment and then to shame. My father finally lifted his hand and whispered, Enough. We backed out of the room and walked down the steps.

Late that afternoon, my father moved a card table into the bedroom. My mother did not react. Then he set up folding chairs at the table and I heard her furiously berating him and begging him to take it away. He came downstairs sweating again, and told me that every night at six o'clock I was to be home for dinner, which we'd bring upstairs and eat together.

Like a family again, he said. We were starting this regimen now. I took a deep breath and carried up the tablecloth. Again, though my mother was angry, my father opened the shades and even a window, to let in a breeze. We brought a salad and a baked chicken up the stairs, plus the plates, glasses, silverware, and a pitcher of lemonade. Perhaps a drop of wine tomorrow night, to make something festive of it, Dad said without hope. He brought a bouquet of flowers he'd picked from the garden that she hadn't seen yet. He put them in a small painted vase. I looked at the green sky on that vase, the willow, the muddy water and awkwardly painted rocks. I was to become overly familiar with this glazed scene during those dinners because I didn't want to look at my mother, propped up staring wearily at us as if she'd just been shot, or rolled into a mummy pretending to be in the afterlife. My father tried to keep a conversation going every night, and when I had exhausted my meager store of the day's doings, he forged on, a lone paddler on an endless lake of silence, or maybe rowing upstream. I am sure I saw him laboring on the muddy little river painted on the vase. After he'd spoken of the day's small events one night, he said he'd had a very interesting talk with Father Travis Wozniak and that the priest had been there in Dealey Plaza on the day that John F. Kennedy was assassinated. Travis's father had taken him into the city to see the Catholic president and his elegant first lady, who was wearing a suit the exact mute pink as the inside of a cat's mouth. Travis and his father walked down Houston Street, crossed Elm, and decided that the best place to view the President would be there on the grassy slope just east of the Triple Underpass. They had a good view and watched the street expectantly. Just before the first motorcycle escorts appeared, someone's black-and-white gundog ran out into the middle of the street and was quickly recalled by its owner. It often bothered Travis afterward to think that if only the dog had got loose at another time, perhaps just as the motorcade passed, messing up the precision and timing of things, or if it had thrown itself under the wheels of the presidential convertible in an act of sacrifice, or leapt into the President's lap, what followed might not have happened. This so gnawed at him on some nights that he lay awake wondering just how many unknown and similarly inconsequential accidents and bits of happenstance were at this moment occurring or failing to occur in order to ensure he took his next breath, and the next. It gave him the sensation that he was tottering on the tip of a flagpole. He was poised on circumstance. He said the feeling has grown stronger and more persistent, too, since the embassy bombing where he'd been injured.

Interesting, my father said. That priest. A flagpole sitter.

Father Travis had gone on describing how the motorcycles preceded the presidential convertible, and there was John F. Kennedy, looking straight ahead. Some women sitting on the grass had brought their lunch to eat and now stood up beside their sandwich boxes and wildly clapped and cheered. They drew the President's attention, and he looked directly at them, and then smiled at Travis, who was dazzled and disoriented to see the portrait in the living room of every Catholic family come to life. The shots sounded like a car had backfired. The first lady stood up and Travis saw her scan the crowd. The car halted. Then more shots. She threw herself down and that was the last he saw, for his father threw him down, too, and covered him with his body. He was slammed into the ground so suddenly, and his father was so heavy, that he bit into the sod. Ever after, thinking of that day, he remembers the grit in his teeth. Soon his father felt the shift of the crowd and the two of them rose. Waves of confusion swirled, turned chaotic when the presidential car streaked forward. People ran back and forth, not certain which direction was safest, and subject to racing rumors. He saw a family of black people cast themselves onto the earth in grief. The speckled gundog was loose again; it trotted right and left, nose high, as if it were actually directing the crowd instead of being buffeted this way and that by surges of people in the grip of conflicting terrors and fascinations. Some tried to run back to the place they had last seen the President and others grappled with people they thought somehow responsible. People sank to their knees and were lost in prayer or shock. The gundog sniffed a fallen woman and then stood beside her, pointing gravely and motionlessly at the stuffed bird on her hat.

On another night, after I tried but at last grew stumped for conversation, my father remembered that of course an Ojibwe person's clan meant everything at one time and no one didn't have a clan, thus you knew your place in the world and your relationship to all other beings. The crane, the bear, the loon, the catfish, lynx, kingfisher, caribou, muskrat—all of these animals and others in various tribal divisions, including the eagle, the marten, the deer, the wolf—people were part of these clans and were thus governed by special relationships with one another and with the animals. This was in fact, said my father, the first system of Ojibwe law. The clan system punished and rewarded; it dictated marriages and regulated commerce; it told which animals a person could hunt and which to appease, which would have pity on the doodem or a fellow being of that clan, which would carry messages up to the Creator over to the spirit world, down through the layers of the earth or across the lodge to a sleeping relative. There were many instances right in our own family, in fact, as you well know, he said to the crease in the blankets that was my mother, your own great-aunt was saved by a turtle. As you remember, she was of the turtle, or the mikinaak, clan. At the age of ten she was put out to fast on a small island. There she stayed one early spring, four days and four nights with her face blackened, utterly defenseless, waiting for the spirits to become her friends and adopt her. On the fifth day when her parents did not return, she knew something was wrong. She broke the paste of saliva that sealed her thirsty mouth, drank lake water, and ate a patch of strawberries that had tormented her. She made a fire, for although she was not allowed to use it on her fast, she carried with her a flint and steel. Then she began to live on that island. She made a fish trap and lived off fish. The place was remote, but still she was surprised at how the time passed, one moon, two, and no one came to get her. She knew by then that something very bad had happened. She also knew that the fish would soon retreat to another part of the lake for the summer and she would starve. So she determined to swim to the mainland, twenty miles away. She set off on a fair morning with the wind at her back. For a long time the waves helped her along, and she swam well enough, even though she had been weakened by her meager diet. Then the wind changed and blew directly against her. Clouds lowered and she was lashed by a cold driving rain. Her arms and legs were heavy as swollen logs, she thought that she would die, and in her struggle called out for help. At that moment she felt something rise beneath her. It was a giant and a very old mishiikenh, one of those snapping turtles science tells us are unchanged for over 150 million years—a form of life frightful but perfect. This creature swam below her, breaking her way through the water, nudging her to the surface when her strength gave out, allowing her to cling to its shell when she was exhausted, until they came to shore. She waded out and turned to thank it. The turtle watched her silently, its eyes uncanny yellow stars, before it sank away. Then she found her brothers and sisters. It was true about the disaster. They had been laid low by the devastations of the great influenza—as with all pandemics this struck reservations hardest. Their parents were dead and there was no way to know where their sister had been left off, in addition to which people were afraid to catch the deadly illness and had moved away from them in haste so that they, too, the children, were living alone.

There are many stories of children who were forced to

live alone, my father went on, including those stories from antiquity in which infants were nursed by wolves. But there are also stories told from the earliest histories of western civilization of humans rescued by animals. One of my favorites was related by Herodotus and concerns Arion of Methymna, the famous harp player and inventor of the dithyrambic measure. This Arion got a notion to travel to Corinth and hired a boat sailed by Corinthians, his own people, whom he thought trustworthy, which just goes to show about your own people, said my father, as the Corinthians were not long out to sea when they decided to throw Arion overboard and seize his wealth. When he learned what was to happen, Arion persuaded them to first allow him to assume his full musician's costume and to play and sing before his death. The sailors were happy to hear the best harpist in the world and withdrew while Arion dressed himself, took up his harp, and then stood on the deck and chanted the Orthian. When he was finished, as promised, he flung himself into the sea. The Corinthians sailed away. Arion was saved by a dolphin, which took him on its back to Taenarum. A small bronze figure was made of Arion with his harp, aboard a dolphin, and offerings were made to it in those times. The dolphin was moved by Arion's music—that's how I take it anyway, my father said. I imagine the dolphin swimming alongside the ship—it heard the music and was devastated, as anyone would be imagining the emotion Arion must have put into his final song. And yet the sailors, though clearly music lovers, as they were happy to postpone Arion's death and listen, did not hesitate. They did not turn and retrieve him but divided up his money and sailed on. One could argue that this was a much worse sin against art than drowning, say, a painter, a sculptor, a poet, certainly a novelist. Each left behind their works even in the most ancient of days. But a musician of those times took his art to the grave. Of course the destruction of a contemporary musician, too, would be a lesser crime as there are always plenty of recordings, except in the case of our Ojibwe and Metis fiddle players. The traditional player, like your uncle Shamengwa, believed that he owed his music to the wind, and that like the wind his music partook of infinite changeability. A recording would cause his song to become finite. Thus, Uncle was against recorded music. He banned all recording devices in his presence, yet in his later years a few people managed to copy his songs as tape recorders were made small enough to conceal. But I have heard and Whitey confirms that when Shamengwa died those tapes mysteriously disintegrated or were erased, and so there is no recording of Shamengwa's playing, which is as he wished. Only those who learned from him in some way replicate his music, but it has become their own, too, which is the only way for music to remain alive. I am afraid, said my father that night, to my mother's stiffened back. The sharp bones of her shoulders pressed against the draped sheet. I'm going to have to leave tomorrow, he said. My mother did not move. She had not spoken one word since we'd begun to eat our dinners with her.

I am going back down to Bismarck tomorrow, my father said. I want to meet with Gabir. He will not decline this. But I have to keep him connected. And it's good to see my old friend. We're going to get our ducks lined up even though there isn't anyone to prosecute yet. But there will be, I am sure of that. We are finding things out little by little and when you are ready to tell us about the file and the telephone call we will certainly know more, I feel certain of it, Geraldine, and there will be justice. And that will help, I think. That will help you even though you seem to believe now that it won't help you, that nothing will help you, even the tremendous love in this room. So yes, tomorrow, we won't have dinner in your room and you can rest. I can't ask Joe to wait you out like this, to make conversation with the walls and furniture, although it is surprising where a person's thoughts go. While I'm in Bismarck, I'll see the governor, too;

we'll have lunch and a conversation. Last time he told me that he'd attended the governors' conference. While there, he spoke with Yeltow, you know, he's still the governor of South Dakota. He found out that he is trying to adopt a child.

What?

My mother spoke.

What?

My father leaned forward, pointing like that gundog, motionless.

What? she spoke again. What child?

An Indian child, my father said, trying to keep his voice normal.

He rattled on.

And so of course the governor of our state, who well understands from our conversations the reasons we have for limiting adoptions by non-Indian parents via the Indian Child Welfare Act, attempted to explain this piece of legislation to Curtis Yeltow, who was very frustrated at the difficulty of adopting this child.

What child?

She turned in the bedclothes, a skeletal wraith, her eyes deeply fixed on my father's face.

What child? What tribe?

Well, actually—

My father tried to keep the shock and agitation out of his voice.

—to be honest, the tribal background of this child hasn't been established. The governor of course is well known for his bigoted treatment of Indians—an image he is trying in his own way to mitigate. You know he does these public relations stunts like sponsoring Indian schoolchildren, or giving out positions in the Capitol, aides, to promising Indian high-school students. But his adoption scheme blew up in his face. He had his lawyer present his case to a state judge, who is attempting to pass the matter into tribal hands, as is proper. All present agree that the child looks Indian and the governor says that she—

She?

She is Lakota or Dakota or Nakota or anyway Sioux, as the governor says. But she could be any tribe. Also that her mother—

Where's her mother?

She has disappeared.

My mother raised herself in bed. Clutching the sheet around her, groping forward in her flowered cotton gown, she gave a weird howl that clapped down my spine. Then she actually got out of bed. She swayed and gripped my arm when I stood to help her. She began to retch. Her puke was startling, bright green. She cried out again and then crept back into the bed and lay motionless.

My father didn't move except to lay a towel on the floor, and so I sat there in stillness too. All of a sudden my mother raised her hands and waved and pushed this way and that as if she was struggling with the air. Her arms moved with disconcerting violence, punching, blocking, pushing. She kicked and twisted.

It's over, Geraldine, my father said, terrified, trying to hush her. It's all right now. You're safe.

She slowed and then stopped. She turned to my father, staring out of the covers as out of a cave. Her eyes were black, black in her gray face. She spoke in a low, harsh voice that grew large between my ears.

I was raped, Bazil.

My father did not move, did not take her hand or comfort her now in any way. He seemed frozen.

There is no evidence of what he did. None. My mother's voice was a croak.

My father bent near. There is, though. We went straight to the hospital. And there is your own memory. And there are other things. We have—

I remember everything.

Tell me.

My father did not look at me because his gaze was locked with my mother's gaze. I think if he'd let go she would have collapsed forever into silence. I shrank back and tried to be invisible. I didn't want to be there, but I knew if I moved I'd snap the pull between them.

There was a call. It was Mayla. I only knew her by her family. She's hardly ever been here. Just a girl, so young! She'd begun the enrollment process for her child. The father.

The father.

She'd listed him, my mother whispered.

Do you remember his name?

My mother's mouth dropped open, her eyes unfocused.

Keep going, dear. Keep going. What happened next?

Mayla asked to meet me at the round house. She had no car. She said her life depended on it, so I went there.

My father drew a sharp breath.

I drove into that weedy lot, parked the car. I started out. He tackled me as I was walking up the hill. Took the keys. Then he pulled out a sack. He dragged it over my head so fast. It was a light rosy material, loose, maybe a pillowcase. But it went down so far, past my shoulders, I couldn't see. He tied my hands behind me. Tried to get me to tell him where the file was and I said there's no file. I don't know what file he's talking about. He turned me around and marched me . . . held my shoulder. Step over this, go that way, he said. He took me somewhere.

Where? said my father.

Somewhere.

Can you say anything about where?

Somewhere. That's where it happened. He kept the sack on me. And he raped me. Somewhere.

Did you go uphill or downhill?

I don't know, Bazil.

Through the woods? Did leaves brush you?

I don't know.

What about the ground—gravel? brush? Was there a barbed-wire fence?

My mother screamed in a hoarse voice until her lungs emptied and there was silence.

Three classes of land meet there, my father said. His voice pulled tight with fear. Tribal trust, state, and fee. That's why I'm asking.

Get out of the courtroom, get the damn hell out, my mother said. I don't know.

All right, said my father. All right, keep going.

Afterward, after. He dragged me up to the round house. It took a while to get there. Was he marching me around? I was sick. I don't remember. At the round house he untied me and pulled off the sack and it was . . . it was a pillowcase, a plain pink one. That was when I saw her. Just a girl. And her baby playing in the dust. The baby put her hands up into the light falling through the chinks in the pole logs. The baby had just learned to crawl, her arms gave out, but she made it to her mother. She was an Indian, she was an Indian girl, and I'd got the call from her. She'd come in on Friday and filed the papers. A quiet girl with such a pretty smile, pretty teeth, pink lipstick. Her hair was cut so nice. She wore a knit dress, pale purple. White shoes. And the baby was with her. I played with that baby in my office. So that's who made the call that day. Her. Mayla Wolfskin.

I need that file, she said. *My life depends on that file,* she said.

She was thrown on the ground. Her hands were taped up behind her. The baby crawled over the dirt floor. She was wearing a ruffled yellow dress and her eyes, so tender. Like Mayla's eyes. Big, brown eyes. Wide open. She saw everything and she was confused but she wasn't crying because her mother was right there so she thought things were all right. But he had Mayla tied up, taped up. Mayla and I looked at each other. She didn't blink just kept moving her eyes to the baby, then me, back to the baby. I knew she was saying to me I should take care of her baby. I nodded to her. Then he came in and he took off his pants, just kicked them off. He wore slacks. Every word sticks with me, every single word he said. The way he said things, in a dead voice, then cheerful, then dead again. Then amused. He said, I am really one sick fuck. I suppose I am one of those people who just hates Indians generally and especially for they were at odds with my folks way back but especially my feeling is that Indian women are—what he called us, I don't want to say. He screamed at Mayla and said he loved her, yet she had another man's baby, she did this to him. But he still wanted her. He still needed her. She had put him in this awkward position, he said, of loving her. You should be crated up and thrown in the lake for what you've done to my emotions! He said we have no standing under the law for a good reason and yet have continued to diminish the white man and to take his honor. I could be rich, but I'd rather have shown you, both of you, what you really are. I won't get caught, he said. I've been boning up on law. Funny. Laugh. He nudged me with his shoe. I know as much law as a judge. Know any judges? I have no fear. Things are the wrong way around, he said. But here in this place I make things the right way around for me. The strong should rule the weak. Instead of the weak the strong! It is the weak who pull down the strong. But I won't get caught.

I suppose I should have sent you down with your car, he suddenly turned on Mayla. But, honey, I couldn't. I just felt so sorry for you and my heart split wide open. That's love, huh? Love. I couldn't do it. But I have to, you know. All your fucking shit's in your car. You don't need anything where you're going. I'm sorry! I'm sorry! He struck Mayla, and struck me, and struck her again and again and turned her over. You want to tell me where the money is? The money he gave you? Oh, you do? Oh, you do now? Where? He ripped the tape away. She couldn't talk, then she gasped out, My car.

He would have killed her then, I think so, but the baby moved. The baby cried out and blinked, looked into his eyes without understanding. Ah, he said, well isn't that. Isn't that.

Don't talk no more. I don't want to hear it, he said to Mayla. You are still money in the bank, he said to the baby. I am taking you back with me . . . unless you, dirt. He rose and kicked me and went over and kicked her so hard she wheezed. Then he bent over and looked into my face. He said to me, I'm sorry. I might be having an episode. I'm not really a bad person. I didn't hurt you, did I? He picked up the baby and said to the baby in a baby voice, I don't know what to do with the evidence. Silly me. Maybe I should burn the evidence. You know, they're just evidence. He put her down gently. He uncapped the gas can. While he had his back turned and was pouring the gas on Mayla, I grabbed his pants and put them between my legs and I urinated on them, that's what I did. I did! Because I'd seen him light his cigarette and put the matches back into his pocket. I was surprised that he didn't notice that the pants were wet with urine, but he was absorbed in what he meant to do. Shaking too. He was saying, Oh no, oh no. He poured more gasoline over her and splashed gas on me, too, but not the baby. Then, then, when he couldn't start the fire with the matches from his pants pocket he turned and gave the baby a heavy look. She began to cry and we—Mayla and I—lay perfectly still as he went to comfort the baby. He said, Sshhh, sshhh. I have another book of matches, a lighter even, down the hill. And you, he shook me and said into my face, you, *if you move an inch I will kill this baby and if you move an inch I will kill Mayla*. You are going to die but if you say one word even one word up in heaven after you are dead I will kill them both.

*

I poured myself a bowl of cornflakes and a glass of milk. I put half the milk on the cereal, sprinkled sugar on the cereal, and ate it. I filled the bowl with cereal a second time and drank the sweet milk from the bottom of the bowl and finished off the glass. I dipped a wide-mouth jar into the bag of dog food in the entry, filled Pearl's bowl, and gave her fresh water. Pearl stood by me as I spray-soaked the garden and the flower beds. Then I got on my bike and went to work. I saw my father before I left. He had stayed in the bedroom with my mother. He'd sat up next to her all night. I asked him about the file, and he told me that my mother wouldn't talk about it. She needed to know the baby was safe. Mayla was safe.

What do you think's in that file? I asked.

Something to work with.

And Mayla Wolfskin? What about her?

She went to school down in South Dakota, said my father. And she's related to your mother's friend LaRose. Maybe that's why your mother won't see LaRose—she's afraid of breaking down, of saying something.

That's not what I meant. What about Mayla Wolfskin, Dad? Is she alive?

That's the question.

What do you think?

I think not, he said softly, looking down at the floor.

I looked down at the floor, too, at the swirls of cream in the gray of the linoleum. And the darker gray and the small black spots a vertigo surprise once you noticed. I perused that floor, memorizing the randomness.

Why would he kill her? Dad?

He put his head to the side, shook his head, stepped forward, and put his arms around me. He held me there, not speaking. Then he let me go and walked away.

*

When I got to Whitey and Sonja's station I parked my bike beside the door, where I could see it, then I started my chores. Whitey had a short-wave receiver that picked up signals all around the area. It was always crackling on and burping garbled messages in the vicinity of the garage. Sometimes, he turned it off and pumped out music. I picked up all of the candy wrappers, cigarette butts, loser pull tabs, and other trash that had accumulated in the gravel gas station yard and the weeds down to the road. I got the hose and watered yet another tractor-tire flower bed, this one painted yellow, ringed with silvery sage leaves and red-hot poker flowers, same as I had planted for my mother.

Whitey pumped gas when customers came, checked oil, and gossiped. I washed the car windows. Sonja had bought a Bunn coffeemaker and Whitey had built two wooden booths in the eastern corner of the store. Sonja's first cup of coffee was a dime and the refills were free, so the booths were always filled with people. Clemence baked for the store every few days and there was banana bread, coffee cake, oatmeal cookies in a jar. Every day at lunchtime, Whitey asked if I wanted a rez steak sandwich and then he made us baloney-whitebread-mayo sandwiches. In the afternoon, Whitey took his break and when he came back Sonja left to go home and take a nap. They'd both work until seven p.m. They were saving payroll for the first couple of years, just to start with. Later on, they planned on hiring a full-timer and staying open until nine. I was paid a dollar an hour, ice cream, soda, milk, and cookies off the bottom of the jar.

When I got home, my father was waiting for me.

How was work?

It was good.

My father looked at his knuckles, flexed his hand, frowned. He started talking to his hand, which was a thing that he did when he didn't want to be saying what he had to say.

I had to take your mother down to Minot this morning. To the hospital. They'll keep her a couple of days. I'm going back down tomorrow.

I asked if I could go, but he said there was nothing I could do.

She just has to rest.

She sleeps all the time.

I know. He paused, then finally looked at me, a relief. She knows who it was, he said. Of course, but she still won't tell me, Joe. She has to overcome his threats.

Do you have an idea?

I can't say, you know that.

But I should know. Is he from around here, Dad?

It would fit . . . but he won't show up here. He knows he'll get caught. There will be someone for your mother to identify, he said, pretty soon. Not soon enough. She's going to be better once that begins. I feel certain she'll remember where, too—where it happened. The shock of telling. But then some resolution.

What about Mayla Wolfskin? Did he keep her with him? And that baby? Was that the baby that the governor was trying to adopt?

My father's face told me yes. But what he said was, I wish you hadn't heard all that was said, Joe. But I couldn't stop your mother. I was afraid she might stop talking.

I nodded. All day my mother's words had seeped up through the surface of all I did, like a dark oil.

In her right mind, she never would have described all that happened in front of you.

I had to know. It's good I know, I said.

But it was a poison in me. I was just beginning to feel that.

I've got to go back down there tomorrow, said my father. Do you want to stay with Aunt Clemence or Uncle Whitey?

I'll stay with Whitey and Sonja. That way they can bring me to work.

Next day after work, I rode back to the old place with Sonja and Whitey. We had Pearl with us. Clemence was going to check in on the house and water the garden, so everything was locked up and I didn't have to go there for a while. And that made me happy. Soon we'd have Mooshum's birthday. Everyone would come for that. I'd see my cousins. But for now, staying with Sonja and Whitey seemed like a vacation to me. Things could be normal. At their house, I would sleep on the couch and watch television. There were different sorts of food that Whitey cooked because he'd been a professional cook; there was the wine or beer at every dinner and the drinks after dinner and music. Noise. I didn't know how bad I'd needed noise.

We got into Whitey's Silverado and he immediately punched the button on the tape deck. The Rolling Stones boiled up from his subwoofers and we drove with the windows rolled down and the wind rushing in until we took the turnoff onto gravel. Then we drove the rest of the way with the windows up against the dust. We were in a pod of noise—us three shouting over the air fan and throbbing bass. Everything was funny with Whitey—well, as I knew, funny for about four hours, funny for six beers or three shots—but for that time we laughed over the day's doings and transactions. Cappy's aunts were so savey that they'd only put a dollar's worth of gas in the car at a time. It cost that much gas anyway to come and go. They each took free coffee every time. A young student from the university had come to study Grandma Thunder. She was taking her for rides every day—first Grandma would do her errands and visit her friends and family. Then sometimes she'd let the girl take out her notebook and write down a teaching. She was having a great old time.

I asked Whitey about Curtis Yeltow and he said, you wouldn't believe the things that old boy has done and got away with. Smashed into a freight train, drunk, and lived. Used the prairie nigger word for Indians. Thought it was funny. Had a mistress in Dead Eye. Bought gold and stored it in the basement of the governor's mansion. And guns? He is a gun lover slash freak. Collects war shields. Indian beadwork. Pays homage to the noble savage but tried to store nuclear waste on sacred Lakota earth. Said the Sun Dance was a form of devil worship. That's Yeltow. Oh, and he's all tanned up. Vain about his looks.

We got to the house and Whitey went inside to get dinner going while Sonja and I did the horse chores. As we shoveled out the barn, music blasted from the open windows of the house and we could hear the TV babbling, too. So there was noise while we put the hay out and lightly grained the horses, and noise if we took out the mower, and noise from the dogs anyway as they greeted us joyously and barked to remind us to fill their dishes with food.

Sonja kept the horses in the barn at night and she checked the dogs for ticks and looked at their gums, eyes, and foot pads critically.

What you been up to today? she asked each dog. She'd scold. Not the burr patch again. You smell like you ate shit. Who the hell you let bite at your pretty tail, Chain? I'm gonna whip you if you leave this yard, you know that.

Sonja spoke the same way to the horses as she put them in their stalls, and then Whitey came out and gave her a cold beer. There was a place right outside where the pasture sloped west and the grass turned golden at sunset. Two lawn chairs were set up there, and they added one for me. I drank an orange soda and they had a beer or two more and now the music came from Whitey's boom box, set out on the steps. Then the mosquitoes whined out in attack formation and we went inside.

Whitey had traded gas for fresh walleye that day, and he'd

cleaned the fish already. The fillets were in the refrigerator, soaking in a pie plate of milk. He'd whipped up a foamy beer batter. There was coleslaw made with horseradish. They always had dessert. Sonja insisted on dessert, said Whitey.

She's got a sweet tooth. Have you ever heard of raspberry fool? I made it for her from a recipe once. Or mayonnaise cake? You can't taste the mayonnaise. But she likes chocolate. She's crazy for chocolate. If I dipped my dick in chocolate she'd never let me alone.

He got looser, of course, as the night went on, said things, and eventually Sonja put him to bed.

After he was tucked in, Sonja came out and fixed up the couch for me. The couch was old and smelled of cigarettes. It was upholstered in scratchy brown stuff scattered through with tired orange nubs. Sonja tucked a sheet across the cushions and gave me a plaid sleeping bag with a broken zipper. She turned the television on, the lights out, and then she curled up on the other end of the couch. We watched TV together for an hour or even two. We talked about the money, whispered about it because of Whitey. Sonja made me swear again and again that I had not—would not—tell anybody.

I'm scared as shit. You should be too. Keep your eyes open. Don't slip up, Joe.

Then we'd talk about what I should do with the money. Sonja made me promise I would go to college. She said she'd wanted her daughter, Murphy, to go. She'd named her baby Murphy because it could never be a stripper name. But her daughter had changed her name to London. If I could go back in time, said Sonja, I never would have left my daughter with my own mother when I was working. My mother had a bad influence on her granddaughter, if you can believe that.

Sonja liked the talk shows, the old movies. Sometimes I fell asleep while we were watching, but before I did I tried to suspend myself for as long as possible between sleep and wakefulness. A door might open momentarily into a dream, but instantly I'd shift back to the couch. Her soft weight on the far cushion. The warmth of her that I could feel if I edged the bare soles of my feet from under the sleeping bag, which became my favorite thing to sleep under because it disguised my hard-on.

Every night, Sonja gave me a pillow off her bed. The pillow smelled of apricot shampoo and also a dusky undertone—some private erotic decay like the inside of a wilted flower. I buried my face to breathe it in. I dozed, dreamed, returning to the flickering TV light. The laugh track, turned low. Sonja tranced in a blue haze, drinking cold water now. Outside, the seething of summer insects. The dogs occasionally rousing to bark once or twice at a deer far across the pasture. And Whitey, thankfully, snoring it off behind the bedroom door. The third or fourth night, when I was passing in and out of heaven, Sonja cupped my heel in her palm and squeezed it. She began absently to rub my instep and a bolt of blind pleasure shot through me too sudden to contain. I came with a gurgle of surprise and she dropped my foot. A moment later, I heard a snap and sneaked a look at her. She was eating a pretzel.

Whitey loved kamikaze pulps. He had a wall of shelves built just the right height for grocery-store samurai romances, ninja attack plots, spy thrillers, Louis L'Amours, sci-fi, Conan. He began his morning at six a.m. with a cup of coffee and a paperback. As I ate beside him, he read selections aloud, murmuring, *her lithe haunches quivered with a predatory anticipation as she fixed on his position in the moonless light bereft of soul and decided exactly how to snap his spine . . . Ragna's dagger-sharp eyeteeth glinted in the reflected beams of the headlights . . . knowing his life would end as soon as his eyes met that implacable obsidian gaze . . .* If he was deeply engaged in a plot, he kept reading as Sonja set down a platter of bacon and a pan of her one breakfast specialty—a mixture of grated potatoes, eggs, diced peppers, and ham, laid out in a baking pan and broiled until the cheddar cheese topping bubbled up and toasted. She called it breakfast casserole. Right after we ate, Whitey marked his page and put the book down. Sonja quickly scrubbed up the dishes, we jumped in the pickup, drove to the gas station, and unlocked the pumps. We opened at seven a.m. There was always someone waiting for gas.

That day, a couple of things happened that were not good. The first thing was Sonja's stud earrings, which Whitey said he'd never seen before.

You have too seen them. She flashed a flirty smile.

The earrings sparkled in the dim kitchen. She had on yellow rubber gloves and she was vigorously scouring the broiler pan before we took off for work.

They're rhinestones, she said.

Nice rhinestones, said Whitey. He gave an underhanded glance. Then he looked at her boldly, meanly, while she was not looking at him. Her blue jeans also looked brand-new and clung to her in a way that made me think of Whitey's book, *haunches quivering in deadly* etc. We got in the truck. Whitey didn't turn on the music. Halfway to town, Sonja reached over to switch on the tape player and Whitey smacked her hand off the controls. I was sitting in the jump seat behind them. It happened right in front of me.

It's okay, said Sonja to me, over her shoulder. Whitey's feeling low. He's hungover.

Whitey's jaw was still set in that mean way. He stared straight ahead.

Yeah, he said. Hungover. Not the kind of hungover you're thinking of.

Whitey had a jailhouse spit—so sleek, so accurate. Like he'd gone a period of his life with nothing to do but spit. He jumped out of the car, slammed the door, spat, hit a can, *ping*, and walked away even though there was someone waiting at the gas pump. Sonja just moved over, parked, and unlocked the station. She gave me the keys to the pumps without looking outside and told me I should handle that car. This was the second bad thing.

I'd seen this person, he was familiar, but I didn't know him. All of his features were neat and regular, but he was not good-looking. He was a brown-haired, sunk-eyed white man with a slack but powerful build, a big man in neat clothing—a white shirt, brown belted pants, leather lace-up shoes. His longish hair was combed back evenly behind his ears so you could see the tracks in it. His ears were oddly small and neat, coiled against his head. His lips were thin, dark red, like he had a fever. When he smiled, I saw his teeth were white and even, like a denture commercial.

I went over to wait on him.

Fill 'er up, he said.

I unlocked the gas tanks and pumped gas. I washed his windows and then asked if he wanted his oil checked. His car was dusty. It was an old Dodge.

Nah. His voice was genial. He began counting fives from a wad of bills. He handed over three of them. My car was thirsty, he said. I drove all night. Say, how are you?

Sometimes grown-ups recognize a kid and talk as if they know you, but they really know your parents or uncle or were somebody's teacher. It is confusing, plus he was a customer. So I was polite and said I was fine, thanks.

Oh, that's good, he said. I hear that you're a real good kid.

I took him in, now, put him together. A good kid? Second white man to say that this summer. My thought was, *This could wreck me.*

You know—he looked at me hard—I wish I had a kid like you. I don't have any children.

Gee, too bad, I said like I meant the opposite. Now I was put off. I still couldn't place him.

He sighed. Thanks. I don't know. I suppose it's luck, starting a good family and all. Having a loving family. It's pretty nice. Gives you an advantage in life. Even an Indian boy like you can have a good family and get that sort of start, I guess. And maybe it will let you draw even with a white kid of your own age, you know? Who doesn't have a loving family.

I turned to walk off.

Oh, I've said too much. Come back here! He tried to give me another five. I kept walking. He looked down and turned the ignition key. The engine coughed and caught. Well, that's me, he called. Always saying too much. But! He slapped the side of the car. Say what you will, you're the judge's son.

I whirled around.

My twin sister had a loving Indian family and they stuck by her when times were hard.

Then he drove off, and because of what Linda had told me, I knew I had spoken with Linden Lark.

I decided that I wanted to quit and go home now. I was mad at Whitey. I'd pumped gas for the enemy. Sonja bothered me too. She came out of the station, chewing gum. As her jaws worked, those earrings twitched and flashed. She'd spun her hair up in a flossy cone held with clips of hot pink enamel. Those jeans fit her like paint. The morning seemed to last forever. I had to stay because Whitey was gone. Then around eleven he returned and I realized he'd had a beer or maybe two. Sonja pretended, insultingly, as though she didn't notice his silence as he came and went.

At noon Sonja made us the sandwiches out of bread and meat from the cooler, so there wasn't any joking about how good our rez steak was or if I wanted mine well done. She just handed me the sandwich and a can of grape Shasta. Later on she gave Whitey's sandwich to me. His had lettuce on it but I ate it anyway as I watched him changing a tire for LaRose. My mother, Clemence, and LaRose had been inseparable once upon a time. In Mom's little photo album there were pictures of them in school shots at their boarding school. Mom always talked about going to school with them. LaRose figured in her stories. But when it came to the present, they didn't visit often, and when they did, it was always just the two of them talking intensely, away from other people. You would have thought they had some secret, except that this had been going on for years. Sometimes Clemence joined in, and again they always went off, the three of them, and nobody else.

LaRose was always there and not there. Even when she looked right at you and spoke, it seemed her thoughts were elsewhere, elusive. LaRose had had so many husbands that nobody kept track of her last name anymore. She had started out a Migwan. She was a skinny, fine-boned, birdlike woman who smoked brown cigarillos and wore her silky black hair in a glistening beaded flower clip. Sonja had come out to stand by LaRose, so there we were. Three pop drinkers watching a sweaty Indian Elvis try to loosen up a set of rusted lug nuts. He strained. His neck bulged, his arms inflated. His gut was padded by those nightly beers, but his arms and chest were still powerful. He sank his weight on the wrench. Nothing. He knelt back on his feet. Even the dust was hot that day. He smacked the wrench in his palm and then he stood up suddenly and winged it into the weeds. Again, he gave Sonja that crafty look.

Don't gimme snake eyes, you bastard, she said, just because you can't turn a damn screw.

LaRose raised her curved eyebrows and turned her back on the two of them.

C'mon, she said to me. I need another pack of smokes.

She put her hand on my back, an auntielike gesture. She steered me forward. We went into the store and were alone together. She reached behind the counter for what she needed. I didn't care how elusive LaRose was, I'd question her. I asked her if she was related to Mayla Wolfskin.

She's my cousin, lots younger than me, said LaRose. Her dad was Crow Creek.

Did you grow up with her?

LaRose lazily lit a cigarillo and snapped out the match with exaggerated wrist swipes.

What's going on?

I just want to know.

You a FBI, Joe? I told that white guy with the dirty eyeglasses that Mayla went to boarding school in South Dakota, then was going on to Haskell. There was this program where they took the smartest ones to have a special job in the government, something like that. Gave a stipend of money, everything. Mayla got in the papers—my aunt clipped the article. Chosen for an internship. She looked so nice. Wearing a white headband, jumper she probably made in Home Ec, knee socks. I know that much. She worked for that one governor, you know. He did all those bad things. Nothing stuck to him.

Sonja walked inside and sold LaRose the cigarillos she was already smoking. I looked outside and saw that Whitey was headed for the Dead Custer.

Ah, shit, said Sonja. That's no good.

LaRose said, My tire.

I'll fix it.

She smiled at me—the reflection of a smile. She had a sad calm face that never really lighted up. Her delicate silken brown skin had fine lines if you were close enough to smell her signature rose powder. A silver tooth glinted when she smoked.

Have a go at it, my boy.

I wanted to ask her more about Mayla, but not with Sonja around. First I went and found the wrench in the weeds. When I came back, I saw that the women had brought lawn chairs and set them up in a crack of shade next to the building. They were sipping cream sodas.

Go ahead! Sonja waved. Smoke drifted from her fingers. I'll take care of customers, if we get any.

I stared at the lug nuts. Then I got up and went into Whitey's garage and got the ratchet.

Oooh, said LaRose when I brought that out.

Good choice, said Sonja.

I got the right-sized socket to fit the wrench on the old nut. I poured all of my strength down on the handle. But it didn't budge. From behind me I heard Cappy, Zack, and Angus take the jump on their bikes and land by the pumps in a swirl of grit.

I turned around. Sweat was dripping off me.

What'cha got? asked Cappy.

They ignored LaRose and, more elaborately, Sonja. They came up to stand around the flat.

Rusted out, man.

They each tried the ratchet. Zack even balanced on the handle and gently bounced, but the nut seemed soldered on. Cappy asked for Sonja's lighter, applied flame. That didn't work either.

You got WD-40?

I showed Cappy where it was on Whitey's tool bench. Cappy squirted a tiny bit around the base and rubbed dust on the nut and inside the socket. He fit the wrench on, tighter.

Step on it again, he said to Angus.

This time it gave, and we left the car jacked up while we rolled the tire into the garage. Whitey had a stock tank set up in there to find the holes in tires, and he was good at putting in a seal, but of course he was over at the Dead Custer.

I came out and looked at Sonja.

Maybe you should get him, she said, looking away, and I noticed that she'd taken out her stud earrings.

We got Whitey out after only three beers. LaRose got her tire fixed. We had a sudden rush and then everything quieted down. We closed the place and got into the truck. Neither of them touched the tape deck. We rode back silently but Sonja and Whitey just seemed tired now, all done in by the heat. At home, things went as usual—I helped Sonja with the chores. We ate, nobody saying much. Whitey drank, morose, but Sonja stuck to 7Up. I fell asleep on the couch with a fan blowing on me and Sonja's hair swirling gently around her profile in the sapphire light.

There was a crash. The lights were out and there was no moon. Everything was black but the fan still stirred the air around me. In the bedroom, low vehemence. Steady grating of Whitey's voice. A heavy thud. Sonja.

Quit that, Whitey.

He give 'em to you?

There's no he. It's just you, baby. Lemme go. The crack of a slap, a cry. Don't. Please. Joe's out there.

Doan fucking care.

Now he was calling her names one after another.

I got up and went to the door. My blood pulsed and swam. The poison that was wasting in me thrilled along my nerves. I thought I'd kill Whitey. I was not afraid.

Whitey!

There was silence.

Come out and fight me!

I tried to remember what he'd taught me about blocking punches, keeping my elbows in, chin down. He finally opened the door and I jumped back with my dukes up. Sonja had put the lamp on. Whitey was wearing yellow boxer shorts patterned with hot red chili peppers. His fifties hairdo hung off his forehead in strings. He put up his hands to slick it back and I punched him in the gut. The punch reverberated up my arm. My hand went numb. I broke it, I thought, and was exhilarated. I swung at him again but he pinned my arms and said, Oh shit, oh shit. Joe. Me and Sonja. This is just between us, Joe. Stay out of it. You ever hear of cheating? Sonja's cheating. Some prick gave her diamond earrings—

Rhinestone, she interjected.

I know diamonds when I see 'em.

He let me go and stepped away. He tried to reclaim some dignity. He put his hands up.

I won't touch her, see? Even though some prick she's stringing along bought her diamond earrings. I won't touch her. But she is dirty. His eyes rolled toward her, red with weeping now. Dirty. Someone else, Joe . . .

But I knew that wasn't true. I knew where those earrings came from.

I gave 'em to her, Whitey, I said.

You did? He swayed. He'd had a bottle in the room. How come you gave her earrings?

It was her birthday.

A year ago.

Asshole, what's it to you! I found those studs in the bathroom at the gas station. And you're right. They aren't rhinestones. I think they are genuine cubic zirconiums.

Okay, Joe, he said. Fancy talk.

He looked tearfully at Sonja. Propped himself against the door. Then he frowned at me. *Asshole, what's it to you!* he muttered. Some way to talk to your uncle. You crossed a line, boy. He held out the hand with the bottle and pointed his middle finger at me.

You. Crossed. A. Line.

Well, she's my aunt, I said. So I can give her a birthday present. Asshole.

He killed the bottle, threw it behind him, swelled big, and leaned forward. You got it coming, little man!

There was a splintering crack, and he sagged, his arms clutching his head. Sonja kicked him out of the doorway onto the living-room floor and said, Step around him. Watch the glass. You come in here, Joe.

Then she locked the door behind me.

Get in, she said, pointing at the bed. Go straight to sleep. I'm sitting up.

She sat down in the rocking chair and put the neck of the broken bottle carefully on the side table at her elbow. I got into the bed between the sheets. The pillow smelled like Whitey's tart hair gel and I pushed it away and lay on my arm. Sonja turned the light off and I stared into the lightless air.

He could be dead out there, I said.

No, he ain't. That was an empty. 'Sides, I know just how hard to hit him.

Bet he says that about you, too.

She didn't answer.

Why'd you say that? she said. Why'd you say you gave me them earrings?

Because I did.

Oh, the money.

I'm not stupid.

She was quiet. Then I heard her crying softly.

I wanted something nice, Joe.

See what happened?

Yeah.

It's like you said. Don't touch the money. And where'd you put the earrings?

I threw them out.

No you didn't. Those are diamonds.

But she didn't answer. She just kept rocking.

The next morning Sonja and I left early. I didn't see Whitey.

He's gonna walk it off in the woods, said Sonja. Don't worry. He'll be good for a long time now. But maybe you better stay with Clemence tonight.

We rode to town, no music. I watched the ditches out the side window.

Let me off right now, I said as we passed by Clemence's and our turnoff. Because I quit.

Oh, honey, no, she said. But she pulled over and stopped the car. Her hair was up in a ponytail, a green bow tied around it. She wore a flashy green track suit with white piping, and spongy shoes. That day she had painted her lips a deep carmine red. I must have given her a very long tragic look because she said, *Oh, honey, no,* again. I was thinking something of this sort: that deep red of her lips, if it were printed on me, kissed on me, would become a burning solidified blood that would brand itself into my flesh and leave a black seared brand shaped like the lips of a woman. I felt sorry for myself. I still loved her, worse than ever, even though she had betrayed me. Her blue eyes had a devious sheen.

Come on, she said. I'm onna need help. Please?

But I got out of the car and walked up the road.

The back kitchen door was open. I walked in and called out.

Auntie C?

She came up from the cellar with a jar of Juneberry jam and said she thought I had a job.

I quit.

That's lazy. You get back there.

I shook my head and wouldn't look at her.

Oh. They at it again? Whitey's back at it?

Yeah.

You stay here then. You can sleep in Joseph's old room —the sewing room now, but anyway. Mooshum's in Evey's room. I set up a cot for him there. He won't sleep on Evey's soft bed.

That day I helped Clemence out. She kept a nice garden like my mother used to and her snap peas were in already.

Uncle Edward was working on his backyard pond, trying to get the drainage and flowage just right, measuring mosquito larvae, and I helped him too. Whitey dropped my bike off, but I never went out and saw him. We ate fried venison with mustard and browned onions. Their television was as usual in the repair shop sixty miles away and I was sleepy. Mooshum tottered off to Evey's room and I went to Joseph's. But when I opened the door to the room and saw the sewing machine wedged in next to the bed and the folded stacks of fabric and the wall board covered with hundreds of spools of bright thread, when I saw the quilt pieces and the shoe box labeled Zippers and the same heart-shaped pincushion only Mom's was dusty green, I thought of my father entering our sewing room every night and how the loneliness had seeped from under the door of the sewing room then spread across the hall and tried to get to my bedroom. I said to Clemence, You think it would bother Mooshum if I bunked with him?

He talks in his sleep.

I don't care.

Clemence opened Evey's door and asked if Mooshum minded, but already he was lightly snoring. Clemence said it was fine, so I shut myself in the room. I shed my clothes and crawled into my grown-up cousin's bed, which was plush and saggy and smelled of dust. Mooshum's snore was a very old man's hypnotizing purr. I fell immediately asleep. Sometime right after moonrise, for there was light in the room, I woke. Mooshum was talking all right, so I rolled over and stuck a pillow over my head. I dozed off, but something he said hooked me in, and little by little, like a fish reeled up out of the dark, I began to surface. Mooshum was not just talking in the random disconnected way people do, blurting out scraps of dream language. He was telling a story.

Akii

At first she was just an ordinary woman, said Mooshum, good at a number of things—weaving nets, snaring rabbits, skinning out and tanning hides. She liked the liver of the deer. Her name was Akiikwe, Earth Woman, and like her namesake she was solid. She had heavy bones and a short, thick neck. Her husband, Mirage, appeared and disappeared. He looked at other women. She had caught him many times but stayed with him. He was a resolute hunter in spite of his ways and the two of them were good at surviving. They could always get food for their children, and even extra meat would come their way, for she especially, Akii, could make out in dreams where to find the animals. She had a shrewd heart and an endless stare, with which she kept her children in line. Akii and her husband were never stingy, and as I say they were always very good at finding food even in the dead of winter—that is, until the year they forced us into our boundary. The reservation year.

A few had broken soil like the white man, and put some seeds in the ground, but a real farm takes many years to build until it keeps you alive in winter. We hunted all the animals before the Moon of Little Spirit and there wasn't even a rabbit left. The government agent had promised supplies to tide us over for the loss of our territory, but these never came through. We left our boundaries and ranged back up into Canada, but the caribou were long gone, there were no beaver left, no muskrats even. The children cried and an old man boiled strips of his moosehide pants for them to chew on.

During this time, every day, Akii went out and she always came back with some small tidbit. She chopped an ice hole and with great effort she and her husband kept it open day and night, so they fished there until she hooked a fish that said to her, *My people are going to sleep now and you shall starve.*

Sure enough, she could not get another fish after that. She saw Mirage looking at her strangely, and she looked strangely back at him. He kept the children behind him as they slept and the axe with him in his blanket. He was tired of Akii so he pretended he could see it happen. Some people in these hungry times became possessed. A wiindigoo could cast its spirit inside of a person. That person would become an animal, and see fellow humans as prey meat. That's what was happening, her husband decided. He imagined that her eyes were starting to glow in the dark. The thing to do was you had to kill that person right away. But not before you had agreement in the matter. You couldn't do it alone. There was a certain way the killing of a wiindigoo must be done.

Mirage got some men together, and persuaded them that Akii was becoming very powerful and would soon go out of control. She had cut her arm for her baby to drink the blood, so that baby might go wiindigoo too. She stared as if she might pounce on her children and followed their every movement. And then, when they tried to tie her up, she struggled. It took six men to do it, and they came out the worse for their work—bitten and gouged. Another woman took the children away so they would not see what was to happen. But one, the oldest boy, was left. The only person who could kill a wiindigoo was someone in the blood family. If her husband killed her, Akiikwe's people might take revenge. It could have been a sister or a brother, but they refused. So the boy was given a knife and told to kill his mother. He was twelve years old. The men would hold her. He should cut her neck. The boy began to weep, but he was told that he must do it anyway. His name was Nanapush. The men urged him to kill his mother, tried to buck up his courage. But he got angry. He stuck the knife into one of the men who was holding his mother. But the man had on a skin coat and the wound wasn't very deep.

Ah, said his mother, you are a good son. You will not kill me. You're the only one I will not eat! Then she struggled so powerfully that she broke away from all of the men. But they wrestled her down.

He knew, Nanapush, that she had just threatened to eat those men because she was being tormented. She was a good mother to her children and had taught them how to live. Now the men brought her back tied in cords. Her husband bound her to a tree and left her there to freeze or starve. She screamed and fought the straps, but then grew quiet. They thought she must be getting weak so they left her alone that night. But the chinook wind came through and the air turned mild. She ate the snow. There must have been some good in the snow, because with her strong fingers she undid the knots and untied the cords. She began to walk away. Her son crawled from the tent and decided to go with her, but they were followed and overtaken when they reached the lake. Again, the men tied her up.

Now Mirage enlarged the very hole Akii had fished, where the ice was thinner. The men decided to put her down into the water, all of them, so no one had to take the blame. They strengthened those bindings and this time they attached a rock to her feet. Then they stuffed her down the hole into the freezing water. When she did not come up, they walked away, except her son, who wouldn't go with them. He sat on the ice there and sang her death song. As his father passed him, the boy asked for his gun and said that he would shoot his mother if she came out.

Maybe at that moment his father wasn't thinking straight, because he gave his gun to Nanapush.

Once the men were out of sight, Akii crashed her head from the hole. She had managed to kick free of the rock, and breathed the air that sits just beneath the surface of the ice. Nanapush helped her out of the water and put his blanket on her. Then they went into the woods and walked until they were too weak to walk anymore. The mother had her flint and striker in a pocket next to her skin. They made a fire and a shelter. Akii told her son that while she was underwater the fish spoke to her and said he felt sorry for her, and that she should have a hunting song. She sang this song to her son. It was a buffalo song. Why a buffalo song? Because the fish missed the buffalo. When the buffalo came to the lakes and rivers on hot summer days, they shed their tasty fat ticks for the fish to eat, and their dung drew other insects that the fish liked too. They wished the buffalo would come back. They asked me where the buffalo had gone, said Akii. I couldn't tell them. The boy learned the song, but said he wondered if it was useless. Nobody had seen a buffalo for years.

The two slept that night. They slept and slept. When they woke, they were so weak that they thought it would be easier to die. But Nanapush had some wire for a snare. He crawled out and set that snare a few feet away from their little shelter.

If a rabbit is snared, it will tell me where the animals are, said Akii.

They went to sleep again. When they woke, there was a rabbit struggling in the snare. The mother crept to the rabbit and listened to what it said. Then she crept back to her son with the rabbit.

The rabbit gave itself to you, she said. You must eat it and throw every single one of its bones out into the snow, so it can live again.

Nanapush roasted the rabbit, ate it. Three times he asked his mother to take some, but she refused. She hid her face in the blanket so he would not see her face.

Go now, she said. I heard the same song from the rabbit. The buffalo used to churn up the earth so the grass would grow better for the rabbits to eat. All the animals miss the buffalo, but they miss the real Anishinaabeg too. Take the gun and travel straight into the west. A buffalo has come back from over that horizon. The old woman waits for you. If you return and I am dead, do not cry. You have been a very good son to me.

So Nanapush went out.

Mooshum stopped talking. I heard his bed creak, and then the light, even rattle of his snoring. I was disappointed and thought of shaking him awake to find out the end of the story. But at last I fell asleep too. When I woke, I wondered again what had happened. Mooshum was in the kitchen, sipping at the soupy maple-syrup-flavored oatmeal he loved in the morning. I asked Mooshum who this Nanapush was, the boy he spoke of in the story. But he gave me another answer entirely.

Nanapush? Mooshum gave a dry, little creaky laugh.

An old man prone to madness! Like me, only worse. He should have been weeded out. In the face of danger, he was sure to act like an idiot. When self-discipline was called for, greed won out with Nanapush. He was aged early on by absurdities and lies. Old Nanapush, as they called him, or akiwenziish. Sometimes the old reprobate worked miracles through gross and disgusting behavior. People went to him, though secretly, for healings. As it happened, when I was a young man I myself brought him blankets, tobacco, and acquired from him secrets on how to please my first wife, whose eyes had begun to stray. Junesse was slightly older than me, and in bed she craved patience from a man that only comes with age. What should I do? I begged the old man. Tell me!

Baashkizigan! Baashkizigan! said Nanapush. Don't be shy. Take your time with the next, and if another stand comes on think about paddling across the lake against a stiff wind and don't stop until you've beached your canoe.

And so I kept my woman and came to respect the old man. He acted crazy to sort his friends from his enemies. But he spoke the truth.

What about his mother? I asked. What about the woman

no man could kill? When she sent him for the buffalo. What happened?

What caca are you talking about, my boy?

Your story.

What story?

The one you told me last night.

Last night? I told no story. I slept the whole night through. I slept good.

Okay then, I thought. I'm going to have to wait for him to fall asleep good and hard again. Maybe this time I'll hear the end.

So I waited the next night, trying to keep awake. But I was tired and kept dropping off. I slept for a good while. Then in my dreams I heard the sound of a light sticklike gnashing, and woke to find Mooshum sitting up again. He'd forgotten to take out his dentures and they were loose. He was clacking his teeth together, not speaking, as he sometimes did when he was very angry. But at last the teeth fell out of his mouth and he found words.

Ah, those first reservation years, when they squeezed us! Down to only a few square miles. We starved while the cows of settlers lived fat off the fenced grass of our old hunting grounds. In those first years our white father with the big belly ate ten ducks for dinner and didn't even send us the feet. Those were bad years. Nanapush saw his people starve and die out, then his mother was attacked as wiindigoo but the men could not kill her. They were nowhere. Dying. But now in his starved condition the rabbit gave him some strength, so he resolved to go after that buffalo. He took up his mother's hatchet and his father's gun.

As he dragged himself along, mile after mile, Nanapush sang the buffalo song although it made him cry. It broke his heart. He remembered how when he was a small boy the buffalo had filled the world. Once, when he was little, the hunters came down to the river. Nanapush climbed a tree to look back where the buffalo came from. They covered the earth at that time. They were endless. He had seen that glory. Where had they gone?

Some old men said the buffalo disappeared into a hole in the earth. Other people had seen white men shoot thousands off a train car, and leave them to rot. At any rate, they existed no longer. Still, as Nanapush stumbled along, mile by mile, he sang the buffalo song. He thought there must be a reason. And at last, he looked down. He saw buffalo tracks! He found it hard to believe. Hunger makes you see things. But after following these tracks for some time, he saw this was indeed a buffalo. An old cow as crazy and decrepit as Nanapush himself would become, and me, and all survivors of those years, the last of so many.

The cold deepened steadily. Nanapush trudged on, following the buffalo's tracks as it staggered into and out of a rough wooded area of brush and heavy cover in which, thought Nanapush, it would surely take shelter. But it did not. It moved out onto a violently flat plain where the wind blew against them both with killing force. Nanapush knew he would have to shoot the cow at once. He gathered every bit of will from his starving body and pushed on, but the buffalo stayed ahead, moving easier than he could against the snow.

Nanapush sang the buffalo song at the top of his lungs, driving onward. And at last, in that white bitterness, the buffalo heard his song. It stopped to listen. Turned toward him. Now the two were perhaps twenty feet apart. Nanapush could see that the creature was mainly a hide draped loosely over rickety bones. Yet she'd been immense and in her brown eyes there was a depth of sorrow that shook Nanapush even in his desperation.

Old Buffalo Woman, I hate to kill you, said Nanapush, for

you have managed to live by wit and courage, even though your people are destroyed. You must have made yourself invisible. But then again, as you are the only hope for my family, perhaps you were waiting for me.

Nanapush sang the song again because he knew the buffalo was waiting to hear it. When he finished, she allowed him to aim point-blank at her heart. The old woman toppled over still watching Nanapush in that emotional way, and Nanapush fell beside her, spent. After a few minutes passed, he roused himself and plunged his knife into the underbelly. A gust of blood-fragrant steam stirred him to life and he worked quickly, wrenching away the guts, cleaning out the rib cavity. As he worked, he chewed on raw slices of heart and liver. Still, his hands shook and his legs kept giving out. He knew he wasn't thinking clearly. Then the snow came down. He was caught in the blind howl.

Hunters on the plains can survive a deadly storm by making a shelter of buffalo hide skinned straight off, but it is dangerous to go inside the animal. Everybody knows that. Yet in his delirium, blinded and drawn by its warmth, Nanapush crawled into the carcass. Once there, he swooned at the sudden comfort. With his belly full and the warmth pressing around him, he passed out. And while unconscious, he became a buffalo. This buffalo adopted Nanapush and told him all she knew.

Of course, once the storm had passed, Nanapush found that he was frozen against the buffalo's ribs. He was held fast by solid blood. Nanapush had dragged in his rifle and kept it where he could shoot, so he managed to blast himself an air hole, though he was deafened for days by the explosion. He could not get his gun to work again. He poked the barrel out the air hole to keep it from freezing over, and waited. To keep up his spirits, he began to sing.

After the storm passed, his mother came out to find him. She had saved herself by knocking a porcupine out of a tree.

She'd killed it with great tenderness, and singed the quills into its flesh so she got the benefit of every part. She'd started looking for her son when the snow stopped. She even made a toboggan and dragged it along in case he'd been hurt or, in the best case, shot an animal. Soon she spotted the dark, shaggy shape swept half bare of snow. She ran, the toboggan bumping along behind, but when she reached the buffalo, her knees gave in fright, she was so surprised to hear it singing the song she'd learned from the fish. Then her mind cleared and she laughed. She knew immediately how her foolish son had trapped himself. So it was, Akii hacked Nanapush out of the buffalo, laced him onto the toboggan, and hauled him to the woods. There she built a brush shelter and a fire to thaw him out. Then with the toboggan they went back many times and transported every bit of the buffalo back to their family and relatives.

When the men were given meat by the woman they had tried to kill, and the son who had protected her, they were ashamed. She was generous, but took her children and did not go back to her husband.

Many people were saved by that old woman buffalo, who gave herself to Nanapush and his unkillable mother. Nanapush himself said that whenever he was sad over the losses that came over and over through his life, his old grandmother buffalo would speak to him and comfort him. This buffalo knew what had happened to Nanapush's mother. She said wiindigoo justice must be pursued with great care. A place should be built so that people could do things in a good way. She said many things, taught Nanapush, so that, as he lived on, Nanapush was to become wise in his idiocy.

Mooshum fell straight back, gave a great sigh, and began his soft rattling snore. I dropped off too, as suddenly as Nanapush inside the buffalo, and when I woke I had forgotten Mooshum's story—although I remembered it later on in the day, when my father came to get me, because he said the word carcass. He was very pale and elated, and he was speaking to Uncle Edward, saying, *They've got his damned carcass in custody.* At that moment, I remembered Mooshum's story entirely, vivid as a dream, and simultaneously knew they'd caught my mother's rapist.

Who is he? Who? I asked my father as we walked up our road.

Soon enough, he said.

At home, my mother was up and about, cleaning, darting around the house with a spidery quickness. Then gasping in a chair, collapsed, leaving jobs started or half done. She got up again, no more than a stick figure. She rushed back and forth, refrigerator to stove to freezer. After her long retreat, this flashing energy was upsetting. She'd gone from zero to a hundred miles an hour and that seemed wrong, although my father seemed pleased and busied himself finishing her projects. They didn't notice me at all, so I left.

Now that they had the carcass in custody, now that something was being done, I felt a lightness. I felt like I could go back just to being thirteen and live my summer. I was glad I'd quit the station. I skimmed along the road.

Cappy's house, surrounded too by unfinished projects, stood about three miles east of the Hoopdance golf course. The golf course cut into the reservation, which was an issue between the town and the tribal council yet to be resolved. Did the tribal council have the right to lease tribal land to a golf course that extended off the reservation and gave most of its profits to non-Indians? And who was responsible if a golfer was struck by lightning? If this issue had come before my father, I was not aware of it, but everybody thought that Indians should get to golf there for free—which of course they couldn't. Sometimes Cappy and I biked over there to look for lost golf balls, which we planned to sell back to the golfers. When I got to Cappy's and suggested this, though, he said he wanted to do something else but he didn't know what. I didn't know what either. So we biked to Zack's and Angus was there and the four of us were together.

The lake beach closest to town had a church on it—or to be more accurate, the church blocked access. The church owned the road to the beach and kept up a cattle gate that could be locked. After the gates, there were signs—no alcohol, no trespassing, no anything. At the Catholic beach there was a faded-out statue of the Virgin Mary surrounded by rocks. She was draped with rosaries, one of which belonged to Angus's aunt. Because of that rosary, I believe we felt we had the right to be there. Of course, as the Catholic church was given the land in a time of our desperation, the very time when Nanapush shot the buffalo, it was true that we not only had a right but owned the land, the church, the statue, the lake, even Father Travis Wozniak's little house. We owned the graveyard that stretched up the hill behind it and the lovely old oak woods pressing in on those graves. But own or not own the whole outfit, once we got there by brazenly riding up the hill, jumping the cattle guard, and racing for the beach, we encountered Youth Encounter Christ—YEC.

As we rode past, they were sitting cross-legged in a circle on the far side of the mowed grass. I could see at a glance they were a mixture of reservation kids, many I knew, and strangers who were probably summer volunteers from Catholic high schools or colleges. I'd seen these volunteers traveling in packs, in their bright orange T-shirts with black sacred heart images printed on the chest. Most people who would talk to them were converted already, which must have been a disappointment. Anyway, we slid past and left our bikes down by the dock. We bushwhacked around a corner to another slice of beach that was more private.

Let's hide our pants, said Angus, in case one of them shows up to steal our clothes. Clothes stealers did not exactly show up, but after we'd been in the water skinny-dipping, horsing around for half an hour, we did get two visitors. One was a tall, stoop-chested dirty blond guy, older, probably in college, with the worst zits you ever saw. The other, well, she was the opposite of him. She was I guess you'd say a dream. Which was what we called her afterward. Dream Girl. Caramel skin. Soft wide eyes of velvet brown. Straight brown fall of hair held back by cute headband. Shorts. Shapey. Breasts that delicately pushed at her ugly orange sacred heart T-shirt. I was relaxing on my back looking at the sky when all of this happened. I turned over and saw my friends were gone. They'd moved closer in to shore and were standing in waist-high water, chopping at the wavelets with their hands. Cappy was slicking back his hair as he talked and suddenly I noticed that he looked much older and stronger than Zack or Angus or me. I swam in, stood up beside my friends.

So I'm gonna ask you again to leave, said pimple guy.

And I'm gonna ask you again how come, said Cappy.

Once again, just to be clear—the YEC guy paused and lifted his first finger and pointed at heaven, a gesture which Angus copied ever after that day. This beach is reserved for church-authorized activities, said YEC. I'm asking you politely to leave.

Naw, said Cappy. We don't wanna go. He squirted water up through his closed fist in a jet. He was squinting lazily at Dream Girl. She hadn't said anything. But her eyes were on Cappy.

What do you think? He nodded at her. Do you think we should go?

Dream Girl said in a clear voice, I think you should go.

Okay, said Cappy, if you say so. And he walked out of the water.

I looked sideways at Cappy as he strode past. His dick hung heavy between his legs. There was a scream. It was from the guy.

Go back!

Then pimple boy rushed forward to grapple Cappy back into the water. Cappy pushed him off and Dream Girl walked away, but she took a good look back. Cappy kicked the God Squadder's legs out from under him, reached around with a wrestler's move, and started dunking him. He didn't dunk him hard, no worse than we did fooling around, but the guy screamed again and Cappy quit.

Hey, man, Cappy held onto his shoulder. The pimple guy puked in the lake and we moved away from him. I'm sorry, man, said Cappy. He reached out to pat the orange back, but the guy's face went a terrible dead purple and we could hear his back teeth grind.

He's shittin' mad or something, Cappy said. And just like that the guy flipped over and began thrashing wildly and jerking his head and he would have drowned right there if we hadn't grabbed him and carried him up onshore. We laid him out. I was the only one with socks. I rolled one up and stuck it in his mouth. We took turns holding the guy, talking to him, and at the same time getting dressed, quick. He quit seizuring and I removed the sock. We sent Angus up to get Father Travis.

While Angus was gone and the guy was breathing okay but still out of it, Cappy said, What do we do now? Think fast, Number One.

Join the YEC, I said.

Yeah, said Zack. Seek out new life-forms. The YEC, a rosary-based primitive people . . .

I get it, Cappy said. We convert. This guy converted us.

Yeah right, said pimple guy, half opening his eyes. He passed out and puked again. We turned him sideways so he wouldn't choke, and he sputtered awake.

We're cool now, man, said Cappy. You showed us the way. We felt a sparkle come down over us.

It happened, I said. The sparkle.

Jesus saves, said Zack, and then he repeated these words over and over in a soft but rising chant that seemed to galvanize the skinny guy, whose name we learned was Neal, into rising with us and putting up a wobbling hand with ours to feel the spirit. Moving forward with the spirit upon us we advanced from the bush, fully dressed, in a little cluster around dripping Neal, calling out whatever Zack did. Holy Spirit is right on! Right *on* upon us. Hallelujah. Praise the Christ Form. Praise His Rez Erection. Holy Mother's Milk. Lamb of Goodness Sakes. Holy Fruity Womb! Zack was a rotten Catholic. Father Travis had left the squad on some urgent business of the moment and was just now hurrying back with Angus. His cassock swirled around his striding thighs. But too late. All he saw was us surrounded by a pack of orange Ts, hugging, weeping, throwing up our hands. All he could do when Cappy fell upon him crying, *Thank you, thank you, Jesus*, was pat Cappy's back hard enough to make him grunt, and eye me like a trapped hawk. I knew better than to meet Father Travis's eyes after that one look. I turned away and bumped up against Dream Girl, who was standing at the edge of things, with the truth and Cappy walking from the water in her thoughts. I saw those things on her face. And I saw there was no conflict. Which is as much as to say that she was in love.

Her name was Zelia and she'd traveled all the way over from Helena, Montana, to convert the Indians, none of whom lived in tipis and many of whom had skin lighter than her own, and this confused her.

Zack asked why she didn't stay in Montana and convert those Indians over there.

What Indians? she asked.

Oh them, said Cappy quickly. They're all Mormons and Witnesses and so on already, those Montana Indians. Nobody goes near them. You should keep on converting over here. Lots of pagans here.

Oh, said Zelia. Well, we don't trespass on other missions so much, anyway.

She was Mexican, from a very close family. They'd been against her mission work to a danger zone, she said, but she got her way eventually.

Actually, you're an Indian too, I told her. She looked offended, so I said, Maybe you're a noble Mayan.

You're probably an Aztec, said Cappy. This was later in the afternoon. We had signed on for the last two days of Father Travis's summer program so that we could see Dream Girl. She and Cappy were starting to flirt.

Yes, I think you are Aztec. Cappy eyed her half-mockingly. You'd reach right into a man's chest and rip out his heart.

She looked away, but she smiled.

Zack put his fist out and pumped it with a squishing noise. Padump. Padump. But neither of them looked at him. The three of us knew we had no hope. Cappy was the only one. But we still wanted to be near her and hoped that she would try converting us for real.

At home, my mother's energy had faded only slightly. She had two streaks of color on her face. I realized she'd smeared on rouge. She was taking iron pills and other pills. There were six bottles of stuff right inside the kitchen cabinet. She had made Juneberry pancakes for dinner. Mom and Dad sat skeptically and listened as I told all about how I had joined Youth Encounter Christ, or YEC, and was due up at the church tomorrow.

Youth Encounter? My father narrowed his eyes. You quit Whitey's to join a youth encounter group?

I quit Whitey's because he pasted Sonja.

My mother went rigid.

All right, said my father quickly. What do you encounter?

We dramatize life situations. Like if we are offered drugs. We imagine that Jesus is there to step between, say, Angus and the drug dealer. Or me and the dealer, say, not that it happens.

That's right, said my father, you're beer drinkers, as I remember. Does Jesus snatch the cans from your paws? Empty them on the ground?

That's what we're supposed to visualize.

Interesting, said my mother. Her voice was neutral, formal, neither caustic nor falsely enthusiastic. I'd thought she was the same mother only with a hollow face, jutting elbows, spiky legs. But I was beginning to notice that she was someone different from the before-mother. The one I thought of as my real mother. I had believed that my real mother would emerge at some point. I would get my before-mom back. But now it entered my head that this might not happen. The damned carcass had stolen from her. Some warm part of her was gone and might not return. This new formidable woman would take getting to know, and I was thirteen. I didn't have the time.

The second day at Youth Encounter Christ was better than the first—we got our T-shirts that morning and put them right on over our clothes, patting the thorn-encircled sacred hearts printed over our own hearts. We went down to the lake and started lip-synching the songs everyone else in the group knew. Neal was our best friend now. The other kids from the reservation, real devout ones whose parents were deacons and pie makers for the funerals, had told Neal that the four of us were the worst bunch in school, which wasn't even true. They were just trying to help Neal feel impressed with himself as from the beginning he had confessed low self-esteem. Unfortunately for us and for our chances of long-term salvation, Youth Encounter Christ was only a two-week camp. We had been converted with only a day left. So we were in wrap-up sessions. And since they were wrapping up the insights gained over the two weeks, we didn't have much to contribute.

One girl whose sister we knew, Ruby Smoke, stated that she had been delivered of a serpent. I felt Zack shaking beside me, and I elbowed him hard. Angus knew the score and murmured praise, but Cappy said, What kind of snake was it, in a deadpan voice, and Father Travis bent forward, giving him a sideways stare.

Ruby was a big girl with short, sprayed hair, streaked with dry red, and hoop earrings. Lots of makeup. Her boyfriend, Toast, I don't recall his real name, nobody did, was there too—very skinny with basketball shorts and a sad slump. He looked over at Cappy not with malice, and said, None of your business. A serpent is a serpent.

Cappy put his hands up, Just asking, man! He fixed his eyes on the ground.

But since you're interested, said Ruby, it was a humungous serpent, brownish, with crisscross lines. And its eyes were golden and it had a wedge head like a rattlesnake.

A pit viper, I said. You were delivered of a pit viper.

Father Travis looked ominous, but Ruby looked pleased.

It's okay, Father, she said. Joe's uncle is a science teacher.

In fact, I went on, encouraged, it sounds to me like you were delivered of the fer-de-lance, which is hands down the deadliest snake in the world. If it bites your hand they chop off your arm. That's the treatment. Or you could have been delivered of the bushmaster, which can get to ten feet and waits to ambush its prey and can take down a cow. You can't see it when the fer-de-lance strikes, it moves at lightning speed.

Everyone nodded in excitement at Ruby and someone said, Way to go, Ruby. She looked proud of herself. Then Father Travis spoke: Sometimes things happen very quickly, like that, which is why in this encounter group we work to prepare you for those lightning-fast moments. Those moments aren't temptation, really. You react on instinct. Temptation is a slower process and you'll feel it more in the morning just after waking and in the evening, when you are at loose ends, tired, and yet not ready to fall asleep. You're tempted then. That's why we learn strategies to keep ourselves occupied, to pray. But a quick-acting poison, that's different. It strikes with blind swiftness. You can be bit by temptation anytime. It is a thought, a direction, a noise in your brain, a hunch, an intuition that leads you to darker places than you've ever imagined.

I sat rooted, struck into an odd panic by his words.

We caught hands all around and put our heads down and prayed the Hail Mary, which you don't have to be a Catholic to know on this reservation as people mutter it at all hours in the grocery store or bars or school hallways. We did ten, mentioning the fruit of thy womb every time, a phrase that Zack found unbearable and couldn't even say for fear he'd laugh. The day went on pretty much like that—confessions, pep talks, tears, drama-praying. Creepy moments when we had to stare into each other's eyes. I say creepy because I had to stare into Toast's eyes, which were burnt holes, unreadable and belonging to a guy, so what was the point anyway. Cappy got to lock eyes with Zelia. This was supposed to be a soul-to-soul encounter. A spiritual thing. But Cappy said he got the worst hard-on of his life.

The flittering energy that had possessed my mother was burnt out and she was resting—but on the couch, not locked in her room. After I got home, my father invited me to sit alongside him on an old rusted kitchen chair next to the garden. The evening was cool and the air stirred the scrub box elder bordering the yard. The big cottonwood clattered by the garage. My father tipped his head back to catch the slow-setting sun on his face.

I had asked him about the damned carcass, and he was trying to think of what to say.

Who is it?

My father shook his head.

The thing is, my father said, the thing is. He was choosing his words very carefully. There will be an arraignment where the judge will decide whether he can be charged. But even now we may be pushing the envelope. The defense attorney is filing a motion for his release. Gabir is hanging in there, but he doesn't have a case. Most rape cases don't get this far but we have Gabir. There's talk by the defense of suing the BIA. Even though we know he did it. Even though everything matches up.

Who is it? Why can't they just hang him?

My father put his head in his hands, and I said I was sorry.

No, he said, broodingly. I wish I could hang him. Believe me. I imagine myself the hanging judge in an old western; I'd happily deliver the sentence. But beyond playing cowboy in my thoughts, there is traditional Anishinaabe justice. We would have sat down to decide his fate. Our present system though . . .

She doesn't know where it happened, I said.

My father tipped his chin down. There is nowhere to stand. No clear jurisdiction, no accurate description of where the crime occurred. He turned over a scrap of paper and drew a circle on it, tapped his pencil on the circle. He made a map.

Here's the round house. Just behind it, you have the Smoker allotment, which is now so fractionated nobody can get much use out of it. Then a strip that was sold—fee land. The round house is on the far edge of tribal trust, where our court has jurisdiction, though of course not over a white man. So federal law applies. Down to the lake, that is also tribal trust. But just to one side, a corner of that is state park, where state law applies. On the other side of that pasture, more woods, we have an extension of round house land.

Okay, I said, looking at the drawing. Fine. Why can't she make up a place?

My father turned his head and gazed at me. The skin beneath his eyes was purple-gray. His cheeks were loose folds.

I can't ask her to do that. So the problem remains. Lark committed the crime. On what land? Was it tribal land? fee land? white property? state? We can't prosecute if we don't know which laws apply.

If it happened anyplace else . . .

Sure, but it happened here.

You knew this ever since Mom talked about it.

So did you, my father said.

Since my mother had broken her silence in my presence and set in motion all that followed, I had insisted to my father that he tell me what was happening. And to some extent he did, although not all of it by any means. For instance, he said nothing about dogs. The day after we spoke, a search-and-rescue outfit came to our reservation. From Montana, is what Zack heard.

We were riding aimlessly around, doing wheelies in the dust, circling the big gravelly yard near the hospital, jumping over stray clumps of alfalfa and jewelweed. It was Saturday and Zelia, along with the other leaders of the camp, was on a final bus trip to the Peace Garden. After their leadership workshop they would all leave. The workshop lasted three days and Cappy was being Worf.

He made his Klingon challenge to me, *Heghlu meh qaq jajvam*, tried to skid into a 360, and bit the dust.

This is a good day to die! he yelled.

Fuck yes! I yelled.

Angus was best at imitating Data. Please continue this petty bickering, he said. It is most intriguing. He raised his finger.

At that moment, Zack rode up and told us what was happening down by the lake with the search-and-rescue teams and the police and the vans towing commandeered fishing boats. By the time we got to the lake, we could see them, the dogs and their handlers in four aluminum boats with outboard motors that couldn't have been more than fifteen hp. The dogs were different breeds; there was a golden one, a runty one that looked like a cross between Pearl and Angus's scabby rez mutt, a sleek black Lab, and a German shepherd.

They're looking for a car that went down, said Zack. At least I know that much.

I knew it was Mayla's car. From what Mom had said, I knew that her attacker had sent it to the bottom of the lake. I also knew they were looking for Mayla. I couldn't help imagining ways that he could have weighted her body and somehow got her back into that car. I didn't want to think of these things, but my mind kept these awful thoughts going. We watched the searchers all day, the dogs choosing the air above the water, and their people watching every move they made. It was a slow business. They moved across the water, calm, methodical, laying an invisible grid down on the lake bottom. They worked until dark, then quit and set up their own tents and mess camp right near the shore.

The next day, we were there early and got closer, in fact spectacularly close. We didn't mean to. We left our bikes and crept toward the camp unnoticed—there was a new bustle of energy there. Some purpose had been established and we saw it when two wet-suited divers went out in one of the boats and lowered themselves into the drop-off we all knew about. There was a steep bank and where it met the shore it was well-known that the water went to an immediate depth of what we grew up thinking was a hundred feet, but turned out to be twenty. There was a cliff above it, where we lodged ourselves and watched through the day. We were hungry, thirsty, and talking about sneaking away, when a tow truck rumbled down the rutted road. It backed down as close to the water as the searchers could safely wave it. We stayed hidden in the brush and were there when the car, a maroon Chevy Nova, was winched up the bank streaming weeds and water. We expected of course to see a body, and Angus whispered to be ready—we'd get nightmares. He'd seen his drowned uncle. But there was no body in the car. We were peering through weeds, but perched directly where we had a perfect view of the car's interior. We saw the sludgy water wash through and away. The windows were all cranked down. The doors were soon opened. Nobody, nothing, I thought at first, except there was one thing.

One thing that sent through me a shock that registered as a surface prickle and then went deeper, all that day, all evening, then that night, until I saw it again the moment I was falling asleep and started awake.

In the back window of the car there was a jumble of toys—some plastic, a mashed-up stuffed bear maybe, all were washed together so you couldn't quite distinguish what each of them was except for a scrap of cloth, a piece of blue-and-white checked fabric that matched the outfit on the doll stuffed with money.

CHAPTER NINE

The Big Good-bye

Mooshum was born nine months after berry-picking camp, a happy time when families got together all through the bush. I went out to pick berries with my father, Mooshum always said, and I came back with my mother. He thought it was a great joke and always celebrated his conception, not his birth, as in fact he had become convinced that he was born at Batoche during the siege in 1885, which my father privately doubted. It was true, however, that Mooshum had still been a child when his family left behind their neat cabin, their lands, their barn and sweet water well, and fled Batoche after Louis Riel was caught and sentenced to be hanged. They came down over the border, where they were not exactly welcomed with open arms. Still, they were taken in by an unusually kindhearted chief who told the U.S. government that maybe it threw away its half-breed children and gave them no land, but that the Indians would take these children into their hearts. The generous full-bloods would have a hard time of it in the years to come, while the mixed-bloods who already knew how to farm and husband animals fared better and eventually began to take over and even looked down on those who had rescued them. Yet as Mooshum went on in life he cast off his Michif ways. First to go was Catholicism, then he started speaking pure Chippewa not mixed with French, and even made himself a fancy powwow outfit to dance in although he still jigged and drank. He went, as they said in those times, back to the blanket. Not that he wore a blanket. But sometimes he threw one over his shoulder and walked out to the round house and participated in the bush ceremonies. He was great friends with all the troublemakers who caroused about as well as those who fought desperately to keep their reservation, ground that kept shifting under their feet according to government whim and Indian agent head counts and something called allotment. Many an agent gained wealth on stolen rations in those years, and many a family turned their faces to the wall and died for lack of what they were promised.

And now, said Mooshum, on the day we gathered to celebrate his birthday, there is food aplenty. Food everywhere. Fat Indians! You would never see a fat Indian back in my time.

Grandma Ignatia sat with him under the old-timey arbor that Uncle Edward and Whitey had built for Mooshum's birthday party. They had laid fresh popple saplings onto posts to make a shady roof, and the leaves were still sweet and bright. The old ones sat in woven plastic lawn chairs and drank hot tea though the day was warm. Clemence had instructed me to sit with Mooshum, to watch him and make sure that the heat did not prostrate him. Grandma Ignatia was shaking her head at the fat Indians.

I had a fat Indian for a husband at one time, she told Mooshum. His pecker was long and big but only the head reached past his gut. And of course I didn't like to get underneath him anyway for fear of getting smashed.

Miigwayak! Of course. What did you do? Mooshum asked.

I bounced around on top naturally. But that belly, yai! It grew big as a hill and I couldn't see over it. I'd call out, Are you still back there? Holler to me! Like most fat Indians he did have a skinny butt. Man, those muscles in his back cheeks were powerful, too. He swung me around like a circus act. So I enjoyed him real well, those times were good.

Awee, said Mooshum. His voice was wistful.

But sadly they were not to last, said Grandma Ignatia. One time we were going hell for leather when he quit. Sometimes he did get tired out of course, being so heavy like he was, so I just keep cranking away on top. His flagpole was still up and hard as steel. But I thought he might have gone to sleep, he was so quiet. Holler to me! I said. But he never did. My, it is strange he sleeps through all of this! He must be having a grand dream, I think. So I don't quit until it's all over—many times over with me, eyyyy. At last I get off him. My, he's lasting! I think. I crawl around to the other end of him. Not long, and I realize that he is not breathing. I pat his face, but no good. He is dead and gone, my sweet fat husband. I mourned for that man a solid year.

Awee, said Mooshum. A happy death. And a noble lover for you, Ignatia, as he satisfied you even from the other side. I wish to die that way, but who will give me the chance?

Does it still stand up? asked Ignatia.

Not by itself, said Mooshum.

Eyyyy, said Ignatia. After a hundred years of hard use it would be a miracle. If you only prayed more, she cackled.

Mooshum's frail shoulders were shaking. Pray for a hard-on! That's a good one. Maybe I should pray to Saint Joseph. He was a carpenter and worked with wood.

Them nuns never mentioned the patron saint of manaa!

Mooshum said, I will say a prayer to Saint Jude, the one who handles lost cases.

And I will pray to Saint Anthony, the one in charge of lost objects. You're so old you probably can't even find your own pecker in those pants Clemence put on you today.

Yes, these pants. They are good material.

One of my other husbands, said Ignatia, the one with the tiny cock, had a pair of pants like yours once. Extremely high quality. He had sex like a rabbit. Quick in-out-in-out but for hours at a time. I would just lay there making things up in my head, thinking my own thoughts. It was restful. I felt nothing. Then one day, something. Howah! I cried. What happened to you? Did it grow?

Yes, I watered it, he said between in-out-in-out. And fertilized it.

Yai! I cried out, even louder. What did you use?

I'm joking, woman. I made it bigger with clay from the river. Oh, no!

All of a sudden I felt nothing again.

It fell off, he said.

The whole wiinag?

No, just the clay part. He was very downhearted. Oh my love, he said, I wanted to make you scream like a bobcat. I'd give my life to make you happy. I said to him, That's all right, I'll show you another way.

So I showed him a thing or two and he learned so good that I made sounds his ears had never heard. One time, anyway, we had this lantern swinging from a hook over the foot of the bed. He was going at me like the rabbit and that lantern fell off the hook and hit him in the ass. I heard him tell his friends about it. They were laughing pretty good, then he says, I was lucky though. If I had been doing the deed my old lady taught me, the one that makes her so happy, that lantern would have hit me in the head.

Yai! Mooshum's tea spluttered from his lips. I gave him a napkin because Clemence had also charged me with keeping food out of his hair, which against her wishes he'd worn the way he liked it, hanging down around his face in greasy strands.

Too bad we never tried each other out when we were young,

said Ignatia. You are much too shriveled up to suit me now but as I remember it, you were damn good-looking.

So I was, said Mooshum.

I blotted away the tea that was rolling down his neck, before it reached the starched white collar of his shirt. I drove a few girls out of their minds, Mooshum continued, but when my pretty wife was living, I did my Catholic duty.

No difficulty there, Ignatia snorted. Were you faithful or not? (They both pronounced the word fateful; in fact, every *th* in this whole conversation was a *t*.)

I was fateful, said Mooshum. To a point.

What point? said Ignatia sharply. She always supported women's extramarital excitements, but was completely intolerant of men's. Oh, wait, my old friend, how could I be forgetting? To a point! Eyyyyy, very funny.

Anishaaindinaa. Yes, of course, she lived out on the point, that Lulu. And you had your son with her.

I started in surprise, but neither one of them noticed. Was it known all over that I had an uncle I never knew about? Who was this son of Mooshum's? I tried to shut my mouth but as I looked around I saw, of course, a large number of the guests were Lamartines and Morrisseys and then Ignatia said his name.

That Alvin did good for himself.

Alvin, a friend of Whitey's! Alvin had always seemed like part of the family. Well. When I tell this story to white people they are surprised, and when I tell it to Indians they always have a story like it. And they usually found out about their relatives by dating the wrong ones, or at any rate, they usually began to figure out family somewhere in their teens. Maybe it was because no one thought to explain the obvious which was always there or maybe as a child I just had not listened before. Anyway, I now realized that Angus was some kind of cousin to me, as Star was a Morrissey and her sister, mother to Angus, was once married to Alvin's younger brother, Vance, and yet as Vance had a different father from Alvin the connection was weakened. Had I heard the name for this type of cousin, I wondered, sitting there, or should I ask Mooshum and Ignatia?

Excuse me, I said.

Oh yes, my boy, how polite you are! Grandma Ignatia suddenly noticed me sitting there and stuck me with her crow-sharp eyes.

If Alvin is my half uncle and Star's sister was married to Vance and they had Angus what does that make Angus to me?

Marriageable, croaked Grandma Ignatia. Anishaaindinaa. Kidding, my boy. You could marry Angus's sister. But you ask a good question.

He is your quarter cousin, Mooshum said firmly. You don't treat him like a whole cousin but he's closer to you than a friend. You would defend him, but not to da dett.

That's how he said it, da dett. Nowadays most of us will say our *th*s unless we grew up speaking Chippewa, but we still drop a lot of them from habit. My father felt that as a judge it was important to pronounce his every last *th*. My mother didn't, however. As for me, I left my *d*s behind when I went to college and I took up the *th*. So did lots of other Indians. I wrote an awful poem once about all of the *d*s that got left behind and floated around on reservations and a friend read it. She thought there was something to that idea and as she was a linguistics major she wrote a paper on the subject. Several years after she wrote that paper, I married her, back on the reservation, and I noticed that as soon as we passed the line we dropped our *th*s and picked up our *d*s again. But even though she was a linguistics major, she didn't have a word for what kind of cousin Angus was to me. I thought Mooshum defined it best with his statement that I was bound to defend Angus, but only so far. I didn't have to die for him, which was a relief.

At this point, more people came and sat with us, a crowd in fact, all around Mooshum, and the whole party directed its attention to where he sat underneath the arbor. People with cameras carefully positioned themselves and my mother and Clemence posed for pictures with their heads on either side of Mooshum's head. Then Clemence ran back into the house and there was a hush broken by the exclamations of small children pushed to the edge of the crowd, The cake! The cake!

As Clemence and Edward were now fiddling with their cameras, my cousins Joseph and Evey got to carry in the extraordinary cake. Clemence had constructed a great sheet cake frosted with whiskey-laced sugar, Mooshum's favorite, and she had iced it onto a piece of masonite covered with tinfoil. The cake was the size of a desktop, elaborately lettered with Mooshum's name and studded with at least a hundred candles, already lighted, brightly burning as my cousins walked gingerly forward. People parted around them. I slipped aside once they held the cake right in front of Mooshum's face. The cake was dazzling. Ignatia looked jealous. The little flames reflected up into Mooshum's dim old eyes as people sang the happy birthday song in Ojibwe and English and then started on a Michif tune. The candles flared more intensely as they burned down, dripping wax onto the frosting until they were mere stubs.

Blow them out! Make a wish! people cried, but Mooshum seemed mesmerized by their light. Grandma Ignatia leaned over and spoke right into his ear. He nodded, finally, and stooped over the cake and at that moment a stray breeze came through the arbor, a little gust. You think it would have extinguished the candles, but on the contrary. It gave them enough oxygen for one last flare and when this happened the little flames fused into a single fire that ignited the mixture of wax and whiskey icing. The cake caught fire with a gentle whoosh and the flames leapt high enough to ravel into Mooshum's locks of greasy hair as he bent over with his lips pursed. I still have the picture in my mind of Mooshum's head surrounded by the blaze. Only his delighted eyes and happy grin showed, as, it seemed, he was consumed. My grandfather and the cake might have been destroyed right there, if Uncle Edward hadn't had the presence of mind to empty a pitcher of lemonade over Mooshum's head. Just as providentially, Joseph and Evelina were still holding on to the masonite and ran the burning cake out onto the driveway, where the flames went out once they had consumed the liquorous frosting. Uncle Edward was again the hero of the day as he simply slicked off the scorched frosting with a long bread knife. He declared the rest of the cake edible, indeed, improved by the scorching. Someone brought gallons of ice cream and the party recommenced. I was told to take Mooshum inside to rest from the thrill. Once there, Clemence tried to cut away his singed locks.

The fire itself hadn't touched his skin or his scalp, but to be on fire had excited him enormously. He was concerned that Clemence cut away only what parts of his hair were hopelessly black and shriveled.

Okay, I'm trying, Daddy. But the pieces stink, you know.

She gave up.

Oh here, Joe. You sit with him!

He was lying on the couch, pillowed, covered with an afghan, just a pile of sticks and a big grin. His white choppers had come loose in the excitement, so I fetched a cup of water and he plunged them in. Unfortunately, I chose an opaque plastic cup of the kind that children were using to drink Kool-Aid. While my back was turned, some four-year-old snatched the cup and ran outside happily drinking the denture water, imitating his older cousins, until apparently this child asked his mother for more Kool-Aid and she saw what was in the bottom. I sat by Mooshum, though, oblivious of these dramas. My cousins were home but much older than me and absorbed in carrying out constant orders from their mother. My friends, who had promised to come, weren't here yet. This party would go on and on. There would be dancing later, fiddles, an electric guitar and keyboard, more food. My friends were probably waiting for Alvin's pit-barbecued venison or the food coming from their own households. Once a party like this started on the reservation it always gained its own life. There was a tradition of the uninvited showing up and every party had provisions for that—as well as for those who would show up drunk and get too rowdy. But from all of this, lying in state on the living-room couch, Mooshum was protected. Part of things but able to snooze. I sat with him as he dropped off and slept. But when Sonja entered he snapped to like a soldier. Her outfit must have penetrated his unconscious. She wore a shirt of softly fringed suede that clung to her breasts like an unforgiven sin. And those jeans, making her legs so long and lean. My eyes popped. New lizard-skin-trimmed cowboy boots! And she wore those studs in her ears. They trembled in the soft light.

I ducked when she tried to kiss the top of my head, moved off so she could sit in my chair, but stayed in the room with my arms folded, glaring at her. I knew that shirt was bought with my doll money and it looked expensive. She'd used a lot of my money again. And those boots! Everybody had to notice.

Sonja bent close to Mooshum. They were speaking in annoying low voices, and she was shaking her head, laughing. He was giving her a toothless pleading look that dripped with besotted admiration. She leaned over and kissed his cheek, then she held his hand and talked some more and both of them laughed and laughed themselves silly until I got disgusted and went away.

My parents were sitting in the grown-up seating area beneath the arbor and my mother, though talking little, was at least nodding as my father spoke to her. The band was setting up out by the storage shed. Behind the shed, Whitey and the other drinkers were sitting on the ground passing a bottle. Whitey was on a morose jag now. He sat in the corner of the yard staring at the party, trying to track things with his double vision, muttering dark thoughts that fortunately were completely incoherent. I saw Doe Lafournais and Cappy's aunt Josey. There was Star and Zack's mom, too, and Zack's baby brother and sister. But no Zack, Angus, or Cappy. I didn't want to ask where they were in case they were up to something, so I got my bike from beside the garage and left. I was pretty sure that Zelia had something to do with Cappy's absence and sure enough, as I went toward the church I met Zack and Angus zigzagging down the hill, slow as they could, no Cappy.

He stayed behind. They're gonna meet in the graveyard at dark, said Zack.

All three of us were crushed by the thought, even though we'd given up on Zelia day one. We rode back to the party, which was ramping up with jiggers stepping out onto the grass and Grandma Ignatia in the middle showing off her fancy steps. We ate as much as we could, then sneaked beers and poured the beer into empty soda cans. We drank and hung out listening to the band, watching Whitey hang on Sonja as they two-stepped until it grew late. My father said I should ride my bike home, and I did, wobbling into the yard. I took Pearl up to my room and was just falling asleep when I heard my parents coming home. I heard them walk up the stairs talking together in low voices and then I heard them enter their bedroom the way they always had before. I heard them shut their door with that final small click that meant everything was safe and good.

If things could stay that way, safe and good, if the attacker would die in jail. If he would kill himself. I couldn't live with the if.

I need to know, I said to my father the next morning. You've got to tell me what the carcass looks like.

I'll tell you when I can, Joe.

Does Mom know he could get out?

My father waved his finger across his lips. Not exactly, no. Well, yes. But we haven't spoken. It would set her back, he said quickly. His face contorted. He put his hand over his features as if to erase them.

I have to look out for her, watch for him.

He nodded, and after a while he rose and with a heavy tread walked to his desk. As he fumbled in his pocket for his keys, I saw the vulnerable brown eggshell of his head, the wisps of white. He had begun to lock this particular drawer, but now he opened it and withdrew a file. He opened the file, walked over to me, and drew out a photograph. A mug shot. He put the photograph in my hands.

You mother hasn't decided whether to tell anybody else, he said. It's her call. So don't talk about this.

A handsome but not good-looking powerful man with a pallid complexion and black shining eyes that showed no white, just the speck of livid life. His half-open mouth was filled with perfect white teeth and his lips were thin and red. It was the customer. The man who'd bought gas the day before I quit.

I've seen him before, I said. Linden Lark. He bought gas at Whitey's.

My father didn't look at me, but his jaw flattened, his lips went hard.

When?

Must have been just before he was picked up.

My father pinched the picture back and slid it into the file. I could see that it hurt his fingers to touch the photograph, that the mute image emitted a jagged force. He slammed the file back in the drawer, then stood staring at the papers scattered over his desk. He unclenched the hand over his heart, opened it, fingered a shirt button.

Bought gas at Whitey's.

We heard my mother outside. She was pounding slim poles she'd cut down into the ground, setting them alongside her tomato plants. Next she would rip old sheets into strips to bind their acrid, musky stems, so that they could safely climb. Already the plants bore star-shaped flowers colored a soft, bitter yellow.

He's studied us, said my father softly. Knows we can't hold him. Thinks he can get away. Like his uncle.

What do you mean?

The lynching. You know that.

Old history, Dad.

Lark's great-uncle was in the lynching party. Thus, I think, the contempt.

I wonder if he even knows how people here keep track of that, I said.

We know the families of the men who were hanged. We know the families of the men who hanged them. We even know our people were innocent of the crime they were hung for. A local historian had dredged that up and proved it.

Outside, my mother was putting away the tools. They jangled in her bucket. She cranked on the hose and began to spray her garden, the water splattering softly back and forth.

We'll get him anyway, I said. Won't we, Dad.

But he was staring at his desk as if he saw through the oak top into the file beneath it and through the manila cover to the photograph and from the photograph perhaps to some other photograph or record of old brutality that hadn't yet bled itself out.

After his mother died, Linden Lark had kept her farmhouse at the edge of Hoopdance. He had been staying in the house, a rickety, peeling two-story that once had flower beds and big vegetable gardens. Now, of course, the whole place had gone to weeds and was cut off by crime tape. Dogs had searched and double-searched the premises, the fields and woods surrounding the house and found nothing.

No Mayla, I said.

Dad was talking with me later on that day—the house was quiet. I'd been playing my game. He'd walked in. This time he told me things. The governor of South Dakota had stated that the child he wished to adopt came from a Rapid City social service agency and that claim was confirmed. The people there said that about a month ago someone, a man it was believed, had left the baby asleep in her car seat, in the furniture section at Goodwill. There had been a note pinned on the baby's jacket informing the finder that her parents were dead.

Is it Mayla's baby?

My father nodded.

Your mother was shown a picture. She identified the baby.

Where is Mom now? I asked.

My father raised his brows, still surprised.

I just dropped her off at work.

A few days after my mother identified the baby, she began regular hours at her office. There was a backlog; blood quantum to parse, genealogy hopefuls curious about their possible romantic Indian Princess grandmothers. There were children returning as adults, adopted-out people cut off from their tribe, basically stolen by the state welfare agencies, and there were also those who had given up on being an Indian but whose children longed for the connection and designed a meaningful family vacation to the reservation to explore their heritage. She had a lot to do, and this was even before casino money roped wannabes in droves. She could apparently work as long as Lark was in custody. As long as the baby was safe. There were a few days when things were normal—but it was holding-your-breath normal. We heard the baby was with her grandparents, George and Aurora Wolfskin. She was placed there permanently or at least until Mayla returned. If she did return. Then on about the fourth day, my mother told my father that she had to talk to Gabir

Olson and Special Agent Bjerke because, now that the baby's safety was no longer an issue, she'd suddenly remembered the whereabouts of that missing file.

All right, my father said. Where?

Where I left it, underneath the front seat of the car.

My father went outside and came back with the manila folder in his hands.

They went to Bismarck again, and I stayed with Clemence and Edward. The birthday banners were all down. The beer cans crushed. The leaves were dried out in the arbor. Things again were quiet at Clemence and Edward's house, but a sort of cheerful quiet as there were always people coming around to visit. Not only relations and friends, but people who came just for Mooshum, students or professors. They would set up a tape recorder and tape him talking about the old days or speaking Michif, or Ojibwe or Cree, or all three languages together. But he really didn't tell them much. All his real stories came at night. I slept in Evey's room with him. About an hour or two into the night I woke to hear him talking.

The Round House

When he was told to kill his mother, said Nanapush, a great rift opened in his heart. There was a crack so deep it went down forever. On the before side his love for his father, and belief in all that his father did, lay crumpled and discarded. And not only that one belief, but others as well. It was true that there could be wiindigoog—people who lost all human compunctions in hungry times and craved the flesh of others. But people could also be falsely accused. The cure for a wiindigoo was often simple: large quantities of hot soup. No one had tried the soup on Akii. No one had consulted the old and wise. The people he'd loved, including his uncles, had simply turned against his mother, so Nanapush could not believe in them or in what they said or did anymore. On the side of the crack where Nanapush was, however, his younger brothers and sisters, who had cried for their mother, existed. And his mother, too. Also the spirit of the old female buffalo who had been his shelter.

That old buffalo woman gave Nanapush her views. She told him that he had survived by doing the opposite of all the others. Where they abandoned, he saved. Where they were cruel, he was kind. Where they betrayed, he was faithful. Nanapush then decided that in all things he would be unpredictable. As he had completely lost trust in authority, he decided to stay away from others and to think for himself, even to do the most ridiculous things that occurred to him.

You can go that way, said the old buffalo woman, but even though you become a fool, people will in time consider you a wise man. They will come to you.

Nanapush did not want anyone to come to him.

That will not be possible, said the buffalo woman. But I can give you something that will help you—look into your mind and see what I am thinking about.

Nanapush looked into his mind and saw a building. He even saw how to make the building. It was the round house. The old female buffalo kept talking.

Your people were brought together by us buffalo once. You knew how to hunt and use us. Your clans gave you laws. You had many rules by which you operated. Rules that respected us and forced you to work together. Now we are gone, but as you have once sheltered in my body, so now you understand. The round house will be my body, the poles my ribs, the fire my heart. It will be the body of your mother and it must be respected the same way. As the mother is intent on her baby's life, so your people should think of their children.

That is how it came about, said Mooshum. I was a young

man when the people built it—they followed Nanapush's instructions.

I sat up to look at Mooshum, but he had turned over and begun his snore. I lay awake thinking of the place on the hill, the holy wind in the grass, and how the structure had cried out to me. I could see a part of something larger, an idea, a truth, but just a fragment. I could not see the whole, but just a shadow of that way of life.

I had been there three or four days when Clemence and Uncle Edward went over to Minot to purchase a new freezer. They started out early in the morning, before I was up. Mooshum had risen at six as usual. He'd drunk the coffee, eaten all the eggs, toast, and buttered hash brown potatoes that Clemence made, even my share. When I went down to the kitchen, I took a slice of cold meat loaf she'd left for lunch, slapped it between two pieces of soft white bread, with ketchup. I asked my Mooshum what he wanted to do that day and he looked vague.

You go off with your own. He waved his hand. I'm all set here.

Clemence said I have to stay with you.

Saaah, she treats me like a puking baby. You go! You go off and have a good time!

Then Mooshum tottered over to Evey's old dresser and rummaged among the things in his top drawer until he came up with an old gray sock. Dangling the sock at me with a significant look, he plunged his hand in. He was wearing his dentures, which usually meant company. With a sly air of triumph he drew a soft ten-dollar bill from the toe of the sock and waved it at me.

Take this! Go on, live it up. Majaan!

I didn't take the bill.

You're up to something, Mooshum.

Up to something, he said as he sat down, up to something. Then he said in low outrage, How can a man be a man!

Maybe I can help you, I said.

Eh, so be it. Clemence keeps my bottle high in the kitchen cabinet. You could fetch me that!

It wasn't even noon, but then I figured what could it hurt? He'd lived long enough to deserve a drink of whiskey when he wanted it. Clemence had given him but one pour on his birthday, then lots of swamp tea to counteract the effect. I was standing on the countertop, trying to find the place where Clemence hid the bottle, when Sonja came in the back door. She was carrying a plastic shopping bag with sturdy handles, and at first I thought she'd shopped again with my money and was coming to show Clemence her purchases. I clambered down with the bottle in my hand and said, in a belligerent tone, So, you went on another spending spree! I stood before her. We're going to dig up those passbooks, I said. We're gonna go around and get all that money back, Sonja.

All right, she said, her blue eyes soft with hurt. That's fine.

Stop this talk of money. Mooshum stumbled close to Sonja. Took her arm. He spoke silkily.

This old man has money and a bottle too, *ma chère* niinimoshenh.

Mooshum steered Sonja and her heavy shopping bag toward the bedroom.

Get out of here now, he said to me. Get! He held his hand out for the bottle.

But I stood my ground.

I'm not going anywhere, I said. Clemence told me to stay.

I followed them into the bedroom. They stared at me in a helpless way. I sat down on the bed.

I'm not leaving, at least, until I see what's in that bag.

Mooshum gave me an outraged snort. He snatched the bottle from my hand and took a quick pull. Sonja sat down sullenly and puffed out her lips. She was wearing one of her tracksuits, plush and pink, and a T-shirt with a plunging neckline; a silver heart at the end of a silver chain pointed to the shadowy swelling line where her breasts were pushed together. Her hair glowed in light from the window behind her.

Joe, she said, this is Mooshum's birthday present.

What is?

What's in the bag.

Well, give it to him, then.

It's . . . ah . . . a grown-up gift.

A grown-up gift?

Sonja made a face that meant *duh*.

My throat shut. I looked from Mooshum to Sonja, back and forth. They wouldn't look at each other.

I'm gonna ask you to leave in a nice way, Joe.

But as she spoke she started taking things from the bag—not exactly clothes—tatters of cloth and sequiny things and glittering tassels and some long strands of hair and fur. Heeled sandals with long leather laces. I'd seen this stuff before, on her, in my folder labeled HOMEWORK.

I'm not leaving. I sat down next to Mooshum, on his low cot.

You are too! Sonja stared at me. Joe! Her face hardened in a way I had not seen before. Get outta here, she ordered.

I won't, I said.

No? She stood, hands on her hips, and puffed air into her cheeks, mad.

I was mad, too, but what I said surprised me.

You're gonna let me stay. Because if you don't, I'll tell Whitey about the money.

Sonja froze and sat back down. She was holding some shiny cloth. She stared at me. A remote, mystified look crept onto her face. A shiny film flooded her eyes, making her look so young.

Really, she said. Her voice was sad, a whisper. Really?

I should have left, right then. In one half hour I'd wish I had, but also be glad I stayed. I've never felt all one way about what happened next.

Money again, saaah, cried Mooshum in disgust. Which made me think about the money and about Sonja's diamond earrings.

I grabbed Mooshum's bottle and drank. The whiskey hit me and my eyes watered too.

He's a good boy, said Mooshum.

Sonja wouldn't take her eyes off me. You think so? You really think he's a good boy? She sat down and slapped the shiny bra she held against her knee.

He takes good care of me. Mooshum drank and offered me the bottle again. I passed it to Sonja.

You'll tell Whitey, huh?

She gave me an ugly smile, a smile that jolted me. Then she knocked back a long swallow. Mooshum took a sip and handed the bottle back to me. Sonja narrowed her eyes until the blueness turned black. So it's you and Whitey. Okay then. I'm onna dress in the bathroom. You boys stay right here. And if you ever say a word about anything to anybody, Joe, I will cut off your puny dick.

My jaw dropped, and she laughed mean. Can't have it both ways, you lying little phony. I'm not momming you anymore.

She took a tape player out of the bottom of her bag, plugged it into the wall, and popped in a cassette.

When I come back in, turn the music on, she ordered. Then she went across the hall to the bathroom with her bag.

Mooshum and I sat silently on the cot. I now remembered the two of them talking low at the party, and how they had annoyed me. My head started buzzing. I took another swig from Mooshum's bottle. After a while, Sonja came back in, shut the door behind her and locked it, then turned around.

I suppose the two of us gaped at her.

Hit Play, Joe, she growled.

The music began, a low faraway series of wails and chants. Sonja's hair was held straight up in a metallic cone that acted as a fountain, spilling tons of hair, more than she really had, down her shoulders and back. She wore heavy makeup—her eyebrows were black wings, her lips a cruel red. A formal gray sheath of silk hung from her neck to her legs and covered her arms. She drew a long wavy dagger from her sleeve. Then she lifted her arms like an ancient goddess about to sacrifice a goat, or a live man tied on a slab of rock. She held the dagger in both hands, then switched to one hand, staring at the dagger. She pushed an invisible switch. The dagger lit up and glowed. The music changed to guttural, grinding moans, then a sudden series of yips. Along with each yip she cut apart a piece of Velcro that held her robe together. She teased us for a while. The robe had slits in the sides. One armor-plated breast would appear. A leg in the sandal laced to her thigh. Finally, after a chorus of chants and howls, there was a sudden shriek. Then silence. She dropped her robes. I grabbed Mooshum's arm. I didn't want to waste a second looking at him but didn't want him to fall over backward, either, and hit his head. I have never, ever, forgotten her in the dim glory of Evey's bedroom. She was tall in those heeled sandals. With her hair in that cone she nearly touched the ceiling. Her legs went up forever and she wore a bikini bottom that looked like it was forged of iron, padlocked shut. Her stomach was pure and lithe, toned I don't know how. I'd never seen her exercise. And my loves, her breasts, also cased in bits of plastic armor, pushed at the seams of the breastplate, which had been made with fake erect nipples. Skins and scarves flowed off her. She held the dagger in her teeth and then she began to rub and work the fur and fabric all over her body. She wore thin vinyl gauntlets. She took one off, lightly whipped herself and scoured her chastity belt with it, and then cracked me across the face. I almost fainted.

I grabbed Mooshum again. He was panting with happiness. Sonja smacked me right in the eye with the other gauntlet. The drums began. Sonja's belly and hips began to gyrate in a different tempo—so fast her movements blurred. Mooshum gave me the bottle. I choked. Sonja whirled. Kicked me in the knee. I bent over in pain but my eyes never left her. The drum fell silent. She played with the leather strips that held her armor bra together and then suddenly she let it drop. And there they were. Wearing only gold tassels that she twirled first one way, then the other, mesmerizing us. I was dizzy by the time the drum quit. Mooshum's breath came ragged. I could hear the tape scratch. She pulled the ties on her sandals and stepped out of them, threw them at my head. She unsnapped the cone from her hair and it fell around her face in a wild waterfall. She threw the cone at me too. Barefoot, she stepped close and began to grind her hips to the howls of wolves, but when she reached down into her iron bikini and slowly pulled out a key on a silken string, Mooshum was ready. He snatched the key from her fingers and without a tremble in his ancient fist he opened the padlock, unhooked and threw it to the side, and there was a G-string made of soft, black, dense fur. Well, it was a rabbit pelt. But so what. She straddled Mooshum's lap but carefully did not let down her weight. Cupped her tasseled breasts in her hands.

Happy birthday, old man, she said.

Mooshum's smile glowed. Tears flowed down the grooves in his cheeks. He put his arms around her waist, rested his forehead between her breasts, and took one deep groaning breath. He did not take another.

Oh no. Sonja lifted her arms away and lowered him cautiously onto his cot. She put her ear to his chest and listened.

I can't hear his heart, she said.

I held on to Mooshum too. Should we do mouth-to-mouth resuscitation? CPR? What? Sonja?

I don't know.

We looked down at him. His eyes were closed. He was smiling. He looked the happiest I'd seen him.

He's in a dream now, Sonja said tenderly. Her words burst through a sob. He's going away. Let's not disturb him. She leaned over Mooshum, smoothing his hair back and murmuring.

He opened his eyes once, smiled at her, closed his eyes again.

Maybe his heart is beating after all! Sonja knelt down and put her ear to his chest again, biting on her lip.

I hear a thump or two, she said, relieved.

Dazed, I watched Mooshum for signs of life. But he did not stir.

Pick my stuff up, said Sonja, her head still on Mooshum's chest. Yes, she said. There's a beat. They're just coming really slow. And I think he took a breath.

I went around the room picking up her things, took them into the bathroom, and put them in the shopping bag. I brought the tracksuit and tennis shoes into the bedroom and turned my back as she put them on. I wouldn't look at her.

When she was all dressed, she picked up the shopping bag holding her stripper outfit and dropped it at my feet.

Keep it, jerk off in it, I don't care, she said. She plucked a fallen tassel I'd missed off the floor and threw it in my face.

I'm really sorry, I said.

Sorry doesn't cut it. But I couldn't care less. You know where I'm from?

No.

Outside Duluth. That's a nice town, right?

Yeah, I guess.

I went to a Catholic school. I finished eighth grade. Know how I made it through?

No.

My mom. My mom was a Catholic. Yeah. She went to

church. She went—she worked the boats. Know what she did?

No.

She went with men, Joe. Know what that means?

I mumbled something.

That's how I came along in the first place. She tried to keep her own money too. Know what that means, Joe?

No.

She got beat up a lot. She took drugs, too. And guess what? I never met my dad. I never saw him, but my mom was good to me sometimes, sometimes not, whatever. I quit school, had my baby. I did not learn nothing. Anything. My mom said if you got nothing, you can strip. Just dance around, right? Don't do nothing more, just dance around. I had a friend, she was doing it, making money. I said yes, I wouldn't do any other stuff. Think I did something else?

No.

I got stuck in that life. Then I met Whitey, see. They open up more bars for dancing during the hunting season. Whitey courted me. Followed me around the circuit. Whitey started protecting me. He asked me to quit. Come live with me, he says. I didn't ask if he would marry me. You know why, Joe?

No.

I'll tell you. I didn't think I was worth marrying, that's why. Not worth marrying. Why should even an over-the-hill Elvis with a bridge for teeth, an old guy no more educated than me, a drunk who hits me, why should even a guy like that marry me, huh?

I don't know. I thought . . .

You thought we were married. Well, no. Whitey did not do me that honor, though I got a cheap ring. I don't give a rat's ass now. And you. I treated you good, didn't I?

Yes.

But all along you just were itching. Sneaking a good look

at my tits when you thought I didn't know. You think I didn't notice?

My face was so red and hot that my skin burned.

Yeah, I noticed, said Sonja. Take a good look now. Close up. See this?

I couldn't look.

Open your frickin' eyes.

I looked. A thin white scar ran up the side and around the nipple of her left breast.

My manager did that with a razor, Joe. I wouldn't take a hunting party. Think your threats scare me?

No.

Yeah, no. You're crying, aren't you? Cry all you want, Joe. Lots of men cry after they do something nasty to a woman. I don't have a daughter anymore. I thought of you like my son. But you just turned into another piece a shit guy. Another gimme-gimme asshole, Joe. That's all you are.

Sonja left. I sat with Mooshum. Time collapsed. My head rang like I'd been clocked. Sometimes with the ancient, their breath comes so shallow it cannot be discerned. The afternoon went on and the air went blue before he finally stirred. His eyes opened and then closed. I ran for water, and gave him a little sip.

I'm still here, he said. His voice was faint with disappointment.

I continued to sit with Mooshum, at the edge of his cot, thinking about his wish for a happy death. I'd had a chance to see about the difference between Sonja's right and left breasts, but I wished I never had. Yet I was glad I did. The conflict in me skewed my brain. About fifteen minutes before Clemence and Edward returned with the freezer, I looked down at my feet and noticed the golden tassel by the leg of the cot. I picked it up and put it in my jeans pocket.

I don't keep the tassel in a special box or anything—anymore. It's in the top drawer of my dresser, where things just end up, like Mooshum's limp stray sock where he kept money. If my wife has ever noticed that I have it, she's said nothing. I never told her about Sonja, not really. I didn't tell her how I stuffed the rest of Sonja's costume in a garbage can by the tribal offices where the BIA was contracted to pick it up. She wouldn't know that I put that souvenir tassel where I'll come across it by chance, on purpose. Because every time I look at it, I am reminded of the way I treated Sonja and about the way she treated me, or about how I threatened her and all that came of it, how I was just another guy. How that killed me once I really thought about it. A gimme-gimme asshole. Maybe I was. Still, after I thought about it for a long time—in fact, all my life—I wanted to be something better.

Doe had built a little deck onto the front of the house and it was filled, as all of our decks tend to be, with useful refuse. There were snow tires stored in black garbage bags, rusted jacks, a bent hibachi grill, banged-up tools, and plastic toys. Cappy slumped amid all that jetsam in a sagging lawn chair. He was running both hands over his hair as he stared at the dog-scratched boards. He didn't even look up when I stepped next to him and sat down on an old picnic bench.

Hey.

Cappy didn't react.

So, aaniin . . .

Still, nothing.

After a lot more nothing it came out that Zelia had gone back to Helena with the church group, which I already knew, and after still more nothing Cappy blurted out, Me and Zelia, we did something.

Something?

We did everything.

Everything?

Everything we could think of . . . well, there might be more, but we tried . . .

Where?

In the graveyard. It was the night of your Mooshum's birthday. And once we did a few things there—

On a grave?

I dunno. We were kind of on the outskirts of the graves, off to the sides. Not right on a grave.

That's good; it could be bad luck.

For sure. Then after, we got into the church basement. We did it a couple more times there.

What!

In the catechism room. There's a rug.

I was silent. My head swam. Bold move, I said at last.

Yeah, then she left. I can't do nothing. I hurt. Cappy looked at me like a dying dog. He tapped his chest and whispered. It hurts right here.

Women, I said.

He looked at me.

They'll kill you.

How do you know?

I didn't answer. His love for Zelia was not like my love for Sonja, which had become a thing contaminated by humiliation, treachery, and even bigger waves of feeling that tore me up and threw me down. By contrast, Cappy's love was pure. His love was just starting to manifest. Elwin had a tattoo gun and traded for his work. Cappy said he wanted to go to his place and get Elwin to etch Zelia's name in bold letters across his chest.

No, I said. C'mon. Don't do that.

He stood. I'm gonna!

I only convinced him to wait by telling him that when his pecs swelled from his workouts, the letters could be bigger. We sat a long time, me trying to distract Cappy, that not working. I finally left when Doe came home and told Cappy to get to work on the woodpile. Cappy walked over to the axe, grabbed it and began splitting wood with such crazed thwacks that I feared he would take off his leg. I told him to take it easy, but he just gave me a dead look and hit a piece of wood so hard it shot up ten feet.

Meandering back toward our house, where my mother and father were supposed to have returned that afternoon, I had that feeling again of not wanting to go home. But I didn't want to go back to anywhere Sonja was, either. Thinking of her made me think of everything. Into my mind there came the picture of that scrap of blue-and-white checked cloth, and the knowledge I kept pushing away about the doll being in that car. By throwing out the doll I'd obviously destroyed evidence, maybe even something that would tell Mayla's whereabouts. Where she lay, in a place so obscure that even the dogs could not find her. I put the thought of Mayla from my mind. And Sonja. I tried also not to think of my mother. Of what had maybe happened in Bismarck. All of these thoughts were reasons I did not want to go home, or to be alone. They came up over me, shrouding my mind, covering my heart. Even as I rode, I tried to get rid of the thoughts by taking my bicycle over the dirt hills behind the hospital. I began to course violently up and down, jumping so high that when I landed my bones jarred. Whirling. Skidding. Raising clouds of grit that filled my mouth until I was sick and thirsty and dripping with sweat so I could finally go home.

Pearl heard my bike approach, and she stood at the end of the drive, waiting. I got off the bike and put my forehead on her forehead. I wished I could change places with her. I was holding Pearl when I heard my mother scream. And scream again. And then I heard my father's low voice grinding between her shrieks. Her voice veered and fell, just the way I'd just been riding, crashing hard, until finally it dropped to an astonished mutter.

I stood outside, holding my bike up, leaning on it. Pearl was next to me. Eventually, my father walked out the back screen door and lit a cigarette, which I had never seen him do. His face was yellow with exhaustion. His eyes were so red they seemed rimmed with blood. He turned and saw me.

They let him go, didn't they, I said.

He didn't answer.

Didn't they, Dad.

After a moment he dragged on the cigarette, looked down.

All of the electric poison that had drained out of me on my bike flooded back and I began to harangue my father, with words. Stupid words.

All you catch are drunks and hot dog thieves.

He looked at me in surprise, then shrugged and tapped the ash off his cigarette.

Don't forget the scofflaws and custody cases.

Scofflaws? Oh sure. Is there anywhere you *can't* park on the rez?

Try the tribal chairman's spot.

And custody. Nothing but pain. You said yourself. You've got zero authority, Dad, one big zero, nothing you can do. Why do it anyway?

You know why.

No, I don't. I yelled it at him and went in to be with my mother, but there was nothing to be with when I got there. She was staring blankly at the blank of the refrigerator and when I stepped in front of her she spoke in a weird, calm voice.

Hi, Joe.

After my father entered, she went upstairs in a slow devotional walk with him holding on to her arm.

Don't leave her, Dad, please. I said this in dread as he came back down alone. But he did not even glance at me to answer. I stood awkwardly across from him, dangling my hands.

Why do you do it? I said to him, bursting out. Why bother?

You want to know?

He got up and went to the refrigerator and rummaged around and pulled something from deep on the back shelf. He brought it over to the table. It was one of Clemence's uneaten casseroles, there so long the noodles had turned black, but stashed near enough to the cold refrigeration coils that it had frozen and so didn't stink, yet.

Why I keep on. You want to know?

With a savage thump he turned the casserole over onto the table. He lifted off the pan. The thing was shot through with white fuzz but held its oblong shape. My father rose again and pulled the box of cutlery from the cabinet counter. I thought he'd gone crazy at last and watching him I could hardly speak.

Dad?

I'm going to illustrate this for you, son.

He sat down and waved a couple of forks at me. Then with cool absorption he laid a large carving knife carefully on top of the frozen casserole and all around it proceeded to stack one fork, another fork, one on the next, adding a spoon here, a butter knife, a ladle, a spatula, until he had a jumble somehow organized into a weird sculpture. He carried over the other four butcher knives my mother always kept keen. They were good knives, steel all the way through the wooden shank. These he balanced precariously on top of the other silverware. Then sat back, stroking his chin.

That's it, he said.

I must have looked scared. I *was* scared. His behavior was that of a madman.

That's what, Dad? I carefully said. The way you'd address a person in delirium.

He rubbed his sparse gray whiskers.

That's Indian Law.

I nodded and looked at the edifice of knives and silverware on top of the sagging casserole.

Okay, Dad.

He pointed to the bottom of the composition and lifted his eyebrows at me.

Uh, rotten decisions?

You've been into my dad's old Cohen *Handbook*. You'll be a lawyer if you don't go to jail first. He poked at the fuzzy black noodles. Take *Johnson v. McIntosh*. It's 1823. The United States is forty-seven years old and the entire country is based on grabbing Indian land as quickly as possible in as many ways as can be humanly devised. Land speculation is the stock market of the times. Everybody's in on it. George Washington. Thomas Jefferson. As well as Chief Justice John Marshall, who wrote the decision for this case and made his family's fortune. The land madness is unmanageable by the nascent government. Speculators are acquiring rights on treaty-held Indian land and on land still owned and occupied by Indians—white people are literally betting on smallpox. Considering how much outright grease is used to bring this unsavory case to court, a case pled by no less than Daniel Webster, the decision was startling. It wasn't the decision itself that still stinks, though, it was the obiter dicta, the extra incidental wording of the opinion. Justice Marshall went out of his way to strip away all Indian title to all lands viewed—i.e., "discovered"—by Europeans. He basically upheld the medieval doctrine of discovery for a government that was supposedly based on the rights and freedoms of the individual. Marshall vested absolute title to the land in the government and gave Indians nothing more than the right of occupancy, a right that could be taken away at any time. Even to this day, his words are used to continue the dispossession of our lands. But what particularly galls the intelligent person now is that the language he used survives in the law, that we were savages living off the forest, and to leave our land to us was to leave it useless wilderness, that our character and religion is of so inferior a stamp that the superior genius of Europe must certainly claim ascendancy and on and on.

I got it then. I pointed at the bottom of the mess.

I suppose that's *Lone Wolf v. Hitchcock.*

And *Tee-Hit-Ton.*

I asked Dad about the first knife he laid on the casserole, stabilizing it.

Worcester v. Georgia. Now, that would be a better foundation. But this one—my father teased a particularly disgusting bit of sludge from the pile with the edge of his fork—this one is the one I'd abolish right this minute if I had the power of a movie shaman. *Oliphant v. Suquamish.* He shook the fork and the stink wafted at me. Took from us the right to prosecute non-Indians who commit crimes on our land. So even if . . .

He could not go on. I hoped we'd clean the mess up soon, but no.

So even if I could prosecute Lark . . .

Okay, Dad, I said, quieted. How come you do it? How come you stay here?

The casserole was starting to ooze and thaw. My father arranged the odd bits of cutlery and knives so they made an edifice that stood by itself. He had suspended Mom's good knives carefully. He nodded at the knives.

These are the decisions that I and many other tribal judges try to make. Solid decisions with no scattershot opinions attached. Everything we do, no matter how trivial, must be crafted keenly. We are trying to build a solid base here for our sovereignty. We try to press against the boundaries of what we are allowed, walk a step past the edge. Our records will be scrutinized by Congress one day and decisions on whether to enlarge our jurisdiction will be made. Some day. *We want the right to prosecute criminals of all races on all lands within our original boundaries.* Which is why I try to run a tight courtroom, Joe. What I am doing now is for the future, though it may seem small, or trivial, or boring, to you.

*

Now it was Cappy and me, the two of us trying to break ourselves on the bike course. I'd ridden over to our construction site with him because he'd chopped up every piece of wood in his yard and reduced length after length to kindling. Still this was not enough and he wanted to go out and ride Sonja's ponies. In his state of mind I thought he'd ride them to death. Besides, I didn't want to see Sonja, or Whitey either, but I was desperate to distract Cappy so I told him that after we had cruised around and found Angus, we'd catch a ride to the horses though I didn't mean it. From time to time, when we paused or wiped out, Cappy folded his hand on his heart and something crackled. I finally asked him what it was.

It's a letter from her. And I wrote one back, he said.

We were breathing hard. We'd raced. He pulled out her letter, waved it at me, and then carefully folded it back into its ripped envelope. Zelia had that cute round writing that all high-school girls had, with little *o*s to dot the *i*s. Cappy waved another envelope, sealed, with her name and address on it.

I need to get a stamp, he said.

So we biked down to the post office. I was hoping Linda would not be working that day, but she was. Cappy put his money out and bought a stamp. I didn't look at Linda, but I felt her sad pop eyes on me.

Joe, she said. I made that banana bread you like.

But I turned my back on her and went out the door and waited for Cappy.

That lady gave me this for you, said Cappy. He handed me a foil-wrapped brick. I hefted it. We got on our bikes and rode over to find Angus. I thought of throwing the banana bread at the side of a wall or in a ditch, but I didn't. I held on to it.

We got to Angus's and he came out, but said his aunt was making him go to confession, which made us laugh.

What is that? He nodded at the brick in my hand.

Banana bread.

I'm hungry, he said. So I tossed it to him and he ate it while we made our way toward the church. He ate the whole thing, which was a relief. He balled up the foil and put it in his pocket. He'd redeem it with his cans. I had assumed that while Angus went inside the church and made his confession, Cappy and I would wait outside under the pine tree, where there was a bench, or down at the playground, though we didn't have a cigarette to smoke. But Cappy put his bike into the bike rack right alongside Angus's and so I parked mine too.

Hey, I said. Are you going inside?

Cappy was already halfway up the steps. Angus said, No, you guys can wait outside, it doesn't matter.

I'm going to confession, said Cappy.

What? Were you even baptized? Angus stopped.

Yeah. Cappy kept on going. Of course I was.

Oh, said Angus. Were you confirmed then?

Yeah, said Cappy.

When was your last confession? Angus asked.

What's it to you?

I mean, Father will ask.

I'll tell him.

Angus glanced at me. Cappy seemed dead serious. His face was set in an expression I'd never seen before, or to be more accurate, his expression and the look in his eyes kept shifting—between despair and anger and some gentle moony rapture. I was so disturbed that I grabbed him by the shoulders and spoke into his face.

You can't do this.

Cappy terrified me then. He hugged me. When he stood back, I could tell that Angus was even more dismayed.

Look, I think I got the time wrong, he said. Please, Cappy, let's go swim.

No, no, you've got the time right, said Cappy. He touched our shoulders. Let's go in.

The church was nearly empty inside. There were a few people waiting for the confessional and a few up front praying at the feet of the Blessed Virgin, where there was a rack of votive candles flickering in red glass cups. Cappy and Angus slid into the back pew, where they knelt hunched over. Angus was closest to the confessional. He looked sideways at me over Cappy's bent head, made a rolling-eyed grimace, and jerked his head at the church door as if to say, Get him outta here! After Angus went into the confessional and closed the velvet drape after him, he poked his head out and made that face again. I squeezed close to Cappy and said, Cousin, please, I beg you, let's get the hell out of here. But Cappy had his eyes closed and if he heard me he made no sign. When Angus emerged, Cappy rose like a sleepwalker, stepped into the confessional, and shut the curtain behind him.

There were arcane sounds—the slide of the priest's window, the whispering back and forth—then the explosion. Father Travis burst from the wooden door of the confessional and would have caught Cappy if he hadn't rolled out from under the curtain and half crawled, half scrambled along the pew. Father ran back, blocking the exit, but already Cappy had sprung past us, hurdling the pews toward the front of the church, landing on the seats with each bound in a breathtaking series of vaulting leaps that took him nearly to the altar.

Father Travis's face had gone so white that red-brown freckles usually invisible stood out as if drawn on with a sharp pencil. He didn't lock the doors behind him before he advanced on Cappy—a mistake. He didn't count on Cappy's speed either, or on Cappy's practice at evading his older brother in a confined space. So for all Father Travis's military training he made several tactical errors going after Cappy. It looked like Father Travis could just walk down the center of the church and easily trap

Cappy behind the altar, and Cappy played into that. He acted confused and let Father Travis stride toward the front before he bolted to the side aisle and pretended to trip, which caused Father Travis to make a right-hand turn toward him down one of the pews. Once the priest was halfway along the pew, Cappy flipped down the kneeler and sped toward the open door, where we were standing alongside two awestruck old men. Father Travis could have cut him off if he'd run straight back, but he tried to get past the kneeler and ended up lunging along the stations of the cross. Cappy exited. Father Travis had the longer stride and gained but, instead of running down the steps, Cappy, well practiced as we all were at sliding down the iron pole banister, used that and gained impetus, a graceful push-off that sent him pell-mell down the dirt road with Father Travis too close behind for him to even grab his bike.

Cappy had those good shoes, but so, I noticed, did Father Travis. He wasn't running in sober clerical blacks but had perhaps been playing basketball or jogging before he dropped in to hear confessions. The two sprinted hotly down the dusty gravel road that led from the church into town. Cappy boldly crossed the highway and Father Travis followed. Cappy cut through yards he knew well and disappeared. But even in his cassock, which he'd hoisted and tucked into his belt, Father Travis was right behind him heading toward the Dead Custer Bar and Whitey's gas station. We marveled at Father's pale thick-muscled calves blurring in the sun.

What should we do?

Stay ready, I said.

Angus and I took our bikes from the rack and held Cappy's between us. We hoped he'd gain enough on Father Travis so he could jump on and we could pedal away. We watched the bit of road we could see far over the trees because it was there Cappy would appear if Father Travis didn't catch him. Soon, Cappy popped across. A moment later, Father Travis. Then they vanished and Angus said, He's trying to lose him by zigzagging through the BIA housing. He knows those yards too. We turned to watch the next patch of road where they would appear and again it was Cappy first, Father Travis not far behind. Cappy knew the front and back entrances of every building, and fled in and out of the hospital, the grocery, the senior citizens, the tiny casino we had back then. He doubled back through the Dead Custer and in and out of Whitey's. He took the road we'd taken past old lady Bineshi's, hoping he'd surprise the dogs and they'd fix their teeth in Father Travis's robe, but they made it through. Cappy hopscotched downhill through the graveyard and then the two of them made a loop that took them through the playground—it was mesmerizing to watch. Cappy set the swings going and sprang through the monkey bars, lightly touching down. Father Travis landed like an ape with knuckles on the ground, but kept going. They sprinted uphill, two tiny ciphers who now enlarged as Cappy ran toward us ready to jump on the bike we held and speed off. We would have made it. He would have made it. He came so close. Father Travis put on a burst of speed that brought him within a handsbreadth of Cappy's shirt collar. Cappy floated out from under that hand. But it came down and grabbed his back wheel.

Cappy jumped off the bike but Father Travis, purple in the face, wheezing, had him by the shoulders and bodily lifted him. Angus and I had dropped our bikes to plead his case. Although we couldn't have known for sure what Cappy planned to confess, it was now obvious. He had confessed what we feared he would confess.

Father, this does not look good, said Angus.

Let him down, please, Father Travis. I tried to imagine my father's voice in this situation. Cappy is a minor, I said. Perhaps that was absurd, but Father Travis had hold of Cappy's shirt now and had raised his fist and his fist stopped in the air.

A minor, I said, who came to you for help, Father Travis.

A Worf-like roar seized Father Travis and he threw Cappy on the ground. His foot went back but Cappy rolled out of range. We picked up our bikes because Father Travis wasn't moving now. He was standing there, breathing in deep gasps, head lowered, glaring from under his brow. We'd somehow gotten the upper moral ground in that moment and we knew it. We got on our bikes.

Good day, Father, said Angus.

Father Travis stared past us as we rode away.

Shit and hell, I said to Cappy later. What were you thinking?

Cappy shrugged.

You told him about the church basement, where you did it?

Everything, said Cappy.

Shit and hell.

Clemence frowned at my language.

Sorry, Auntie, I said. We had gone to Clemence and Edward's in hopes they were eating, which they weren't, but that didn't matter because Clemence knew why we came around and she immediately warmed up her usual hamburger macaroni, poured her usual swamp tea, only mixed, for us specially, with a can of lemonade. She fed Mooshum because he ate whenever anybody else ate, but his tremor had become so pronounced that he couldn't eat soup.

Why'd you tell him? I asked.

I dunno, said Cappy, maybe what he said about his woman. Or what he said to me about *You be the one to notice her*, remember?

He said notice her, not, you know. I was delicate around Cappy, even though Clemence wasn't listening right then. Although Cappy had had sex, it was on a higher plane, so I didn't use any sex words. He got upset when they were associated with anything that had happened between himself and Zelia.

You could have gone to your dad, gone to your older brother, talked with them, I said.

I'm glad I went to Father Travis though, said Cappy, grinning.

Cappy's run was already becoming history and his reputation would soar. Father Travis was not damaged by it either, as we'd never had a priest in such fine athletic shape.

The size of his calf muscles! said Clemence.

The last priest could not have run ten yards, said Mooshum. I saw him laid out in our yard once, dead drunk. That old priest weighed more than you and your skinny friends all put together. He cackled. But this new one has his pride. It will take him many prayers to get over Cappy's run.

God help the gophers this week, said Uncle Edward as he passed through the room.

Clemence brought a dish towel and tied it around Mooshum's neck. Between bites, he said, I ever tell you boys about the time I outrun Liver-Eating Johnson? How that old rascal used to track down Indians and kill us and take and eat our livers? That was a white wiindigoo, but when I was young and fleet, I run him down and whittled him away bite by bite and paid him back. I snapped off his ear with my teeth, and then his nose. Want to see his thumb?

You told them, said Clemence, who was intent on getting nourishment into his old gullet. But Mooshum wanted to talk.

Listen here, you boys. People say Liver-Eating Johnson was supposed to have escaped some Indians by chewing through a rawhide that bound his hands. The story had it he killed the young Indian who was guarding him and cut off that poor boy's leg. Supposedly that scoundrel run off with that leg into the wilderness and survived by eating it until he made his way into friendlier territory.

Open up, said Clemence, and filled his mouth.

But that was not how it happened, said Mooshum. For I was

there. I was hunting with some Blackfeet warriors when they caught Liver Eater. They planned on delivering him to the Crow Indians because he had killed so many of their people. I was sitting with that young Blackfeet who was supposed to guard him, but he wanted to kill Johnson so bad his hands twitched.

I talked to Liver Eater in the Blackfeet language, which he sort of understood. Liver Eater, I said, half the Blackfeet hate you so much they're gonna stake you down buck-naked and skin you alive. But they'll cut off your balls first and feed them to their old ladies right in front of your eyes.

Say there! said Clemence.

The Blackfeet's eyes just glowed, said Mooshum. I said to Liver Eater that the other half of the Blackfeet wanted to tie him securely between their two best war ponies and then charge in opposite directions. The Blackfeet boy's eyes sparked like candles at that. I told Liver-Eating Johnson that he was supposed to decide which of these fates he would prefer, so that the tribe could make preparations. Then we turned our backs on Liver Eater and warmed our hands over the fire. We left him to work on the rawhide thongs that bound his wrists. His ankles, too, were bound with strong ropes. Another rawhide at his waist fixed him to a tree. He had plenty to work on with his teeth, which were none too sturdy and that's the point. You never saw a white trapper's teeth, but they hadn't the habits we Indians had of scrubbing our teeth clean with a birch twig. They let their teeth rot. You could smell his breath a mile before a trapper came into view. His breath generally smelled worse than the rest of him and that is saying a lot, eh? Liver Eater's teeth were no different from any trapper's. And now he was trying to chew off his cords. Every so often, we would hear him curse and spit—there went one tooth, then another broke off. We panicked him into chawing until he was all gum. Never again could he bite into an Indian. But we planned to make him helpless altogether. This young

Blackfeet and me. He had a potion from his grandma that would make your eyes cross. As soon as Liver Eater fell asleep and snored, we dabbed that medicine onto his eyes. Now he couldn't shoot straight. He would have to become a sheriff. That is, if the Crows did not kill him. Still, you don't leave a rattlesnake alive to bite you next time you walk the path, I said to the Blackfeet, even if he don't have fangs.

I wish we didn't have to give him to the Crows, said the young man.

They need their fun, I said. But just in case he gets loose we should make sure he cannot pull the trigger on a gun. We could chop off his fingers, but then the Crow would say we'd stolen some of him.

There is a centipede if it bites a man his hands will swell up like mittens for the rest of his life, the Blackfeet told me. So we made little torches for ourselves and went around hunting for this bug, but while we were away Liver Eater did manage to escape. When we returned all we saw was the chewed straps on the ground surrounded by broken brown teeth. He got away. Then he made up the story about eating the Indian's leg because unless he had a good story who'd believe a toothless cross-eyed old bugger?

Exactly, said Clemence.

Awee, I'm going to miss that Sonja, said Mooshum, winking at me.

What?

Oh, said Clemence. Whitey says she cleared out. She played sick yesterday and he came home to find her closet empty and one of the dogs gone with her. She took off in her old rattletrap car he'd just fixed to run smooth.

Is she coming back? I said.

Whitey told me her note said never. He said he slept with the other dog, he was so broke up. She said he'd best clean up his act. Amen to that.

The news made me dizzy and I told Cappy we needed to go somewhere. He said his usual polite and traditional thank-you to Clemence and then we biked away together, slow. Finally we got to the road that led, though it was a long ride off, to the hanging tree where Sonja and I had buried the passbook savings books. We stopped our bikes and I told Cappy the entire story—finding the doll, showing it to Sonja, her helping me stash the money in those bank accounts, and then where we put the passbooks in the tin box. I told him about how Sonja insisted I keep quiet so as to not put him in danger. Then I told him about Sonja's diamond stud earrings and the lizard-skin boots and about the night Whitey beat on her and how it looked like she was planning to get away from him and I told him how much money I had found.

She could get real far on that, he said. He looked away, offended.

Yeah, I should have told you.

We didn't talk for a while.

We should go dig up the little box anyway, he said. Just to make sure. Maybe she left you some money, said Cappy. His voice was neutral.

Enough for shoes like yours, I said as we rode along.

I offered to trade, said Cappy.

It's okay. I like mine now. I bet she left me a goddamned note. That's what I bet.

We both turned out to be right.

There was two hundred dollars, one passbook, and a piece of paper.

Dear Joe,
Cash is for your shoes. Also I am leaving you saving acct. to spend on an IV education out east.

I looked inside the passbook. It was ten thousand.

Treat your mom good. Some day you might deserve how good you grew up. I can have a new life with the $. No more of what you saw.
Love anyways,
Sonja

What the hell, I said to Cappy.

What's she mean, what you saw?

I struggled. I wanted to tell the whole dance, every howl, every gliding move, and show him the tassel. But my tongue was stopped by obscure shame.

Nothing, I said.

I split the cash with Cappy and put the passbook and letter in my pocket. At first, he wouldn't take the money and then I said it was so he could get a bus ticket to visit Zelia in Helena. Travel money, then. He folded the bills in his hand.

We started back home and halfway there we scared up a pair of ducks from a watery ditch.

After a couple miles, Cappy laughed. I got a good one. How come ducks don't fly upside down? He didn't wait for me to answer. They're afraid of quacking up! Still happy with his wit, he left me at the door to have dinner with my mother and father. I went in and although we were quiet and distracted and still in a form of shock, we were together. We had candied yams, which I never liked but I ate them anyway. There was farmer ham and a bowl of fresh peas from the garden. My mother said a little prayer to bless the food and we all talked about Cappy's run. I even told them Cappy's joke. We stayed away from the fact of Lark's existence, or anything to do with our actual thoughts.

CHAPTER TEN

Skin of Evil

Linda Wishkob rolled out from her car and trudged to our door. I let my dad answer her knock and slipped out the back way. I'd finally worked out my thoughts in regard to Linda and her banana bread; although these thoughts did not make sense, I couldn't argue myself out of them. Linda was responsible for the existence of Linden. She'd saved her brother, even though she knew by then he was a skin of evil. She now repelled me like she'd repelled him and her birth mother, though my parents didn't feel the same way. As it turned out, while I was in the backyard running this way and that with Pearl, playing tag, though we never touched but whirled around each other in an unceasing trot, Linda Wishkob was giving my father information. What she told him would cause him to accompany my mother to her office and back home for the next two days. On the third day my father asked her to write him out a list for the grocery.

He insisted that we go instead of her and that she lock the door behind us and keep Pearl in the house. From all of this I gathered that Linden Lark was back in the area. My mind wouldn't go any farther. I wasn't thinking about it—I couldn't stand thinking about it. It was out of my mind entirely when my father asked me to go to the grocery store with him. I had been on my way to meet up with Cappy and carve out a newer and faster series of jumps in the dirt. I resented going with my father to the grocery, but he said it would take two of us to decipher and find all of the exact things my mother wanted—which, when I saw her slanted script with even the brand names listed and tiny bits of advice in choosing properly, looked like the truth.

That we have a real grocery store on our reservation is no small thing. It used to be that, besides the commodity warehouse, food came from the tiny precursor store—Puffy's Place. The old store sold mainly nonperishable items—tea, flour, salt, peanut butter—plus surplus garden vegetables or game meat. It sold beadwork, moccasins, tobacco, and gum. For real food our people had traveled off reservation twenty miles or more to put our money in the pockets of store clerks who watched us with suspicion and took our money with contempt. But with our own grocery now, run by our own tribal members and hiring our own people to bag and stock, we had something special. Even though the pop machine out front was banged in, the magic doors swished shut on slow grandmas, and children smudged the gumball machine until you couldn't see the colors of the candy, it was our very own grocery. Trucks came to it, like a regular store, stocked it, and then drove away.

My father and I walked in past the wall of tattered powwow posters and ads for cars to sell. We got a grocery cart. Dad unfolded the list.

Dried pinto beans.

I pointed out that Mom had instructed us to shake and examine the plastic bag of beans and make sure it contained no small rocks. We located the beans in the pasta aisle.

A spotted pebble is going to look just like a bean, I said to my father, turning the rectangular package this way and that.

We should stock up, said my father, throwing six or seven bags into the cart. These are cheap. We can spread the beans in a pan and check for rocks when we get home.

Tomato paste, canned tomatoes—Rotel, the kind with chilies—4 cans each. Five pounds of hamburger meat. Lean if you can get it, the list said.

Lean? Why would she want lean?

Less grease, said my father.

I like grease.

Me too.

He threw some packages into the cart.

Cumin, I read. In the spice aisle we found cumin.

She was making extra food to bring to Clemence, to pay her back for all the dinners.

I read. Lettuce, carrots, then onions and we're supposed to smell the onions first to make sure they aren't rotten inside.

Fruit. Whatever fruit is good, said my father, peering over my shoulder at the list. I guess we are able to make that decision, anyway, regarding the fruit. What do you think?

We looked at a pile of muskmelons. Some had spots. There were grapes. All had spots. There was a bucket of local berries and some plums. Dad chose a melon and filled paper bags with plums and a plastic mesh bucket with the berries.

We bought chicken, an anemic-looking fryer, cut up, and we counted all the packaged pieces like she said. We bought another package that contained only thighs. We bought barbecue sauce and Old Dutch potato chips, for me. A couple of cans of mushroom soup went into the cart. At the bottom of the list was milk and butter, a 1-pound box of wrapped sticks, salted, and 1 pound wrapped whole, sweet. Cream.

What does she mean wrapped whole? My father stopped beside me, frowning at the paper. He held a carton of cream in one hand. Why sweet? Why salted?

I was pushing the cart in front of my dad, and so I saw

Linden Lark first. He was leaning into the cold light of the open meat case. My father must have looked up just after I did. There was a moment where all we did was stare. Then motion. My father threw the cream, surged forward, and grabbed Lark by the shoulders. He spun Lark, jamming him backward, then gripped Lark around the throat with both hands. As I've said before, my dad was somewhat clumsy. But he attacked with such an instinct of sudden rage it looked slick as a movie stunt. Lark banged his head against the metal racks of the cooler. A carton of lard smashed down and Lark slipped in the burst cream, scraping the back of his head down the lower edge of the case, ringing the shelves. The glass doors flapped against my father's arms as he fell with Lark, still pressing. Dad kept his chin down. His hair had fallen in strings about his ears and his face was dark with blood. Lark flailed, unable to put a similar grip on my father. I was on him too, now, with the cans of Rotel tomatoes.

The thing was, Lark seemed to be smiling. If you can smile while being choked and can-beaten, he was doing it. Like he was excited by our attack. I smashed the can on his forehead and opened a cut just over Lark's eye. A pure black joy in seeing his blood filled me. Blood and cream. I smashed as hard as I could and something—maybe the shock of my happiness or Lark's happiness—caused my father to let go of Lark's throat. Lark kicked upward and pushed with all his might. My father went skidding backward. With a hard jolt my father landed in the aisle, and Lark fled in a scrambled crouch.

That was when my father had his first heart attack—it turned out to be a small one. Not even a medium one. Just a small one. But it was a heart attack. In the grocery store aisle in the spilt cream and rolling cans, next to the Prell shampoo, my father's face went a dull yellow color. He strained for breath. He looked up at me, perplexed. And because he had his hand on his chest, I said, Do you want the ambulance?

When he nodded *yes*, everything went out of me. I went down on my knees, and Puffy made the call.

They tried to tell me I couldn't ride with him to the hospital but I fought. I stayed with him. They couldn't make me leave him. I knew what happened if you let a parent get too far away.

We stayed down in Fargo for almost a week and spent the days at St. Luke's Hospital. On the first day, my father had an operation that is now routine, but which at the time was new. It involved inserting stents into three arteries. He looked weak and diminished in the hospital bed. Although the doctors said that he was doing well, of course I was afraid. I could only look in at him, at first, from the hall. When he was moved into his own room, things were better. We all sat together and talked about nothing, everything. This seems odd, but it soon became a kind of a vacation to be there, safe, together, our conversation vague. We'd walk the halls, pretend shock at the mushy food, talk some more about nothing.

At night, my mother and I went back to the room we shared at the hotel. We had twin beds. On other trips, the three of us had always bunked together, Mom and Dad in a double. I would sleep on a rollaway in some corner. This was the first time I could remember staying alone anywhere with just my mother. There was an awkwardness; her physical presence bothered me. I was glad she'd brought Dad's old blue bathrobe made of towel cloth, the one she'd kept pestering him to get rid of. The nap was worn down in places, the sleeve unraveling, the hem frayed. I'd thought that she brought it for him, but then she put it on the first night. I imagined she had forgotten her own robe, which was printed with golden flowers and green leaves. But the second morning I woke early and looked over at her, still sleeping. She was wearing my father's robe. I checked that night to see if she was wearing his robe on purpose, and sure enough she got into bed wearing it. The room wasn't cold. It occurred to me the next day, as I was wandering around the park outside the hospital, that it would feel good if I had something of Dad's to wear, too. It would tie us together somehow.

I needed him so much. I couldn't really go into it very far, this need, nor could my mother and I talk about it. But her wearing his robe was a sign to me of how she had to have the comfort of his presence in a basic way that I now understood. That night, I asked her if she'd packed Dad an extra shirt, and she nodded when I asked if I could wear it. She gave it to me.

I still have many of his shirts, and his ties as well. He purchased everything he wore at Silverman's in Grand Forks. They carried the very best men's clothing, and he didn't buy much, but he was particular. I wore my father's ties to get me through law school at the University of Minnesota, and the bar exam after. For the time I was a public prosecutor, I wore his ties for the last week of every jury trial. I used to carry around his fountain pen, too, but I became afraid of losing it. I still have it, but I don't sign my tribal court opinions with it the way he did. The unfashionable ties are enough, the golden tassel in my drawer, and that I have always had a dog named Pearl.

I was wearing my father's shirt on the day he stopped being vague, the second-to-last day we were there. He saw his shirt on me and looked quizzical. My mother left to get some coffee and I sat with him. This was the first time I was really alone with him. It did not surprise me that even while his incisions were healing he chose to revisit the situation, to ask if I knew anything of Lark's whereabouts. I had been thinking the same way, but of course I didn't. If Clemence had told my mother in their phone conversations from the hotel room, I didn't know about it. But then that night I did get a call; it was while my mother was out buying a newspaper. It was Cappy.

Some members of our family paid a visit, he said.

I didn't know what he was talking about.

Here?

No, *there.*

Where?

They brought him around.

What?

The Holodeck, dummy. It was a situation like when Picard was the detective. Remember? The persuasion?

Right. I was flooded, tingling with relief. Right. Is he dead?

No, just persuaded. They messed him up good, man. He won't come around you. Tell your mom and dad.

After the call, I was thinking how to tell them. How to make it sound like I didn't know it was Doe and Randall and Whitey, even Uncle Edward, who went to Lark's, when another call came in. My mother had come back. I could tell the call was from Opichi when my mother asked if there was something wrong at the office. The cadence of the voice, tiny in the receiver, was shrill and intense. My mother sat down on the bed. Whatever she heard wasn't good. Eventually, she put the receiver in its cradle, and then she curled up on the bed, her back to me.

Mom?

She didn't answer. I remember the buzz of lights on in the bathroom. I walked around to the other side of the bed and knelt down beside it. She opened her eyes and looked at me. At first she seemed confused and her eyes searched my face almost as if she were looking at me for the first time, or at least after a long absence. Then she focused and her mouth creased in a frown. She whispered.

I guess people beat him up.

That's good, I said. Yeah.

And then, Opichi says, he drove back all crazy and blasted up to the gas station. He said something to Whitey about his rich girlfriend. How Whitey's rich girlfriend had herself a nice setup and he was thinking of joining her. He drove through, yelling, making fun of Whitey. He got away. Whitey chased him with a wrench. What was he talking about? Sonja isn't rich.

I sat there with my mouth open.

Joe?

I put my head down in my hands, my elbows on my knees. After a while, I lay down and put a pillow over my head.

This room's hot, said my mother. Let's get the blower going.

We cooled off and went to a little restaurant called the 50s Cafe for hamburgers, french fries, chocolate shakes. We ate silently. Then all of a sudden, my mother put down the hamburger. She laid it on her plate and said, No.

Still chewing, I stared at her. The slight droop of her eyelid gave her a critical air.

Is there something wrong with that burger, Mom?

She gazed past me, transfixed by a thought. The knife crease shot up between her eyebrows.

It's something Daddy told me. A story about a wiindigoo. Lark's trying to eat us, Joe. I won't let him, she said. I will be the one to stop him.

Her determination terrified me. She picked up her food and deliberately, slowly, began to eat. She didn't stop until she'd finished all of it, which also frightened me. This was the first time since the attack she ate all the food on her plate. Then we went back to the room, got ready for bed. My mother took a pill and fell asleep at once. I stared at the feeble soundproofing insulation tiles on the ceiling. If I watched them closely enough, I could feel my own heart wind down. My chest opened and my stomach stopped grinding. I counted out, slowly and evenly, 78 random holes in the tile just over my head, and 81 in the next. If my mother went after Lark, he'd kill her. I knew this. I counted the holes again and again.

On the day we left Fargo, I woke early. My mother was up, in the bathroom making brushing and washing sounds. I listened to the shower water rattle down. The hotel curtains were so heavy I didn't know that it was pouring outside too. One of those rare August rains that tamp down the dust flares on the roads had just begun. A rain that washes the whitened dust-coated leaves. A rain that fills the cracks in the earth and revives the brown grasses. That grows the corn by a foot and makes a second cutting of hay possible. A gentle rain that lasts for days. There was a chill in the air that persisted all the way home. My mother drove with the windshield wipers going. The coziest of sounds to a boy drowsing in the backseat. My father stayed alert beside my mother, covered with a quilt. From time to time I'd open my eyes, just to see them. He had his hand across the seat, resting on her leg above the knee. Occasionally she took one hand off the wheel, reached down, and rested her hand on top of his.

During this ride of peace, so like my earliest memories of going places with my parents, it came to me what I must do. A thought descended into me as I lay beneath my own soft old quilt. I pushed it out. The thought fell back. Three times I pushed it out, each time harder. I hummed to myself. I tried to talk, but my mother put her finger to her lips and pointed at my father, who was asleep. The thought came again, more insistent, and this time I let it in and reviewed it. I thought this idea through to its conclusion. I stood back from my thought. I watched myself think.

The end of thinking occurred.

When we got home, Clemence had fixed the chili. Puffy had delivered all of the groceries that we had picked out. Everything we needed was stowed in the cupboards and the refrigerator. I saw my box of potato chips right away, sitting on the counter. I thought of the cans of tomatoes I had used as weapons. Clemence had probably opened them and added them to the chili. Every day since the grocer, I wished I had brained Lark. I imagined myself killing him over and over. But since I hadn't, I was going to visit Father Travis first thing in the morning. I decided I would join his Saturday morning catechism class. I thought he would let me do that. I also hoped that if I made myself useful afterward up at the church, he might notice how the gophers had been driven from the tunnels by the rain and now were fattening on the new grass. They needed to be dealt with. I hoped that Father Travis might teach me how to shoot gophers, so that I could get some practice.

I wasn't exactly starting from scratch when it came to being a Catholic. Priests and nuns have been here since the beginning of the reservation. Even the most traditional Indians, the people who'd kept the old ceremonies alive in secret, either had Catholicism beaten into them in boarding school, or had made friends with some of the more interesting priests, as Mooshum had for a time, or they had decided to hedge their bets by adding the saints to their love of the sacred pipe. Everybody had extremely devout or at least observant family members; I had been lobbied over and over, for instance, by Clemence. She had persuaded my mother (she hadn't bothered with my father) to have me baptized and had campaigned for my first communion and confirmation. I knew what I was in for. The God Squad had not been doctrinal, but my classes would be filled with lists. Confession: i. Sacramental. ii. Annual. iii. Sacrilegious. iv. Legal. Grace: i. Actual. ii. Baptismal. iii. Efficacious. iv. Elevating. v. Habitual. vi. Illuminating. vii. Imputed. viii. Interior. ix. Irresistible. x. Natural. xi. Prevenient. xii. Sacramental. xiii. Sanctifying. xiv. Sufficient. xv. Substantial. xvi. At meals. xvii. There were also Actual, Formal, Habitual, Material, Moral, Original, and Venial Sin. There were special types of sins: those against the Holy Ghost, Sins of Omission, Sins of Others, Sin by Silence, and the Sin of Sodom. There were Sins Crying Out to Heaven for Vengeance.

There were, of course, definitions of each of these categories on the lists. Father Travis taught like Vatican II had never happened. Nobody looked over his shoulder way up here. He said Latin mass if he felt like it and for several months the previous winter had turned the altar away from the congregation and conducted the Mysteries with a sort of wizardy flourish, Angus said. When it came to teaching catechism, he added subject matter or dismissed it. Saturday morning, he let me into the church basement and told me to take a seat in the cafeteria. I did, trying not to look down at the rug and think of Cappy. Bugger Pourier, reforming again after years of a stumblebum life in the Cities, was the only other student in the dim room. He was a skinny sorrowful man, with the fat purple clown nose of a longtime drinker. His sisters had dressed him in clean clothes, but he still smelled musty, like he'd been sleeping in a moldy corner. I looked over the handouts and listened to Father Travis talk about each member of the Holy Trinity. After class was done and Bugger wandered off, I asked Father Travis if I could take personal instruction all next week.

Do you have some goal in mind?

I want to be confirmed by the end of summer.

We get one visit from the bishop in the spring and everybody gets confirmed at that time. Father Travis looked me over. What's your rush?

It would help things.

What things?

Things at home, maybe, if I could pray.

You can pray without being confirmed. He handed me a pamphlet.

Plus, he said, you can pray by just talking to God. You can use your own words, Joe. You don't have to be confirmed in order to pray.

Father, I have a question.

He waited.

I had heard a phrase mentioned long ago and had stored it

in my mind. I asked, What are Sins Crying Out to Heaven for Vengeance?

He cocked his head to the side as though he was listening to a sound I couldn't hear. Then he flipped through his catechism book and pointed out the definition. The sins that cried out for vengeance were murder, sodomy, defrauding a laborer, oppressing the poor.

I thought I knew what sodomy was and believed it included rape. So my thoughts were covered by church doctrine, a fact I had found out the very first day.

Thanks, I said to Father Travis. I'll see you Monday.

He nodded, his eyes thoughtful.

Yes, I'm sure you will.

On Sunday, I sat through mass with Angus and on Monday morning I was at church right after breakfast. It was raining again, and I had eaten a huge bowl of my mother's oatmeal. It had weighed me down on my bike and sat warm and heavy in my stomach now. I wanted to go back to sleep, and so, probably, did Father Travis. He looked pallid and maybe hadn't slept so well. He hadn't shaved yet. The skin beneath his eyes was blue and the coffee was harsh on his breath. The cafeteria counter was stacked with neatly boxed-up food and the trash cans were stuffed.

Was there a wake down here? I asked.

Mr. Pourier's mother died. Which means we have probably seen the last of him. He was hoping to reconcile with the church while she was still conscious. By the way, I have a book for you. He handed me a soft old splayed paperback of *Dune*. So. Shall we start with the Eucharist? I saw you at mass with Angus. Did you understand what was happening?

I had memorized the pamphlet, so I said yes.

Can you tell me?

There was a sharing of the grace-producing food of our souls.

Very good. Anything else?

The body and blood of Christ were present in the wine and crackers?

Communion wafers, yes. Anything else?

As I wracked my mind the rain quit. A sudden flare of sunshine hit the dusty glass of the basement windows and spun motes of dust in the air. The basement was aslant with shimmering veils of light.

Uh, spiritual nutrition?

Right. Father Travis smiled at the dancing slashes of air around us and up at the windows. Since it's just us two, whaddya say we take our class outside?

I followed Father Travis up the steps, out the side door, and along the path that led through dripping pines. The grass path made a loop behind the gym and school, down through the rows of trees and over again to the road where Cappy and Father Travis had made the most dramatic part of their run. As we walked he told me that in order to prepare for the Eucharist when I would become part of the Mystical Body of Christ, I would have to purify myself via the sacrament of confession.

In order to purify yourself, you have to understand yourself, Father Travis went on. Everything out in the world is also in you. Good, bad, evil, perfection, death, everything. So we study our souls.

All right, I said faintly. Look, Father! There's a gopher.

Yes. He stopped and looked at me. How's your soul doing?

I glanced around as if my soul would appear so I could check on it. But there was only Father Travis's carefully planed, too handsome face, his grave, pale eyes shining uncannily, his sculpted lips.

I don't know, I said. I'd like to shoot some gophers.

He started walking again and from time to time I glanced at him, but he didn't speak. Finally, when we turned into the trees, he said, Evil.

What?

We've got to address the problem of evil in order to understand your soul or any other human soul.

Okay.

There are types of evil, did you know that? There is material evil, that which causes suffering without reference to humans but gravely affecting humans. Disease and poverty, calamities of any natural sort. Material evils. These we can't do anything about. We have to accept that their existence is a mystery to us. Moral evil is different. It is caused by human beings. A person does something deliberately to another person to cause pain and torment. That is a moral evil. Now you came up here, Joe, to investigate your soul hoping to get closer to God because God is all good, all powerful, all healing, all merciful, and so on. He paused.

Right, I said.

So you have to wonder why a being of this immensity and power would allow this outrage—that one human being should be allowed by God to directly harm another human being.

Something hurt in me, shot straight through me. I kept walking, my head down.

The only answer to this, and it isn't an entire answer, said Father Travis, is that God made human beings free agents. We are able to choose good over evil, but the opposite too. And in order to protect our human freedom, God doesn't often, very often at least, intervene. God can't do that without taking away our moral freedom. Do you see?

No. But yeah.

The only thing that God can do, and does all of the time, is to draw good from any evil situation.

I went cold.

He does, said Father Travis, his voice rising a little. In every instance, Joe. In every heart-soaking instance. As the priest here you know well I have buried infants and whole families killed in car accidents and young people who made terrible choices, and even people who got lucky enough to die old. Yes, I've seen it. Every time there is an evil, much good comes of it—people in these circumstances choose to do an extra amount of good, show unusual love, become stronger in their devotion to Jesus, or to their own favorite saint, or attain an unusual communion of some sort in their families. I have seen it in people who go their own ways, your traditionals, and never come to mass except for funerals. I admire them. They come to the wakes. Even if they are so poor they have nothing, they give the last of their nothing to another human. We are never so poor that we cannot bless another human, are we? So it is that every evil, whether moral or material, results in good. You'll see.

I stopped walking. I looked at the field, not at Father Travis. I shifted the book he'd given me from hand to hand. I felt like throwing it. Gophers were popping up and down, uttering their cheerful tweets.

I'd sure like to shoot some gophers, I said through my teeth.

We won't be doing that, Joe, said Father Travis.

Our dusty old midsummer reservation town sparkled all washed clean as I rode down the hill, past the BIA houses, up the road past the water tower place toward the Lafournais spread. There were three Lafournais allotments bordering on one another and although they were divided many times they never did go out of the family. The houses were connected by threads of roads and trails, but Doe's was the main house, the ranch style closest to the road, and Cappy was there leaning on the deck rail with his shirt open and a set of free weights on the decking by his feet.

I stopped, sat back on my bike seat.

Any girls come by to watch you pump iron?

Nobody came by, said Cappy. Nobody worth this vision.

He pretended to rip his shirt open and pounded his smooth

chest. He was better since last week—he had got two letters from Zelia.

Here. He made me come up on the deck and lift his weights for a while.

You should get your dad to buy you some weights. You can lift in your bedroom until you're presentable.

Presentable like you think you are. Is there any beer?

Better than that, said Cappy.

He reached into his jeans pocket and took out a sandwich bag rolled carefully around a lone joint.

Hey, blood brother!

Me sparkum up, kemo sabe, said Cappy.

We decided to smoke it on the overlook. If we walked along the spine of a small wooded ridge down Cappy's road we could climb to a higher spot from which we could see the golf course from close up, though we were hidden. We had watched the earnest players before—Indians and whites—as they wiggled their hips, gave shrewd looks, swung well or disastrously. Everything they did was funny: puffing out their chests or smashing down their golf clubs. We always watched the arc of the ball in case they couldn't find it. We still had our bucket full of golf balls. Cappy put some bannock, two soft apples, pop, plus a lone beer in a plastic bag and tied it to his handlebars. We rode off, dragged our bikes into the brush at the turnoff, and walked up the hill and along the ridge to our lookout spot.

The ground was almost dry. The rain had been sucked into the porous leaves and thirsty earth. The ticks were mostly gone. We leaned our backs against an oak tree that gave perfect shade. I held the joint too long. Quit chiefin' it, said Cappy. I'd got lost in my thinking. The weed was harsh and stale. We drank the beer. A little party of big-bellied men in white hats and yellow shirts, a team of some sort, came into view and we laughed at every move they made. But they were good golfers and didn't lose any golf balls. There was a lull after they passed. We smoked the roach and ate the tar bits with our food. Cappy turned to me. His hair was so long now, he flung it back with a certain head shake. Angus and Zack were already trying to fling the hair from their eyes, but couldn't bring off the imitation. It was a gesture sure to drive girls crazy.

How come you went to mass and took catechism from that asshole?

News flies fast, I said.

Yeah, said Cappy, it sure does. He wouldn't let up. Why? he asked again.

Wouldn't you think, I said, a guy whose mom suffered what she did and the skin of evil shows up.

The skin of evil, oh yeah, the tar guy who killed Yar. So, Lark.

For no reason. The skin of evil shows up in the fucking grocery and his dad has a fucking heart attack trying to kill him. Wouldn't you think that a kid who witnessed all this would need spiritual help?

Cappy looked me over. Nah.

Right. I brooded down at the clipped green for a while.

Nah, he said again. There's something else.

Okay, I said. I needed practice shooting. Like I thought he'd let me help shoot the gophers. But he just gave me a book.

Cappy laughed. You dumb-ass!

Yeah. I imitated Father Travis talking: *We won't be doing that, Joe. Good will always come out of evil. You'll see.*

You'll see? He said that?

Yeah.

Butt-fucker. If that was true, all good things would start in bad things. If you wanna shoot, said Cappy, you coulda gone to your uncle.

I'm off Whitey.

Better me. You shoulda come to me. Anytime. Anytime,

my brother. I been hunting since I was two. I got my first buck when I was nine.

I know it. But it wasn't just shooting gophers. You know that.

I might. I might know that.

You know what it is. What I'm talking about.

I do. I guess I do. Cappy nodded, looking down at a new set of golfers, Indian ones this time, who didn't match.

So if you know, you also know I won't implicate anybody else.

Implicate. Big lawyer word.

Should I define it?

Fuck you. I'm your best friend. I'm your number one.

I'm your number one, too. I do it alone or I don't do it.

Cappy laughed. He reached around to his back pocket suddenly and took out a squashed pack of his brother's cigarettes. Shit, I forgot about these.

They were crumpled but not torn apart. This time I noticed the matches had Whitey's station on them.

Now he's got matches, I said.

My brother got 'em. I never went there. But Randall said he's moving on, he's gonna rent out movies. Anyway, back to the subject.

What subject.

I don't need to know. We'll take my dad's deer rifle out and practice, because, Joe, you can't hit the side of a truck.

Maybe not.

And then where would you be when the side of the truck gets pissed off and runs you down? Shit outta luck. I can't let that happen to you.

Except his rifle. I can't use his rifle.

Just to practice. Then Doe's gun gets stolen while we're gone. While the house is empty. We hide the gun, the ammunition. And we're not here anyway to laugh at geezers, are we.

No.

We're scouting.

In case he comes along. I know he golfs, used to anyway. Linda told me.

Everybody knows Lark golfs, which is good. Anyone can miss a deer and hit a golfer.

We rode back to Cappy's and went out back where Cappy had started practicing when he was five years old.

My dad taught me on a .22, said Cappy, just gophers or squirrels, hardly no kick to speak of. Then the first time we went deer hunting he hands me his 30.06. I tell him I'm worried it'll kick, but he says no more than the .22, I promise you, my boy, just go easy. So I get my first deer on one shot. Know why?

'Cause you're an Emperor?

No, my son, because I didn't feel the kick. I wasn't worried about the kick. I shot smooth. Sometimes you learn on a 30.06 and you flinch while you jerk the trigger, 'cause you can't help anticipate the kick. I wish I could teach you on a .22 like my dad did, but you're ruined already.

I did feel ruined. I knew I'd jerk the trigger, knew I'd flinch, knew how awkwardly I'd work the bolt action, how I'd probably jam it up, knew how I might as well cross my eyes as sight a target.

There was a rail fence where we set out cans and shot them down, and set up cans and shot them down. Cappy shot the first off neatly, showing me exactly how, but I couldn't hit a single one of the rest. I was probably the only boy on the whole reservation who couldn't shoot. My father hadn't cared, but Whitey had tried to teach me. I was just no good at it. I couldn't aim straight.

Lucky you're not an old-time Indian. You woulda starved, said Cappy.

Maybe I need glasses. I was discouraged.

Maybe you should close one eye.

I'm doing that.

The other eye.

Both eyes?

Yeah, you might do better.

I hit three out of ten. I shot until we used most of the expensive ammunition, a problem as Cappy pointed out. We couldn't let anybody know I was practicing. He couldn't ask Doe for ammunition without explaining why. We also decided I should only practice when there was nobody home. In fact, Cappy said we had to find a more remote place for me to practice—we could go two pastures over and be out of sight, although people would hear us.

We have to get money though, hitch over to Hoopdance or get a ride. We'll go into the hardware and I'll buy the ammo.

No, I said, I should go myself.

So we argued back and forth until I had to leave. I had strict hours—my mother had told me she would send the police out after me if I was not home at six.

The police?

Just a figure of speech, she'd said. Maybe Uncle Edward. You wouldn't want him out looking for you, would you?

No, I didn't want Uncle Edward out looking for me in his big car, riding slow and rolling down his window, questioning everyone who happened to be out. So I went home. I had the money that Sonja left me. One hundred dollars hidden in my closet in that folder labeled HOMEWORK. Thinking of Sonja was like punching a bruise. As I rode back I decided on a plan to get my mother to drive me to Hoopdance. She still thought I was taking catechism classes. I'd need candles, maybe. Or dress shoes to be an altar boy.

The shoes were a good touch. After work the next day she drove me to the shoe store and bought the dress shoes, which

I regretted for the waste of money. But I got into the hardware and sporting goods store on a casual excuse, and she waited outside while I bought forty dollars' worth of ammunition for Doe's rifle. The clerk did not know me and examined the large bill closely. I looked over at the paints, the basketballs and baseballs, the golf corner, the nail bins and spools of wire, at the home canning section, the shovels, rakes, chain saws, and I noticed gas cans for sale. Exactly like the one I'd found in the lake.

I guess it's okay, the clerk said, giving me change.

When I came back out, I told my mother that I'd bought a surprise for Dad, who was supposed to take it easy. Besides the ammo, I had bought spinners for bass, our favorite fish to catch. I was building lie upon lie and it all came naturally to me as honesty once had. As we were driving home, I realized that my deceits were of no consequence as I was dedicated to a purpose which I'd named in my mind not vengeance but justice.

Sins Crying Out to Heaven for Justice.

I might have murmured this aloud. I was in a kind of trance, looking at the road, imagining the amount of practice it would take.

What did you say?

My mother had kept that edge. She was protective of my father and it gave her an intent authority, but more than that, there was what she had told me in Fargo when she put down the hamburger. *I will be the one.* No you won't, I thought. But she was keen as a blade, as if during that time she lay dull in her closed room she had actually been sharpening herself. And then in Fargo, we'd talked about Dad, about things the doctors said. We'd weighed facts and questions together. She had treated me like someone older than I was, and this, too, had continued. She saw too much, didn't have the same mild patience with me. She had quit indulging me. Never laughed at things I did. It was as if she had expected me to grow up in those weeks and now to not need her. If she expected me to act alone on my instincts, I was doing just that. But I still needed her. I had needed her to drive me to Hoopdance. No, I needed her in ways that now were lost to me. On the drive back from Hoopdance that day, after I had muttered that phrase about Sins Crying Out to Heaven, I asked her directly the thing my father would not ask. It was a childish thing, but also grown-up.

Mom, I said, why couldn't you have lied? Why couldn't you have said that sack slipped? You stumbled over something and you put your hand up, pulled it out, saw the ground? That you knew where it happened? It wouldn't matter *where*, if you had just said where.

She was quiet for so long that I thought she wouldn't answer. I felt no anger from her, no surprise, no embarrassment, merely a period of concentration.

I wish I knew, she said at last, why I could not lie. Last week, in the hospital, I sat there looking at your father and I suddenly wished that I had lied from the beginning. *I wish I had lied, Joe!* But I didn't know where it happened. And your father knew I didn't know. And you knew, too. I told you both. How could I change my story later on? Commit perjury? And remember, I knew that I didn't know, too. What would happen to my sense of who I am? But if I had understood all that would come of my not knowing, exactly what happened, him going free, him with the sick gall to show himself, I would have.

I'm glad you would have.

She looked straight ahead.

Clearly, she was done talking. I looked at the road coming at us, thinking: If you had lied, if you had changed your story, so what. You're my mom. I'd love you. Dad would love you. You lied to save Mayla and her baby. You did that easy. If they could prosecute Linden Lark, I would not have to lie about the ammunition or practice to do what someone had to do. And quickly, before my mother figured out her version of *stopping him*. There was no one else who could do it. I saw that. I was only thirteen and if I got caught I would only be subject to juvenile justice laws, not to mention there were clearly extenuating circumstances. My lawyer could point out my good grades and use that good-kid reputation I had apparently developed. Yet, it was not that I wanted to do it, or even thought I could do it. I was a bad shot and I knew that. I might not get much better. Plus, the reality of the thing. So I didn't let the whole of it enter my mind at any one time. I only let one piece and then another piece fall into place. We fell silent again. After a while, I realized the next piece: I was going to have to go to Linda Wishkob. I was going to have to find out if her brother played golf anymore, for sure, and if he had some kind of schedule. I was going to have to get some soft and spotted bananas, or buy some firm bananas and allow them strategically to rot.

Three days of shooting practice later, I showed up at the post office with a bag of bananas I'd watched carefully in my room. They were soft and spotted, but not black.

Linda peered over the scale at her window, her round eyes glistening. And that unbearable, doggy grin. I bought six stamps for Cappy, and gave her the bag of bananas. She took the bag with her chubby little paws, and when she opened it her whole face glowed as though I'd given her something precious.

Are they from your mother?

No, I said, from me.

She flushed with pleasure and wonder.

They are perfect, she said. I'll bake when I get home and drop them by tomorrow after work.

I left. I'd learned from my mistake with Father Travis that unusual politeness from a boy my age is an instant suspicion-raiser. I would have to maintain my course until the moment was right. I would have to have more than one conversation, maybe several conversations, before I would dare fit in a question or two about Linda's brother. So I made sure I was hanging around the house the next day at five o'clock when Linda pulled her car into the driveway. I looked out the window and said to Dad, There's Linda. I'll bet you a buck she has banana bread.

You win, he said without looking up.

He was sipping water. Reading yesterday's *Fargo Forum*. Mom walked downstairs. She was wearing black pants and a pink T-shirt. Her hair was fluffy and tinted to a shiny darkness. She wore black-and-pink-beaded earrings and her feet were bare. I saw she'd painted her toenails pink. There was the subtle coloring of makeup—her features more dramatic. And that light lemon lotion as she passed by. I got close to her. Stood behind her as she opened the door and accepted the familiar foil brick. She was dressing up for Dad. I wasn't too dumb to figure that out. She was looking nice to keep his spirits up. Linda entered, sat down in the living room, and Dad put down his newspaper.

Joe, here's another loaf for you. She pulled another brick from the bag. She didn't thank me for the bananas in front of my parents, which surprised me. Most grown-ups think everything a young person does should be common knowledge. They brag about the slightest gesture from a boy. I'd been prepared to play down my banana giving, but Linda didn't put me in that position. She did, however, start in on the weather chatter with my father. Just the way they had before, they pulled out their favorite all-eternal commonplace-choked subject. Sure enough, my mother folded and went into the kitchen to make tea and slice up the banana bread. I decided to try a whole other ploy and sat down across from them on the couch. Sooner or later, they would slog through the atmosphere and say something important. Or Dad would leave and I could bring up golf. They were on rain: inches fallen in which county, and whether we might see hail. They got to hail they'd seen and various forms of hail damage, when I yawned, lay back, and closed my eyes.

I pretended to fall into a deep, impermeable slumber, twitching once and then breathing with such deep regularity I was sure they would be convinced. I let myself go limp and heavy. They were talking hail big as golf balls, perfectly round as peas, hail that penetrated roof shingles like BB shot. The couch was wide, the pillows giving. I woke an hour later. Mom was calling my name softly, sitting on the edge of the couch, patting my shin. As happens sometimes drifting out of an unexpected sleep, I did not know exactly where I was. I kept my eyes closed. My mother's voice and the childhood sensation of her hand stroking my ankle, which was always how she woke me, flooded me with peace. I allowed my consciousness to sink to an even younger hiding place where nothing could touch me.

When I finally did wake, all was dark, the house silent. Pearl panted in her sleep, curled on the braided oval rug across the room. A knitted afghan had been thrown over me. I'd kicked it off and I was cold. I had missed supper and was hungry, so I wrapped myself in the afghan and padded into the kitchen. Pearl rose and followed me. A tinfoil-covered plate of food glinted on the table. The moon was full again and the kitchen was alive with pale energy. Now that I have lived some, I understand what happened to me in the kitchen that night, and why it happened when it happened. During my sleep I'd dropped my guard. The thoughts that protected my thoughts had fallen away. I was left with my real thoughts. My knowledge of what I planned. With those thoughts came fear. I had never really been afraid before, not for myself. For my mother and father, yes, but that fear had been shared and immediate, not secret. And my worst terrors of loss had not materialized. Though damaged, my parents were sleeping upstairs, in the same room, the same bed. But I understood their peace was temporary. Lark would appear again. Unless they found Mayla dead, or she showed up alive and filed a kidnapping charge, he was free to walk this earth.

I had to do what I had to do. This act was before me. In the uncanny light a sense of dread so overwhelmed me that tears started in my eyes and a single choking sound, a sob maybe, a wrench of hurt, burst from my chest. I crossed my fists in the knitting and squeezed them against my heart. I didn't want to blurt out the sound. I didn't want to give a voice to this roil of sensation. But I was naked and tiny before its power. I had no choice. I muffled the sounds I made so that I alone could hear them come out of me, gross and foreign. I lay on the floor, let fear cover me, and I tried to keep breathing while it shook me like a dog shakes a rat.

I lay under this spell for maybe half an hour, and then it went away. I hadn't known whether it would or not. I had clenched my whole body so tightly that it hurt to let go. I was sore when I got up off the floor, like an old man with joint pains. I shuffled slowly up the stairs to my bed. Pearl had stayed by me all along. She'd huddled next to me. I kept her with me now. As I fell into a darker sleep, I understood that I had learned something. Now that I knew fear, I also knew it was not permanent. As powerful as it was, its grip on me would loosen. It would pass.

I could not use the bananas a second time, so I decided to run into Linda around noon. I knew that she brought her own lunch most days, but treated herself once a week to what women always got at Mighty's—the soup and salad bar. I checked the window every day, or went inside and had a grape pop. On the third day, I saw Linda approach the café with her cheerful Tonka Truck walk. She waved at Bugger, who was sitting on the narrow strip of stained grass between the two buildings. She stopped and gave him a cigarette. It was a surprise to me that she smoked, but I found out later she carried around a pack just to give a mooch to people when they asked. I parked my bike where I could see it from inside and followed her in. Of course, she knew everyone and talked to everyone. She didn't notice me until she sat down. I pretended to suddenly see her. Her eyes popped with the thrill of it.

Joe!

I came over and stood looking around, as if for my friends, until she asked if I was hungry.

Kinda.

Then sit down.

She ordered a shrimp basket. Then without asking me, another shrimp basket. The most expensive thing on the menu. And a coffee for herself and a glass of milk for me because I was growing right before her eyes. I shrugged. I tried to look trapped as I sat there.

Don't worry, said Linda. When your buddies show up you can go sit with them. I won't mind.

Geez, I said. I didn't mean to . . . anyway, thanks. I only had enough for a pop. Do you always get the shrimp basket?

I never do! Linda twinkled at me. It's a kind of treat. It's a special day, Joe. It is my birthday.

I told her happy birthday. Then it occurred to me this was her twin brother's birthday, too. Could I bring him up? Then I remembered something about the story of her birth.

Wasn't it winter, though, when the two of you were born?

Why yes, you've got a good memory. But I was only physically born that day, you see. The way my life has gone, I was born several other times. I picked a date out of those important turning points to be my birthday.

I nodded. Snow Goodchild brought our drinks. I could hear the sizzle of our shrimps and fries. All of a sudden I was very hungry. I was happy that Linda was buying me lunch. I forgot I hated her and remembered that I'd liked talking to her and that she had always loved my parents and was trying to help even now. The tense prickling left my throat. The right moment would come for questions. I took a drink of cold milk and then a drink of cold water from the ripply plastic glasses.

What day did you pick? The day that Betty brought you home from the hospital?

No, said Linda, I picked the day the social worker brought me home the second time. It was marked on Betty's calendar. She only put the most special things on her calendar. So I knew she loved me, Joe.

That's good, I said. Then I didn't know what to say. We were in a grown-up conversation and I could only go so far. I was stuck. I expected Linda would ask me either how my summer was going or if I was looking forward to getting back to school, the way grown-ups were doing if they did not ask after my dad. Nobody ever asked after my mother, exactly. Instead, they made some comment—I saw your mother going in to work, or I saw your mother at the gas station. The tribal council had given Lark notice that he was barred from the reservation, but there was really no way that could be enforced. It wouldn't work any better than the persuasion. When people said they saw my mother, it meant they were keeping an eye out for her. I thought that Linda might make such a comment. But she startled me.

Listen, Joe, I've got to tell you this. I am sorry that I saved my brother's life. I wish that he was dead. There, I said it.

I paused a moment, and then said, Me too.

Linda nodded and looked at her hands. Her eyes popped again. Joe, he says he's gonna get rich. He says he'll never have to work again. He's sure he'll have money in the bank now, he says, and he's going to fix up the house and live here forever.

Oh? I was dizzy at the thought of Sonja.

That was all in a phone message on my machine. He said a woman would give it to him in exchange for something, and he laughed.

No, she won't, I said. My brain cleared and I saw the broken bottle on Sonja's side table. I saw the look on her face when she threw her Red Sonja bag down. Lark would not get to her.

These are grown-up things, said Linda. They probably

make no sense to you. That don't make sense to me, either.

Our shrimp baskets came and she tried to put ketchup on the side. She shook the bottle with both hands like a little kid. I took the bottle from her and hit the bottom carefully with the heel of my hand, the way my father did, setting a precise glop of ketchup down.

Oh, I can never do that, said Linda.

This is the way. I put some ketchup on my plate. Linda nodded and tried the technique.

You learn something new, she said, and we started eating, piling the little plastic-looking pink tails at the sides of our baskets.

What she'd said about her brother was so full of adult complexity that it threw me off. This was not the way I'd meant to bring up Linden Lark. I didn't know if I could take any more information. So I said the safest thing to deflect her honesty.

Wow, it's hot.

But she wouldn't go to the weather with me. She nodded, closed her eyes, and said, Mmmm, as she ate her birthday shrimp.

Slow down, Linda, she told herself. She laughed and dabbed her lips.

I've got to do this, I thought.

Okay, I said. I get it about your brother. Sure. Now he thinks he'll be a rich piece of scum. I'm just wondering, though, could you tell me when he plays golf? If he does play golf? Anymore?

She kept her napkin at her lips and blinked at me over the white paper.

I mean, I said, I need to know because—

I crammed a fistful of fries into my mouth and chewed and thought furiously.

—because what if my dad wants to golf or something? I was thinking it would be good for him to golf. We can't run the risk of Lark being out there, too.

Oh, gosh, said Linda. She looked panicked. I never thought about that, Joe. I don't know how often, but yes, Linden does golf and he likes to get out there very early, right after the course opens at seven a.m. Because he doesn't sleep, hardly. Not that I know his habits anymore. I should talk to your . . .

No!

How come?

We were frozen, staring across the food. This time I picked up two shrimp and ate each one, frowning, and picked apart their tails, and ate that little bit too.

This is something I want to do on my own. A father-and-son thing. A surprise. Uncle Edward has golf clubs. I'm sure he'll let us use them. We'll go out there. Just me and Dad. It's something I want to do. Okay?

Oh, certainly. That's nice, Joe.

I ate so quickly, in relief, that I finished the whole plate and even ate some of Linda's fries and the remains of her salad before I understood I had all I needed—the information and an agreement to keep it secret. Which gave me both a sense of relief and the return of that whirling dread.

Bugger floated by the window. He was riding my bicycle.

I have to go, I said to Linda. Thank you, but Bugger's stealing my bike.

I ran outside and caught up to Bugger, who was only halfway across the parking lot. He meandered along slowly and didn't get off the bike, just glanced at me with his wobbly eye. I walked beside him. I actually didn't mind walking because I didn't feel so well. I'd eaten so much, so fast, maybe on a nervous stomach like my father sometimes said he did. Plus, after all, those frozen shrimp had traveled a couple of thousand miles from where they had started to land on my plate. I'd had to cover the piled tails with a napkin while Linda waited for the check. Now the walk seemed better than the jolting of a bicycle. I wanted to get away from other people, too, in case I had to puke.

As I walked beside Bugger in the hot sun, I started feeling better and within a mile I was okay. Bugger didn't seem to have a destination that made any sense to me.

Can I have my bike now?

I've gotta get somewhere first, he said.

Where?

I needa see if it was just a dream.

What was just a dream?

What I saw was just a dream. I needa see.

Whatever it was, it was, I said. You snaked out. Can I have my bike?

Bugger was getting too far out of town, going the opposite of the way to Cappy's house. I was worried that he might swerve into a passing car. So I persuaded him to turn around by talking up Grandma Ignatia and her generous handouts.

True. A man gets hungry from all this bicycling, said Bugger.

We got to the senior citizens and he dropped the bike in front of me. He staggered away like a man in the grip of a magnetic force. I turned around and rode back to Cappy's. We had planned to practice shooting, but Randall was there, off work early, fixing his bustle at the kitchen table. The long, elegant eagle feathers were carefully spread out from the circle where they joined, and he was working on a loose one. Randall had a handsome traditional powwow outfit, which he had mostly inherited from his father, though his aunties had beaded flower patterns on the velvet armbands and aprons. When he was all fitted out, he was a magnificent picture. All kinds of ordinary and extraordinary things had gone into his regalia. Two giant golden eagle tail feathers topped his roach, his headpiece. Stabilized by lengths of a car antenna, the feathers bobbed on the springs of ballpoint pens. The elastic garters of one aunt's old girdle were covered with deerskin and sewn with ankle bells. He had a dance stick that was supposedly taken from a Dakota warrior, though it was actually made in boarding-school shop class. Wherever the components of Randall's outfit had originated, they were all adapted to him now, each feather fixed and strengthened with carved splinters of wood and Elmer's glue, the soles of his moccasins soled and resoled with rawhide. Randall won prize money sometimes, but he danced because Doe had danced, and also because those moving pieces caught girls' eyes pretty good. He was getting ready for our annual summer powwow this coming weekend. Doe as usual would be up behind the MC's microphone making jokes and making sure that things ran along, as he always said, in a good way.

C'mon, let's go pick grandfathers for Randall's sweat lodge, said Cappy. We always put down tobacco for those ancient rocks. That's why they were grandfathers. We didn't always get the rocks. We liked being fire keepers better, but Randall had promised if Cappy could start his old red rez car, he could drive it.

There was a collapsed gravelly place on their land that filled with water in the spring and had the right kind of stones if you kicked around for them. Randall always needed a specific number dictated by the type of sweat he would give. We dragged an old plastic toboggan out to collect the rocks. They took a while to find. They had to be a certain kind of rock that would not crack too easily or explode when red hot and splashed with water in the sweat-lodge pit. They had to be a certain size that Randall could pick off our shovel with his deer antlers. Finding twenty-eight grandfathers was a good afternoon's work and more often, especially if Randall was in a hurry, we'd go out to the rock piles in the fields off reservation and load up Doe's pickup. But this time we needed to be alone.

I told Cappy what I'd learned from Linda about the morning golf.

Cappy kicked his feet around in the grass and bent to dislodge a rounded gray rock.

You gotta move then, Cappy said, before Lark changes his habits. You should take Doe's rifle while we're at the powwow.

Just to think about stealing from Doe gave me a black, sinking feeling and those shrimp began to perk around in my gut. But Cappy was right.

You have to break in between eight and ten on Saturday night, said Cappy. There's the off chance that Doe or Randall will need to come back for something after they retire the flags. But for sure Randall will be out there pounding his hooves until then. Or snagging. And for sure Dad can't leave that microphone. So you go in, Joe. And I really mean break in. Leave a mess. You've got to take a crowbar to the closet where the guns are. I've thought about this. And steal a couple of other things or pretend to. Like the TV.

I can't carry that!

Just unplug it, knock the junk off it. Take Randall's boom box—no, he'll have that—take the good toolbox. But leave it scattered on the porch like a passing car scared you off.

Yeah.

And then the gun. Make sure you get the right one from the closet. I'll show you.

Okay.

And you bring a couple black plastic bags to wrap it in because you're gonna hide it.

I can't bring it home, I said. I'll have to hide it someplace else.

Like the overlook, in the brush behind the oak tree, said Cappy.

After we piled the grandfathers by the fire pit, we spent the rest of the afternoon marking out the trail I'd use and deciding on a hiding place that I could find in the dark. The moon was going to be three quarters, but of course there might be cloud cover. We wanted to make sure I could do it all without using a flashlight. And also, after that, I would have to make it to the powwow grounds—three miles away—walking fields and trails without using my bike so nobody would see me. I'd camped out for the last two years with Cappy's family—an RV for the aunts and a tent for the men. A fire. Randall tipi-creeping. Sneaking off. We'd wake up in the morning next to him passed out, scented low with some girl's perfume. My parents would expect that I'd go again this year. And even if they said no this time, I'd slip out anyway. I had to.

Those shrimp or something else I'd eaten stayed with me all that week. I felt sick when I looked at food and dizzy when I looked at my mother or my father, so I didn't look at anyone and hardly ate. Mostly, I slept. I fell asleep like I was knocked out and couldn't get out of bed in the morning. Once, on waking, I picked up the book Father Travis had given me. *Dune* was a fat paperback with three black figures walking a desert beneath a massive rock. I opened it at random and read something about a boy filled with a terrible sense of purpose. I flung the book across the room and left it there. Many months after that morning I would read that book, once, then again, and again. It was the only book I read for a solid year. My mother said I must be getting my growth. I overheard her. Or listened in on her. Eavesdropping was a habit now. My sneaking came of needing to know that there was no other way, that I had to do this. If Lark moved or skipped out or was poisoned like a dog or caught for some reason, I would be free. But I didn't trust my parents to tell me any of these things, so I had to slip behind doors and sit underneath open windows and listen, never hearing what I wanted. Of course, powwow weekend came.

Mom and Dad had agreed to let me camp out with Doe's boys, as they said, and I hitched a ride out with them in back of Randall's pickup, sitting on my sleeping bag. Five dollars in my pocket for food. Randall drove us so fast on the gravel road that our teeth clacked and we nearly bounced out of the back, but we got there in time to set up in our usual place. Cappy's family always parked their RV to the south at the edge of the powwow camp circle, right up against the unmowed fields. At that time of the year the hay was usually ready to cut again. Standing at the edge of the grass, I watched it ripple gently up a soft rise, parting and reparting like a woman's hair. The family liked camping at the edge so they could get away from what Suzette and Josey called "the goings-on." Doe's sisters were stout and jolly. They danced women's traditional, and when they were getting ready in their small RV camper it shook with their heavy movements and bursts of laughter. Their husbands did not dance but helped out with organization and security.

The first thing we did on arriving was lift the webbed lawn chairs out of the back of the pickup. We decided where to dig a fire pit and put the lawn chairs up around the hole. It was important to have a little place where visitors could come and get brewed tea, or drink Kool-Aid from one of the giant plastic thermos jugs Suzette and Josey filled before they came. They also had coolers—one stuffed with sandwiches, pickles, tubs of baked beans and potato salad, bannock, jelly, crab apples, blocks of commodity cheese. The other cooler was full of hot dogs and cold fried rabbit. Soon, around the camp, Suzette and Josey's married children started pulling up in their low-slung old cars. When the car doors opened, the grandchildren bounced out like Super Balls. They gathered other children from the neighboring camps and moved through the powwow grounds in a tornado of whirling hair and chasing legs and pumping arms. Occasionally an announcement came over the loudspeaker—these were just test announcements. Doe did not come on for real until noon. He did the welcome several times and reminded dancers that Grand Entry was at one.

Put on your dancin' shoes! His announcer voice was smooth

as warm maple syrup. He loved to say Oh mercy, as well as Gee willikers, I'll be doggone, and Howah! He loved to joke. His jokes were friendly and awful.

Just yesterday a white guy asked me if I was a real Indian. No, I said, Columbus goofed up. The real Indians are in India. I'm a genuine Chippewa.

Chip a what? How come you got no braids?

They got chipped off, I told him. The old word for us is Anishinaabe, you know. Eyyyy. Sometimes you can't tell a real Anishinaabe woman something. She gives you that look and you got to tell her *everything*. Eyyyy.

Doe announced lost children. Papoose on the loose! Here's a little boy looking for his family. Don't be scared when you come claim him, Mama, he's not covered with war paint. It's just ketchup and mustard. He's been fixing himself to face the Fifth Cavalry over at the hot-dog stand.

When he introduced the drums, he rolled one to the next with a good word for each: Beartail, Enemy Wind, Green River. The bleachers started filling with people and Suzette and Josey sent their husbands to set up lawn chairs at the edge of the arena on the south side to avoid the long and blinding brilliance of the sun as it would set, it seemed, forever into the night. Cappy and I set up our tent with its square canopy where Randall could dress and preen. Suzette and Josey loved having a male dancer to fuss over and kept asking Cappy and me when we were going to start. Cappy had danced until he was ten years old.

I'm making you a new grass dance outfit. Josey shook her finger at him.

Cappy just smiled at her. He never said no to anyone. He and Randall had cut young popple saplings on their land and we set up a cooling arbor where the aunties could take the breeze. The day was heating up and their beaded yokes and the tanned hides, the bone breastplates and the woolen shawls, the heavy silver concho belts and figured ornaments and all that long leather fringe must have weighed sixty pounds or more. Suzette and Josey were round but phenomenally strong, so they could move with dignity under the weight of all this tradition, and not collapse. Randall was hardly weighed down at all by contrast, but he was covered with so many feathers Cappy said it looked like he'd rolled in a flock of eagles. He had a pair of red long johns with aprons or breechcloths that hung fore and aft.

Be sure you get your modesty panel set just right, said Cappy. You don't want anyone to know what you ain't got.

Shut up, bobtail, he said to Cappy. And don't you even start, shrimpy, he said to me.

He held up a mirror and painted two black stripes down his forehead to his eyebrows, then continued underneath his eyes and down his cheeks. Randall's eyes suddenly became impenetrable warrior eyes. He glowered at us from under his guard hair roach and swaying feathers.

Give us your smolder, said Cappy.

That was it, said Randall. Observe its effect.

He went out into the sunlight and stretched beside the cotton candy vendor's trailer. Randall said his red long johns were traditional, but Cappy and I thought they ruined his look.

A girl in a leather halter top leaned away from her friends. Sipping soda through a straw, she watched all kissy face as Randall practiced his moves. He put his foot up on the trailer hitch, and strained to touch his toes like he was stretching his hamstrings. He did this twice and on the third time cracked a boogid. He tried to saunter off as though it hadn't happened. The girl laughed so hard she choked and spurted her pop.

Learn from the master, said Cappy. Whatever Randall does, do the opposite.

Angus's family was there, spilling out of and around a car,

so we went to get him and find Zack. When we were all four together, we needed frybread, went and got some, and were eating in the shade of the stands when some girls from school came up to us. They always talked to Angus first, then Zack, then me, then focused on their real target, Cappy. The girls from our year were mainly named some version of Shawn. There was Shawna, Dawna, Shawnee, Dawnali, Shalana, and just plain Dawn and Shawn. There was also a girl named Margaret, named after her grandmother, who worked at the post office. I ended up talking to Margaret. Dawn, Shawn, and the others had their hair curled back from their faces and sprayed stiff, eye shadow, lip gloss, two pairs of earrings in each ear, tight jeans, little striped T-shirts, and shiny silver necklaces. I tease Margaret to this day about what she wore to that powwow—that's because I remember every detail, down to the silver locket that contained not a photo of her boyfriend, but a picture of her baby brother.

What Cappy did to attract girls was just be Cappy. He didn't smolder like Randall, he didn't wear a single feather. He was dressed as usual in a faded T-shirt and jeans. His hair naturally fell down over one eye and he didn't bother tucking it behind his ear, but used that head toss. Otherwise, he just talked, and drew us all in. The thing I noticed was, he asked the girls about themselves almost like a teacher would. How their summer was going, what their families were doing. The conversation put us on an easy footing and we walked, circling the arena behind the stands, the girls being noticed, us noticing them being noticed. We went around a few times. The girls bought cotton candy. They peeled off strips of fluff for us. We drank pop and tried to crush the cans in our fists. Things started up. Veterans brought in the American flag, the MIA-POW flag, the flag of our Tribal Nation, our traditional Eagle Staff. The head dancers followed and then the Grand Entry dancers lined up and moved into the arena by category, all the way down to the tiny tots. We stood on the top tier to watch it all: the drums, the rousing synchrony of bells, rattles, deer clackers, and the flashing music of the jingle dancers. Grand Entry always caught my breath and made me step along with the dancers. It was big, contagious, defiant, joyous. But tonight all I could think of was how to grab my pack and slip away.

I went as the crow flies, took the woods paths, crossed a couple of pastures, cut down the back roads. When I got to the house there was still light. The outdoor dog barked at me and recognized me. Hey, Fleck, I said, and he licked my hand. We waited half an hour, behind the shed, until dusk. I waited for a while after that, until it was really dark, and then I put on a pair of my mother's leather gloves, tight ones, and walked up to the back door carrying the crowbar Cappy had left out.

When I jimmied the door the indoor dog barked, but she wagged her tail when I entered and followed me to the gun cabinet. The shatter of glass startled her, but she whined with excitement when I took out the gun. She thought we were going hunting. Instead, I put ammunition in my backpack, messed up the TV, scattered the toolbox, then said good-bye to the dogs. I walked across the road and found the path Cappy and I had marked out. I had to use my flashlight but switched it off when a car crested the rise on the gravel road. Up near the overlook, we'd already made the hole. I wrapped the rifle and ammo tight in the garbage bags and buried it, scattered leaves, brush, twigs back over the top. At least by the light of a three-quarter moon the place looked undisturbed. I drank some water and started walking back to the powwow grounds. I went back along the same paths, around the same sloughs, down the old two-track dirt roads, the woods paths that a few still cleared to log out their firewood. I crossed a horse pasture and could hear the drums from there, still going, now forty-nine songs and moccasin games. People stayed awake all night gambling in some of the tents. I made it back to our tent and unzipped the bug-proof screen. Cappy was awake. Randall gone. Cappy asked me how it went.

Smooth, I said. I think it went smooth.

Good, he said. We lay on our backs, awake. Doe would have gone home by now and found his house broken into, his rifle gone. He'd have called the BIA/tribal police. There wasn't any way he'd know it was me. But I didn't know how I could face him anyway.

Mornings were always the best times—waking with the cool air stirring along the fabric walls. Smelling coffee, bannock, eggs, and sausage. Outside, sun and fresh alfalfa cut for the horses. Suzette and Josey were making their plans for the day and feeding their grandchildren on flimsy paper plates, which always bent or disintegrated beneath the load of food.

Ey! Here. Put another plate underneath, you.

The children walked hunched over to the edge of the grass and ate close to the ground. Every bite was good. The sisters had a Coleman gas stove and a propane tank. They fried bacon and cooked bannock with the grease. Their scrambled eggs were light, fluffy, never burnt. Bread was toasted on the hot griddle. There was a open jar of Juneberry jam. Another of wild plum. They knew how to feed boys. A couple hours after hot breakfast there was cold breakfast—watermelon, cereal, cold bannock, soft butter, and meat. They owned a magnificent blue-speckled enameled tin coffeepot, and a stainless steel one, too, just for tea. The lawn chairs at the camp were always full of gossiping men, and the RV started out crawling with children until one of the sisters put a stop to it and locked them out. After cold breakfast, the sisters made piles of sandwiches, stashed them in the cooler under supervision of their daughters. They retired into the RV to prepare themselves for the day's Grand Entry. Nothing could disturb them. Not pleas to use their bathroom, screams of vengeance from fighting boys, or their daughters' feigned panic. The scent of burning sweetgrass wafted from the little pull-down screen windows. Suzette and Josey took their regalia very seriously and made sure all of the bad looks from other women, the grudge thoughts or snapping eyes, were removed from their cloth and beads by the smoke. And their own thoughts, too, perhaps, for their husbands' eyes were known to roam although they had no proof. The interior of the RV, so cunningly fitted with cabinets and fold-up beds, drawers, cupboards, hidden chests, a tiny toilet, was neatened and perfected. When they emerged, one of them padlocked the door shut from the outside and stashed the key in the beaded striker purse or knife sheath that hung from her belt. They moved off in unison, their hair braided long with mink pelts, gray only at the temples. Grandly, gracefully, they entered the flow of the dancers. Their buckskin fringe swayed with dreamlike precision. Everybody liked to watch them, to see if they'd be thrown off by the swirl of intertribal, when anybody and everyone entered the arena. Little boys in half a grass dance outfit copied big boy moves and knocked against Suzette and Josey. Little girls with eyes glazed in concentration jingle-hopped after their glamorous sisters and tripped into their path. Suzette and Josey did not falter. They talked to each other, broke into laughter, never missed a beat or disrupted the even sway of fringe on their sleeves, shawls, and yokes.

Two skins for each dress, said Cappy. And probably another skin's worth of fringe. If they fell on top of each other, they'd get snarled up and never break apart.

C'mon down, all you spectators, called Doe, this is intertribal! Put your feet on the ground in whatever you got—boots, moccasins, even hippie sandals. What are those? Birkenstocks, somebody tells me. We found a Birkenstock outside of Randall's tent last night. Ohhhh, yes. Howah.

Doe was always teasing Randall and his friends about their continual efforts at snagging women.

Fuck, said Randall, behind us. Some fuckers broke into our house last night and stole one a Dad's deer rifles.

They get anything else? asked Cappy. He didn't turn around to look at Randall, but frowned out at the dancing.

Nah, said Randall. That rifle shows up, I'll coldcock somebody.

How's Doe taking it?

He's mad, Randall shrugged, but not that mad. He says it's odd they just took that one rifle. They might of tried to take the TV, dropped the toolbox. Amateurs. Couldn't find any tracks or nothing. Drugheads.

Yeah, said Cappy.

Yeah, I said.

Either the dogs weren't doing their jobs or they knew who did it.

Or somebody coulda thrown them a piece of meat, said Cappy.

Randall made a disgusted noise. Wasn't his favorite rifle anyway. If they got his favorite, he'd be mad.

That's good, I said.

I felt so low I wanted to slide under the bleachers and crouch there with the dead cigarettes, melted snow-cone wrappers, balled-up diapers, and brown splats of spit snoose.

From now on we're gonna keep the house better locked, Cappy said.

I'm going home tonight, said Randall. Sleeping on the couch with my shotgun until we fix the door.

Don't shoot your nuts off, said Cappy.

Don't worry, nutless. Fuckers show up to finish the job, they'll be sorry.

You're the man, said Cappy. He clapped his brother's shoulder and we sauntered off. We walked around and around the arena. After a while he clapped my shoulder too.

You did it smooth.

I hate myself though.

Brother, you must get over that, said Cappy. He will never know, but if he did know, Doe would understand.

Okay, I said after a while, but when I do it, the rest of it, I do it alone.

Cappy sighed.

Listen, Cappy, I said, hoarse, nearly whispering. I'm going to call this like it is. Murder, for justice maybe. Murder just the same. I had to say this a thousand times in my head before I said it out loud. But there it is. And I can take him.

Cappy stopped. Okay, you said it. But that's not the whole point. If you ever hit five, no, three cans in a row, just once, I'd say maybe. But Joe.

I'll get close to him.

He'll see you. Worse, you'll see him. You've got one chance, Joe. I'll just be there to steady your mind, your aim. I won't get implicated, Joe.

Okay, I said out loud. No way, I thought. I had decided I would not tell Cappy what morning I was going to the overlook. I would just go there and do it.

The weather the first part of that week was forecast clear and hot. Linda had said her brother played early, before anybody else was out. So just after sunrise I rose and sneaked downstairs. I told my parents that I was getting in shape for fall cross-country—and I did run. I ran the woods trails where I would not be seen. I was getting good at skirting yards and using windbreaks for cover. I took a washed-out pickle jar of water in one hand and a candy bar in my shirt pocket. I made sure the stone Cappy gave me was in my jeans pocket. I wore a brown plaid shirt over a green T-shirt. The best I could do for camouflage. When I got to the overlook, I scraped the sticks and leaves away and set them aside. Then, I took the earth off the gun in the bags and set that aside too. I took the rifle out of the bags and loaded it. My fingers shook. I tried deep breaths. I wrung my hands and brought the rifle to the oak tree, sat down, and held it. I put the jar of water next to me. Then I waited. I would see any golfer on the fifth tee well before he came to the place where I planned to shoot. Then while Lark was starting down the fairway behind a screen of young pine trees, I would walk down the hill with the rifle and hide behind a riffle of chokecherry bush and box elder. From there, I'd aim and wait until he got close enough. How close he came would depend on where he hit the ball and which way it rolled, where he stood to putt, and other things. There were many variables. So many that I was still weighing possibilities when the sun got so high I knew I'd been sitting there for hours. Once the regular stream of golfers began, I got up and unloaded the rifle. I packed it in its bag, rolled the other bag around it, reburied it, and scattered the leaves and twigs over the ground. On the way home, I ate the candy bar and put the wrapper in my pocket. My stomach had stopped jumping. Done for the day, I felt almost euphoric. I drank the last of the water and carried the empty jar along and didn't think. I looked at every tree I passed and it amazed me with its detail and life. I stopped and watched two horses browse in the weedy pasture. Born graceful. When I got home, I was so cheerful that my mother asked what had got into me. I made her laugh. I ate and ate. Then I went upstairs and fell asleep for an hour and woke into the same great wash of dread I began with every time I woke up. I'd have to do the same thing tomorrow morning. And I did. As I sat against the oak tree there were moments I forgot why I was there. I would get up to leave, thinking I was crazy. Then I remembered my mother stunned and bleeding in the backseat of the car. My hand on her hair. Or how she had stared from her bedcovers as if from a black cave. I thought of my father helpless on the linoleum floor of the grocery. I thought of the gas can in the lake, on the hardware store shelf. I thought of other things.

Then I was ready. But he did not show up that Tuesday. He did not show up on Wednesday either. On Thursday rain was forecast, so I thought maybe I'd stay home.

I went anyway. Once I got to the overlook, I went through all of the actions that had become routine by now. I sat under the oak tree with the rifle, safety on. The water beside me. There was low cloud cover and the air smelled like rain. I had been there for maybe an hour, waiting for the clouds to break, when Lark walked onto the tee dragging his clubs in a stained old canvas wheeled cart. He disappeared behind the planted pines. Cradling the rifle the way Cappy had taught me, I stepped down the hill. I'd told myself exactly what to do so often that at first I thought I'd be all right. I found the spot marked out just at the edge of the bushes where I could stand, nearly hidden. From there I could sight and aim just about any place Lark might be on the green. I thumbed off the safety. I gulped in air and let it out explosively. I held the rifle gently the way I'd practiced, and tried to control my breathing. But each breath got stuck. And there was Lark. He hit from a low rise near the pine trees. The ball arced and landed at the edge of the clipped circle with a bounce that took it another yard toward the hole. Lark walked down quickly. The scent of minerals began to seep out of the earth. I brought the rifle to my shoulder and followed him with the barrel. He stood sideways, staring down at his golf ball, squinting his eyes, opening them, squinting again, completely absorbed. He wore tan pants, golf shoes, a gray cap, and a brown short-sleeved T-shirt. He was so close I could read the logo of his defunct grocery store. Vinland. The golf ball rolled to a spot half a foot from the hole. He'd tap it in, I thought. He'd bend over to scoop it out. When he straightened up I'd shoot.

Lark walked forward and before he could tap it in I shot at the logo over his heart. I hit him someplace else, maybe in the stomach, and he collapsed. There was a loud silence. I lowered the rifle. Lark rolled over on his knees, staggered to his feet, found his balance, and began to scream. The sound was a high squeal like nothing I'd ever heard. I got the rifle back to my shoulder, reloaded. I was shaking so hard I rested the barrel on a branch, held my breath, and shot again. I couldn't tell where that shot went. Once again I worked the bolt, reloaded, aimed, but my finger slid off the trigger—I couldn't shoot. Lark pitched forward. There was another silence. My face was drenching wet. I wiped my eyes on my sleeve. Lark began to make noise again.

Please, no, please, no. I thought I heard those words, but I could have said them. Lark was trying to get up again. He pedaled one foot in the air, rolled over, onto his knees, and rose in a crouch. He locked eyes with me. Their blackness knocked me backward. The rifle was lifted from my arms. Cappy stepped forward beside me. I didn't hear the shot. All sound, all motion, had stalled in the sullen air. My brain was ringing. Cappy picked up the ejected casings from around my feet and put them in the pockets of his jeans.

C'mon, he said, touching my arm. Turning me. Let's go.

I followed him uphill in the first drops of rain.

CHAPTER ELEVEN

The Child

At the oak tree, we turned and looked down. Lark was lying on his back, the golf clubs neatly waiting in their cart. His putter cast down at his heels. He hadn't moved. Beside me, Cappy dropped to his knees. He leaned over until his forehead touched the earth and put his arms over his head like a child in a tornado drill. After a while, he lifted his head and shook it. We wrapped the rifle back up in its bag, and set it aside as we tried to restore the ground where it had been buried. Cappy used a branch to brush up the grass I had trampled.

Nobody's home at my place, said Cappy. We gotta hide this. He had the rifle.

We waited until a passing car was out of sight before we crossed the road. Now the rain was misting down. When we got to Cappy's, we went straight to the kitchen tap. We washed our hands, put water on our faces, and drank glass after glass of water.

I should have thought of where to hide it, I said. I don't know why I didn't think of this.

I don't know why I didn't either, said Cappy.

He went and rummaged around on the junk-laden coffee

table until he came up with a set of keys. Doe had taken his car to work and Randall had gone off in his pickup, but Randall also had the red beater Olds that Cappy tinkered with. It had a black driver's-side door and a cracked windshield. We went out, put the rifle in the trunk, and got into the front.

The starter's bad, said Cappy.

It groaned the first time he turned it over. He gave it a spurt of gas. It died.

You gotta sneak up on it, Cappy said. While I'm psyching out this car, you think of where we're going.

I know where we're going.

He tried again. It nearly caught.

Where are we going?

To Linda's. To the old Wishkob homestead.

We sat back, looking out at the shed through the two halves of the windshield.

That makes weird sense, said Cappy. Suddenly, he leaned forward, cranked the key hard, and pumped the gas pedal.

Engage, he said. The engine roared.

The rain was coming down like sixty now. Cappy opened his window and craned his neck to peer out as he drove. The windshield wiper worked on the passenger side, but not the driver's side. He drove slowly and sedately as an old man. The Wishkob land was at the other end of the reservation in the dunelike brown hills of grass that were mostly good for grazing. It was a nice old place with plantings of lilac and a few twisted oak, battered shrubs that could stand the heavy wind. On the way there we'd passed maybe two cars and there was nobody to see us turn into Linda's drive—the place was isolated. Cappy eased the car into Park and kept it idling because he didn't know if it would start again. We got out and walked around the house to decide where. Linda's old dog set up an asthmatic barking inside the house. We ended up pulling off a piece of the tan latticework tacked to the underside of Linda's front porch. I crawled in and shoved the gun as far back as I could. We used a tire iron to pound the lattice back in place, then we noticed all the lattice was gone on the other side where the dog liked to sleep. We got back in the car and pulled out. We didn't talk. Cappy paused the car to let me out on the road to my house. On the upper road leading out of town, we saw the tribal police car driving east, toward the golf course, lights going. No siren.

He's dead for sure, said Cappy.

Otherwise, they'd rocket.

Their sirens would be going off.

We sat in the idling car. The rain was hardly a sprinkle now.

You saved my ass, brother.

Not really. You would have shot that—

Cappy stopped. Around here we don't speak badly of the dead and he caught himself.

He would've died though, I said. You didn't kill him. This is not on you.

Sure. Okay.

We were speaking without emotion. Like we were talking of other people. Or as if what we did had just happened on television. But I was choking up. Cappy swiped at his face with the heel of his palm.

We can't talk about it after this, he said.

Affirmative.

Isn't that how your dad says people get caught? Bragging to their friends?

They get drunk, whatever.

I feel like getting drunk, Cappy said.

With what?

The car's idle faltered and Cappy pressed tenderly on the gas pedal.

I don't know. Randall's on the wagon.

I could make it up with Whitey, I said.

Yeah? Cappy glanced at me.

I nodded at him and looked away.

After you bring the car back . . .

Right.

Meet me at the gas station. I'll go talk to him.

I got out. I stood away from the car, then reached out and hit my palm on the window. Cappy drove off and I walked slowly over to the gas station, past the old BIA school and the community center, past the one stop sign and past Clemence and Edward's house. Over the highway and down the weedy ditch and back up. By the time I got there, the rain had completely dried off except for some random dark patches on the gravel or cement. Whitey stood in the doorway of the garage wiping his hands on the greasy rag. He watched me for a moment and then faded back into the darkness. Came out dangling two cold open bottles of grape Crush. I walked up to him and took a bottle. His receiver was crackling police signals. I took a gulp of pop and it nearly came back up.

Your stomach must be turned over, said Whitey. You need a slice a bread.

He got me some white bread from the cooler and after I ate a slice I felt better. We sat down in the lawn chairs in the shadow the garage cast, where Sonja and LaRose had sat what seemed a very long time ago.

Remember when I was little, I asked, you used to give me a swig now and then?

Your mom sure hated that, said Whitey. Hungry? Fancy a rez steak sandwich?

Not yet, I said. I sipped the grape pop.

This time it went down good, said Whitey. He was looking at me closely. He opened his mouth a couple of times before he spoke.

Someone dusted Lark, he said. On the golf course. Made a

mess of him like a kid shooting at a hay bale. Then one clean head shot.

I tried to sit very still, but couldn't. I jumped up and ran around back. I just got there in time. Whitey didn't follow me. He was helping a customer when I came back. My knees were weak as water and I needed the lawn chair.

I'm switchin' you to ginger ale, my boy. He went into the store and came out with a warm can.

This ain't been in the cooler and it should go easy on your gut.

I think I got the summer flu.

The summer flu, he agreed. It's going around. Your friends catch it too?

I don't know. I haven't seen 'em.

Whitey nodded and sat down beside me.

I been listening to the squawk-box. Whoever did it left no traces, he said. There's nothing to go on. Nobody seen it. Nobody seen nothin'. Then it rained so hard. You'll be getting over this flu quickly. Still, maybe you should take a lay-down, Joe. There's a little cot in the office. Sonja used to nap there, and she will again. She's coming home, Joe. I tell you?

Did she call you? I asked, hating him.

Damn right, she called me. Gonna be different now, she said, her game. But I don't care. I don't care. Whatever you think—he looked away from me carefully—I'm stone in love with that old girl. You understand? She's coming back to me, Joe.

I walked in and lay down on the cot for a good half hour. It didn't smell like Sonja. I was glad because I couldn't have taken that. When I got up and went back out, Cappy still had not shown up.

I could maybe eat that sandwich now, Uncle.

Whitey went to the cooler and took out the baloney, cheese, and bread. There was a head of iceberg lettuce in there and he carefully tore off three pale green leaves and placed them on the meat before closing the sandwich.

Lettuce? I asked.

I'm on a health kick, me.

He handed over the sandwich and made one for himself. Then he gave me that one too.

Your friend's here.

Cappy came in the door and I handed him a sandwich.

The three of us went back outside and ate sitting in the lawn chairs.

Uncle, I said, we could use a little something.

He ate his whole sandwich. I don't wonder, he said when it was gone. But if you tell Geraldine or Doe, it is my saggy old red ass on the line here. Plus any future supply of stuff for you. And you have to drink it out back behind the station in those shade trees where I can keep my eye on the botha youse.

We'll abide by your conditions, said Cappy in a formal tone. His face was expressionless.

Handle the trade, said Whitey. There was no one in sight. He went back to open the safe, where he kept his booze. He brought out half a quart of Four Roses and pointed it toward the trees. Cappy took the bottle and put it underneath his shirt. A customer pulled up. Whitey waved and walked over to the car.

Does he know?

I think so, I said. I puked when he told me about Lark.

I puked riding over here, said Cappy.

It's just the summer flu, I said.

Is that a medical opinion, Joe?

We looked at each other and tried to smile, but instead our mouths dropped open. Our faces fell into our real expressions.

What are we? asked Cappy. What are we now?

I don't know, man. I don't know.

Let's sterilize our insides.

Right on.

Beneath the trees there were four or five cement blocks, a litter of crushed cans, a circle of ash. We sat down on the blocks and opened the bottle. Cappy took a cautious drink, then handed it to me. I took a fiery mouthful and let it trickle down. The burning mellowed as the stuff reached inside of me, loosening my chest with a slow warmth and easing my gut. After the next sip I felt better. Everything looked amber. I took my first deep breath.

Oh, I said, bowing my head and passing the bottle back to Cappy. Oh, oh, oh.

Yes? said Cappy.

Oh.

He drank more deeply. I picked up a branch and scraped the bits of charred wood and speckled gravel away from the ash, destroying the circle. Cappy watched the movements of my branch and I kept moving the branch until we'd finished the bottle. Then we lay down in the weeds.

Brother, I said, what made you come to the overlook?

I was always there, said Cappy. Every morning. I always had your back.

I thought so, I said. And then we slept.

After we woke up, Whitey made us rinse out our mouths, gargle with mouthwash, and eat another sandwich.

Gimme your shirt, Joe, he said. Leave it here. Touch the bottle again. You, too, Cappy.

I gave him my shirt and walked home. Cappy coasted beside me. We did not feel particularly drunk. We did not feel anything. But we wove from side to side on the road, unable to keep on a straight course. We thought that Angus and Zack would be looking for us.

We should all four be hanging out all the time, now, together, said Cappy.

We'll keep training for cross-country in the morning.

That's right.

Pearl came out from beneath her bush and walked with me up to the house. Before I went in the door, I played with her and made myself laugh. I took her inside with me because I was afraid that my parents would be sitting at the kitchen table, waiting for me, as indeed they were. When I opened the door and saw them, I bent over and rubbed Pearl's neck and talked to her. I stood up to greet them and let the smile drop off my face.

What? I said.

Whitey's booze had settled inside of me by then, separating me from who I was, say, when I'd dug those seedlings out of the foundation, when I had wept outside my mother's bedroom door, when I had watched the angel, my doodem, cross the sun-grazed walls of my bedroom. I knelt down with my arm around Pearl's neck and disregarded my parents' endless stare. I stayed across the room hoping that they would not smell me, but I felt my mother look at my father.

Where were you? asked my mother.

Running.

All day?

At Whitey's, too.

Some small thing eased between them.

Doing what?

Just hanging around. Whitey fed us lunch. Me and Cappy.

They wanted to believe me so much that I saw they'd make every effort to believe. All I had to do was stay plausible. Not break. Not puke.

Sit down, son, said my father. But although I drew a step closer, I did not take a chair. He told me Lark was dead. I let all my feelings cross my face.

That's good, I finally said.

Joe, said my father, his hand on his chin, his eyes on me, the weight intolerable. Joe, do you know anything, even the slightest thing, about this?

This? This what?

He was murdered, Joe.

But I'd used the word before. I'd hardened myself. I'd used it with Cappy and I'd used it in my head. I had prepared to answer this question and to answer it the way the old Joe from before this summer would answer. I spoke childishly, in a sudden fury of excitement that wasn't fake.

Dead? I wanted him dead, okay? In my thoughts. If you're telling me he's murdered, then I'm happy. He deserved it. Mom is free now. You're free. The guy who killed him should get a medal.

All right, my father said. Enough. He pushed back his chair. My mother's eyes did not leave my face. She was intent on believing anything I said. But she shuddered all over, suddenly. A ripple passed over her body. The shock of it reached me.

She sees the murderer in me, I thought.

Dizzy, I reached down for Pearl, but she had crept to my father's leg. I sat back up.

I won't lie. I'm glad he's dead. Can I go now?

I walked past them and continued until I reached the stairs. I carefully took the steps. As I went up, drawn in my weariness as if by a rope, I felt their eyes on me. I recalled this happening before at some time and me watching. I was halfway to my room before I remembered my mother climbing to that place of loneliness from which we feared she never would descend.

No, I thought, as I crept into my bed, I've got Cappy and the others. I've done what I had to do. There is no going back. And whatever happens, I can take.

I was down. I was sick for real now, with the summer flu, just as I had pretended. Whitey vouched for us. When first Vince Madwesin, then another tribal police officer, then finally Agent Bjerke, pressed him, Whitey gave up that we'd gotten into his booze stash and passed out behind the station.

He showed them our hideout in the weeds, the bottle, which was fingerprinted, and my shirt. My mother identified it as the one she'd washed for me to wear that day. But the rifle. Doe's 30.06. I was running a fever of alternating sweats and chills and my sheets were sodden. While I was ill, I watched the golden light pass across my walls. I could feel nothing, but my thoughts ran wild. Always I kept going back to the day I dug the trees out of the foundation of our house. How tough those roots had clung. Maybe they had pulled out the blocks that held our house up. And how funny, strange, that a thing can grow so powerful even when planted in the wrong place. Ideas too, I muttered. Ideas. Dad's case law, the Cohen, and then that hot dish. I'd think of the black noodles. The noodles became a carcass—the human, the buffalo, the body subject to the laws. I'd wonder how my mother got her spirit to return to her body, and if it had returned, and if mine was fleeing now because of what I'd done. Would I become a wiindigoo? Infected by Lark? And it occurred to me how even pulling trees that day, just months ago, I was in heaven. Unaware. I had known nothing even as the evil was occurring. I hadn't been touched yet. Thinking finally exhausted me. I turned over, away from the light, and slept.

Dad, I said, once, when he came into the room. Does Linda know? Is she okay?

He'd brought me a glass of Whitey's cure—warm ginger ale.

I don't know, he said. She won't pick up her telephone. She's not at work.

I've got to get to her, I thought. And then I slept hard again until late the next morning. When I woke from that sleep everything was clear. I had no fever, no sickness at all. I was hungry. I got up and took a shower. Put fresh clothes on and came downstairs. The trees at the edge of the yard swayed and the leaves showed their dull silvery undersides. I ran myself a glass of tap water and stood at the kitchen window. My mother was outside, kneeling in the dirt of the garden with a colander, picking the bush beans that my father and I had planted late. She dropped down and crawled the row on all fours sometimes. Sat back on her heels. She gave the colander a little jounce, to settle the beans. That's why I did it, I thought. And I was satisfied right then. So she could give her colander a shake. She didn't have to look behind her, or fear he would sneak up on her. She could pick her bush beans all day and nobody was going to bother her.

I poured out a bowl of cereal and added milk. I ate it slowly. The cereal felt good going down. I rinsed my bowl and went outside.

My mother got up and walked over to me. She put her stained palm on my forehead.

Your fever's gone.

I'm fine now!

You should take it easy, just stay home and read or . . .

I won't do much, I said. It's just that school starts up in two weeks. I don't want to waste any of my last days.

I guess they would sure go to waste if you stayed home with me. She wasn't angry, but she didn't smile.

I didn't mean it that way, I said. I'll come back early.

Her eyes, one sadder than the other with its sinking squint, moved softly over me. She pushed back my hair. I looked over her shoulder and saw an empty pickle jar sitting on the kitchen step. I froze. The jar. I'd left the jar on the hill.

What's that?

She turned around. Vince Madwesin came by. He gave me the jar and said to wash it out. He said he likes my home-canned pickles. I guess it's a hint. She looked back at me, closely, but I didn't change my expression.

I am worried over you, Joe.

It was a moment I still linger on in my thoughts. Her

standing before me in the riot of growth. The warm earth smell of her hands, a slick of perspiration on her neck, her searching eyes.

Whitey said you boys got drunk.

It was an experiment, I said, and the results came back negative. I wasted good vacation being sick, Mom. I think my drinking days are done.

She laughed in relief and the laugh stuck in her throat. She said she loved me and I mumbled back at her. I looked down at my feet.

Are you okay now? I asked, low.

Oh sure, my boy. I'm really good; I'm back to myself. Everything is fine now, fine. She tried to persuade me.

At least he's dead, Mom. He paid, whatever else.

I wanted to add that he did not die easy, that he knew what he was getting killed for, that he saw who was killing him. But then I'd have to say it was me.

I couldn't look at her and got on my bike. I rode away with her silent gaze heavy on my back.

First, I rode over to the post office. There was a chance I might run into Dad if it was lunchtime, so I wanted to slip in before noon and see if Linda was working. She was not. Margaret Nanapush, the grandma of the Margaret in my class at school, the girl at the powwow I turned out to marry, told me that Linda was using up some sick leave. As far as Mrs. Nanapush knew, she was at home. So I went there.

I was weak enough to feel that ride as endless. Out on that edge of the reservation, the wind cuts hard. I pedaled against its flow for a good hour before I came to Linda's road, and then finally swerved into her driveway. Linda's car was parked in a wooden carport. She drove, surprising to say, a cute blue Mustang. I remembered that she'd said she enjoyed taking to the road. I leaned my bike against her porch. I am *winded*, I said out loud, and wished Cappy was there to laugh at my bad joke. I dragged myself to the door and knocked, rattling the loose screen in its aluminum frame. She appeared behind it.

Joe! You snuck up on me!

She touched the screen, frowning at it. Shook it.

I've gotta fix this. Come in, Joe.

Her dog started barking, too late. He ran up the hill from a field below the sloping ledge of yard where the house sat. By the time he reached the house he was wheezing—a stumpy old black dog with a whitened face.

Buster, smile, said Linda. He lolled out his tongue, grinning and panting in a comical way. I thought of how I'd heard people looked like their dogs. It was true. Linda let him in with me.

I suppose we shouldn't be laughing, considering what happened, she said as she led me into her kitchen. Sit down, Joe. What can I get you? She listed everything she had. Every kind of drink and sandwich possibility. I didn't stop her. Finally, Linda said she was fond of a fried egg sandwich with horseradish mayonnaise, and that if I picked that one she'd make it for the both of us. I said that sounded good. While she was frying up the eggs, she told me I could look around and so I wandered into the living room and took in the odd order of her place. At my house, although we kept it neat enough, there were always piles of papers and other interesting stuff here and there. Or books that had gotten off the shelves. Not everything was put away immediately. There might be a jacket draped over a chair. Our shoes weren't lined up by the door. Linda's house was extremely neat in the usual way, but also in a way that disoriented me until I figured it out. Everything had a double, though not an identical. Her bookshelf had two books by each author, not the same book, though sometimes a hardback with its companion paperback. They were mostly historical romances. She had chosen collections of objects to display, also two by two. Glass figurines of Disney characters on her end tables, paired in different colors, circled the lamps on which she'd glued fake leaves sorted by the same principle. There were swamp-willow baskets hanging on the wall behind the television. Each held nearly the same arrangement of dried grasses and empty seedpods. She also had a gabled Victorian dollhouse that only a grown-up could have owned. I was afraid to look inside but did, and sure enough every room was completely furnished down to toothpick-fine candles and in the bathroom two infinitesimal toothbrushes and tubes of toothpaste. I had the creeps and we hadn't even talked. She called me back into the kitchen and I went in, tongue-tied. We sat down at her table, which was old and made of scarred wood. At least it was the only table. There was not another almost like it. She had covered it with a bright cloth and set out plates and glasses. She poured some iced tea. The bread was toasted crisp. There was an extra plate. I pointed at it.

What's it for?

Doe told me in that sweat lodge, Joe, that since I had a double spirit around me I should just welcome it. I set up my house for two people, see, even the little people. And when I eat I always set out an extra plate and I put a bit of the food I'm eating on it.

There was a crust of bread on the plate.

Spirits don't eat much?

Not this one, said Linda comfortably.

And suddenly it all seemed okay by me. I was hungry the way you get after an illness. Suddenly ravenous.

Linda munched away, beaming at me, then at the sandwich. She put the eggy bread down almost lovingly and addressed it.

Is it a sin to enjoy you when my own twin brother is lying dead in a morgue? I don't know, but you sure taste good.

I gulped. The other sandwich made a lump in my throat.

Wash it down with some tea?

She poured a bit more into my glass from a plastic pitcher bobbing with cut lemons and ice.

I didn't take off work to mourn, you know me better than that, she said. I took off work for other reasons. I had sick leave coming so I thought, hey, I'll use this time to straighten a few things out.

What things? I thought of her neatly duplicate living room, but then I knew she meant her thoughts.

I'll tell you, said Linda, if you'll tell me why you came here.

I put down my sandwich, wishing I had eaten it all before we got to this.

Wait, said Linda. As if she'd read my mind, she said that we should eat first and talk later. She apologized for being a bad hostess. Then she lifted her food in her chubby little hands, the sharp nails newly shellacked, and gave me such a look—it was a merry twinkle but at the same time it suggested insanity. I ate slowly, but eventually I had to take the final bite.

Linda patted her lips with her paper napkin and folded it into squares.

The golf course, she said. You pumped me for information. She wagged her finger at me. Two and two makes three. However, I have decided that you are too young to have accomplished this. Maybe you're not, but I've decided you are. My theory is you gave the information about Linden golfing to someone older. But someone nearsighted, not your father. Your father is a very good shot.

He is?

This was of course a big surprise to me.

Everybody knows that. He brought down anything he aimed at as a young man. Kids don't know their parents' history. What did you come here for?

Can I trust you?

If you have to ask me that? No.

I was stuck. That mad sparkle came back and lighted up

her tiny round eyes. She seemed about to explode with laughter. Instead, she leaned toward me and peered around as if the walls were bugged, then she whispered.

I would do anything in the world for your family. I am devoted to you guys. Though you've been using me, Joe, and you want something from me now. What is it?

Right then, I thought I was going to ask about the rifle. Instead, I heard myself ask the question I knew had no answer.

Why, Linda? Why did he do it?

I caught her off guard. Her eyes bulged and filled. But she answered. She answered like she thought it was so obvious I wouldn't need to ask.

He hated your family, I mean, your father mostly. But Whitey and Sonja too. His thinking was all crooked, Joe. He hated your father but he was afraid of him. Still, he wouldn't have come for Geraldine except for he became a monster when it came to Mayla. By filling out that form in Geraldine's office, Mayla had named old Yeltow as father of her child—meaning she got pregnant while she worked for him. A high-school girl. From that old lech, excuse me, she got a car to travel home with, and payoff money not to talk, but she still insisted on enrolling her baby. Linden worked for the governor, but he was always jealous, always possessive, sick, smitten to death with Mayla. He wanted to run away with her on that money, and here she won't share. Won't go with him. Probably hates him, scared of him. Tries to get Geraldine to help her—so now both of them know the truth. All this eats at him. He idolized Yeltow. Maybe he thought if he had that file he'd save Yeltow. Or maybe he'd blackmail Yeltow. I could see him doing either. And of course your mother wouldn't give him that file. But why he did this to your mother had more to do with a man who set loose his monster. Not everybody's got a monster, and most who do keep it locked up. But I saw the monster in my brother way back in the hospital and it made me deathly ill. I knew that someday he would let it loose. It would lurch out with part of me inside. Yes. I was part of the monster too. I gave and gave, but know what? It was still hungry. Know why? Because no matter how much it ate, it couldn't get the right thing. There was always something it needed. Something missing in his mother, too. I'll tell you what it was: me. My powerful spirit. Me! His mother couldn't face what she did to her baby, but even more: that what she did could not destroy me. Still, Linda brooded, she could call me after telling the doctor to let me die. All those years later. Call me and say, *Hello, it's your mother.*

I was silent.

And he could not let go, she said at last. Because he came back and he came back like he *wanted* his monster killed, though another reason has occurred to me also.

What's that?

He was nervous about Mayla. I just know she's somewhere on the reservation. He had to keep checking on her, make sure she wasn't found.

Do you think she's alive?

No.

After a while, dread stole into me. I asked, Am I like him?

No, she said. This'll get to you. Or whoever, I mean. This could wreck you. Don't let it wreck you, Joe. What could you do? Or whoever do?

She shrugged. But me, that's another story. It's me who is not so different, Joe. It's me who should have shot him with Albert's old twelve-gauge. Though if Linden had his druthers, I think he'd rather have got shot with the deer rifle.

Yeah, it's about that rifle, I said.

The rifle.

It's under your porch. Can you hide it? Get it off the reservation?

She grinned at me in a way fit to burst and I thought *crazy*, but then she bit her lip modestly and blinked.

Buster found it already, Joe. He knows when anything new enters his territory. I thought he was interested in a skunk. Then I looked underneath and saw the edge of that black Hefty bag.

She saw my shock.

Don't worry, Joe. Want to know where I've been on my sick leave? To Pierre, to my brother Cedric's. He got his training down in Fort Benning, Georgia, and sure knew how to disassemble that rifle. We threw a couple of pieces in the Missouri. I drove back here in a zigzag I can't even remember, down back roads, and ditched the rest of it in sloughs. She held up her empty palms and said, Tell whoever did it to rest easy. Her eyes clouded, her look gentled.

Your mom? How is she?

She was out in the garden, picking bush beans. She said she was fine, but I mean she said it over and over so I'd believe her.

I'll come see her. I want you to give her this.

Linda took something from her pocket and held her fist over my hand. When she opened it a small black screw fell out.

Tell her she can keep this in her jewelry box. Or bury it. Whatever she likes.

I put the screw in my pocket.

Halfway home, blown along all the way back with the usual frozen foil-wrapped brick of banana bread numbing my armpit, I realized of course that the screw in my pocket was part of the rifle. Steadied by the wind, I didn't have to pause or use my handlebars. I fished it out and winged it into the ditch.

This time it was Angus's bottle of Captain Jack's stolen from his mother's boyfriend with a handful of Valium pills and a grocery bag halfway filled with cans of cold Blatz.

We were drinking at the edge of the construction site. After the lazy bulldozers and the Bobcats stopped moving the same dirt piles around, the place was ours. Some days they left our bike tracks alone, other days they obliterated our work. We had no idea what was going to be built. There was always the same amount of dirt.

A federal project, said Zack.

Cappy tipped the beer down with a pill, lay back, and stared up into the leaves. The light was turning gold.

This here is my favorite time of day, he said. He took a small wallet-size school photo of Zelia from his cowboy shirt pocket and held it to his forehead.

Ssshhh, they're communicating, Angus said.

I miss you too, baby, said Cappy after a few moments. He put the photo back in his pocket, pressed down the pearl snaps, and patted his heart.

It's a beautiful love, I said. I turned on my side and leaned into the earth and threw up a little. I buried the puke with dirt. Nobody noticed. I mumbled, I wouldn't mind a beautiful love.

Cappy handed me a pamphlet. Her last letter, man. It was about the Rapture. This was in it. Cappy smiled upward.

I looked at the pamphlet steadily, reading the words several times to get their meaning

Rapture, yeah man, said Zack.

Not that kind of rapture, said Cappy. It's a mass liftoff. There's only a certain number of people who can go. They don't apparently take Catholics so Zelia's family is thinking of converting before the Tribulation. She wants me to convert along with them so we get raptured up together.

Stairway to heaven, laughed Zack.

Raptured as one, I said. As one. My brain had started on a repeating loop and I had to force my mouth to stop saying everything I thought fifty times.

I don't think you'll make it, you two, said Angus dreamily. You guys can't get in now with that mortal stain.

It was like an icicle jabbed into my thoughts. The subject hadn't come up with the four of us. We hadn't spoken of Lark's death. The cold spread. My brain was clear, but the rest of me was just too comfortable. Cappy handled the moment and melted the fear out of me as usual.

Starboy, said Cappy, holding out his hand. Angus clasped it in a brother shake. The truth is, none of us will get there. They only take you stone-cold sober.

All your life? said Angus.

All your life, Starboy, said Cappy. You cannot slip even one time.

Ah, said Angus, we're screwed. My whole family is screwed. No rapture.

We don't need no rapture, Zack said. We got confession. Tell your sins to Father and you're wiped clean.

I did that, said Cappy. Father tried to clock me.

We all laughed and talked for a while about Cappy's run. Then we fell silent and watched the flickering leaves.

Zelia probably confessed at home, Cappy said after a while. Zelia probably got wiped clean.

Unless she got pregnant. I hadn't meant to say a thing like that, but I could not stop the *Star Wars* quote: Luke, at that speed do you think you'll be able to pull out in time?

If only I hadn't, said Cappy. If only she was. We would have to get married then.

You're thirteen, I remembered.

Zelia said so were Romeo and Juliet.

I hate that movie, said Zack.

Angus was asleep, his breath whining evenly as a cicada.

Food. My voice again. But the others were sleeping. I stood up after a time because someone was moaning. It was Cappy. He was weeping, heartbroken, then frightened, shouting Please, no, in his sleep. I shook his arm and he passed on to some other dream. I watched over him until he seemed more peaceful. I left them sleeping there and wobbled home on my bike, but when I got into the yard the space under Pearl's bush looked so comfortable that I crept into the dark leaves with her and slept until the sun faded. I woke up, alert, and walked in the kitchen door.

Joe? Where you been? Mom called from the other room. I felt that she had been waiting for me the whole time.

I grabbed a glass and poured some milk and drank it fast.

Out biking around, I said.

You missed dinner. I can warm up some spaghetti.

But I was already eating it cold, straight from the refrigerator. Mom came in and shooed me aside.

At least can you put it on a plate? Joe, have you been smoking? You stink like cigarettes.

The other guys were.

Same old line I gave my folks.

I like spaghetti cold.

She made me a dish and begged me not to smoke.

I won't anymore, I promise.

She sat down watching me eat.

There's something I wanted to tell you this morning, Joe. You called out in your sleep last night. You yelled.

I did?

I got up and I went to your door. You were talking to Cappy.

What'd I say?

I couldn't make out what you said. But you called Cappy's name twice.

I kept eating. He's my best buddy, Mom. He's like a brother to me.

I thought about him crying in his sleep out at the construction site and put my fork down. I wanted to leave our house, find Cappy again. I felt that I should not have left him sleeping. The crack of light beneath my father's door widened and he came out and sat down at the table with us. He had stopped drinking coffee from dawn till dusk and on into the night. My mother gave him a glass of water. He was neatly shaven, never in his bathrobe anymore. He kept reduced hours at work.

I started today, Joe.

Started what? I was still distracted. If I called Cappy's house, maybe he could get a ride over here and stay the night. We'd be together in the dark. My father kept on talking.

I started my walking regimen, around the high-school track. I made it a half mile. I'll be going every day. You'll be out running too. I guess you'll lap me a few times.

My mother reached out and took his hand. He smoothed his hand over her fingers and touched her wedding ring.

She won't let me go alone, he said, looking at her. Oh, Geraldine!

They were both thinner and the lines along the sides of their mouths had deepened. But the knifelike mark between my mother's eyebrows was gone now. I had stopped them from living in the fear cloud. I should have felt happy watching them across the table, but instead I was angered by their ignorance. Like I was the grown-up and the two of them holding hands were the oblivious children. They had no idea what I had gone through for them. Or Cappy. Me and Cappy. I stubbed my foot sullenly against the table leg.

Something's fighting in me, Joe, my father said.

My foot stopped kicking.

Maybe you'll understand if I talk to you about it?

Okay, I said, though I was jumping out of my skin. I didn't want to listen.

I feel relief at Lark's death, my father said. Just like you said when you first heard, I feel that way too. Your mother is safe from him, he will not show up in the grocery store or at Whitey's. We can go on now, can't we?

Yeah, I said. I tried to get up, but he spoke.

Yet the question of who killed Lark must be asked. There was no justice for your mother, his victim, or for Mayla, and yet justice exists.

Unevenly applied, Dad. But he got what he deserved. My

voice was flat. My heart sickly pounding.

My mother had dropped my father's hand. She did not want to listen to us argue.

I feel that way too, said my father. Bjerke will interview us tomorrow—it's routine. But nothing is routine. He'll want to know where each of us was when Lark was killed. Here is my fight, Joe. I ask myself in this situation, as one sworn to uphold the law in every case, what I would do if I had any information that could lead to the identity of the killer. Last time I talked to your mother about this, I wasn't sure what I would do.

I looked at Mom and her lips were pressed together in a straight dark line.

But I've decided that I would do nothing. I would offer up no information. Any judge knows there are many kinds of justice—for instance, ideal justice as opposed to the best-we can do justice, which is what we end up with in making so many of our decisions. It was no lynching. There was no question of his guilt. He may have even wanted to get caught and punished. We can't know his mind. Lark's killing is a wrong thing which serves an ideal justice. It settles a legal enigma. It threads that unfair maze of land title law by which Lark could not be prosecuted. His death was the exit. I would say nothing, do nothing, to muddy the resolution. Yet—

My father stopped and tried to give me that old look he used to fix on me, and others, from the bench. I could feel it, but I would not meet his gaze.

—yet, he said gently, this too is an abandonment of my own responsibility. That person who killed Lark will live with the human consequences of having taken a life. As I did not kill Lark, but wanted to, I must at least protect the person who took on that task. And I would, even to the extent of attempting to argue a legal precedent.

What?

Traditional precedent. It could be argued that Lark met the

definition of a wiindigoo, and that with no other recourse, his killing fulfilled the requirements of a very old law.

I felt my mother's attention on me keenly.

I just wanted you to know that, my father prodded.

Lots of people had it in for Lark, I said.

I looked from one of my parents to the other. Behind them in the next room the shelves of old books stood mellow in the dip of shadow at twilight. The scuffed brown leather. *Meditations*. Plato. *The Iliad*. Shakespeare in sober dark red and the essays of Montaigne. Then below, a matching Great Books collection they subscribed to by mail. There was a free Book of Mormon from a passing LDS missionary. There was William Warren, Basil Johnston, *The Narrative of the Captivity and Adventures of John Tanner*, and everything by Vine Deloria Jr. There were the novels they read together—fat paperbacks thumbed and stacked. I looked at the books as if they could help us. But we had moved way far past books now into the stories Mooshum told in his sleep. There were no quotations in my father's repertoire for where we were, and it was beyond me at the time to think of Mooshum's sleeptalking as a reading of traditional case law.

So if you hear anything, Joe, said my father.

If I hear anything, yeah, Dad. He'd gotten my attention. There was some relief for me, even, in what he said. But my father was also wrong, and about one thing in particular. He'd said I was now safe, but I was not exactly safe from Lark. Neither was Cappy. Every night he came after us in dreams.

We are back at the golf course in the moment I locked eyes with Lark. That terrible contact. Then the gunshot. At that moment, we exchange selves. Lark is in my body, watching. I am in his body, dying. Cappy runs up the hill with Joe and the gun, but he doesn't know Joe contains the soul of Lark. Dying on the golf course, I know that Lark is going to kill Cappy when they reach the overlook. I try to call out and warn Cappy, but I feel my life bleed out of me into the clipped grass.

I either have that dream, or one where I see the backyard ghost again. The same ghost Randall saw in the sweat lodge—his sour gaze and rigid mouth. Only this time, like with Randall, the ghost is leaning over me, talking to me through a veil of darkness, backlit, his white hair shining. And I know he's the police.

As always I woke shouting Cappy's name. To muffle sound, I'd stuffed a towel at the base of my door. I peered out in the fresh light hoping no one had heard me. I listened. It sounded like Mom and Dad had gone downstairs already, or gone out. I lay back in the covers. The air was cool but I was sweating and still full of adrenaline. My heart was jumping. I rubbed my hand on my chest to calm it and tried to slow down my breathing. Each dream was more real every time it occurred, like it was wearing a track into my brain.

I need medicine, I said out loud, meaning Ojibwe medicine. Old-time medicine people knew how to handle dreams, that's what Mooshum had said. But his spirit was far away now, trying to shed the body in the cot by the window. The only other medicine person I knew was Grandma Thunder. Maybe we could ask her what to do. Not tell her details, of course, or reveal what had happened. Just get advice about these dreams. Bugger Pourier, of all people, stepped into my thoughts right then. Probably because the last time I'd thought of Grandma Thunder, I sent him to her, and right before that Bugger had stolen my bike. Something about a dream.

I sat up. He'd wanted to see if something he saw was a dream. My own dream's reality, which always clung to me, and Bugger's intent drunken fixation fused. What had he seen? I had worked on Bugger's hunger and turned him around so I could get back my bicycle. But I'd never asked him what he saw. I got up and got dressed, ate some breakfast, and went out. To look for Bugger you looked behind places, starting with the Dead Custer. I searched all morning and asked everyone I met, but no one knew. I finally went to the post office. That was where I should have gone first, it turned out. I didn't think of it, as poor Bugger hadn't had an address.

He's in the hospital, said Linda. Isn't he? she called back to Mrs. Nanapush, sorting letters.

He busted his foot stealing a case of beer. Dropped it on his foot. So now he's laid up and his sisters say it's a blessing in disguise—could dry him out.

I rode over to the hospital to visit Bugger. He was in a room with three other men. His foot was in a cast and rigged for traction, though I wondered if that was necessary for his foot to heal or meant to tie him to the bed.

My boy! He was glad to see me. Did you bring me a drop?

No, I said.

His avid face fell into a pout.

I came to ask you something.

Not even a little flower arrangement, he grumped. Or a pancake.

You want a pancake?

I been seeing pancakes. Whiskey. Spiders. Pancakes. Lizards. Pancakes are the only good thing I see. But they just feed an old man the damn oatmeal. Coffee and oatmeal. It's a plain breakfast.

Not even toast? I asked.

I could have it if I wanted, but I keep asking for pancakes. Bugger looked at me fiercely. I am holding out for pancakes!

I have to ask you something.

Ask away then. I'll give you the answer for a pancake.

Okay.

And whiskey. He leaned forward secretively. Bring me a

drop, but don't let those others know about it. Keep the bottle in your shirt.

All right.

Bugger sat back, ready, his face expectant.

Remember when you took my bike?

His face turned blank. I spoke slowly, pausing after each sentence for him to nod.

You were sitting outside Mighty Al's. You saw my bike. You got on my bike and started riding. I came out and asked where you were going. You said you wanted to check and see if something was a dream.

Bugger's face lighted up.

Remember now?

No.

I reset the scene five or six times before Bugger's mind finally turned back and began to riffle through the recent past. He held very still and concentrated now, so hard I could almost hear the gears grind. As his thoughts collected, his expression changed, but so gradually that it was only after I'd looked away impatiently and then looked back that I noticed he was petrified. He stared at something between us on the bedcover. I thought he was having a hallucination, not of the pancakes, which would have filled him with joy, but some sort of reptile or insect. But then his look changed to pity and he gasped, Poor girl!

What girl?

Poor girl.

He began to sob in dry wrenches. He kept crying about her. He mumbled about construction and I knew. She was in the construction site, the earth mounded over her. I couldn't help the picture from forming. Us jumping our bikes, flying back and forth, and her below. I stood up, jolted. I knew, down to the core of me, that he had seen Mayla Wolfskin. He had seen her dead body. If we hadn't killed Lark, he'd have gone to jail for life anyway. I spun around thinking I should go to the police, then stopped. I could not let the police know I was even thinking this way. I had to get off their radar entirely, with Cappy, disappear. I couldn't tell anyone. Even I didn't want to know what I knew. The best thing for me to do was forget. And then for the rest of my life to try and not think how different things would have gone if, in the first place, I'd just followed Bugger's dream.

I needed to find Cappy. Not to tell him. I never would tell him. I'd never tell anyone. There was in me as I rode toward the Lafournaises a disconnect so profound I could think of nothing but obliteration. I would somehow find the means to get drunk. The world would take on that amber tone. Things would soften to brown as if in old photographs. I would be safe.

Zack and Angus were hanging out in the grocery store parking lot. Their bikes were there, and Cappy's too, but they were sitting in Zack's older cousin's car. They got out when they saw me, and told me that Cappy had gone into the post office to see if there was a letter.

He should've come out by now, said Zack.

I went to get Cappy and finally found him out back of the building, sitting on a busted chair where the post office employees took smoke breaks in the summer. His hair was flung down over his face. He was smoking and didn't look at me when I stood next to him. Just held out a piece of paper.

> ***You will cease and desist from any contact with our daughter. My wife found the package of letters Zelia was hiding. You should have to consider that in this case we may persecute you to the full axtent of the law.***
>
> ***Also currently Zelia is being punished and also in short order we will be changing residence. You***

have stolen our daughter's innocence and wracked our life.

Cappy's arms and legs were splayed out, limp and despairing. His face was the color of ashes and there was a cloud of smoke around his head. I sat down beside him on a cardboard box. There was nothing to say about anything at all. I put my head in my hands.

Yeah, said Cappy wildly. Fuck yeah. Punish her? I bet they're keeping her locked up until they move. So she can't go over to the post office. Wrack their lives! I'll wrack their lives? By loving their daughter with a true love?

Look at me, brother, he begged.

I did.

Look at me. He threw his hair back, tapped the tips of his fingers on his chest. Would I wreck her life? The Creator made us for each other. Me here. Zelia there. Space was put between us by human error. But our hearts listened to divine will. Our bodies, too. So fucking what? Every bit of what we did was made in heaven. The Creator is goodness, brother. In his mysterious mercy he gave me Zelia. The gift of our love—I can't throw it back in the face of the Creator, can I?

No.

That's what her parents are asking me to do. But I won't do it. I will not throw our love back in God's face. It will exist for all time whether or not her parents can see that. Nothing they do can get between us.

Okay.

Yeah, said Cappy. His hair flopped down again. He set fire to the letter with the burning coal of his cigarette. Watched it catch, flare, and burn to the tip of his fingers. He dropped the scrap and the flimsy films of burnt paper floated down around his feet.

I'm going home to get that bus money, said Cappy. And

then I'm gassing up Randall's car. I'll come and get you at your house.

Where are we going?

I can't sit still, Joe. I can't stay here. And I know there will be no rest for me until I see her.

We left Zack and Angus drinking pop in Zack's cousin's car and went home. My place was empty. I filled a backpack with a change of clothes and all the money I had, which came to $78.00. I still had some from Sonja, and I'd never spent the cash Whitey paid me for the week I'd worked—he'd overpaid me, maybe to try and keep my mouth shut. I took a jacket. Because I was still waiting for Cappy, and because in spite of what I'd done I was still the kind of person who thought ahead and made lunch, I put together a dozen peanut butter pickle sandwiches. I ate one and drank some milk. He still did not come. I remembered how hard it was to start Randall's car. Engage, I thought. Pearl followed me around. I went into my father's office. I tried the desk drawer my father had been locking for a while now, and it caught, but he hadn't quite turned the key all the way and I jiggled it open. In the drawer was a manila file folder. It was filled with greasy Xeroxes. There was the copy of a tribal enrollment form. On the form it said Mayla Wolfskin. She was listed as seventeen years old and the mother of a child named Tanya. Curtis W. Yeltow was listed as the father, just as Linda had said. I closed the file and put it back in the drawer. I managed to turn the lock with a paper clip so it would seem that the drawer had not been opened; what that mattered anyway, I don't know. I was glad that I wouldn't have to talk to Bjerke. I took a sheet of writing paper from a leather box. My father kept a cup of sharpened pencils on his desk. I took one and wrote my parents that I was going on a camping trip. They should not worry, I'd be with Cappy and I was sorry for the short notice. I said that we'd be gone for three or four days. I'd call them.

I imagined writing: ask Bugger Pourier about his dream. But I didn't. There was some noise outside. Pearl barked. It was Angus and Zack. They wanted to know why we'd ditched them and so I told them about the letter, and about how Cappy was going to get Randall's car.

I've got something, Angus said.

He showed me an ID. It was a driver's license, which his cousin had pretended to lose and got another one. He'd sold the ID to Angus although the picture didn't look like him at all.

Don't you think it looks like Cappy though? He could buy for us.

It looks like him enough, I said. Right about then Cappy drove up and we all got into the idling car. I sat in front and Zack and Angus took the back.

Where we going? asked Zack.

Montana, Cappy said.

The two in back laughed, but I looked out the window, at Pearl. She wouldn't take her eyes off me.

I know there's lots of world over and above Highway 5, but when you're driving on it—four boys in one car and it's so peaceful, so empty for mile after mile, when the radio stations cut out and there's just static and the sound of your voices, and wind when you put your arm out to rest it on the hood—it seems you are balanced. Skimming along the rim of the universe. We had half a tank when we left home and we filled it up again twice before we got across the line to Plentywood. We dropped down there and edged along the bottom of Fort Peck to Wolf Point. Cappy turned the wheel over to me, and we sat there idling outside a liquor store while he bought a fifth and a case and another fifth. Zack had brought his guitar. He sang cry in your beer C&W, one after the next, making us laugh every time. And we kept going, the talk passing this way and that, turning funny and then ridiculous as Cappy made his plan to spring Zelia from her house at the return address in Helena—still far off.

Zack and Angus got nervous at a gas station and called home. That's when Zack got his ear scorched off. He slunk back to the car, looked over at me, said, Oops! We ate the sandwiches. We ate beef jerky, spicy sausages, bags of chips, and cans of nuts from the gas stations. We guzzled water at a rest stop and the car died. We had to push it to a downhill slope, take it out of gear, and jump in while it rolled. The engine turned over and we war-whooped, high and fine. Zack and Angus passed out in back, leaning on each other and snoring. Cappy and I started talking and kept on driving west through the long dusk. The sun burned forever and stayed balanced on the horizon for an age, then flared red from below that dark line for another eternity. So it seemed that time stopped. We rolled effortlessly in a dream.

I told Cappy about the file I found in my father's desk drawer. I told him everything on the enrollment form. I told him about the governor of South Dakota.

So that's where the money came from, he said.

For sure. She was one of those smart high-school girls who get picked to bring coffee and file papers. Get their pictures in the news, especially a pretty Indian with the governor's arm around her shoulder. LaRose told me. Linda knew it too. That's where Yeltow got to her. And Lark, he kept the secret, but he was jealous. Thought he owned her.

The governor gave her money to keep her mouth shut. Start a new life?

She put the cash in her little girl's doll to keep it safe.

Safe from Lark.

I told Cappy that I'd seen that doll's outfit in the car as it came out of the lake, that the doll must have floated out of that opened window and washed onto the opposite shore.

After this, I think, said Cappy, it will all come out. There's still that file with his name on it. So why not? She was jailbait, Mayla.

He'll go down for sure, I said then.

But Yeltow never did.

The silence of wind around us, the car cutting through the night along the Milk River, where Mooshum had once hunted, driven out farther and farther into the west, where Nanapush had seen buffalo straight back to the horizon, and then the next year not a single one. And after that Mooshum's family had turned back and taken land on the reservation. He'd met Nanapush there and together they had built the round house, the sleeping woman, the unkillable mother, the old lady buffalo. They'd built that place to keep their people together and to ask for mercy from the Creator, since justice was so sketchily applied on earth.

Hinsdale went by. Sleeping Buffalo, too. Malta. We'd turn south far ahead at Havre. We'd traced our route on the gas station map.

Let's keep going, said Cappy. I feel good. Let's drive all night.

Make it so.

We laughed and Cappy slowed the car down and idled it while I ran around the front end, jumped in, started driving. The air was cool and green with sage. The lights hit coyote eyes slipping along the ditches, in and out of fence lines. Cappy balled up my jacket under his head, leaned on the window, and slept. I kept driving on until at last I got tired and switched off again with Cappy. This time Zack and Angus climbed in front to keep Cappy awake. I crawled in back. There was an old horse blanket that smelled of dust. I laid my head down and put the belt on because the buckle was cutting into my hip. As I dozed back there, listening to the three up in front talk and laugh, I had that same drifting sense of peace I got in my parents' car. The guys passed the bottle back and I drank deep, to put myself out. I slipped away easily. I slept without dreaming even as the car hurtled off the road, flipped, rolled, threw its doors wide, and came to rest in an unplowed field.

I had the sense of a vast and violent motion. Before I could grasp its significance, all was still. I nearly fell back asleep thinking we had stopped. But I opened my eyes just to see where we were and the air was black. I called for Cappy, but there was no answer. There was the distant sound of distress, not weeping, but a laborious panting. I unbuckled myself and crept out the open door. The sounds came from Zack and Angus, tangled together, moving on the ground, then staggering up and falling. My brain clicked on. I searched the car—empty. One headlight flickered. I climbed out and made a widening circle around the car, but Cappy seemed to have vanished. He left for help, I thought in relief as I stepped along slowly. There was only the light of stars, and the car's one beam; parts of the ground were so black they were like pits reaching down into the earth. For one disoriented moment, I thought I stood at the entrance to a mine shaft, and I feared that Cappy had been flung in. But it was only shadow. The deepest shadow I have ever known. I went down on my hands and knees and crawled into the shadow. I felt my way through invisible grass. The wind came up and blew my friends' cries away from me. The sounds I made, too, when I found Cappy, were taken into the boom of air.

I sat in the police station, attached to the chair. Zack and Angus were in the Havre hospital. They'd taken Cappy someplace else to fix him up for Doe and Randall. The ghost had brought me here. I had seen him in the field as I held Cappy—my ghost had bent over me, backlit by the flashlight he held cocked over his shoulder, silver haloed, looking at me with a sour contempt. He shook me lightly. His lips had moved but the only words I could make out were *Let go* and I would not. I slept and woke in the chair. I must have eaten, drunk water, too. None of it do I remember. Except that again and again I looked at the round black stone that Cappy had given me, the thunderbird egg. And there was that moment when my mother and father walked in the door disguised as old people. I thought the miles in the car had bent them, dulled their eyes, even grayed and whitened their hair and caused their hands and voices to tremble. At the same time, I found, as I rose from the chair, I'd gotten old along with them. I was broken and fragile. My shoes were lost in the accident. I walked between them, stumbled. My mother took my hand. When we got to the car, she opened the back door and crawled in. There was a pillow and the same old quilt. I sat in the front with my father. He started the engine. We pulled out just like that and started driving home.

In all those miles, in all those hours, in all that air rushing by and sky coming at us, blending into the next horizon, then the one after that, in all that time there was nothing to be said. I cannot remember speaking and I cannot remember my mother or my father speaking. I knew that they knew everything. The sentence was to endure. Nobody shed tears and there was no anger. My mother or my father drove, gripping the wheel with neutral concentration. I don't remember that they even looked at me or I at them after the shock of that first moment when we all realized we were old. I do remember, though, the familiar sight of the roadside café just before we would cross the reservation line. On every one of my childhood trips that place was always a stop for ice cream, coffee and a newspaper, pie. It was always what my father called the last leg of the journey. But we did not stop this time. We passed over in a sweep of sorrow that would persist into our small forever. We just kept going.

Afterword

This book is set in 1988, but the tangle of laws that hinder prosecution of rape cases on many reservations still exists. "Maze of Injustice," a 2009 report by Amnesty International, included the following statistics: 1 in 3 Native women will be raped in her lifetime (and that figure is certainly higher as Native women often do not report rape); 86 percent of rapes and sexual assaults upon Native women are perpetrated by non-Native men; few are prosecuted. In 2010, then North Dakota senator Byron Dorgan sponsored the Tribal Law and Order Act. In signing the act into law, President Barack Obama called the situation "an assault on our national conscience." The organizations highlighted in **boldface** below are working to restore sovereign justice and ensure safety for Native women.

Thank you to the many people who advised me as I wrote this book: Betty Laverdure, former tribal judge, Turtle Mountain Reservation; Paul Day, Gitchi Makwa, former tribal judge, Mille Lacs, and executive director of **Anishinabe Legal Services**; Betty Day, wisdom keeper and doulah; Peter Meyers, Psy.D., forensic psychologist; Terri Yellowhammer, former child welfare consultant for the state of Minnesota, and technical assistance specialist and associate judge for White Earth Ojibwe; N. Bruce Duthu, Dartmouth College, author of *American Indians and the Law*; the members of Professor Duthu's Native American Law and Literature class; the Montgomery Fellow Program at Dartmouth College, and Richard Stammelman; Philomena Kebec, staff attorney for the Bad River Band of Lake Superior Chippewa Indians; Tore Mowatt Larssen, attorney; Lucy Rain Simpson, **Indian Law Resource Center**; Ralph David Erdrich, R.N., Indian Health Service, Sisseton, South Dakota; Angela Erdrich, M.D., Indian Health Board, Minneapolis; Sandeep Patel, M.D., Indian Health Service, Belcourt, North Dakota; Walter R. Echo-hawk, author of *In the Courts of the Conqueror: The Ten Worst Indian Law Cases Ever Decided*; Suzanne Koepplinger, executive director of **Minnesota Indian Women's Resource Center**, who gave me the report she coauthored with Alexandra "Sandi" Pierce, "Shattered Hearts: The Commercial and Sexual Exploitation of American Indian Women and Girls in Minnesota"; Darrell Emmel, TNG consultant; my copy editor, Trent Duffy; Terry Karten, my editor at HarperCollins; Brenda J. Child, historian and chair of the American Indian Studies Department at the University of Minnesota; Lisa Brunner, executive director of **Sacred Spirits First Nation Coalition**; and Carly Bad Heart Bull, attorney. Additional thanks are due to Memegwesi; chi-miigwech to Professor John Borrows, whose most recent book, *Drawing Out Law: A Spirit's Guide*, helped greatly in my understanding the process of wiindigoo law, as did Hadley Louise Friedland's 2010 thesis "The Wetiko (Windigo) Legal Principles: Responding to Harmful People in Cree, Anishinabek and Saulteaux Societies."

My cousin Darrell Gourneau, who died in 2011, gave his eagle feather, his songs, and his hunting stories. His mother, my aunt Dolores Gourneau, gave me his quilt for my writing chair.

Finally, thank you to everyone who got me through 2010–2011: first of all, to my daughter Persia, for her many thoughtful readings of this manuscript, her honest, valuable suggestions, and her loving care for me especially during the uncertain weeks of my diagnosis. Everyone rallied wonderfully during my treatment for breast cancer: thanks to Drs. Margit M. Bretzke, Patsa Sullivan, Stuart Bloom, and Judith Walker for matter-of-factly saving my life. My daughter Pallas advocated for me, drove me to treatments, and provided her own treatment—*Battlestar Galactica*, music, and food with mysterious powers of restoration. She kept the family together. Aza fought her own difficult battle and won it for us all with her art. She was also a consultant on the manuscript and a close, discriminating reader. Nenaa'ikiizhikok brought laughter and courage. Dan stayed the center of gravity for us all with his patience and good heart.

The events in this book are loosely based on so many different cases, reports, and stories that the outcome is pure fiction. This book is not meant to portray anyone alive or dead and, as always, any mistakes in the Ojibwe language are mine and do not reflect on my patient teachers.

About the Author

Louise Erdrich is a member of the Turtle Mountain Band of Chippewa and the author of thirteen novels as well as volumes of poetry, short stories, children's books, and a memoir of early motherhood. Her novel *Love Medicine* won the National Book Critics Circle Award. *The Last Report on the Miracles at Little No Horse* was a finalist for the National Book Award. Most recently, *The Plague of Doves* won the Anisfield-Wolf Book Award and was a finalist for the Pulitzer Prize. Louise Erdrich lives in Minnesota and is the owner of Birchbark Books, an independent bookstore.

About the Author

[illegible] of the Turtle Mountain Band of [illegible] and [illegible] of [illegible] novels as well as volumes [illegible] and a [illegible] the National Book [illegible] Book Award [illegible] *The* [illegible] the Anisfield-Wolf Book [illegible] Pulitzer Prize [illegible]